Cover Girl

COVER GIRL — published by Boom! Studios. Cover Girl © copyright Boom Entertainment, Inc. All Rights Reserved. Boom! Studios™ and the Boom! logo are trademarks of Boom Entertainment, Inc., registered in various countries and categories. All rights reserved. Office of publication: **6310 San Vicente Blvd Ste 404, Los Angeles CA 90048.**

FIRST PRINTING: April 2008   PRINTED IN KOREA
Collecting Cover Girl #1-5
10 9 8 7 6 5 4 3 2 1

ISBN-13: 978-1-934506-27-1
ISBN-10: 1-934506-27-3

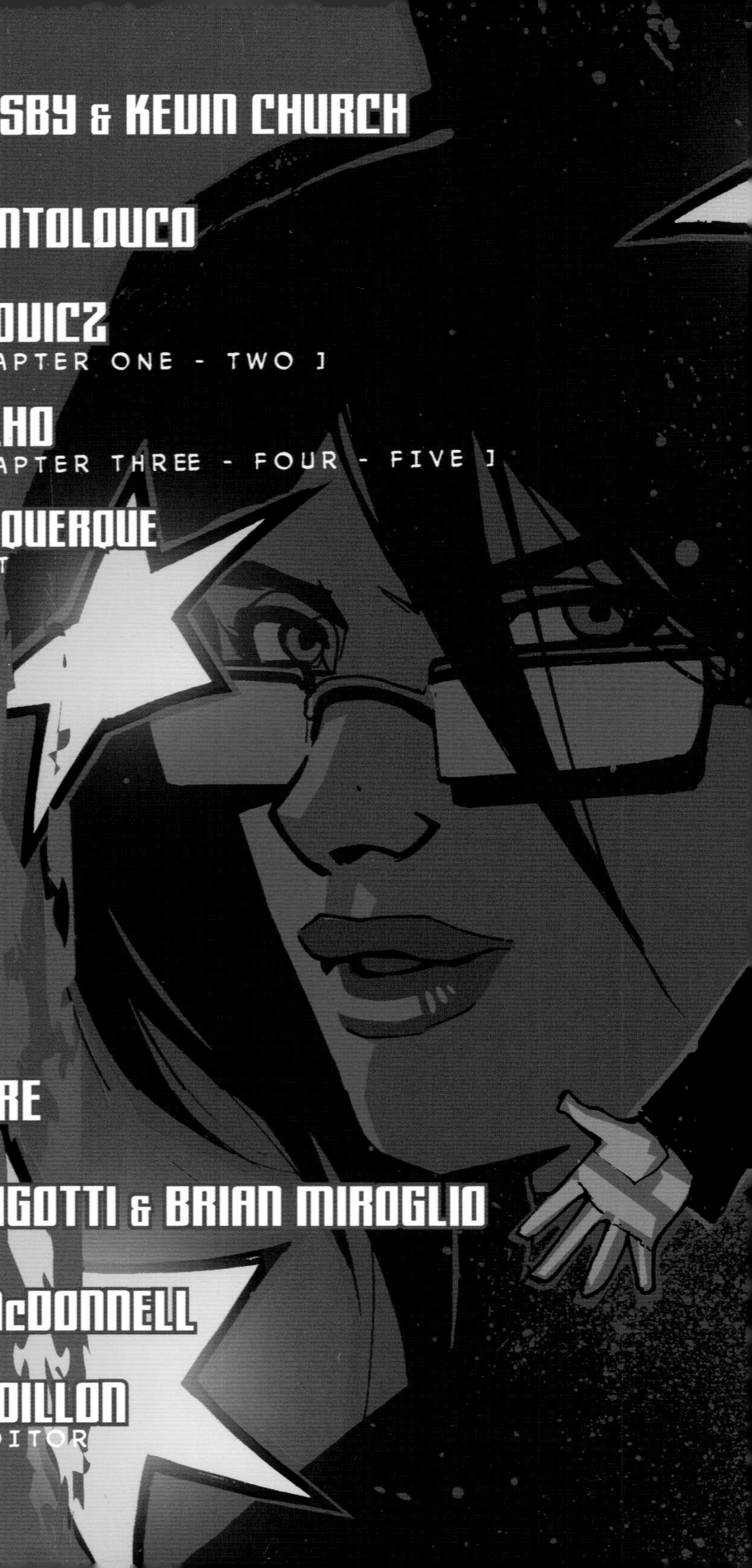

ANDREW COSBY & KEVIN CHURCH
WRITERS

MATEUS SANTOLOUCO
PENCILS

R. M. YANKOVICZ
INKER [CHAPTER ONE - TWO]

ANDRE COELHO
INKER [CHAPTER THREE - FOUR - FIVE]

RAFAEL ALBUQUERQUE
COVER ARTIST

ED DUKESHIRE
LETTERER

PABLO QUILIGOTTI & BRIAN MIROGLIO
COLORISTS

SHANNON McDONNELL
COPY EDITOR

MARSHALL DILLON
MANAGING EDITOR

Cover Girl

ANDREW COSBY
ROSS RICHIE
founders

MARK WAID
editor-in-chief

TOM FASSBENDER
vice president,
publishing

ADAM FORTIER
vice president,
new business

CHIP MOSHER
marketing &
sales director

MICHAEL ALAN NELSON
associate editor

ED DUKESHIRE
designer

DANIEL VARGAS
publishing coordinator

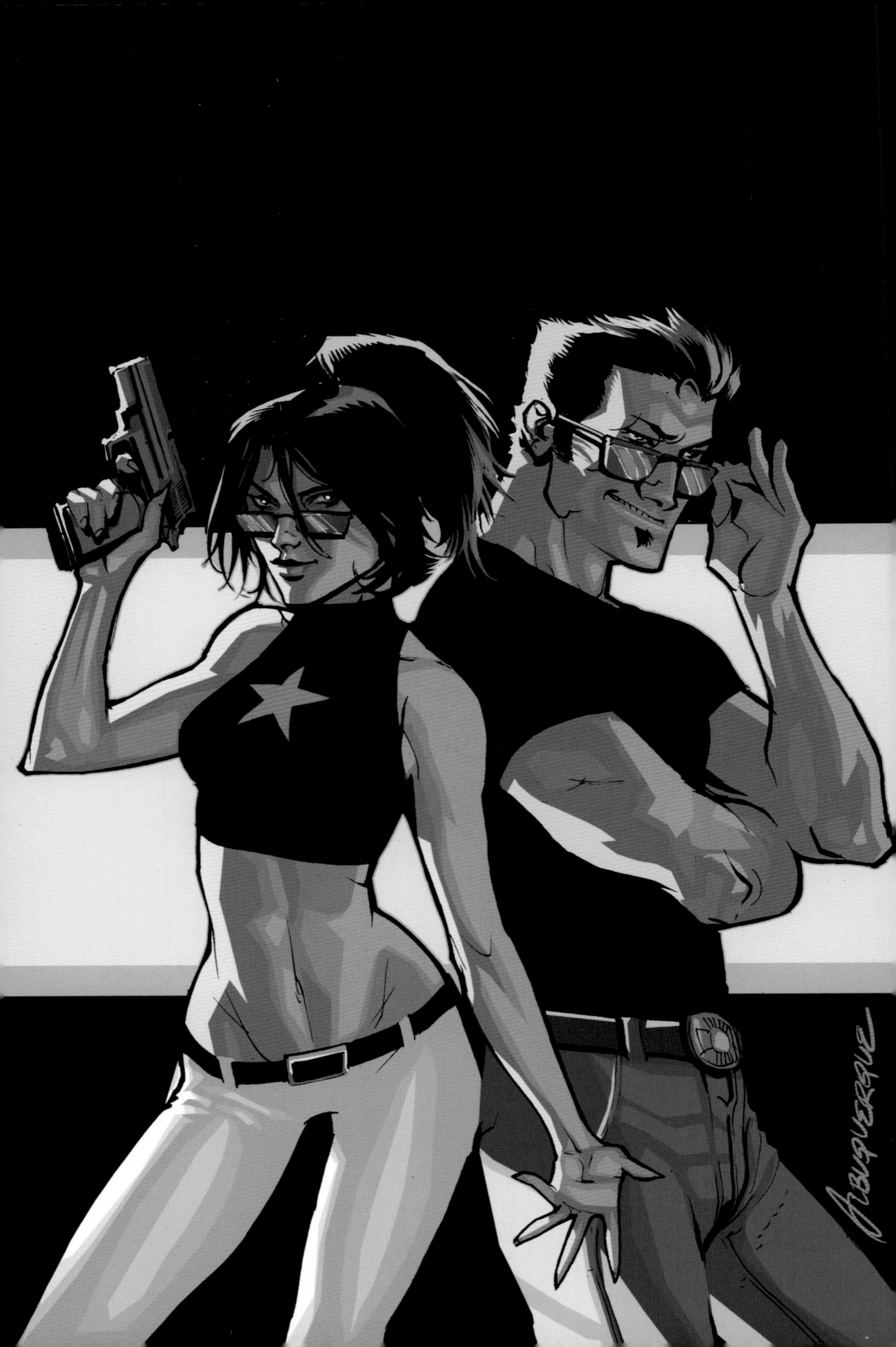
ALBUQUERQUE

CHAPTER ONE

HOLLYWOOD SHUFFLE

ANDREW COSBY & KEVIN CHURCH — WRITERS
MATEUS SANTOLOUCO — PENCILS
R.M. YANKOVICZ — INKER
ED DUKESHIRE — LETTERER
PABLO QUILIGOTTI & BRIAN MIROGLIO — COLORISTS
RAFAEL ALBUQUERQUE — COVER ARTIST
MARSHALL DILLON — MANAGING EDITOR

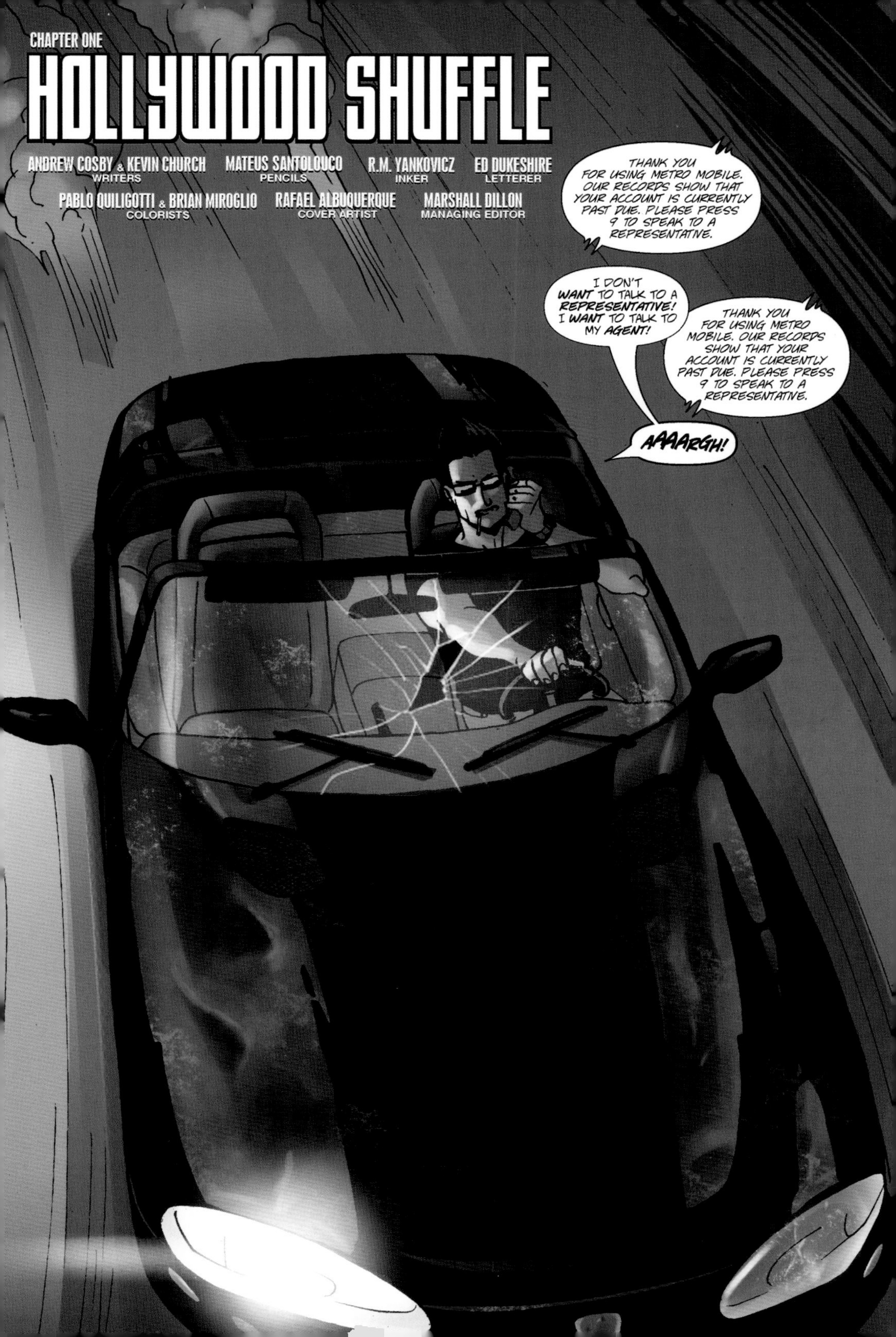
THANK YOU FOR USING METRO MOBILE. OUR RECORDS SHOW THAT YOUR ACCOUNT IS CURRENTLY PAST DUE. PLEASE PRESS 9 TO SPEAK TO A REPRESENTATIVE.
I DON'T WANT TO TALK TO A REPRESENTATIVE! I WANT TO TALK TO MY AGENT!
THANK YOU FOR USING METRO MOBILE. OUR RECORDS SHOW THAT YOUR ACCOUNT IS CURRENTLY PAST DUE. PLEASE PRESS 9 TO SPEAK TO A REPRESENTATIVE.
AAAARGH!

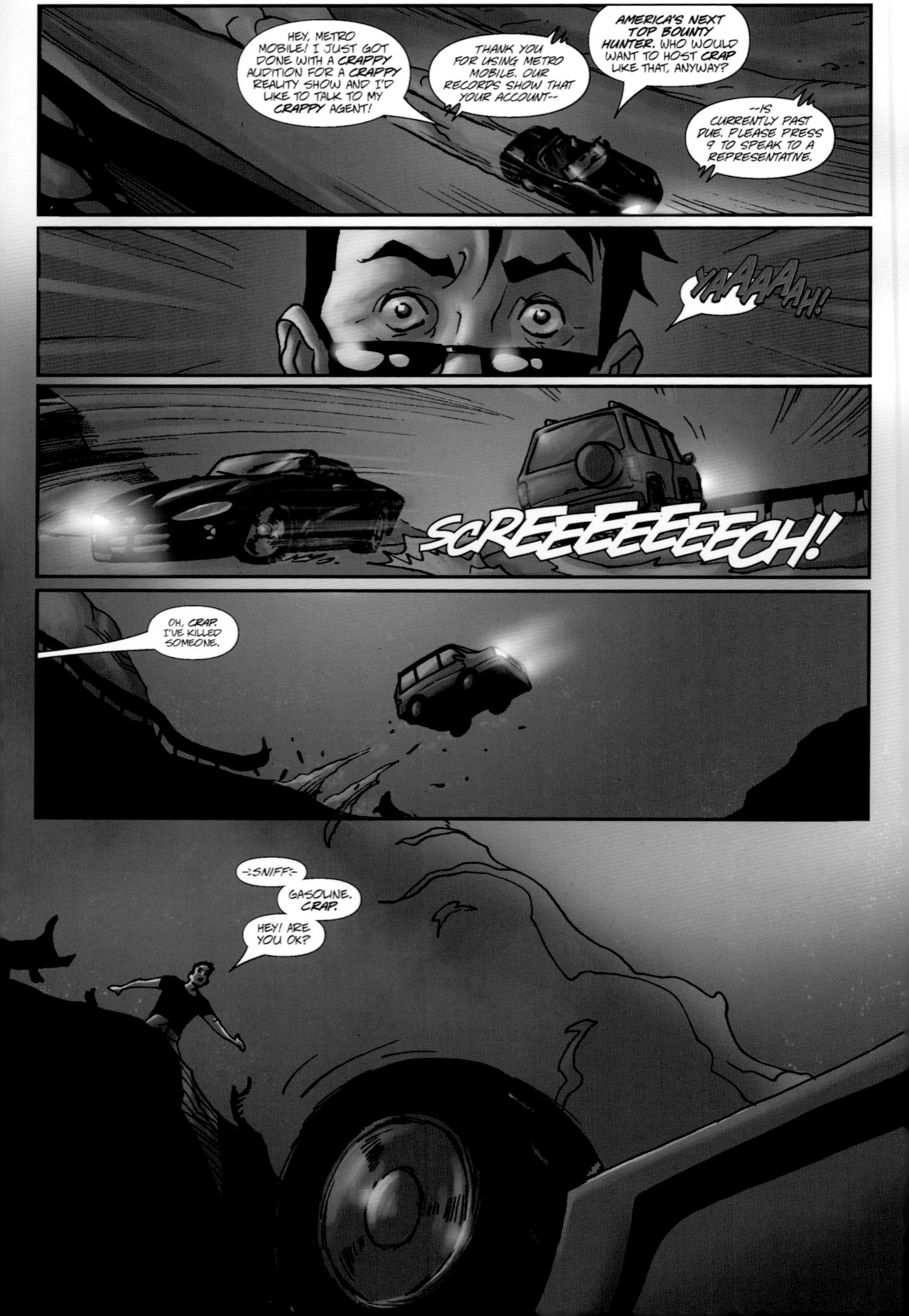
HEY, METRO MOBILE! I JUST GOT DONE WITH A CRAPPY AUDITION FOR A CRAPPY REALITY SHOW AND I'D LIKE TO TALK TO MY CRAPPY AGENT!
THANK YOU FOR USING METRO MOBILE. OUR RECORDS SHOW THAT YOUR ACCOUNT--
AMERICA'S NEXT TOP BOUNTY HUNTER. WHO WOULD WANT TO HOST CRAP LIKE THAT, ANYWAY?
--IS CURRENTLY PAST DUE. PLEASE PRESS 9 TO SPEAK TO A REPRESENTATIVE.
YAAAAAAH!
SCREEEEEEEECH!
OH, CRAP. I'VE KILLED SOMEONE.
-SNIFF-
GASOLINE. CRAP.
HEY! ARE YOU OK?

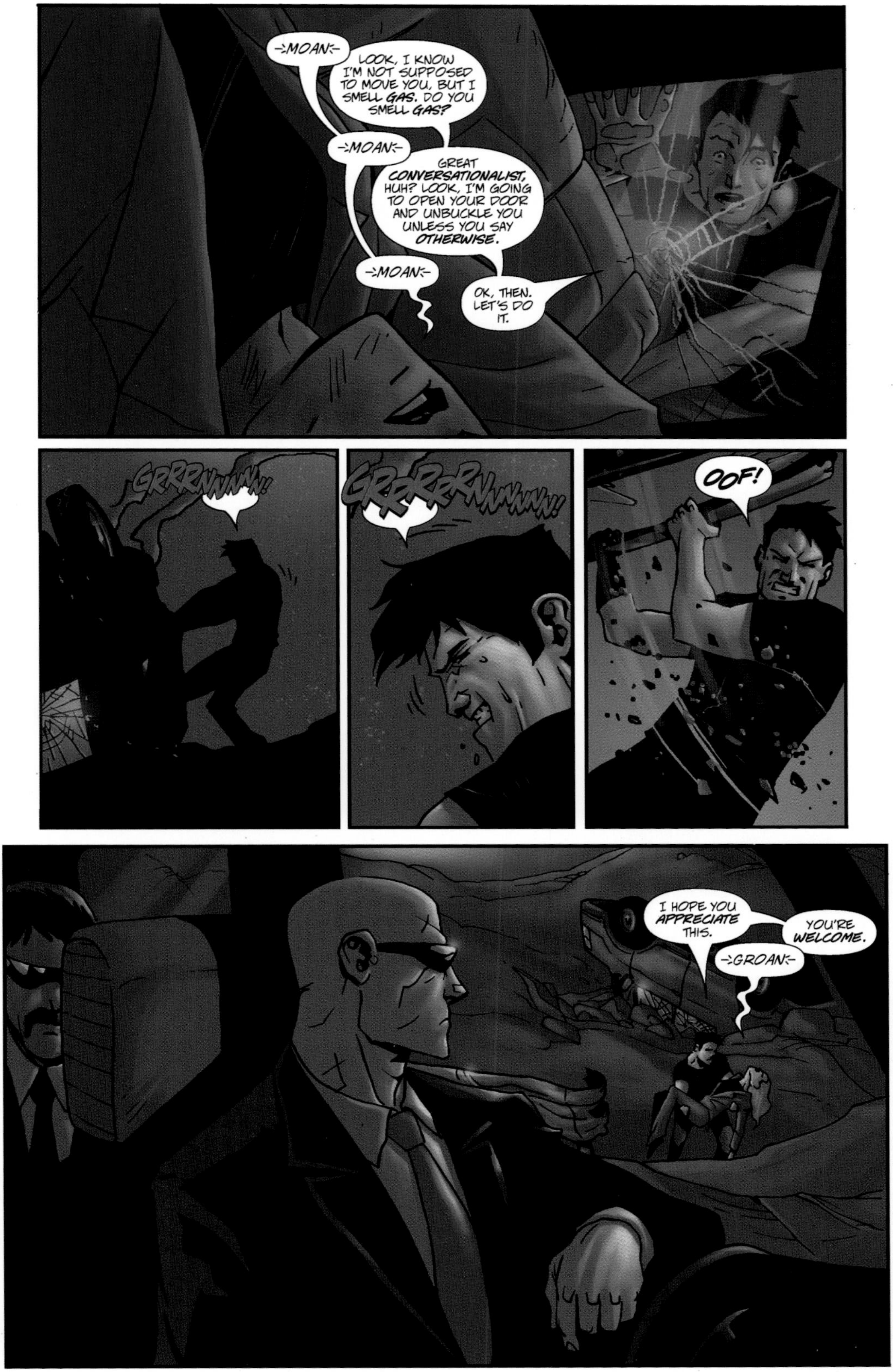
-MOAN-
LOOK, I KNOW I'M NOT SUPPOSED TO MOVE YOU, BUT I SMELL GAS. DO YOU SMELL GAS?
-MOAN-
GREAT CONVERSATIONALIST, HUH? LOOK, I'M GOING TO OPEN YOUR DOOR AND UNBUCKLE YOU UNLESS YOU SAY OTHERWISE.
-MOAN-
OK, THEN. LET'S DO IT.
GRRRNNNNN!
GRRRRRNNNNNN!
OOF!
I HOPE YOU APPRECIATE THIS.
YOU'RE WELCOME.
-GROAN-

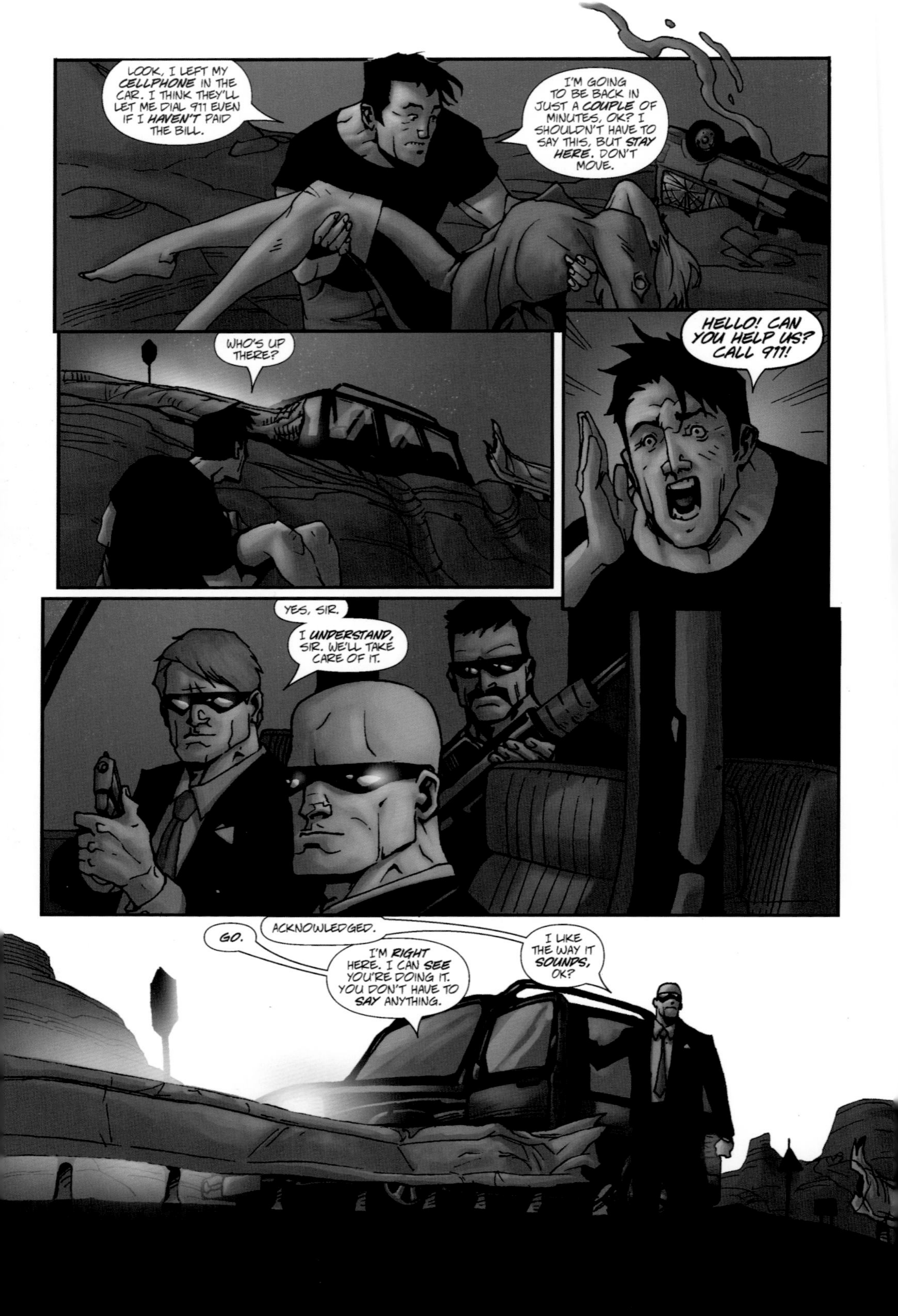
LOOK, I LEFT MY CELLPHONE IN THE CAR. I THINK THEY'LL LET ME DIAL 911 EVEN IF I HAVEN'T PAID THE BILL.
I'M GOING TO BE BACK IN JUST A COUPLE OF MINUTES, OK? I SHOULDN'T HAVE TO SAY THIS, BUT STAY HERE. DON'T MOVE.
WHO'S UP THERE?
HELLO! CAN YOU HELP US? CALL 911!
YES, SIR.
I UNDERSTAND, SIR. WE'LL TAKE CARE OF IT.
GO.
ACKNOWLEDGED.
I'M RIGHT HERE. I CAN SEE YOU'RE DOING IT. YOU DON'T HAVE TO SAY ANYTHING.
I LIKE THE WAY IT SOUNDS, OK?

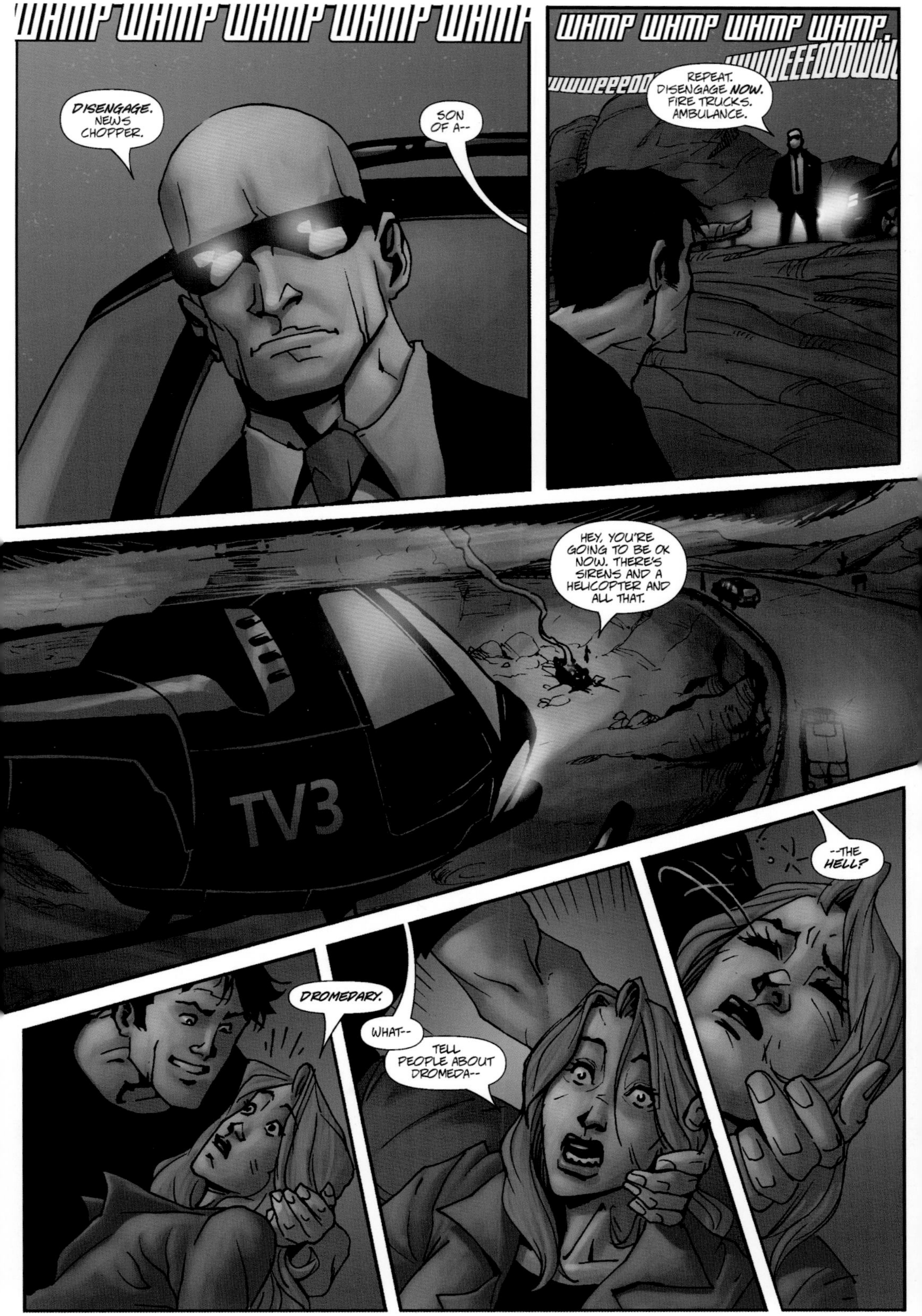
WHMP WHMP WHMP WHMP WHMP
DISENGAGE. NEWS CHOPPER.
SON OF A--
WHMP WHMP WHMP WHMP.
REPEAT. DISENGAGE NOW. FIRE TRUCKS. AMBULANCE.
HEY, YOU'RE GOING TO BE OK NOW. THERE'S SIRENS AND A HELICOPTER AND ALL THAT.
TV3
DROMEDARY.
WHAT--
TELL PEOPLE ABOUT DROMEDA--
--THE HELL?

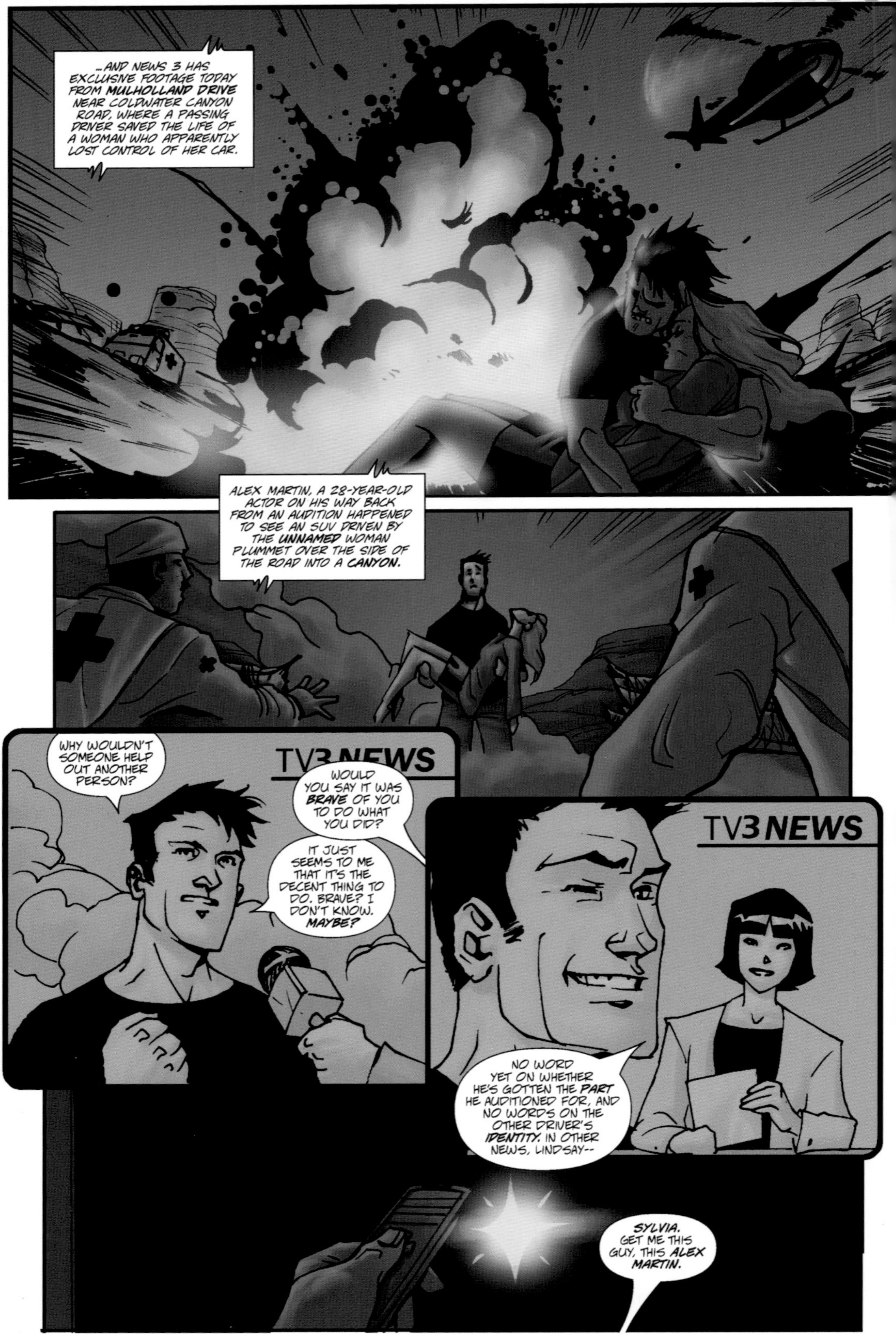
...AND NEWS 3 HAS EXCLUSIVE FOOTAGE TODAY FROM MULHOLLAND DRIVE NEAR COLDWATER CANYON ROAD, WHERE A PASSING DRIVER SAVED THE LIFE OF A WOMAN WHO APPARENTLY LOST CONTROL OF HER CAR.
ALEX MARTIN, A 28-YEAR-OLD ACTOR ON HIS WAY BACK FROM AN AUDITION HAPPENED TO SEE AN SUV DRIVEN BY THE UNNAMED WOMAN PLUMMET OVER THE SIDE OF THE ROAD INTO A CANYON.
TV3 NEWS
WHY WOULDN'T SOMEONE HELP OUT ANOTHER PERSON?
WOULD YOU SAY IT WAS BRAVE OF YOU TO DO WHAT YOU DID?
IT JUST SEEMS TO ME THAT IT'S THE DECENT THING TO DO. BRAVE? I DON'T KNOW. MAYBE?
TV3 NEWS
NO WORD YET ON WHETHER HE'S GOTTEN THE PART HE AUDITIONED FOR, AND NO WORDS ON THE OTHER DRIVER'S IDENTITY. IN OTHER NEWS, LINDSAY--
SYLVIA. GET ME THIS GUY, THIS ALEX MARTIN.

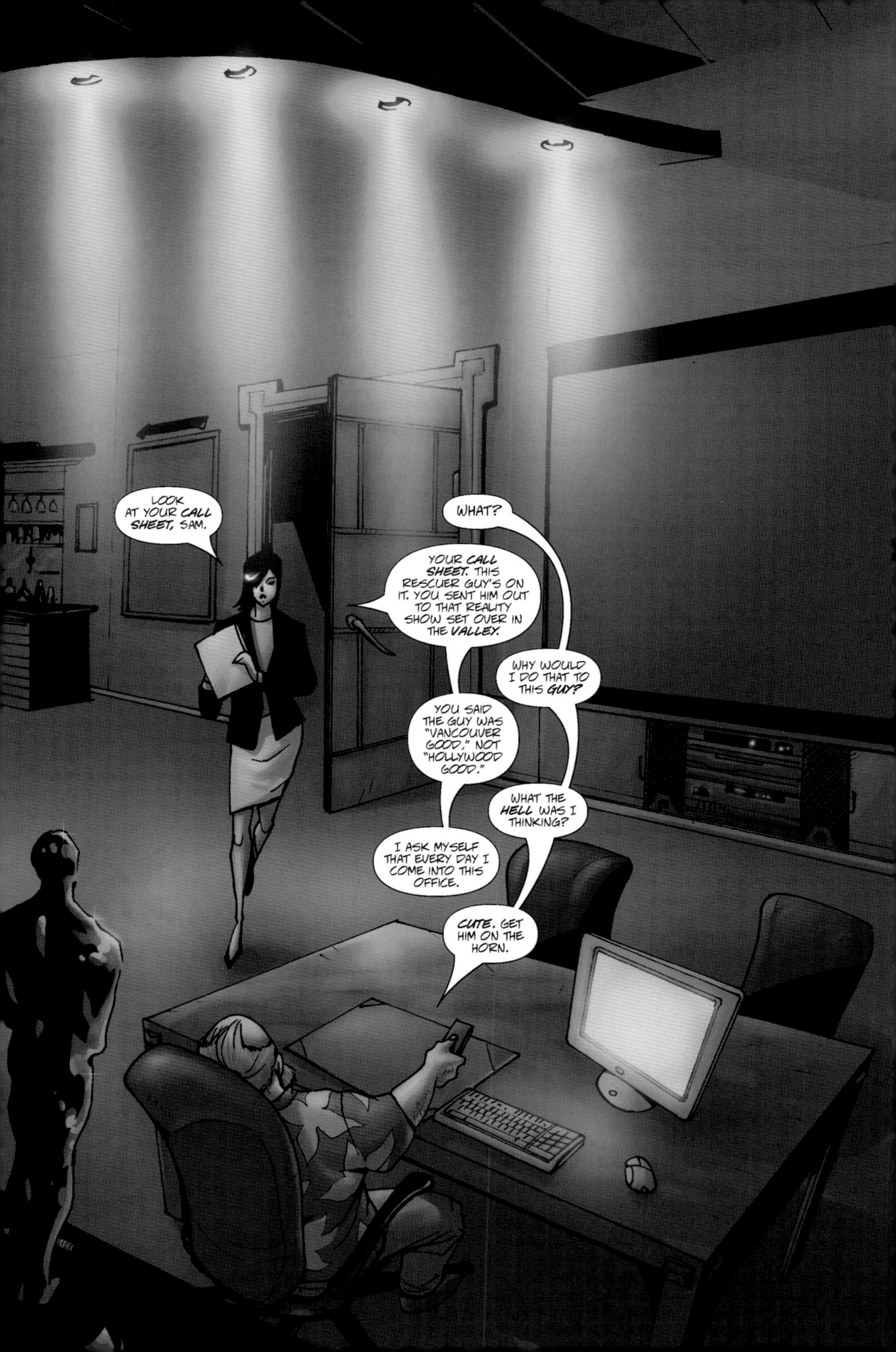
LOOK AT YOUR CALL SHEET, SAM.
WHAT?
YOUR CALL SHEET. THIS RESCUER GUY'S ON IT. YOU SENT HIM OUT TO THAT REALITY SHOW SET OVER IN THE VALLEY.
WHY WOULD I DO THAT TO THIS GUY?
YOU SAID THE GUY WAS "VANCOUVER GOOD," NOT "HOLLYWOOD GOOD."
WHAT THE HELL WAS I THINKING?
I ASK MYSELF THAT EVERY DAY I COME INTO THIS OFFICE.
CUTE. GET HIM ON THE HORN.

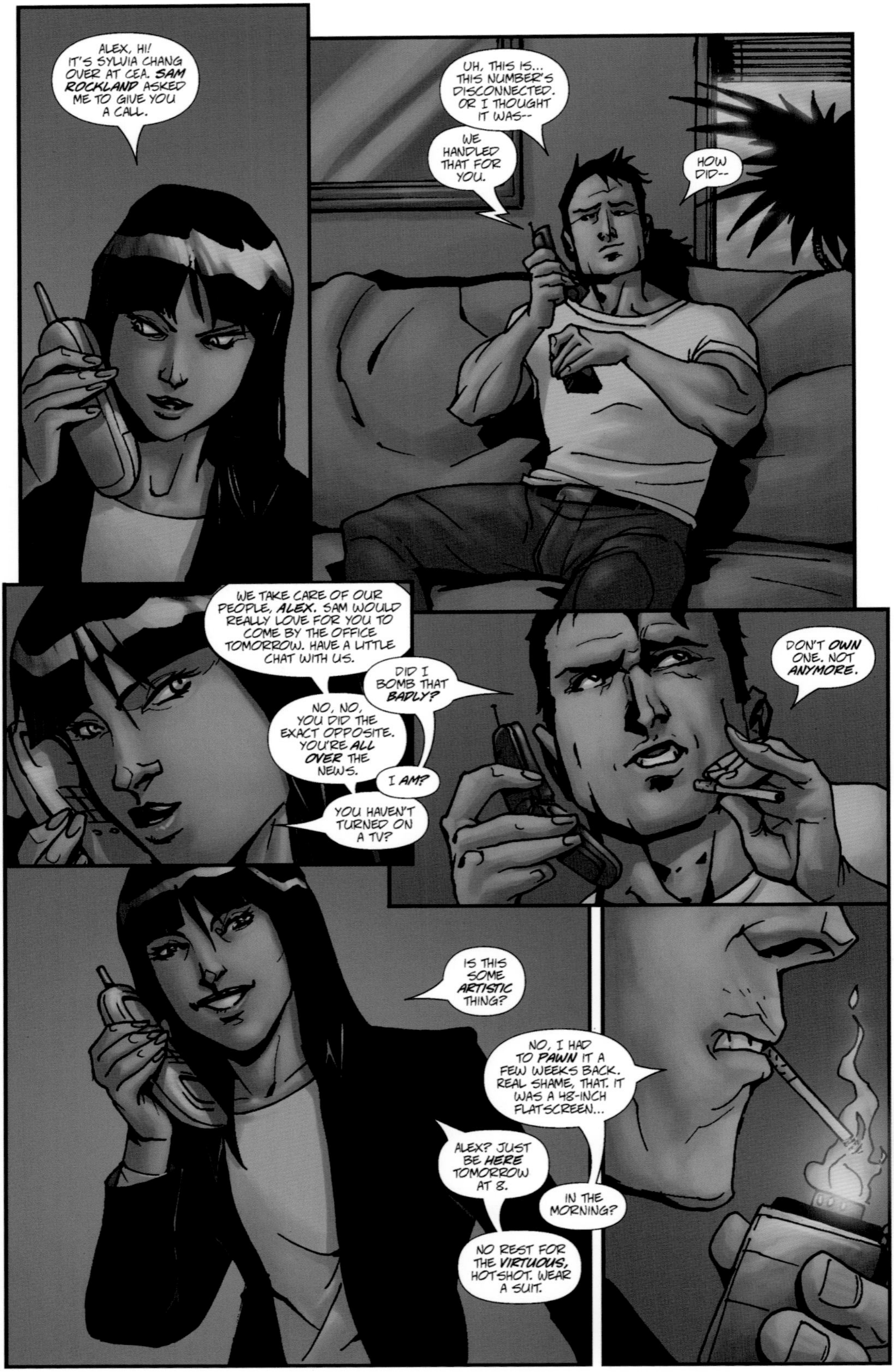
ALEX, HI! IT'S SYLVIA CHANG OVER AT CEA. SAM ROCKLAND ASKED ME TO GIVE YOU A CALL.
UH, THIS IS... THIS NUMBER'S DISCONNECTED. OR I THOUGHT IT WAS--
WE HANDLED THAT FOR YOU.
HOW DID--
WE TAKE CARE OF OUR PEOPLE, ALEX. SAM WOULD REALLY LOVE FOR YOU TO COME BY THE OFFICE TOMORROW. HAVE A LITTLE CHAT WITH US.
DID I BOMB THAT BADLY?
NO, NO, YOU DID THE EXACT OPPOSITE. YOU'RE ALL OVER THE NEWS.
I AM?
YOU HAVEN'T TURNED ON A TV?
DON'T OWN ONE. NOT ANYMORE.
IS THIS SOME ARTISTIC THING?
NO, I HAD TO PAWN IT A FEW WEEKS BACK. REAL SHAME, THAT. IT WAS A 48-INCH FLATSCREEN...
ALEX? JUST BE HERE TOMORROW AT 8.
IN THE MORNING?
NO REST FOR THE VIRTUOUS, HOTSHOT. WEAR A SUIT.

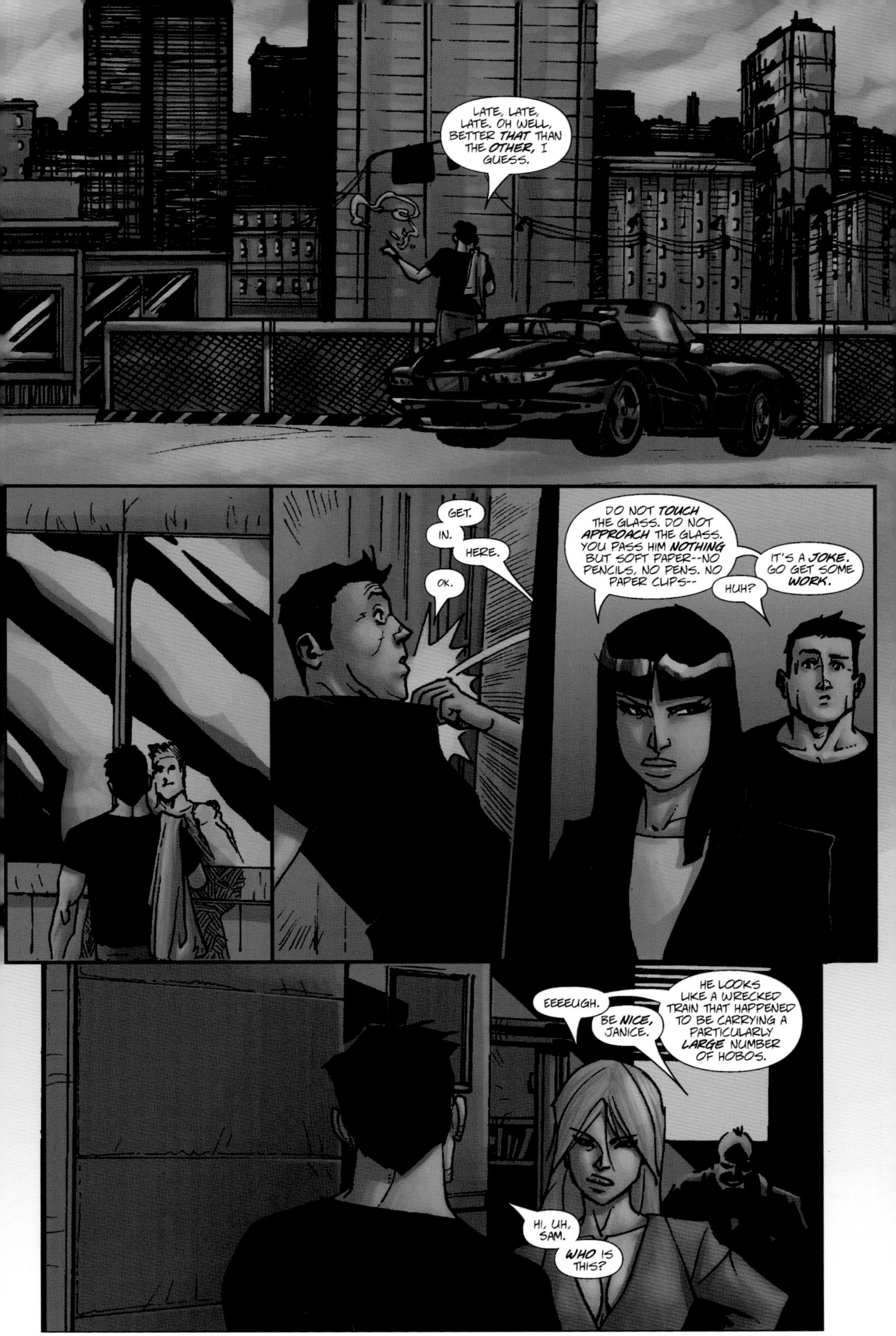
LATE, LATE, LATE. OH WELL, BETTER THAT THAN THE OTHER, I GUESS.
GET.
IN.
HERE.
OK.
DO NOT TOUCH THE GLASS. DO NOT APPROACH THE GLASS. YOU PASS HIM NOTHING BUT SOFT PAPER--NO PENCILS, NO PENS. NO PAPER CLIPS--
HUH?
IT'S A JOKE. GO GET SOME WORK.
EEEEUGH.
BE NICE, JANICE.
HE LOOKS LIKE A WRECKED TRAIN THAT HAPPENED TO BE CARRYING A PARTICULARLY LARGE NUMBER OF HOBOS.
HI, UH, SAM.
WHO IS THIS?

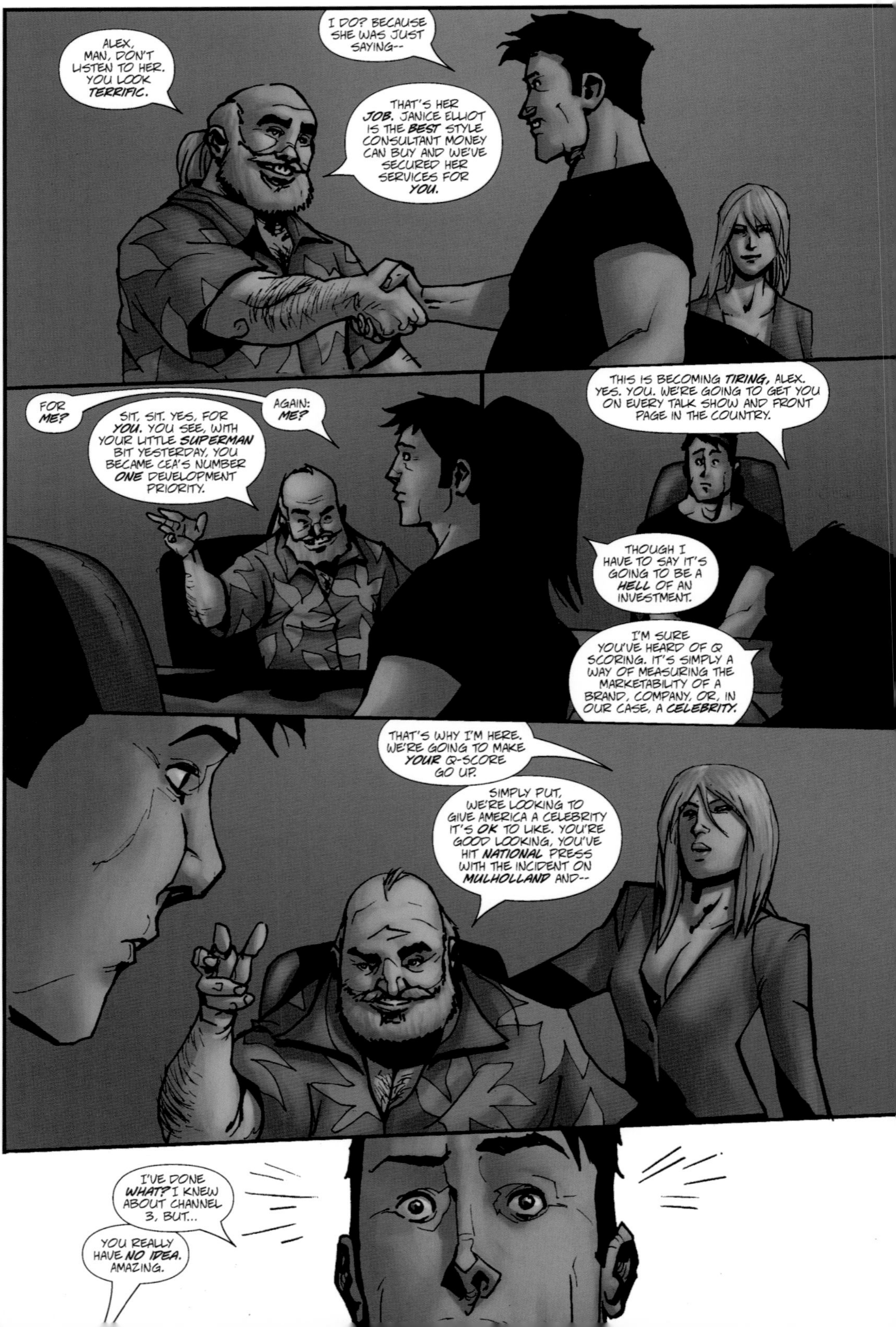
ALEX, MAN, DON'T LISTEN TO HER. YOU LOOK **TERRIFIC**.
I DO? BECAUSE SHE WAS JUST SAYING--
THAT'S HER **JOB**. JANICE ELLIOT IS THE **BEST** STYLE CONSULTANT MONEY CAN BUY AND WE'VE SECURED HER SERVICES FOR **YOU**.
FOR **ME?**
SIT, SIT. YES, FOR **YOU**. YOU SEE, WITH YOUR LITTLE **SUPERMAN** BIT YESTERDAY, YOU BECAME CEA'S NUMBER **ONE** DEVELOPMENT PRIORITY.
AGAIN: **ME?**
THIS IS BECOMING **TIRING**, ALEX. YES. YOU. WE'RE GOING TO GET YOU ON EVERY TALK SHOW AND FRONT PAGE IN THE COUNTRY.
THOUGH I HAVE TO SAY IT'S GOING TO BE A **HELL** OF AN INVESTMENT.
I'M SURE YOU'VE HEARD OF Q SCORING. IT'S SIMPLY A WAY OF MEASURING THE MARKETABILITY OF A BRAND, COMPANY, OR, IN OUR CASE, A **CELEBRITY**.
THAT'S WHY I'M HERE. WE'RE GOING TO MAKE **YOUR** Q-SCORE GO UP.
SIMPLY PUT, WE'RE LOOKING TO GIVE AMERICA A CELEBRITY IT'S **OK** TO LIKE. YOU'RE GOOD LOOKING, YOU'VE HIT **NATIONAL** PRESS WITH THE INCIDENT ON **MULHOLLAND** AND--
I'VE DONE **WHAT?** I KNEW ABOUT CHANNEL 3, BUT...
YOU REALLY HAVE **NO IDEA**. AMAZING.

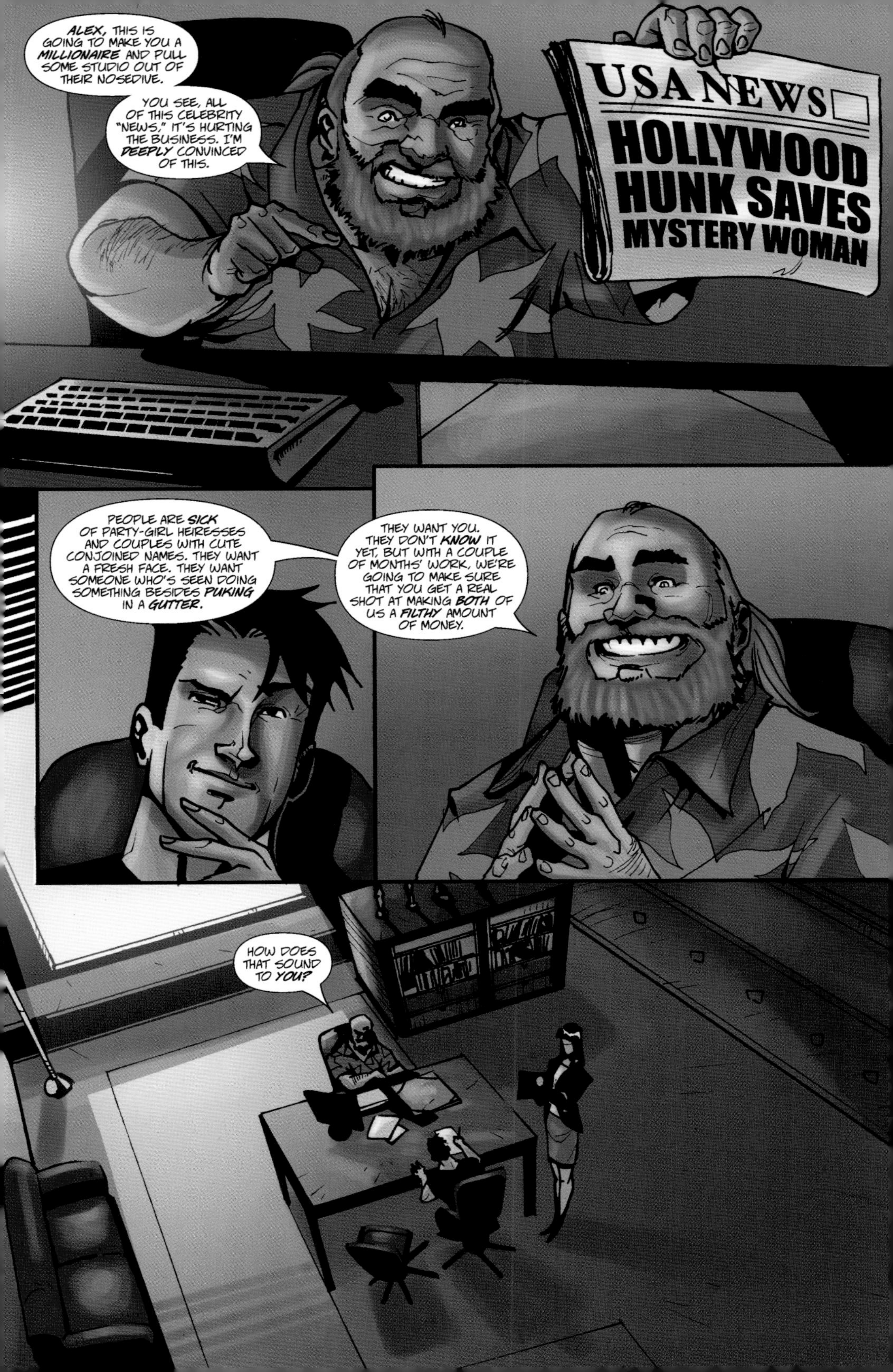

ALEX, THIS IS GOING TO MAKE YOU A MILLIONAIRE AND PULL SOME STUDIO OUT OF THEIR NOSEDIVE.
YOU SEE, ALL OF THIS CELEBRITY "NEWS," IT'S HURTING THE BUSINESS. I'M DEEPLY CONVINCED OF THIS.
USA NEWS
HOLLYWOOD HUNK SAVES MYSTERY WOMAN
PEOPLE ARE SICK OF PARTY-GIRL HEIRESSES AND COUPLES WITH CUTE CONJOINED NAMES. THEY WANT A FRESH FACE. THEY WANT SOMEONE WHO'S SEEN DOING SOMETHING BESIDES PUKING IN A GUTTER.
THEY WANT YOU. THEY DON'T KNOW IT YET, BUT WITH A COUPLE OF MONTHS' WORK, WE'RE GOING TO MAKE SURE THAT YOU GET A REAL SHOT AT MAKING BOTH OF US A FILTHY AMOUNT OF MONEY.
HOW DOES THAT SOUND TO YOU?

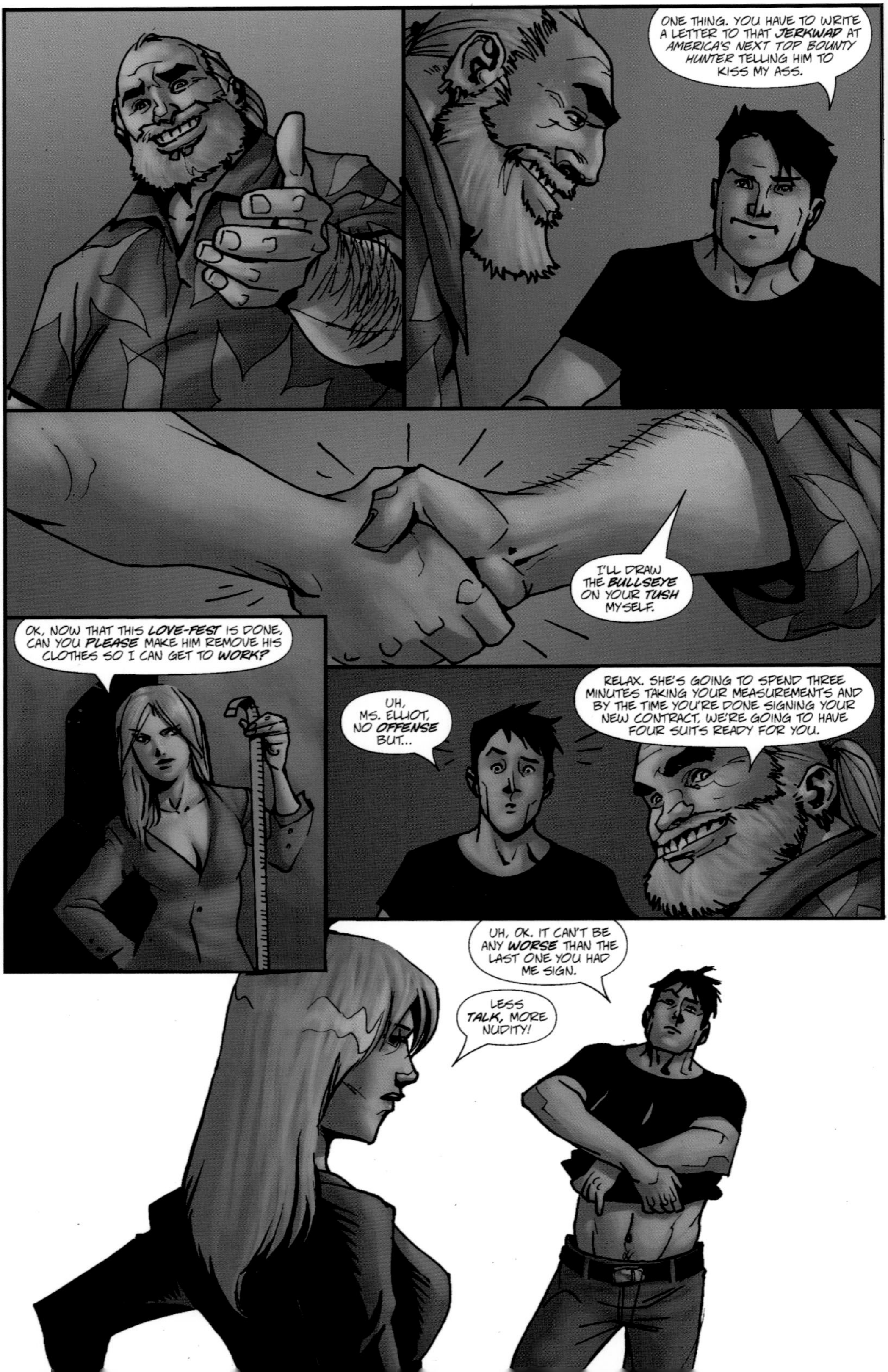

ONE THING. YOU HAVE TO WRITE A LETTER TO THAT JERKWAD AT AMERICA'S NEXT TOP BOUNTY HUNTER TELLING HIM TO KISS MY ASS.
I'LL DRAW THE BULLSEYE ON YOUR TUSH MYSELF.
OK, NOW THAT THIS LOVE-FEST IS DONE, CAN YOU PLEASE MAKE HIM REMOVE HIS CLOTHES SO I CAN GET TO WORK?
UH, MS. ELLIOT, NO OFFENSE BUT...
RELAX. SHE'S GOING TO SPEND THREE MINUTES TAKING YOUR MEASUREMENTS AND BY THE TIME YOU'RE DONE SIGNING YOUR NEW CONTRACT, WE'RE GOING TO HAVE FOUR SUITS READY FOR YOU.
UH, OK. IT CAN'T BE ANY WORSE THAN THE LAST ONE YOU HAD ME SIGN.
LESS TALK, MORE NUDITY!

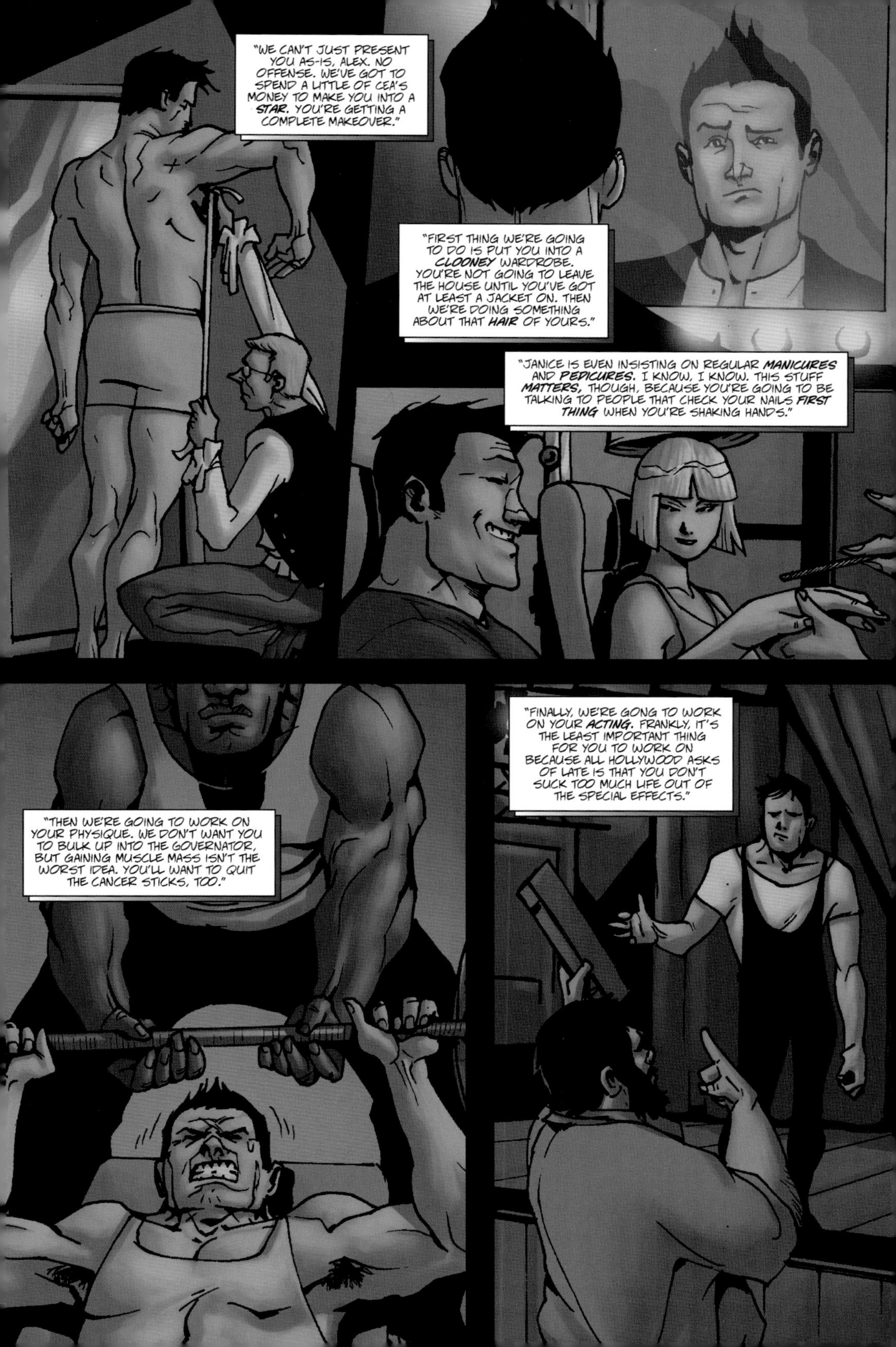
"WE CAN'T JUST PRESENT YOU AS-IS, ALEX. NO OFFENSE. WE'VE GOT TO SPEND A LITTLE OF CEA'S MONEY TO MAKE YOU INTO A STAR. YOU'RE GETTING A COMPLETE MAKEOVER."
"FIRST THING WE'RE GOING TO DO IS PUT YOU INTO A CLOONEY WARDROBE. YOU'RE NOT GOING TO LEAVE THE HOUSE UNTIL YOU'VE GOT AT LEAST A JACKET ON. THEN WE'RE DOING SOMETHING ABOUT THAT HAIR OF YOURS."
"JANICE IS EVEN INSISTING ON REGULAR MANICURES AND PEDICURES. I KNOW, I KNOW. THIS STUFF MATTERS, THOUGH, BECAUSE YOU'RE GOING TO BE TALKING TO PEOPLE THAT CHECK YOUR NAILS FIRST THING WHEN YOU'RE SHAKING HANDS."
"THEN WE'RE GOING TO WORK ON YOUR PHYSIQUE. WE DON'T WANT YOU TO BULK UP INTO THE GOVERNATOR, BUT GAINING MUSCLE MASS ISN'T THE WORST IDEA. YOU'LL WANT TO QUIT THE CANCER STICKS, TOO."
"FINALLY, WE'RE GONG TO WORK ON YOUR ACTING. FRANKLY, IT'S THE LEAST IMPORTANT THING FOR YOU TO WORK ON BECAUSE ALL HOLLYWOOD ASKS OF LATE IS THAT YOU DON'T SUCK TOO MUCH LIFE OUT OF THE SPECIAL EFFECTS."

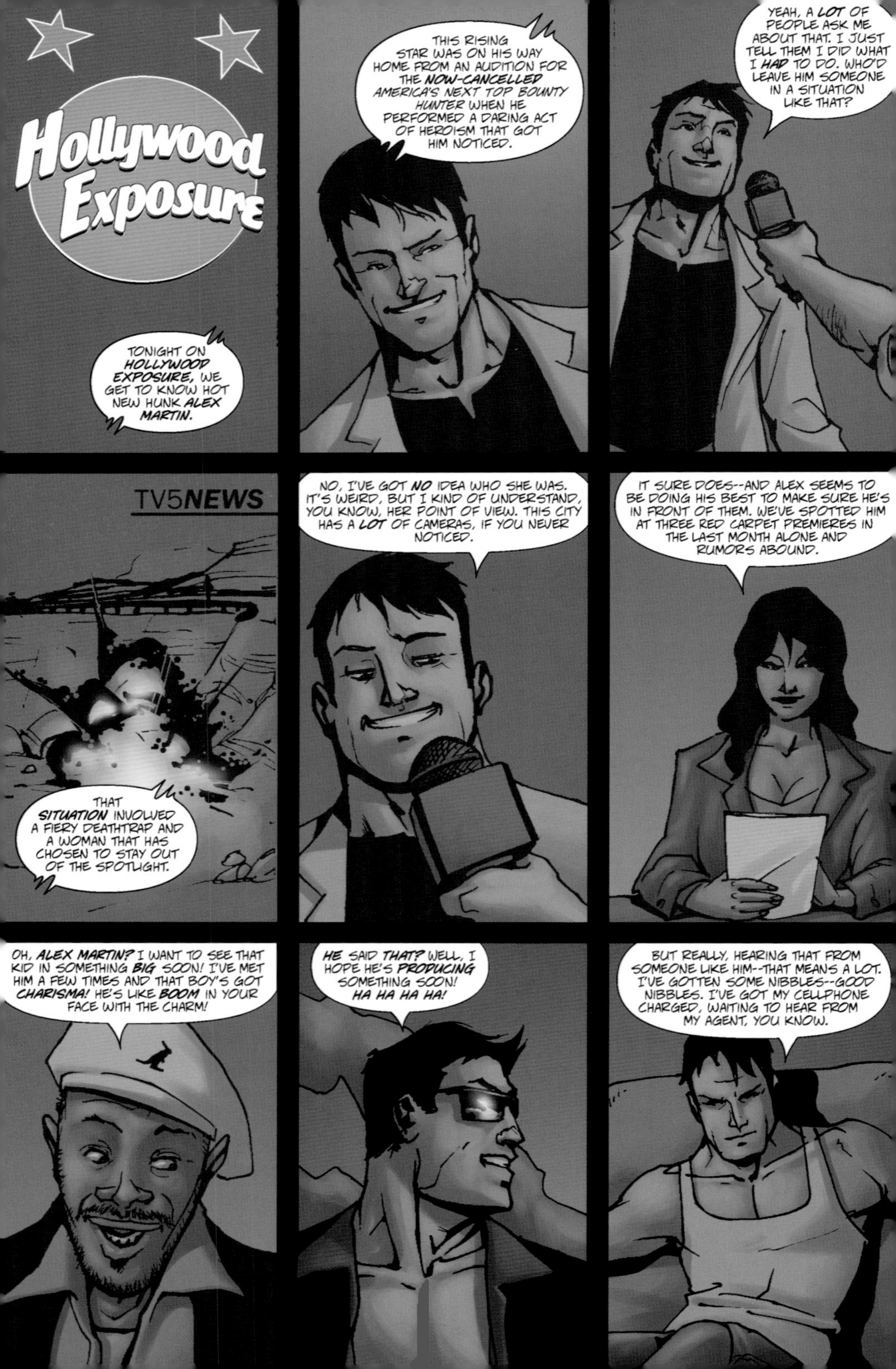
Hollywood Exposure
TONIGHT ON HOLLYWOOD EXPOSURE, WE GET TO KNOW HOT NEW HUNK ALEX MARTIN.
THIS RISING STAR WAS ON HIS WAY HOME FROM AN AUDITION FOR THE NOW-CANCELLED AMERICA'S NEXT TOP BOUNTY HUNTER WHEN HE PERFORMED A DARING ACT OF HEROISM THAT GOT HIM NOTICED.
YEAH, A LOT OF PEOPLE ASK ME ABOUT THAT. I JUST TELL THEM I DID WHAT I HAD TO DO. WHO'D LEAVE HIM SOMEONE IN A SITUATION LIKE THAT?
TV5NEWS
THAT SITUATION INVOLVED A FIERY DEATHTRAP AND A WOMAN THAT HAS CHOSEN TO STAY OUT OF THE SPOTLIGHT.
NO, I'VE GOT NO IDEA WHO SHE WAS. IT'S WEIRD, BUT I KIND OF UNDERSTAND, YOU KNOW, HER POINT OF VIEW. THIS CITY HAS A LOT OF CAMERAS, IF YOU NEVER NOTICED.
IT SURE DOES--AND ALEX SEEMS TO BE DOING HIS BEST TO MAKE SURE HE'S IN FRONT OF THEM. WE'VE SPOTTED HIM AT THREE RED CARPET PREMIERES IN THE LAST MONTH ALONE AND RUMORS ABOUND.
OH, ALEX MARTIN? I WANT TO SEE THAT KID IN SOMETHING BIG SOON! I'VE MET HIM A FEW TIMES AND THAT BOY'S GOT CHARISMA! HE'S LIKE BOOM IN YOUR FACE WITH THE CHARM!
HE SAID THAT? WELL, I HOPE HE'S PRODUCING SOMETHING SOON! HA HA HA HA!
BUT REALLY, HEARING THAT FROM SOMEONE LIKE HIM--THAT MEANS A LOT. I'VE GOTTEN SOME NIBBLES--GOOD NIBBLES. I'VE GOT MY CELLPHONE CHARGED, WAITING TO HEAR FROM MY AGENT, YOU KNOW.

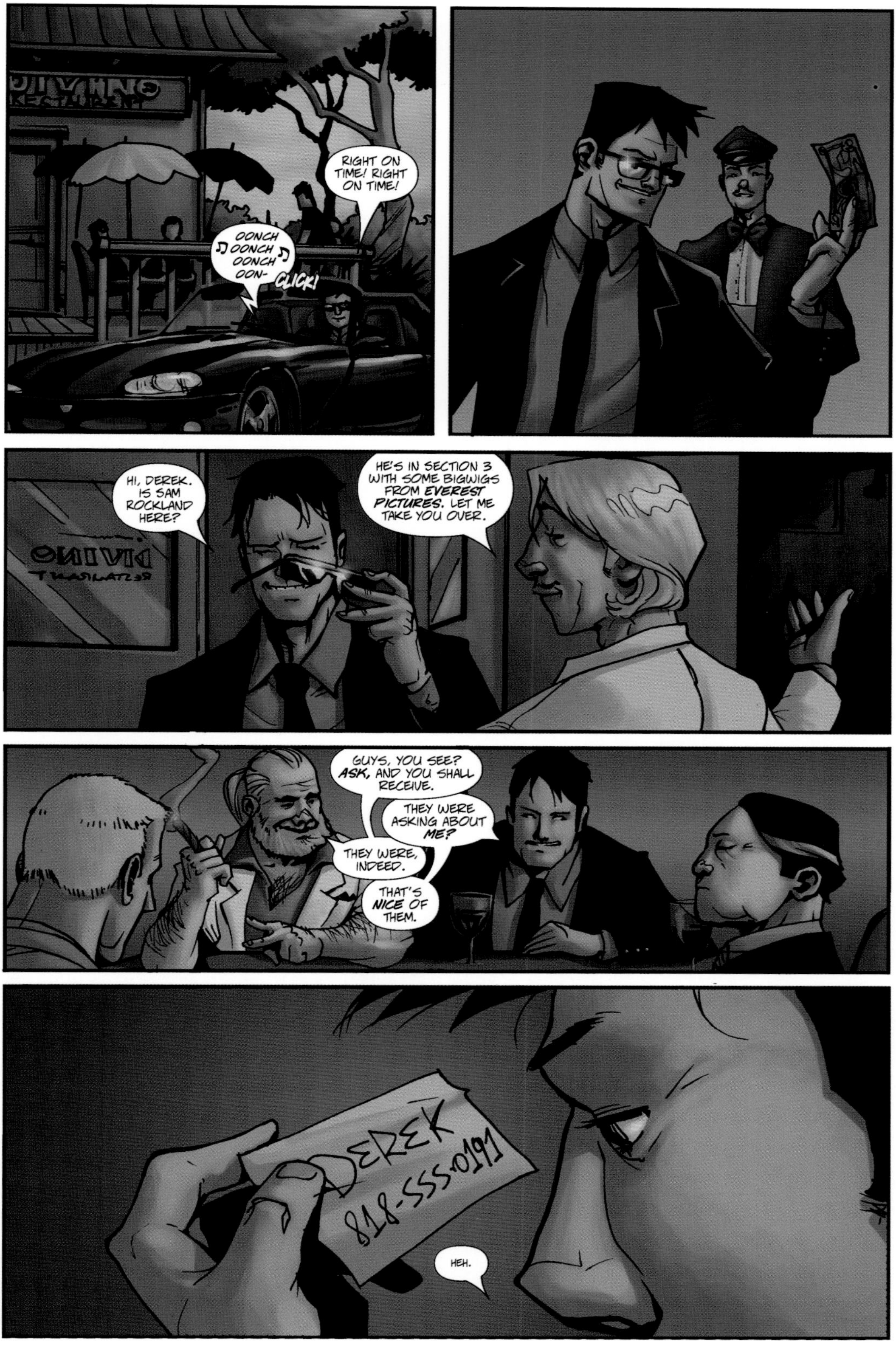
RIGHT ON TIME! RIGHT ON TIME!
OONCH OONCH OONCH OON-
CLICK!
HI, DEREK. IS SAM ROCKLAND HERE?
HE'S IN SECTION 3 WITH SOME BIGWIGS FROM EVEREST PICTURES. LET ME TAKE YOU OVER.
GUYS, YOU SEE? ASK, AND YOU SHALL RECEIVE.
THEY WERE ASKING ABOUT ME?
THEY WERE, INDEED.
THAT'S NICE OF THEM.
DEREK
818-555-0191
HEH.

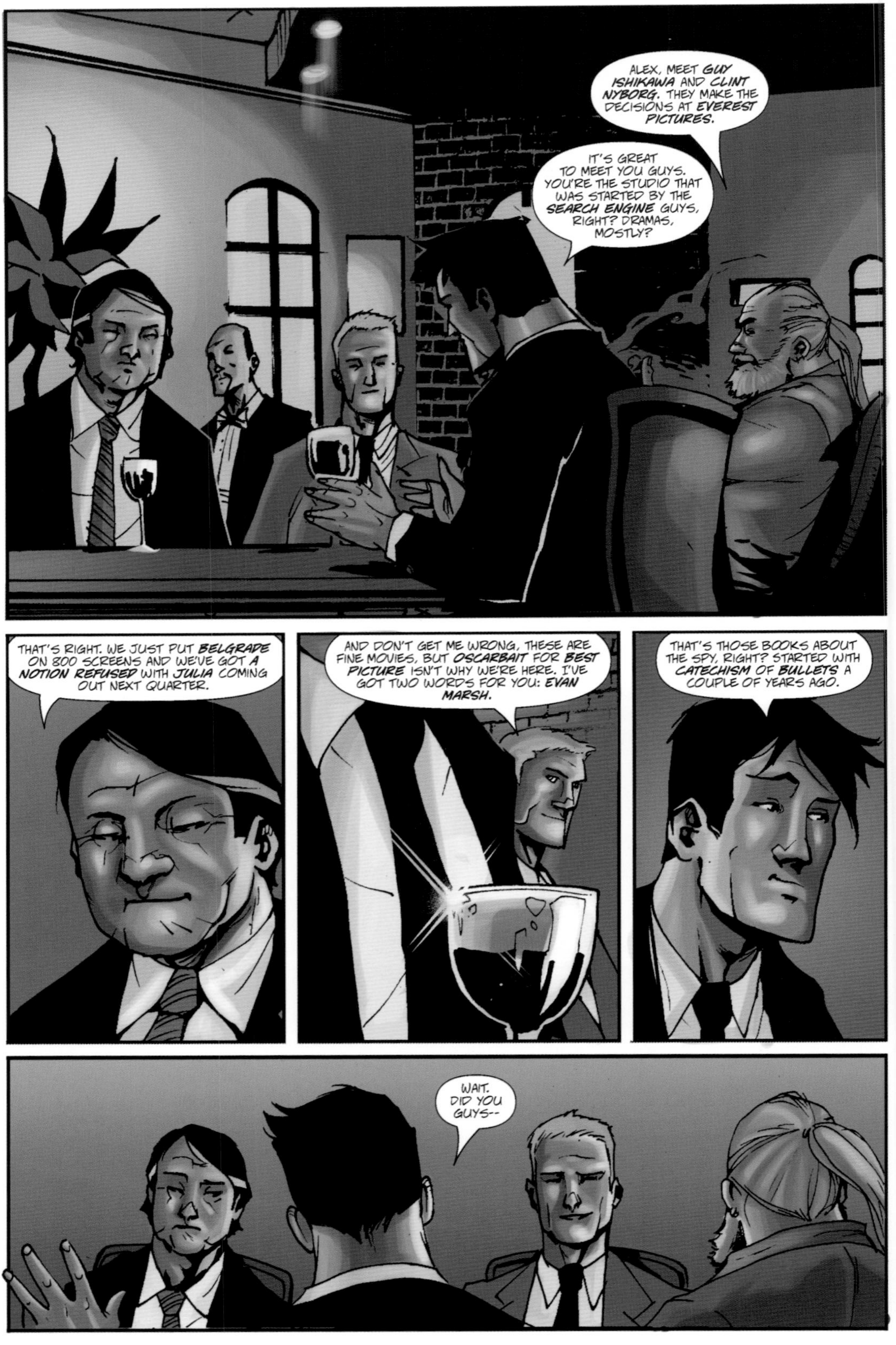
ALEX, MEET GUY ISHIKAWA AND CLINT NYBORG. THEY MAKE THE DECISIONS AT EVEREST PICTURES.
IT'S GREAT TO MEET YOU GUYS. YOU'RE THE STUDIO THAT WAS STARTED BY THE SEARCH ENGINE GUYS, RIGHT? DRAMAS, MOSTLY?
THAT'S RIGHT. WE JUST PUT BELGRADE ON 800 SCREENS AND WE'VE GOT A NOTION REFUSED WITH JULIA COMING OUT NEXT QUARTER.
AND DON'T GET ME WRONG, THESE ARE FINE MOVIES, BUT OSCARBAIT FOR BEST PICTURE ISN'T WHY WE'RE HERE. I'VE GOT TWO WORDS FOR YOU: EVAN MARSH.
THAT'S THOSE BOOKS ABOUT THE SPY, RIGHT? STARTED WITH CATECHISM OF BULLETS A COUPLE OF YEARS AGO.
WAIT. DID YOU GUYS--

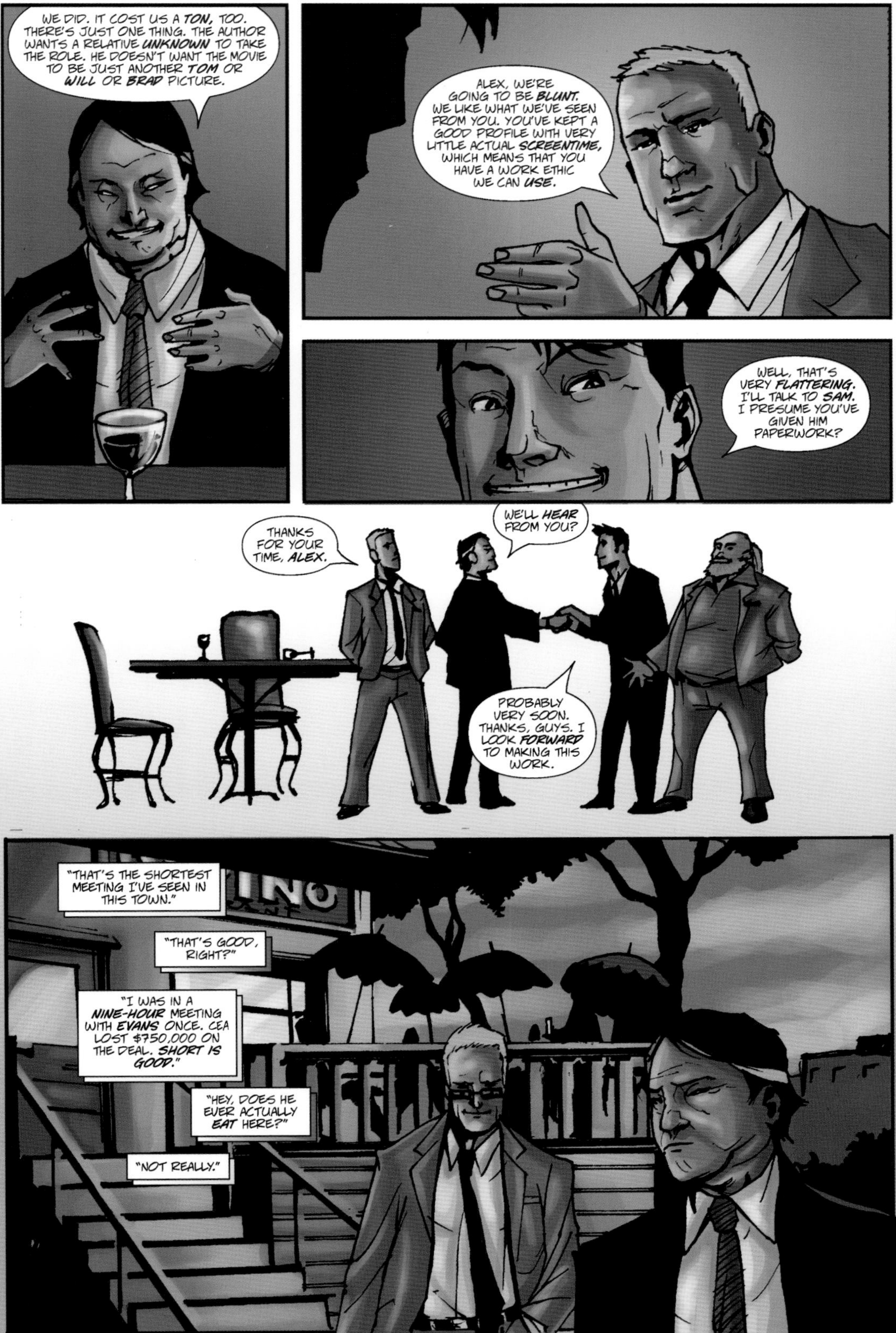
WE DID. IT COST US A TON, TOO. THERE'S JUST ONE THING. THE AUTHOR WANTS A RELATIVE UNKNOWN TO TAKE THE ROLE. HE DOESN'T WANT THE MOVIE TO BE JUST ANOTHER TOM OR WILL OR BRAD PICTURE.
ALEX, WE'RE GOING TO BE BLUNT. WE LIKE WHAT WE'VE SEEN FROM YOU. YOU'VE KEPT A GOOD PROFILE WITH VERY LITTLE ACTUAL SCREENTIME, WHICH MEANS THAT YOU HAVE A WORK ETHIC WE CAN USE.
WELL, THAT'S VERY FLATTERING. I'LL TALK TO SAM. I PRESUME YOU'VE GIVEN HIM PAPERWORK?
THANKS FOR YOUR TIME, ALEX.
WE'LL HEAR FROM YOU?
PROBABLY VERY SOON. THANKS, GUYS. I LOOK FORWARD TO MAKING THIS WORK.
"THAT'S THE SHORTEST MEETING I'VE SEEN IN THIS TOWN."
"THAT'S GOOD, RIGHT?"
"I WAS IN A NINE-HOUR MEETING WITH EVANS ONCE. CEA LOST $750,000 ON THE DEAL. SHORT IS GOOD."
"HEY, DOES HE EVER ACTUALLY EAT HERE?"
"NOT REALLY."

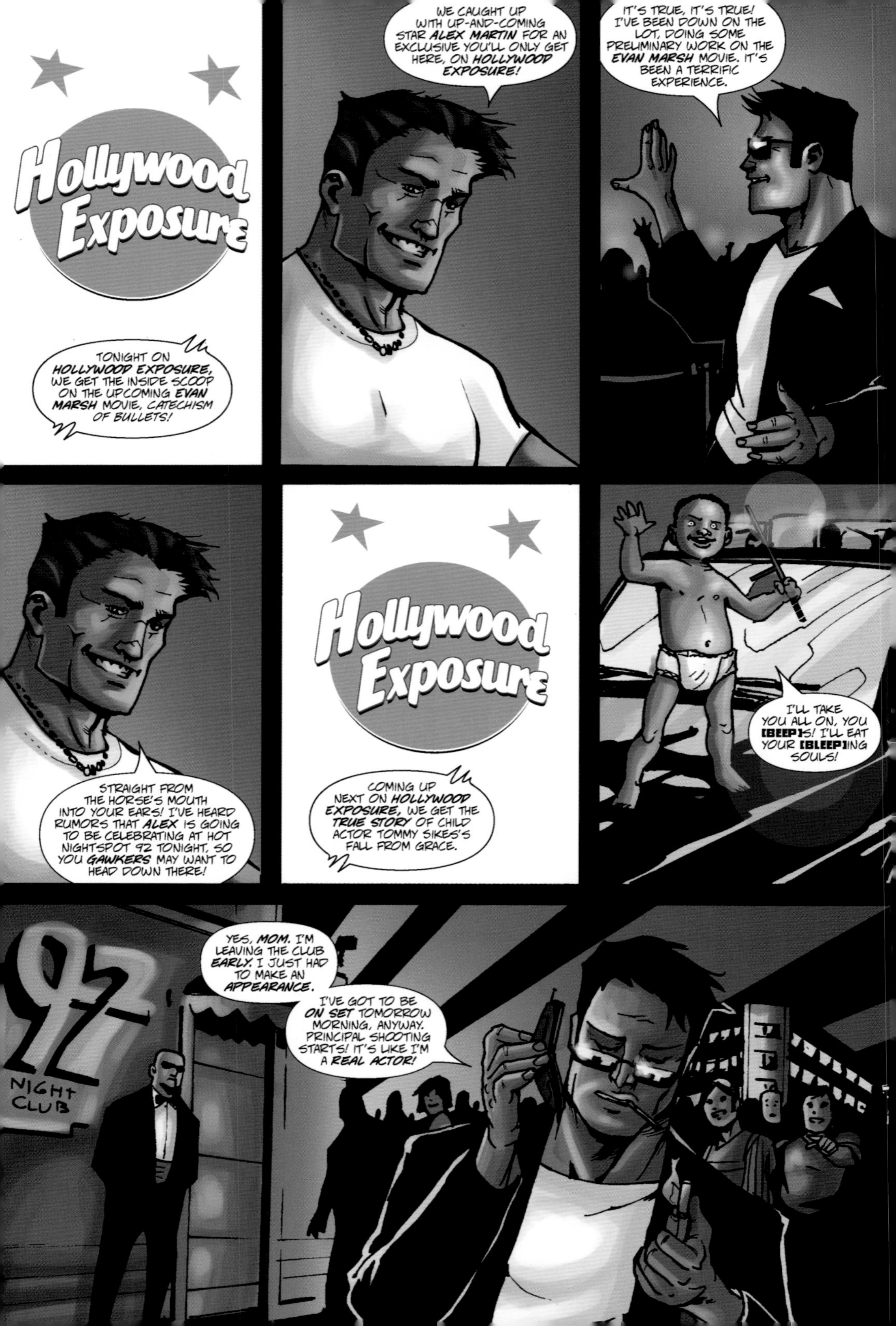
Hollywood Exposure
TONIGHT ON HOLLYWOOD EXPOSURE, WE GET THE INSIDE SCOOP ON THE UPCOMING EVAN MARSH MOVIE, CATECHISM OF BULLETS!
WE CAUGHT UP WITH UP-AND-COMING STAR ALEX MARTIN FOR AN EXCLUSIVE YOU'LL ONLY GET HERE, ON HOLLYWOOD EXPOSURE!
IT'S TRUE, IT'S TRUE! I'VE BEEN DOWN ON THE LOT, DOING SOME PRELIMINARY WORK ON THE EVAN MARSH MOVIE. IT'S BEEN A TERRIFIC EXPERIENCE.
STRAIGHT FROM THE HORSE'S MOUTH INTO YOUR EARS! I'VE HEARD RUMORS THAT ALEX IS GOING TO BE CELEBRATING AT HOT NIGHTSPOT 92 TONIGHT, SO YOU GAWKERS MAY WANT TO HEAD DOWN THERE!
Hollywood Exposure
COMING UP NEXT ON HOLLYWOOD EXPOSURE, WE GET THE TRUE STORY OF CHILD ACTOR TOMMY SIKES'S FALL FROM GRACE.
I'LL TAKE YOU ALL ON, YOU [BEEP]S! I'LL EAT YOUR [BLEEP]ING SOULS!
92 NIGHT CLUB
YES, MOM. I'M LEAVING THE CLUB EARLY. I JUST HAD TO MAKE AN APPEARANCE.
I'VE GOT TO BE ON SET TOMORROW MORNING, ANYWAY. PRINCIPAL SHOOTING STARTS! IT'S LIKE I'M A REAL ACTOR!

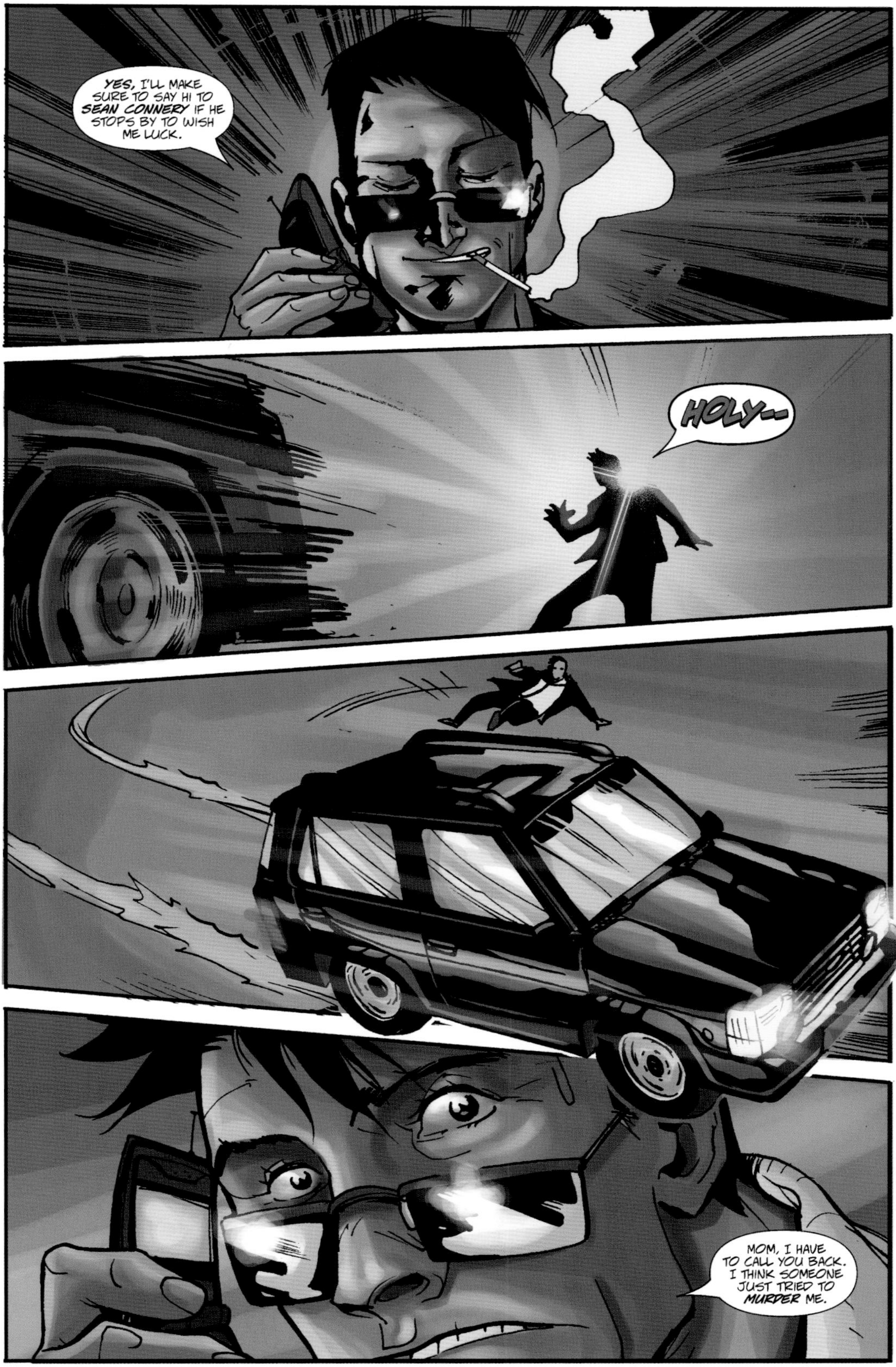
YES, I'LL MAKE SURE TO SAY HI TO SEAN CONNERY IF HE STOPS BY TO WISH ME LUCK.
HOLY--
MOM, I HAVE TO CALL YOU BACK. I THINK SOMEONE JUST TRIED TO MURDER ME.

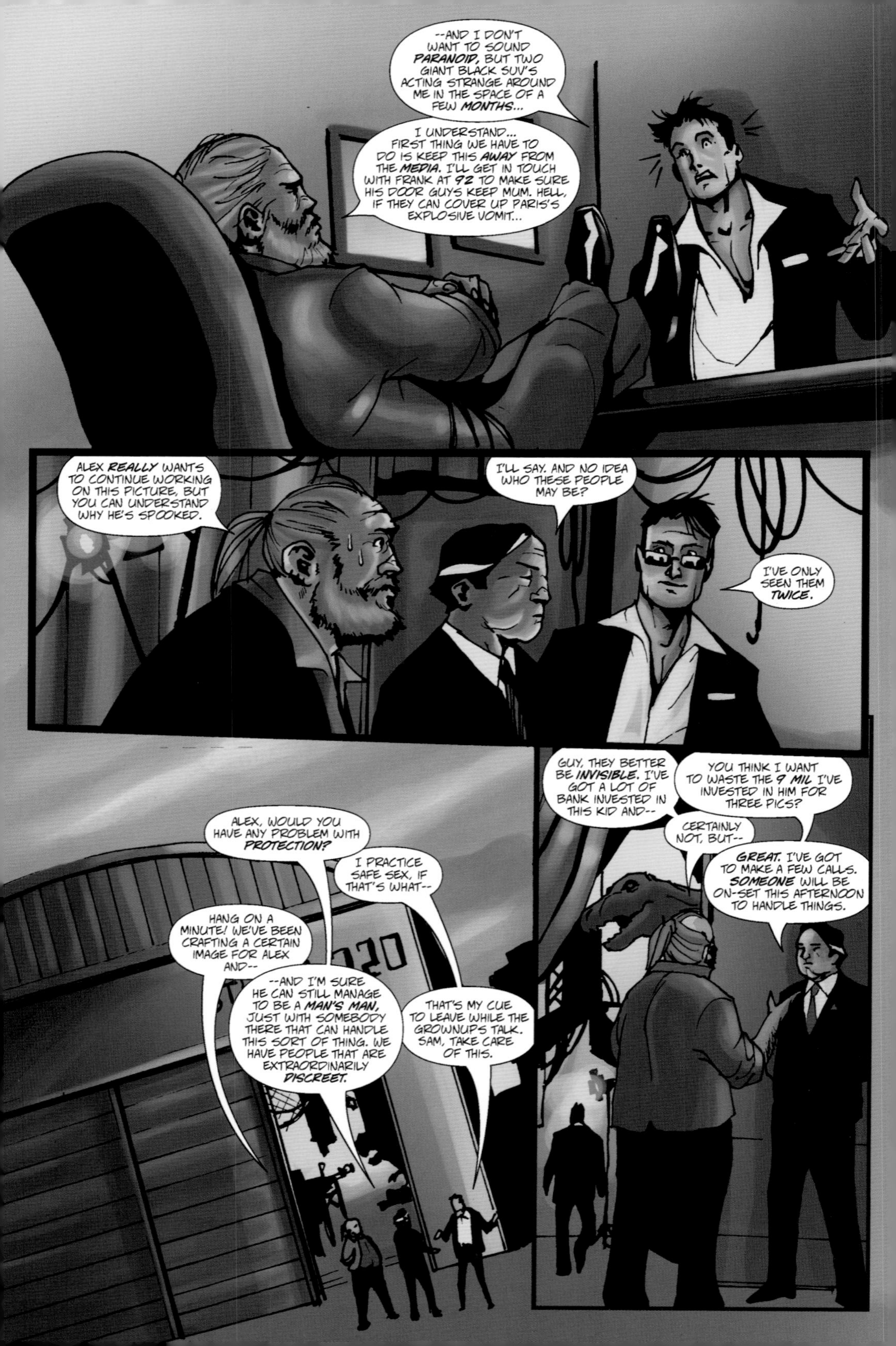
--AND I DON'T WANT TO SOUND PARANOID, BUT TWO GIANT BLACK SUV'S ACTING STRANGE AROUND ME IN THE SPACE OF A FEW MONTHS...
I UNDERSTAND... FIRST THING WE HAVE TO DO IS KEEP THIS AWAY FROM THE MEDIA. I'LL GET IN TOUCH WITH FRANK AT 92 TO MAKE SURE HIS DOOR GUYS KEEP MUM. HELL, IF THEY CAN COVER UP PARIS'S EXPLOSIVE VOMIT...
ALEX REALLY WANTS TO CONTINUE WORKING ON THIS PICTURE, BUT YOU CAN UNDERSTAND WHY HE'S SPOOKED.
I'LL SAY. AND NO IDEA WHO THESE PEOPLE MAY BE?
I'VE ONLY SEEN THEM TWICE.
ALEX, WOULD YOU HAVE ANY PROBLEM WITH PROTECTION?
I PRACTICE SAFE SEX, IF THAT'S WHAT--
HANG ON A MINUTE! WE'VE BEEN CRAFTING A CERTAIN IMAGE FOR ALEX AND--
--AND I'M SURE HE CAN STILL MANAGE TO BE A MAN'S MAN, JUST WITH SOMEBODY THERE THAT CAN HANDLE THIS SORT OF THING. WE HAVE PEOPLE THAT ARE EXTRAORDINARILY DISCREET.
THAT'S MY CUE TO LEAVE WHILE THE GROWNUPS TALK. SAM, TAKE CARE OF THIS.
GUY, THEY BETTER BE INVISIBLE. I'VE GOT A LOT OF BANK INVESTED IN THIS KID AND--
CERTAINLY NOT, BUT--
YOU THINK I WANT TO WASTE THE 9 MIL I'VE INVESTED IN HIM FOR THREE PICS?
GREAT. I'VE GOT TO MAKE A FEW CALLS. SOMEONE WILL BE ON-SET THIS AFTERNOON TO HANDLE THINGS.

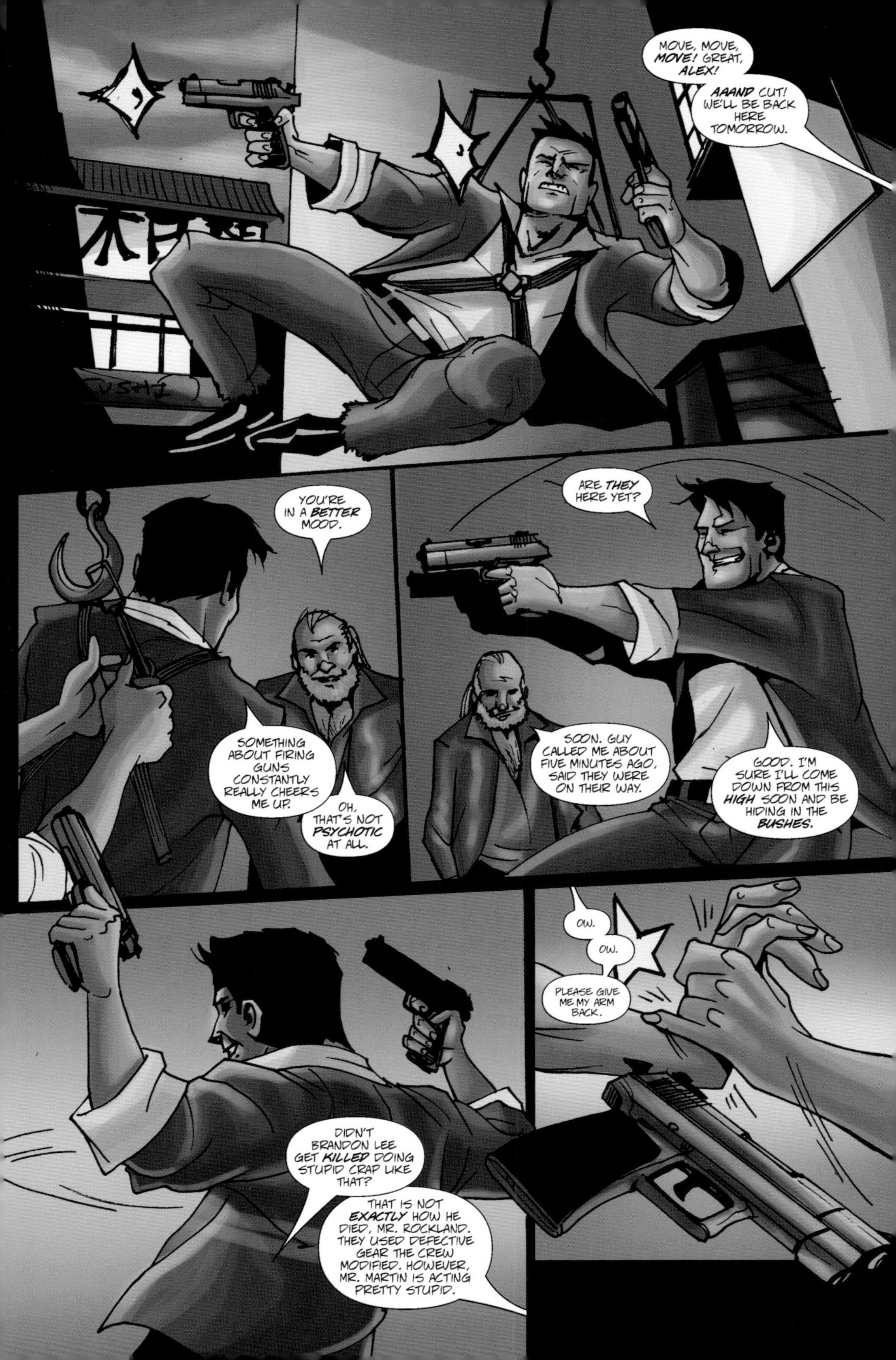
MOVE, MOVE, MOVE! GREAT, ALEX!
AAAND CUT! WE'LL BE BACK HERE TOMORROW.
YOU'RE IN A BETTER MOOD.
SOMETHING ABOUT FIRING GUNS CONSTANTLY REALLY CHEERS ME UP.
OH, THAT'S NOT PSYCHOTIC AT ALL.
ARE THEY HERE YET?
SOON. GUY CALLED ME ABOUT FIVE MINUTES AGO, SAID THEY WERE ON THEIR WAY.
GOOD. I'M SURE I'LL COME DOWN FROM THIS HIGH SOON AND BE HIDING IN THE BUSHES.
DIDN'T BRANDON LEE GET KILLED DOING STUPID CRAP LIKE THAT?
THAT IS NOT EXACTLY HOW HE DIED, MR. ROCKLAND. THEY USED DEFECTIVE GEAR THE CREW MODIFIED. HOWEVER, MR. MARTIN IS ACTING PRETTY STUPID.
OW.
OW.
PLEASE GIVE ME MY ARM BACK.

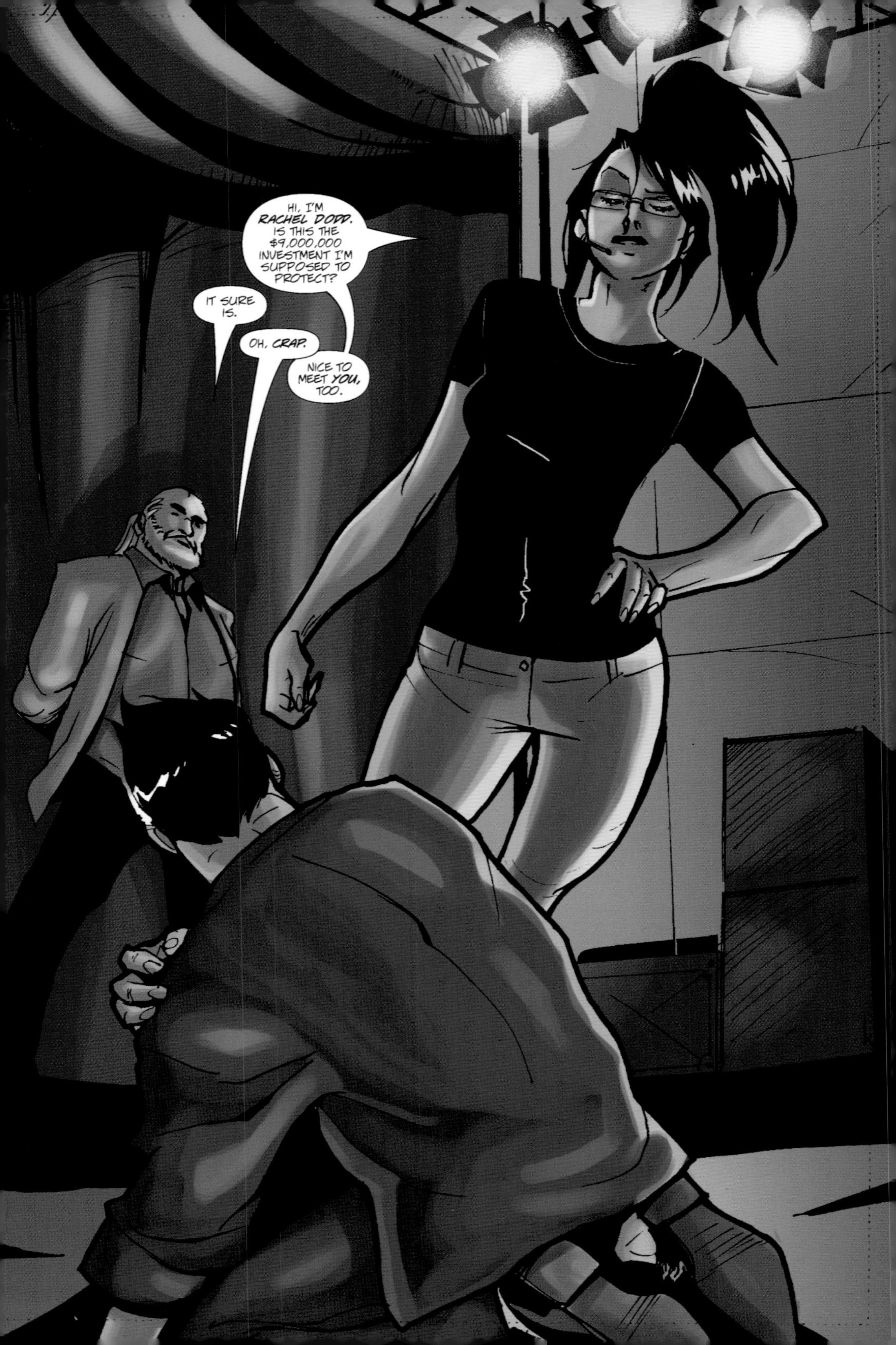
HI, I'M RACHEL DODD. IS THIS THE $9,000,000 INVESTMENT I'M SUPPOSED TO PROTECT?
IT SURE IS.
OH, CRAP.
NICE TO MEET YOU, TOO.

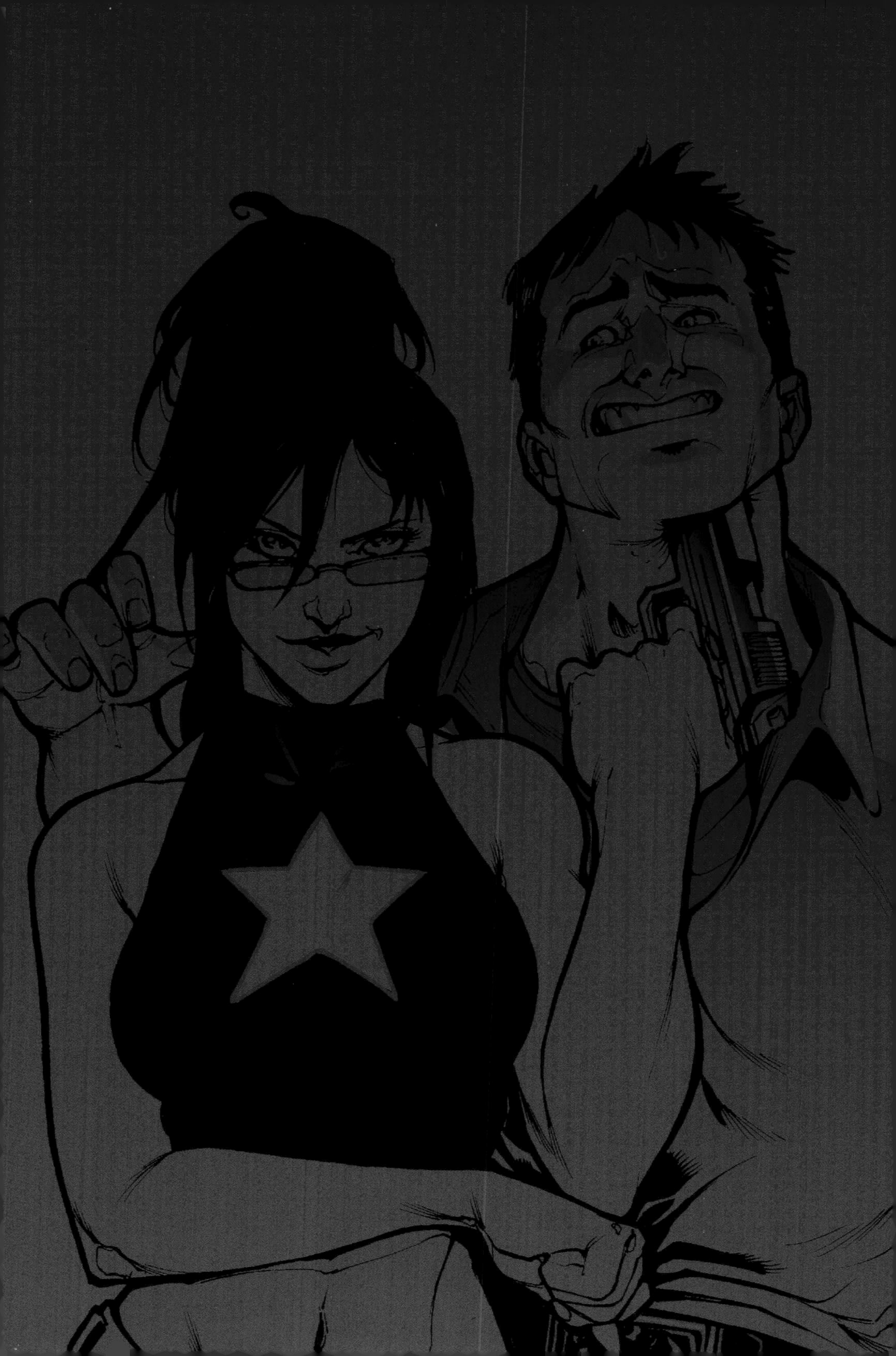

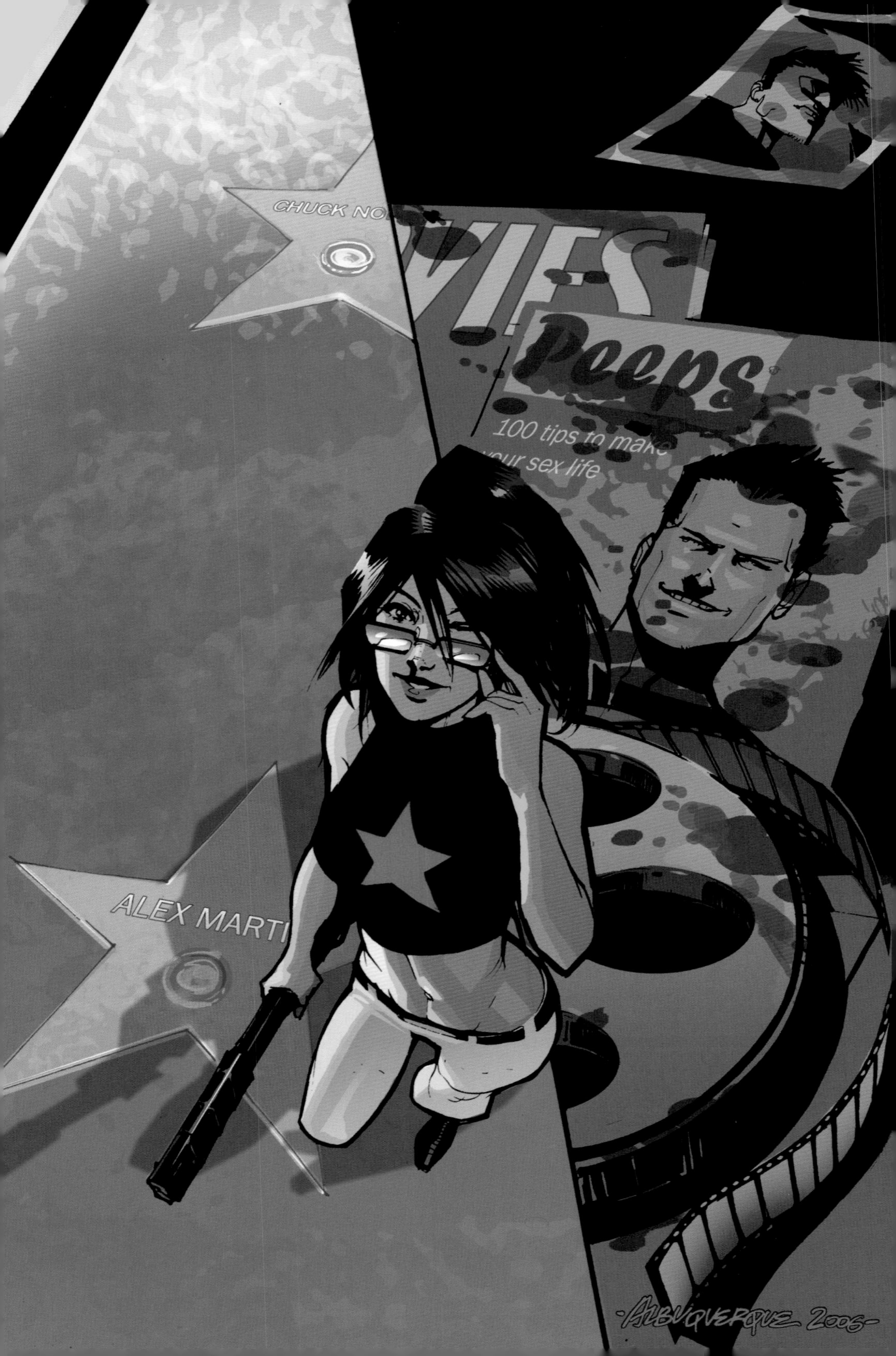
CHUCK NO
VIES
Peeps
100 tips to make
your sex life
ALEX MARTI
-ALBUQUERQUE 2006-

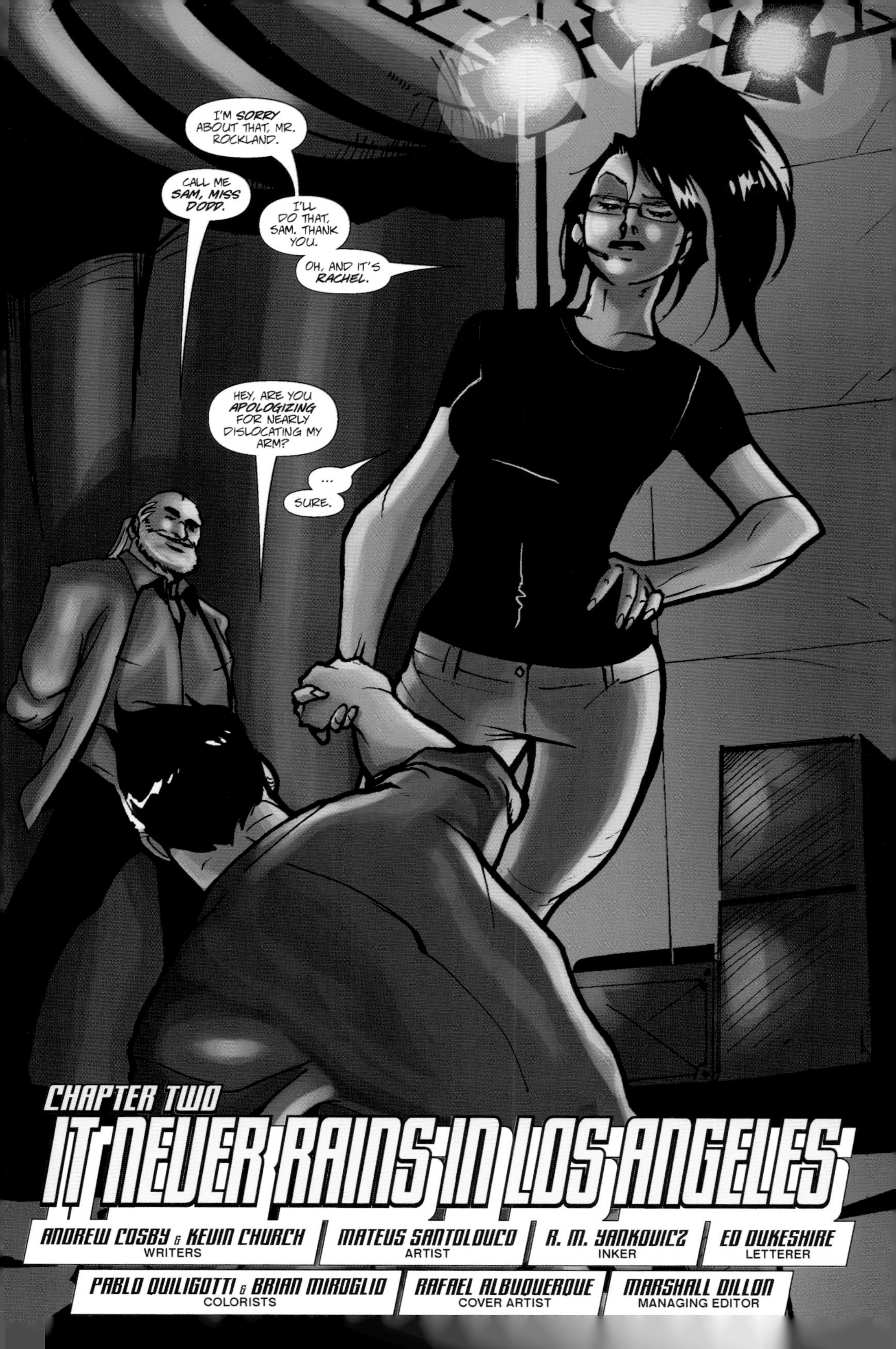
I'M SORRY ABOUT THAT, MR. ROCKLAND.
CALL ME SAM, MISS DODD.
I'LL DO THAT, SAM. THANK YOU.
OH, AND IT'S RACHEL.
HEY, ARE YOU APOLOGIZING FOR NEARLY DISLOCATING MY ARM?
... SURE.
CHAPTER TWO
IT NEVER RAINS IN LOS ANGELES
ANDREW COSBY & KEVIN CHURCH WRITERS
MATEUS SANTOLOUCO ARTIST
R. M. YANKOVICZ INKER
ED DUKESHIRE LETTERER
PABLO QUILIGOTTI & BRIAN MIROGLIO COLORISTS
RAFAEL ALBUQUERQUE COVER ARTIST
MARSHALL DILLON MANAGING EDITOR

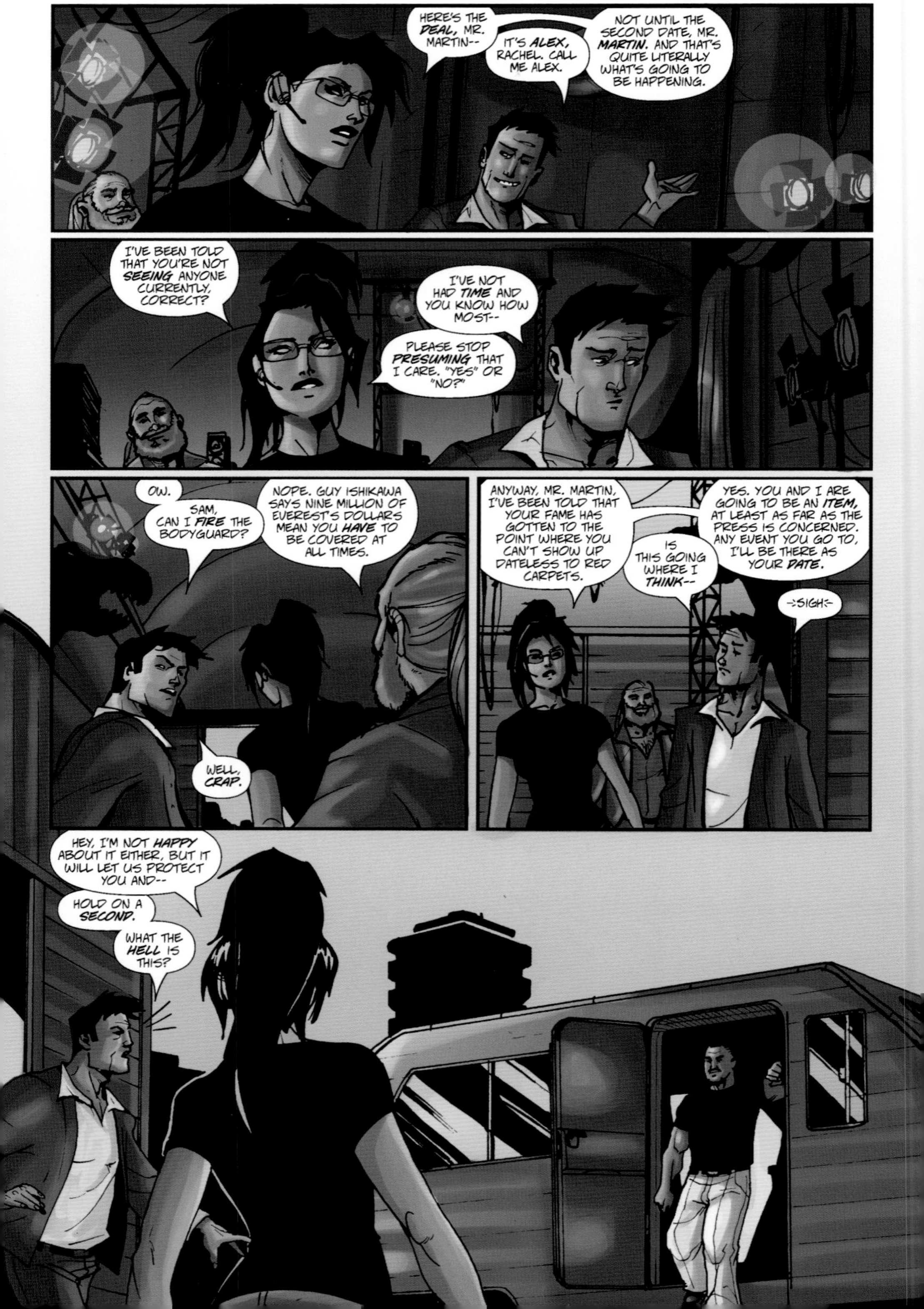
HERE'S THE DEAL, MR. MARTIN--
IT'S ALEX, RACHEL. CALL ME ALEX.
NOT UNTIL THE SECOND DATE, MR. MARTIN. AND THAT'S QUITE LITERALLY WHAT'S GOING TO BE HAPPENING.
I'VE BEEN TOLD THAT YOU'RE NOT SEEING ANYONE CURRENTLY, CORRECT?
I'VE NOT HAD TIME AND YOU KNOW HOW MOST--
PLEASE STOP PRESUMING THAT I CARE. "YES" OR "NO?"
OW.
SAM, CAN I FIRE THE BODYGUARD?
NOPE. GUY ISHIKAWA SAYS NINE MILLION OF EVEREST'S DOLLARS MEAN YOU HAVE TO BE COVERED AT ALL TIMES.
WELL, CRAP.
ANYWAY, MR. MARTIN, I'VE BEEN TOLD THAT YOUR FAME HAS GOTTEN TO THE POINT WHERE YOU CAN'T SHOW UP DATELESS TO RED CARPETS.
IS THIS GOING WHERE I THINK--
YES. YOU AND I ARE GOING TO BE AN ITEM, AT LEAST AS FAR AS THE PRESS IS CONCERNED. ANY EVENT YOU GO TO, I'LL BE THERE AS YOUR DATE.
-SIGH-
HEY, I'M NOT HAPPY ABOUT IT EITHER, BUT IT WILL LET US PROTECT YOU AND--
HOLD ON A SECOND.
WHAT THE HELL IS THIS?

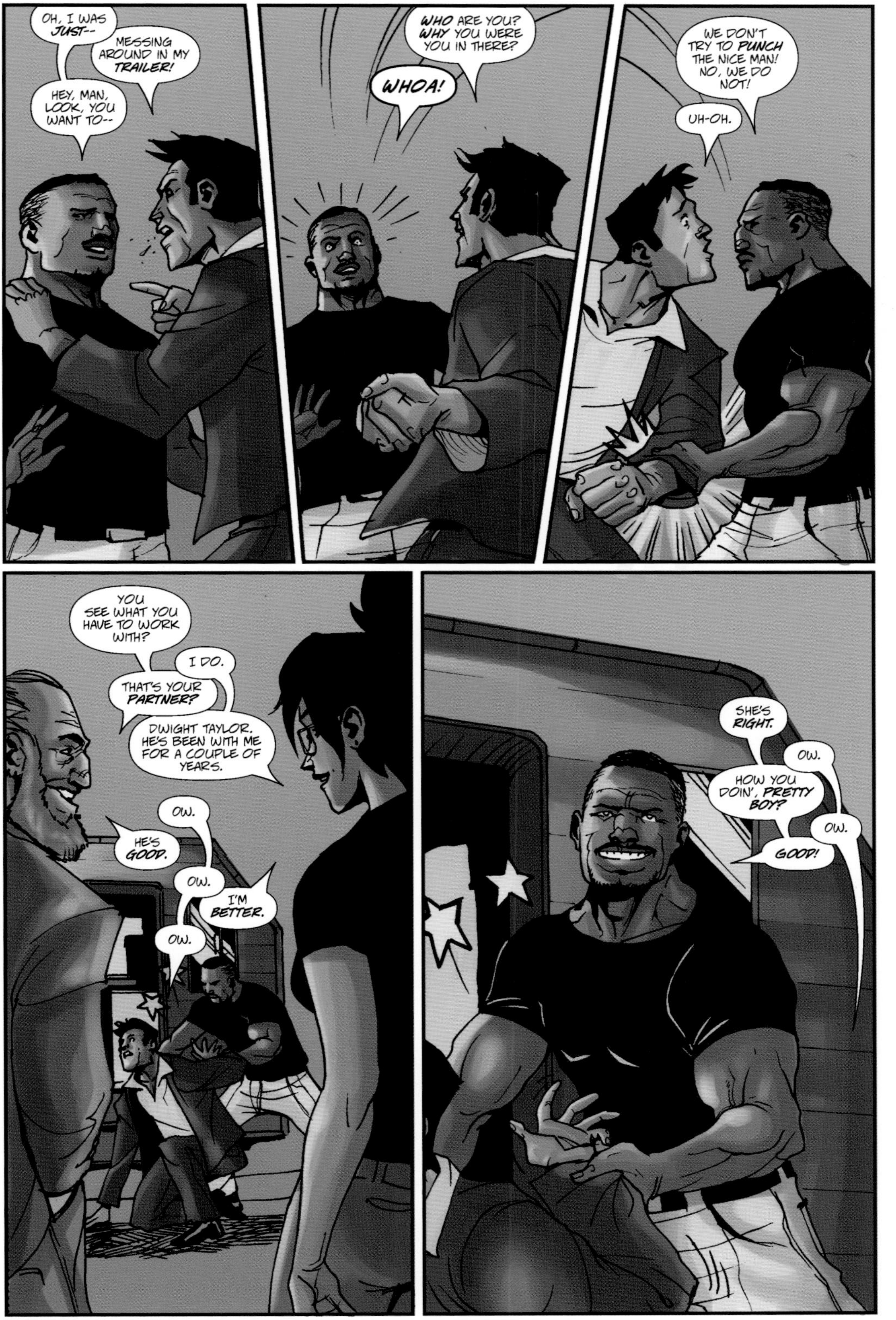
OH, I WAS JUST--
MESSING AROUND IN MY TRAILER!
HEY, MAN, LOOK, YOU WANT TO--
WHO ARE YOU? WHY YOU WERE YOU IN THERE?
WHOA!
WE DON'T TRY TO PUNCH THE NICE MAN! NO, WE DO NOT!
UH-OH.
YOU SEE WHAT YOU HAVE TO WORK WITH?
I DO.
THAT'S YOUR PARTNER?
DWIGHT TAYLOR. HE'S BEEN WITH ME FOR A COUPLE OF YEARS.
OW.
HE'S GOOD.
OW.
I'M BETTER.
OW.
SHE'S RIGHT.
OW.
HOW YOU DOIN', PRETTY BOY?
OW.
GOOD!

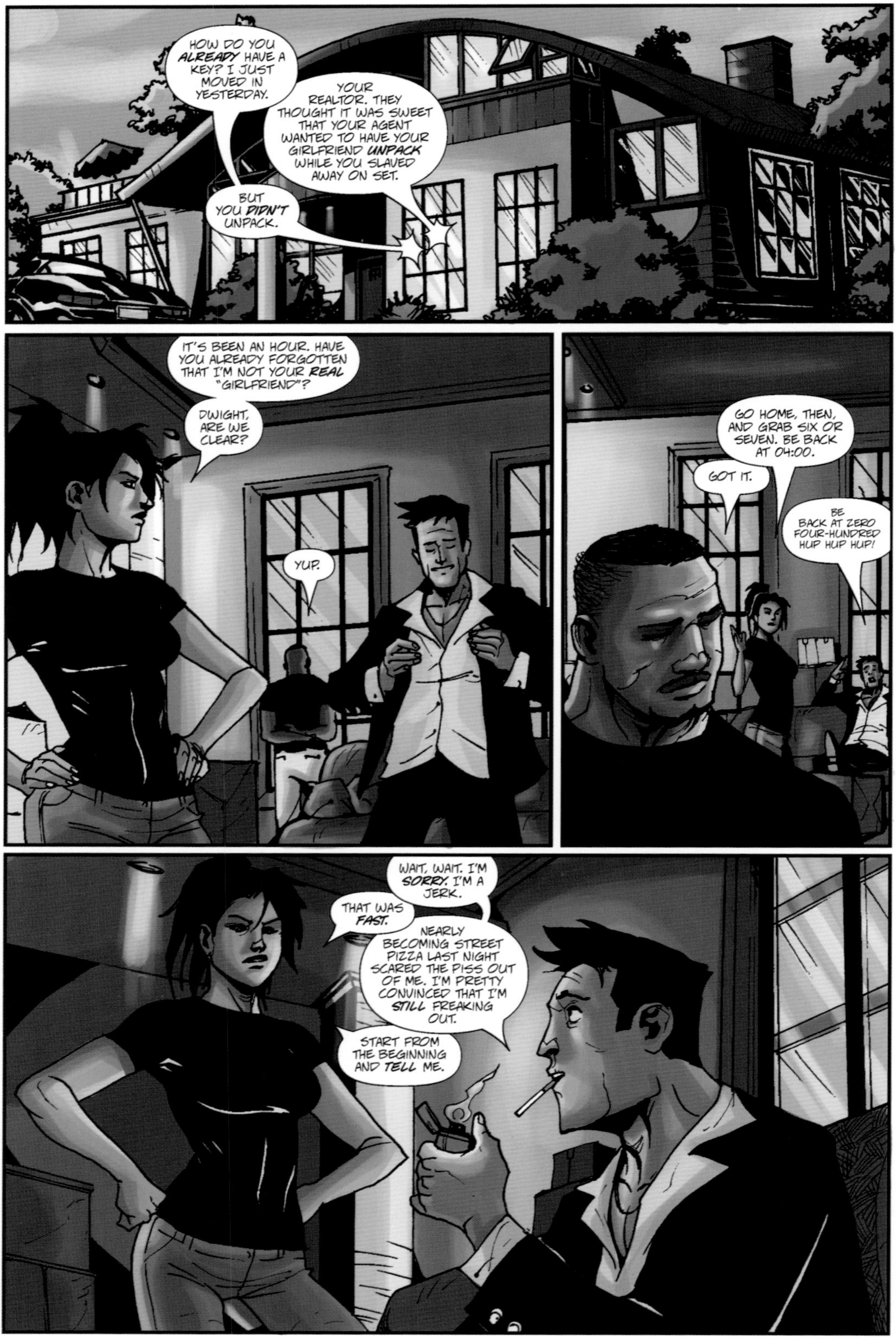
HOW DO YOU *ALREADY* HAVE A KEY? I JUST MOVED IN YESTERDAY.
YOUR REALTOR. THEY THOUGHT IT WAS SWEET THAT YOUR AGENT WANTED TO HAVE YOUR GIRLFRIEND *UNPACK* WHILE YOU SLAVED AWAY ON SET.
BUT YOU *DIDN'T* UNPACK.
IT'S BEEN AN HOUR. HAVE YOU ALREADY FORGOTTEN THAT I'M NOT YOUR *REAL* "GIRLFRIEND"?
DWIGHT, ARE WE CLEAR?
YUP.
GO HOME, THEN, AND GRAB SIX OR SEVEN. BE BACK AT 04:00.
GOT IT.
BE BACK AT ZERO FOUR-HUNDRED HUP HUP HUP!
WAIT, WAIT. I'M *SORRY.* I'M A JERK.
THAT WAS *FAST.*
NEARLY BECOMING STREET PIZZA LAST NIGHT SCARED THE PISS OUT OF ME. I'M PRETTY CONVINCED THAT I'M *STILL* FREAKING OUT.
START FROM THE BEGINNING AND *TELL* ME.

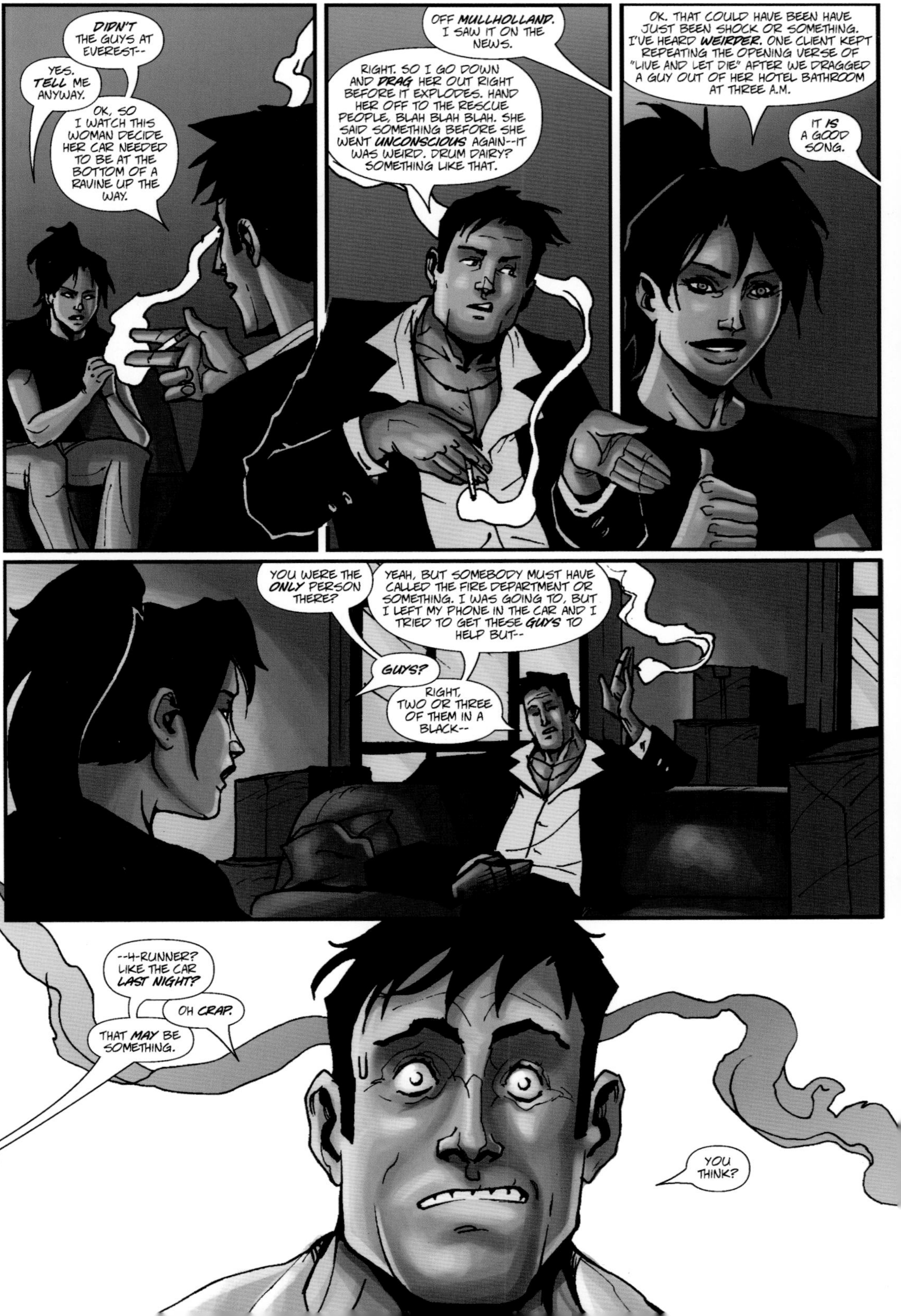

DIDN'T THE GUYS AT EVEREST--
YES. TELL ME ANYWAY.
OK, SO I WATCH THIS WOMAN DECIDE HER CAR NEEDED TO BE AT THE BOTTOM OF A RAVINE UP THE WAY.
OFF MULLHOLLAND. I SAW IT ON THE NEWS.
RIGHT. SO I GO DOWN AND DRAG HER OUT RIGHT BEFORE IT EXPLODES. HAND HER OFF TO THE RESCUE PEOPLE, BLAH BLAH BLAH. SHE SAID SOMETHING BEFORE SHE WENT UNCONSCIOUS AGAIN--IT WAS WEIRD. DRUM DAIRY? SOMETHING LIKE THAT.
OK. THAT COULD HAVE BEEN HAVE JUST BEEN SHOCK OR SOMETHING. I'VE HEARD WEIRDER. ONE CLIENT KEPT REPEATING THE OPENING VERSE OF "LIVE AND LET DIE" AFTER WE DRAGGED A GUY OUT OF HER HOTEL BATHROOM AT THREE A.M.
IT IS A GOOD SONG.
YOU WERE THE ONLY PERSON THERE?
YEAH, BUT SOMEBODY MUST HAVE CALLED THE FIRE DEPARTMENT OR SOMETHING. I WAS GOING TO, BUT I LEFT MY PHONE IN THE CAR AND I TRIED TO GET THESE GUYS TO HELP BUT--
GUYS?
RIGHT, TWO OR THREE OF THEM IN A BLACK--
--4-RUNNER? LIKE THE CAR LAST NIGHT?
OH CRAP.
THAT MAY BE SOMETHING.
YOU THINK?

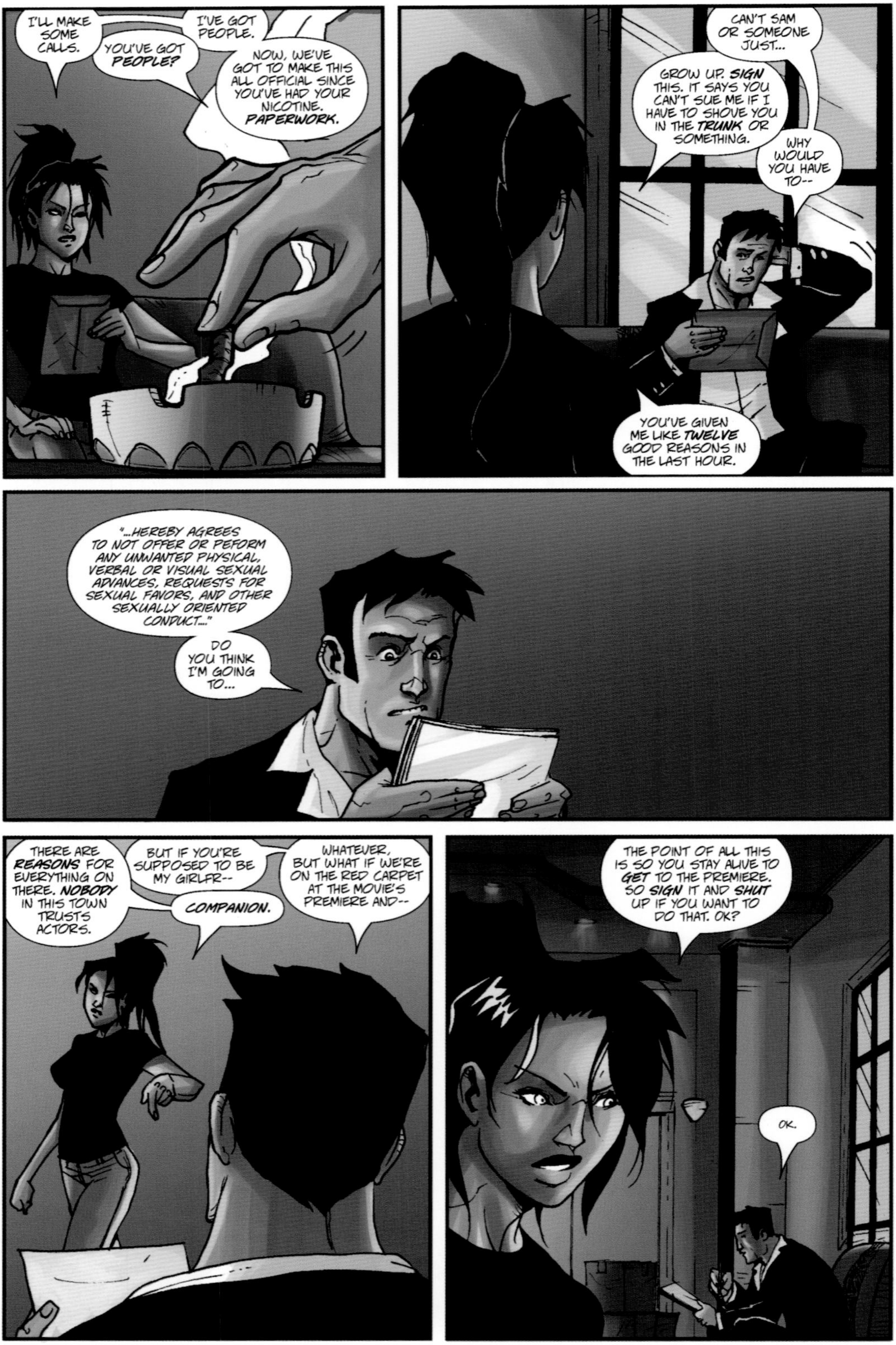
I'LL MAKE SOME CALLS.
I'VE GOT PEOPLE.
YOU'VE GOT PEOPLE?
NOW, WE'VE GOT TO MAKE THIS ALL OFFICIAL SINCE YOU'VE HAD YOUR NICOTINE. PAPERWORK.
CAN'T SAM OR SOMEONE JUST...
GROW UP. SIGN THIS. IT SAYS YOU CAN'T SUE ME IF I HAVE TO SHOVE YOU IN THE TRUNK OR SOMETHING.
WHY WOULD YOU HAVE TO--
YOU'VE GIVEN ME LIKE TWELVE GOOD REASONS IN THE LAST HOUR.
"...HEREBY AGREES TO NOT OFFER OR PEFORM ANY UNWANTED PHYSICAL, VERBAL OR VISUAL SEXUAL ADVANCES, REQUESTS FOR SEXUAL FAVORS, AND OTHER SEXUALLY ORIENTED CONDUCT..."
DO YOU THINK I'M GOING TO...
THERE ARE REASONS FOR EVERYTHING ON THERE. NOBODY IN THIS TOWN TRUSTS ACTORS.
BUT IF YOU'RE SUPPOSED TO BE MY GIRLFR--
COMPANION.
WHATEVER, BUT WHAT IF WE'RE ON THE RED CARPET AT THE MOVIE'S PREMIERE AND--
THE POINT OF ALL THIS IS SO YOU STAY ALIVE TO GET TO THE PREMIERE. SO SIGN IT AND SHUT UP IF YOU WANT TO DO THAT. OK?
OK.

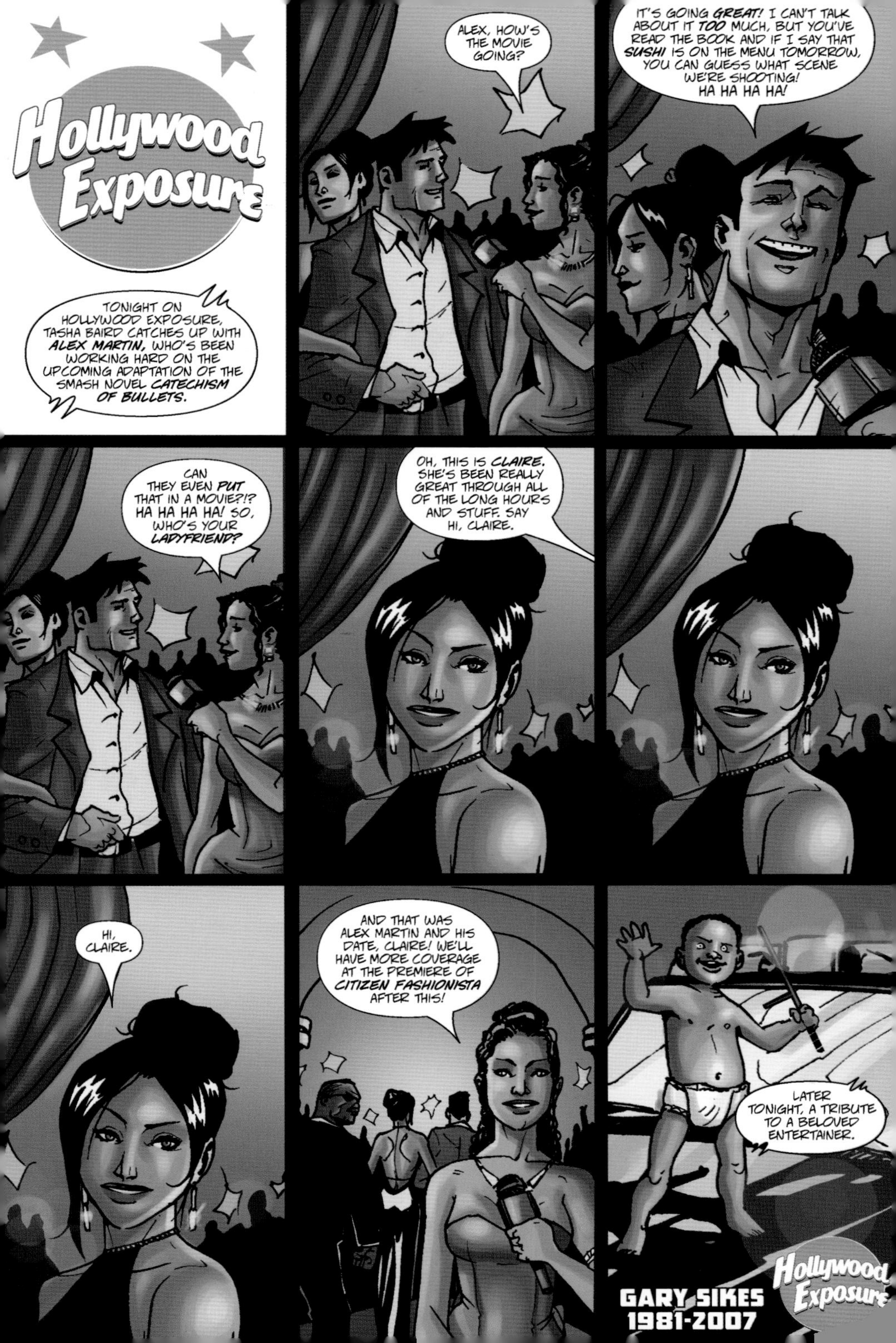

Hollywood Exposure
TONIGHT ON HOLLYWOOD EXPOSURE, TASHA BAIRD CATCHES UP WITH ALEX MARTIN, WHO'S BEEN WORKING HARD ON THE UPCOMING ADAPTATION OF THE SMASH NOVEL CATECHISM OF BULLETS.
ALEX, HOW'S THE MOVIE GOING?
IT'S GOING GREAT! I CAN'T TALK ABOUT IT TOO MUCH, BUT YOU'VE READ THE BOOK AND IF I SAY THAT SUSHI IS ON THE MENU TOMORROW, YOU CAN GUESS WHAT SCENE WE'RE SHOOTING! HA HA HA HA!
CAN THEY EVEN PUT THAT IN A MOVIE?!? HA HA HA HA! SO, WHO'S YOUR LADYFRIEND?
OH, THIS IS CLAIRE. SHE'S BEEN REALLY GREAT THROUGH ALL OF THE LONG HOURS AND STUFF. SAY HI, CLAIRE.
HI, CLAIRE.
AND THAT WAS ALEX MARTIN AND HIS DATE, CLAIRE! WE'LL HAVE MORE COVERAGE AT THE PREMIERE OF CITIZEN FASHIONISTA AFTER THIS!
LATER TONIGHT, A TRIBUTE TO A BELOVED ENTERTAINER.
GARY SIKES 1981-2007
Hollywood Exposure

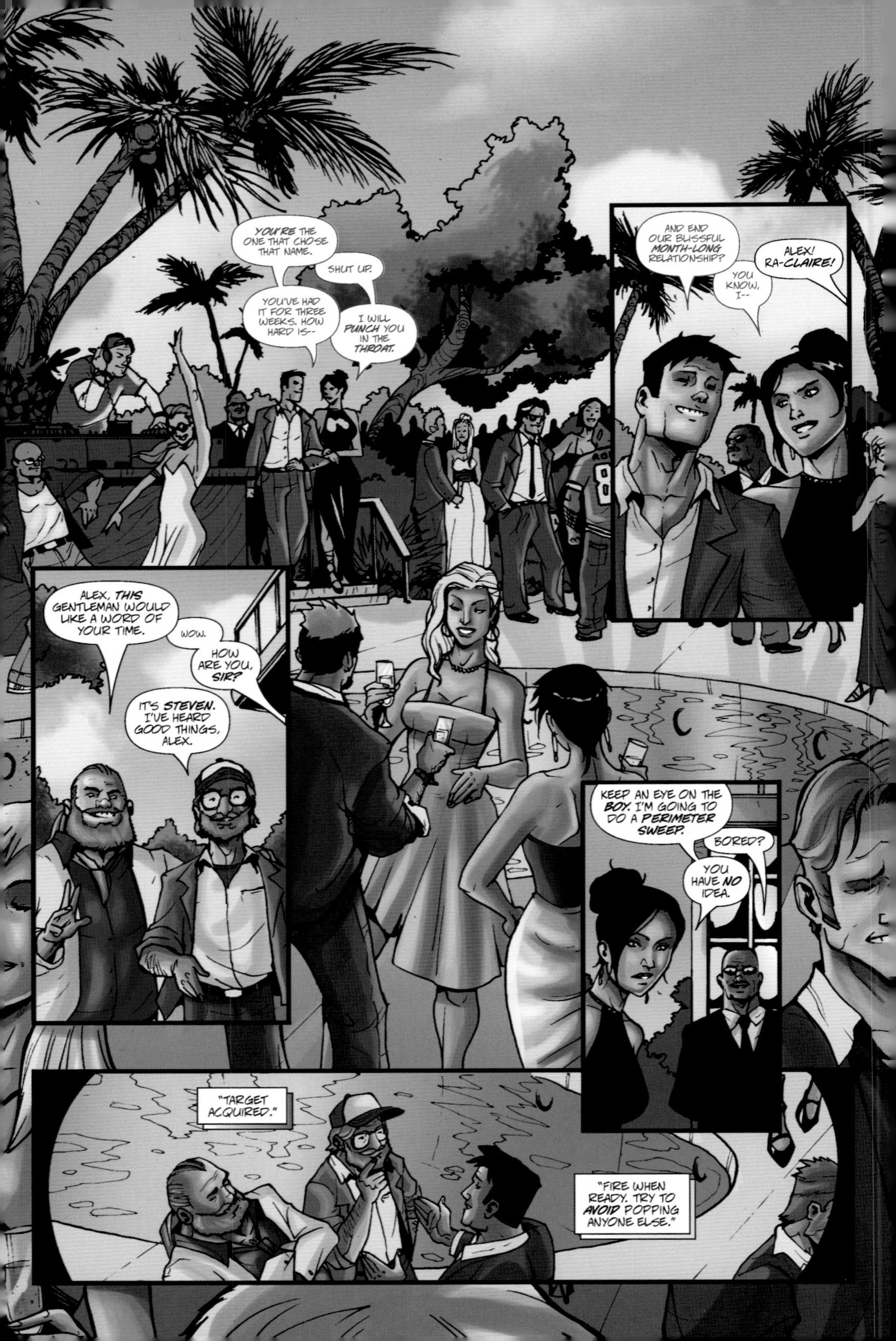
YOU'RE THE ONE THAT CHOSE THAT NAME.
SHUT UP.
YOU'VE HAD IT FOR THREE WEEKS. HOW HARD IS--
I WILL PUNCH YOU IN THE THROAT.
AND END OUR BLISSFUL MONTH-LONG RELATIONSHIP?
YOU KNOW, I--
ALEX! RA-CLAIRE!
ALEX, THIS GENTLEMAN WOULD LIKE A WORD OF YOUR TIME.
WOW.
HOW ARE YOU, SIR?
IT'S STEVEN. I'VE HEARD GOOD THINGS, ALEX.
KEEP AN EYE ON THE BOY. I'M GOING TO DO A PERIMETER SWEEP.
BORED?
YOU HAVE NO IDEA.
"TARGET ACQUIRED."
"FIRE WHEN READY. TRY TO AVOID POPPING ANYONE ELSE."

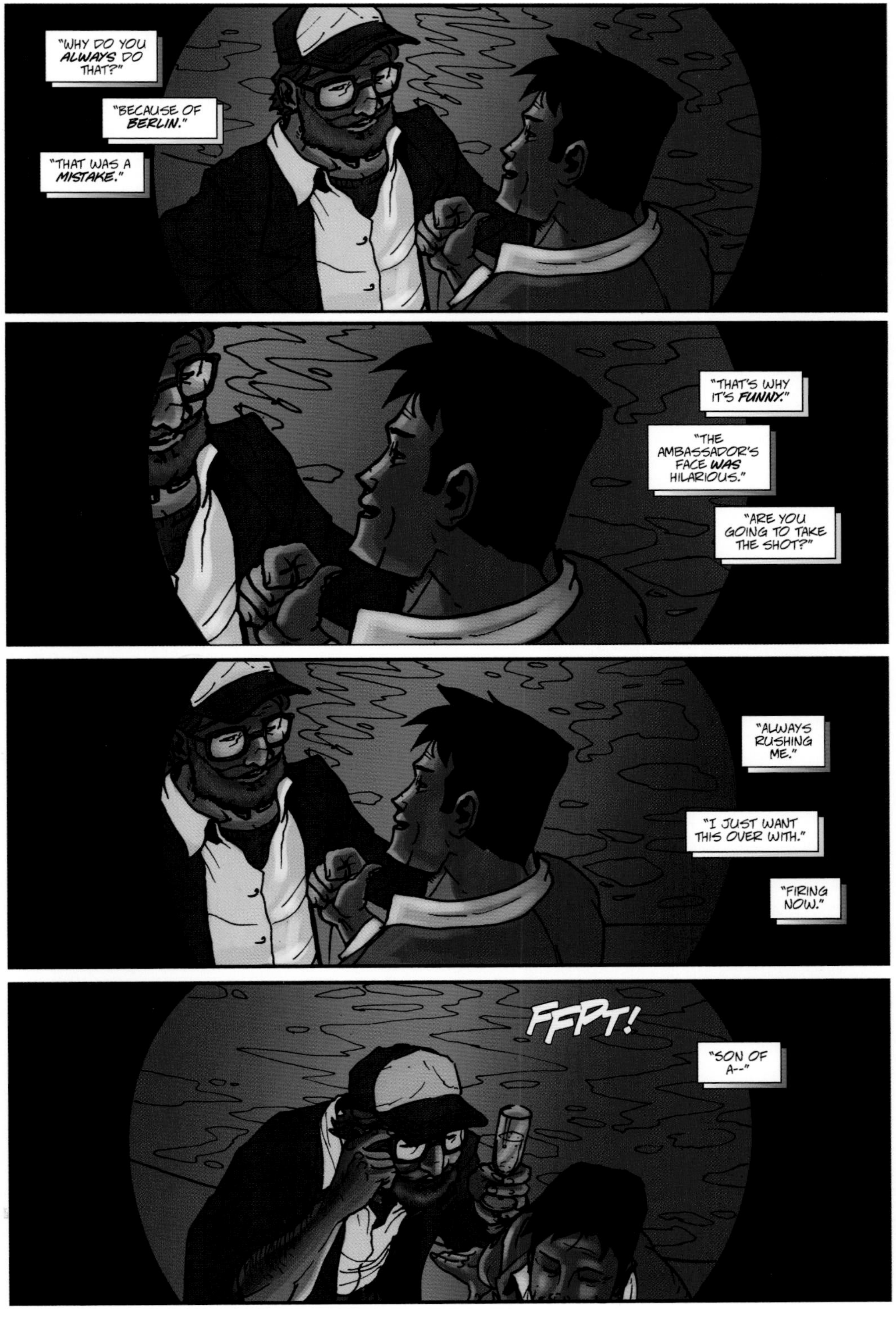
"WHY DO YOU ALWAYS DO THAT?"
"BECAUSE OF BERLIN."
"THAT WAS A MISTAKE."
"THAT'S WHY IT'S FUNNY."
"THE AMBASSADOR'S FACE WAS HILARIOUS."
"ARE YOU GOING TO TAKE THE SHOT?"
"ALWAYS RUSHING ME."
"I JUST WANT THIS OVER WITH."
"FIRING NOW."
FFPT!
"SON OF A--"

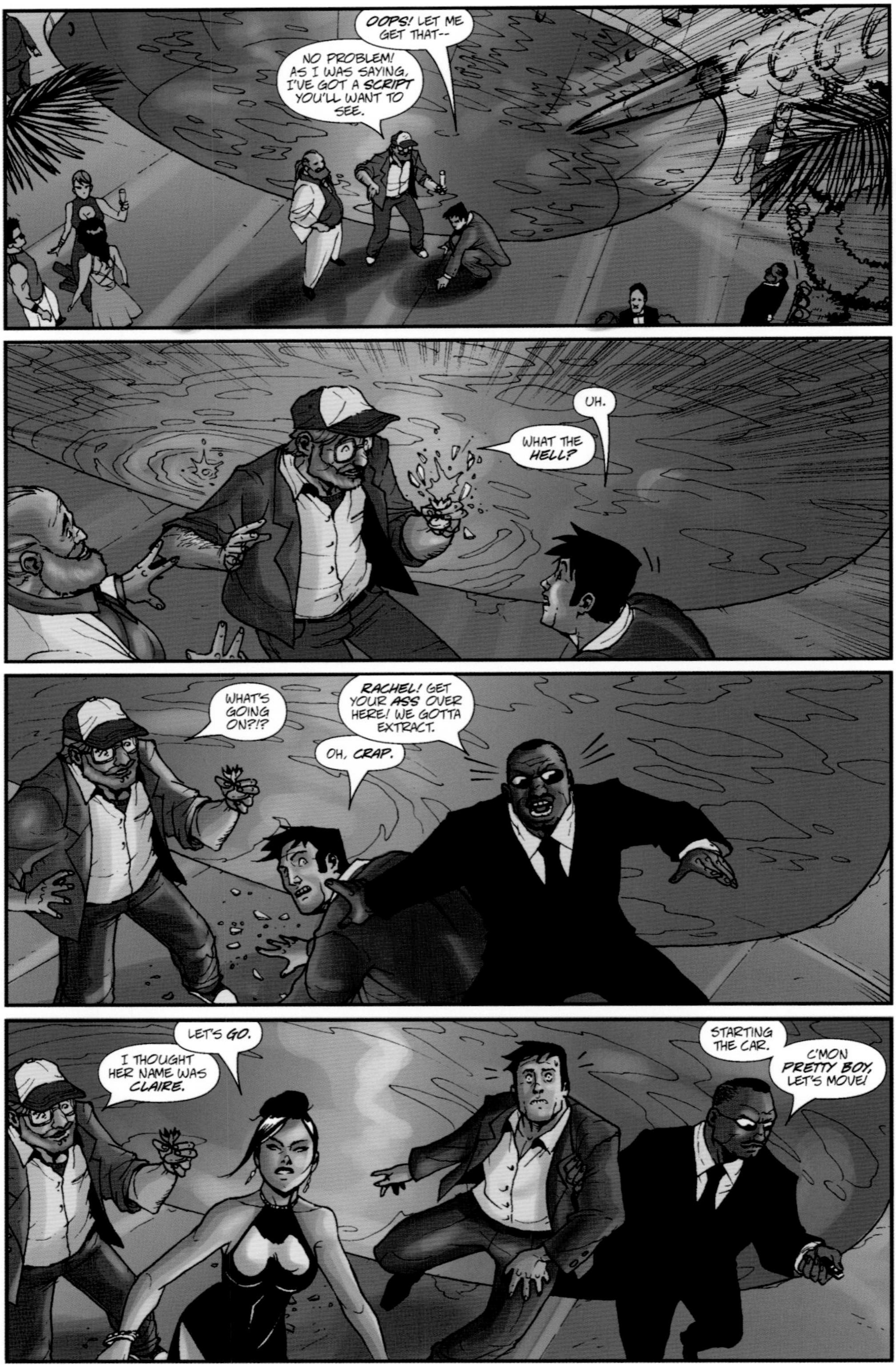
OOPS! LET ME GET THAT--
NO PROBLEM! AS I WAS SAYING, I'VE GOT A SCRIPT YOU'LL WANT TO SEE.
UH.
WHAT THE HELL?
WHAT'S GOING ON?!?
RACHEL! GET YOUR ASS OVER HERE! WE GOTTA EXTRACT.
OH, CRAP.
LET'S GO.
I THOUGHT HER NAME WAS CLAIRE.
STARTING THE CAR.
C'MON PRETTY BOY, LET'S MOVE!

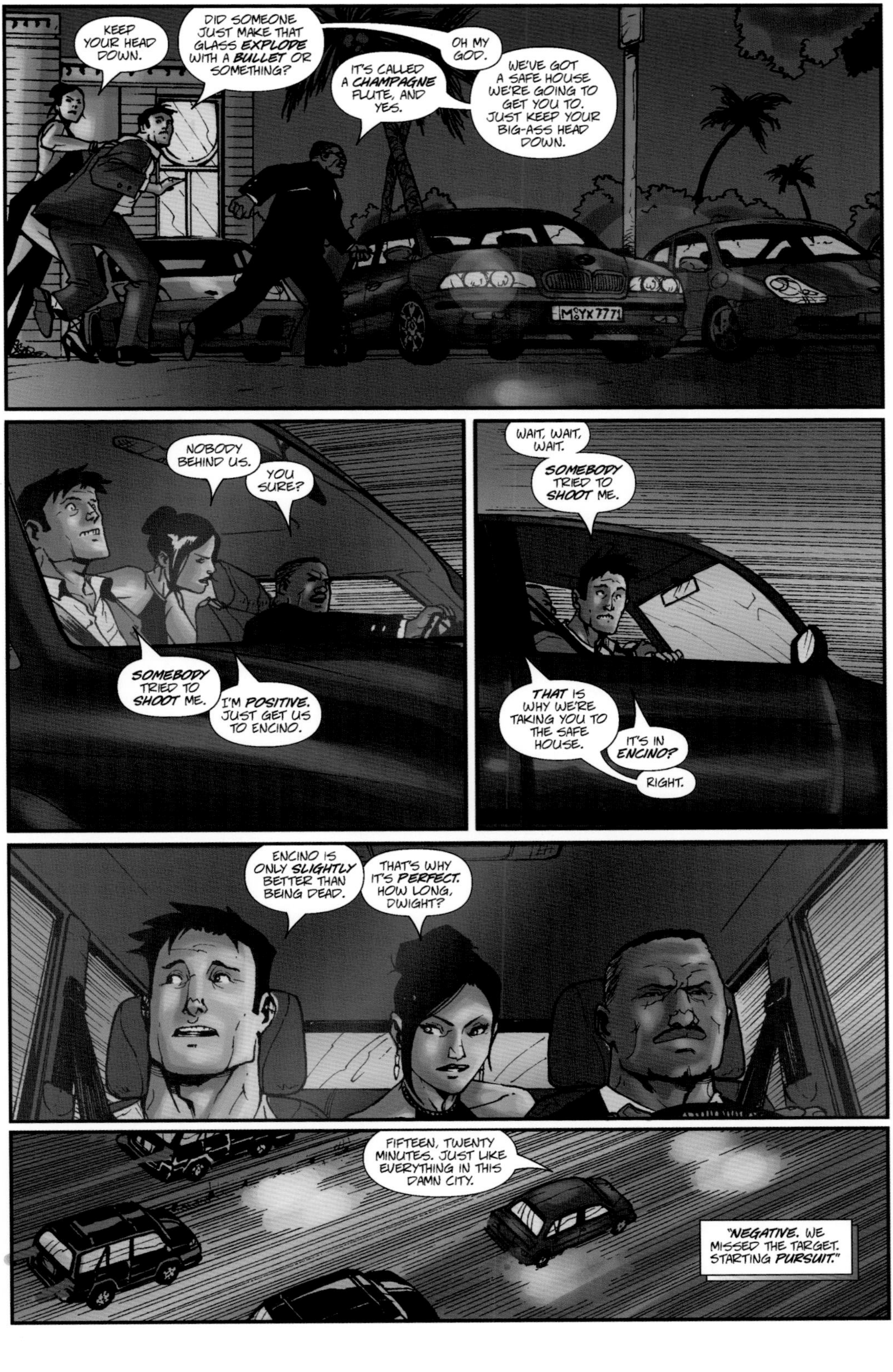
KEEP YOUR HEAD DOWN.
DID SOMEONE JUST MAKE THAT GLASS EXPLODE WITH A BULLET OR SOMETHING?
OH MY GOD.
IT'S CALLED A CHAMPAGNE FLUTE, AND YES.
WE'VE GOT A SAFE HOUSE WE'RE GOING TO GET YOU TO. JUST KEEP YOUR BIG-ASS HEAD DOWN.
NOBODY BEHIND US.
YOU SURE?
SOMEBODY TRIED TO SHOOT ME.
I'M POSITIVE. JUST GET US TO ENCINO.
WAIT, WAIT, WAIT.
SOMEBODY TRIED TO SHOOT ME.
THAT IS WHY WE'RE TAKING YOU TO THE SAFE HOUSE.
IT'S IN ENCINO?
RIGHT.
ENCINO IS ONLY SLIGHTLY BETTER THAN BEING DEAD.
THAT'S WHY IT'S PERFECT. HOW LONG, DWIGHT?
FIFTEEN, TWENTY MINUTES. JUST LIKE EVERYTHING IN THIS DAMN CITY.
"NEGATIVE. WE MISSED THE TARGET. STARTING PURSUIT."

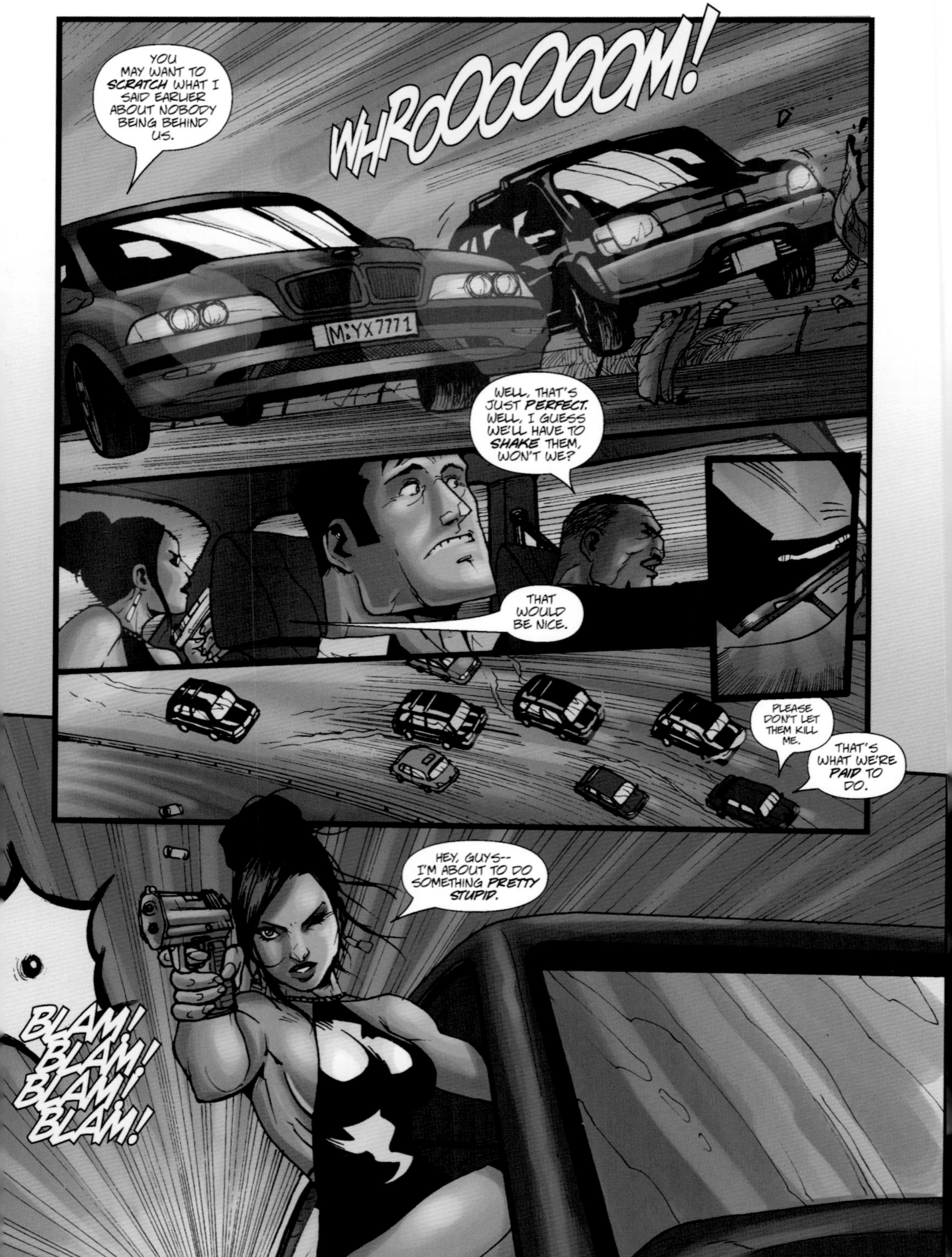

YOU MAY WANT TO SCRATCH WHAT I SAID EARLIER ABOUT NOBODY BEING BEHIND US.
WHROOOOOOM!
M'YX 7771
WELL, THAT'S JUST PERFECT. WELL, I GUESS WE'LL HAVE TO SHAKE THEM, WON'T WE?
THAT WOULD BE NICE.
PLEASE DON'T LET THEM KILL ME.
THAT'S WHAT WE'RE PAID TO DO.
HEY, GUYS-- I'M ABOUT TO DO SOMETHING PRETTY STUPID.
BLAM! BLAM! BLAM! BLAM!

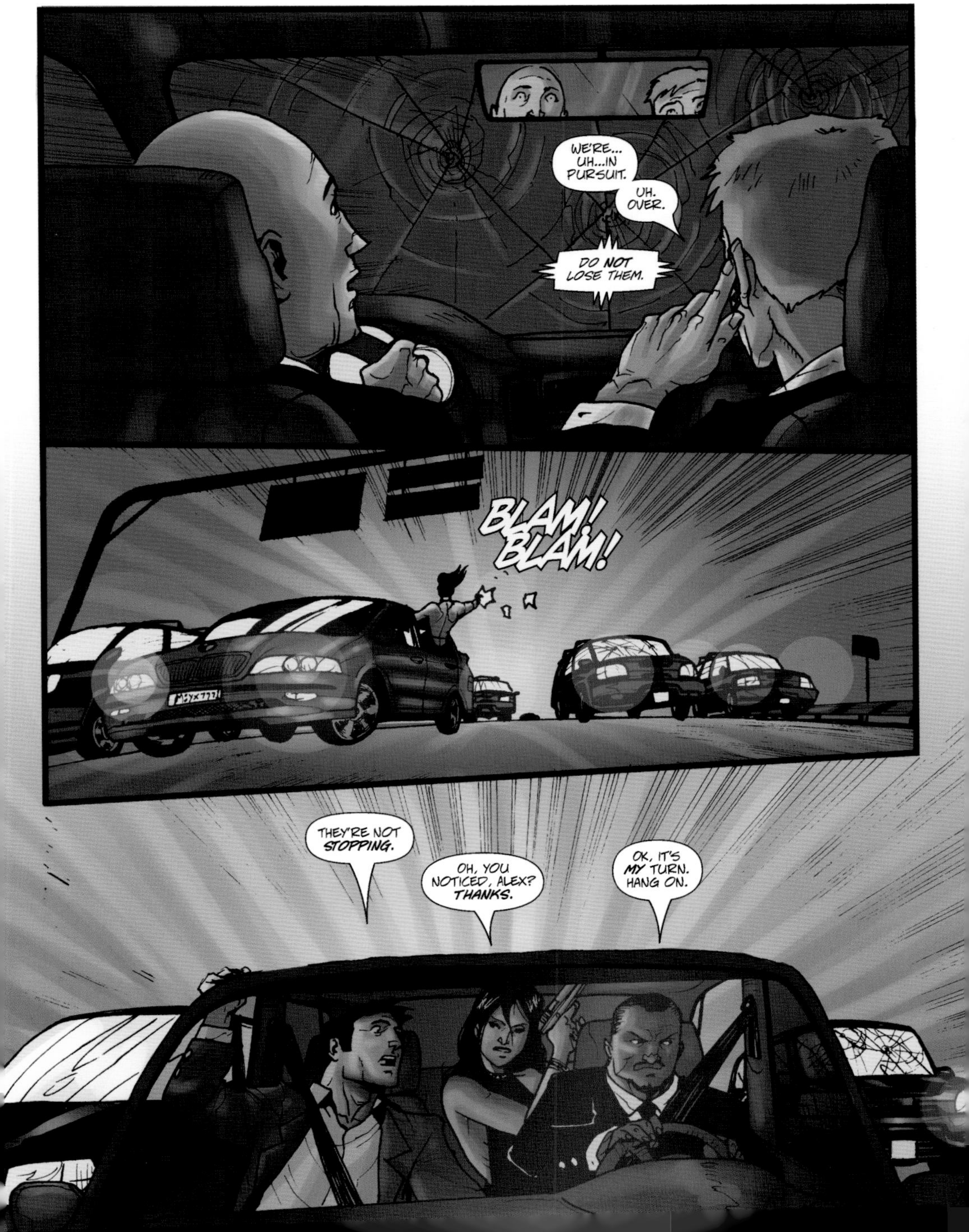
WE'RE... UH...IN PURSUIT.
UH. OVER.
DO NOT LOSE THEM.
BLAM! BLAM!
THEY'RE NOT STOPPING.
OH, YOU NOTICED, ALEX? THANKS.
OK, IT'S MY TURN. HANG ON.

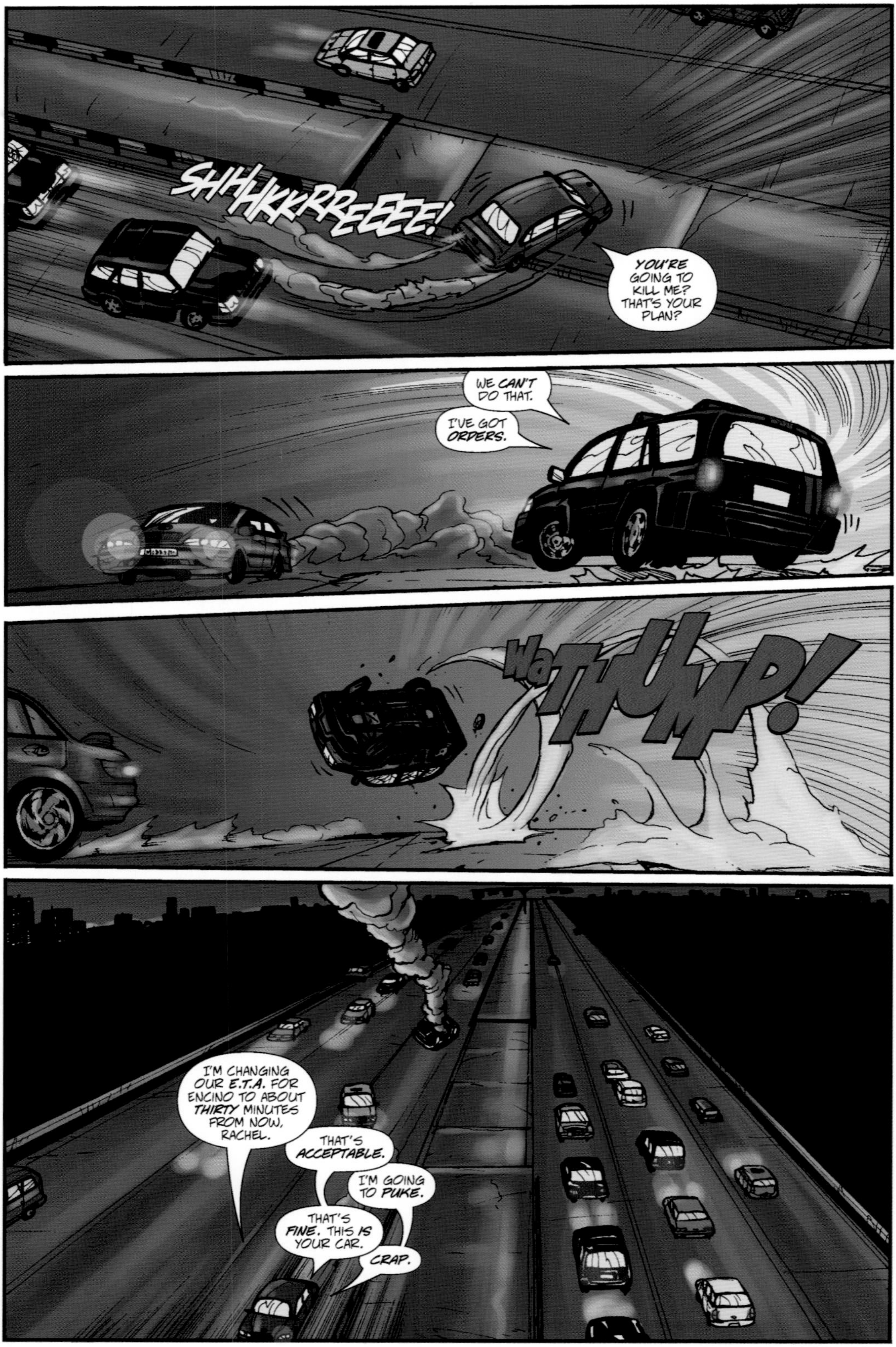
SHHHKKRRREEEEE!
YOU'RE GOING TO KILL ME? THAT'S YOUR PLAN?
WE CAN'T DO THAT.
I'VE GOT ORDERS.
WaTHUMP!
I'M CHANGING OUR E.T.A. FOR ENCINO TO ABOUT THIRTY MINUTES FROM NOW, RACHEL.
THAT'S ACCEPTABLE.
I'M GOING TO PUKE.
THAT'S FINE. THIS IS YOUR CAR.
CRAP.

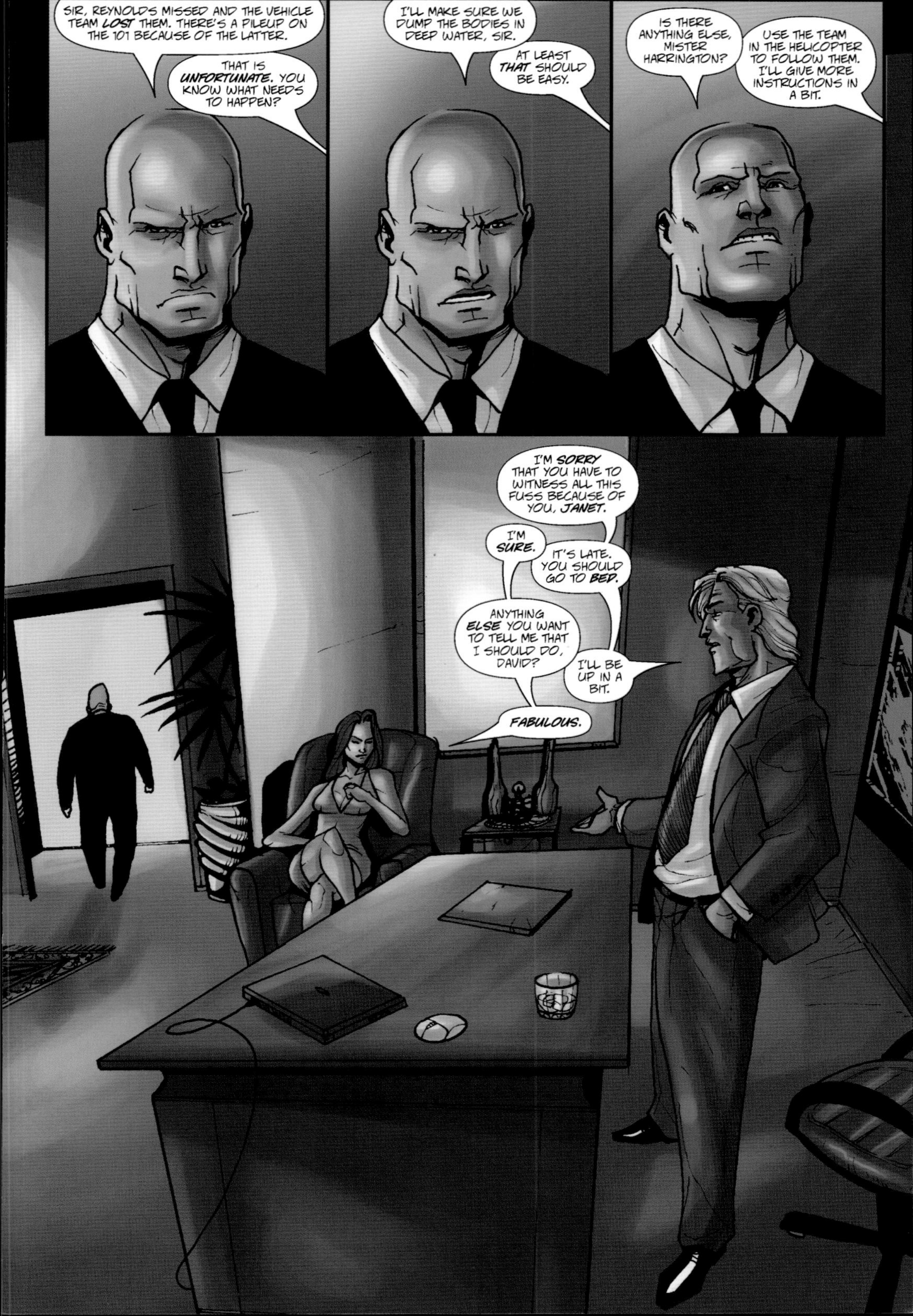
SIR, REYNOLDS MISSED AND THE VEHICLE TEAM LOST THEM. THERE'S A PILEUP ON THE 101 BECAUSE OF THE LATTER.
THAT IS UNFORTUNATE. YOU KNOW WHAT NEEDS TO HAPPEN?
I'LL MAKE SURE WE DUMP THE BODIES IN DEEP WATER, SIR.
AT LEAST THAT SHOULD BE EASY.
IS THERE ANYTHING ELSE, MISTER HARRINGTON?
USE THE TEAM IN THE HELICOPTER TO FOLLOW THEM. I'LL GIVE MORE INSTRUCTIONS IN A BIT.
I'M SORRY THAT YOU HAVE TO WITNESS ALL THIS FUSS BECAUSE OF YOU, JANET.
I'M SURE.
IT'S LATE. YOU SHOULD GO TO BED.
ANYTHING ELSE YOU WANT TO TELL ME THAT I SHOULD DO, DAVID?
I'LL BE UP IN A BIT.
FABULOUS.

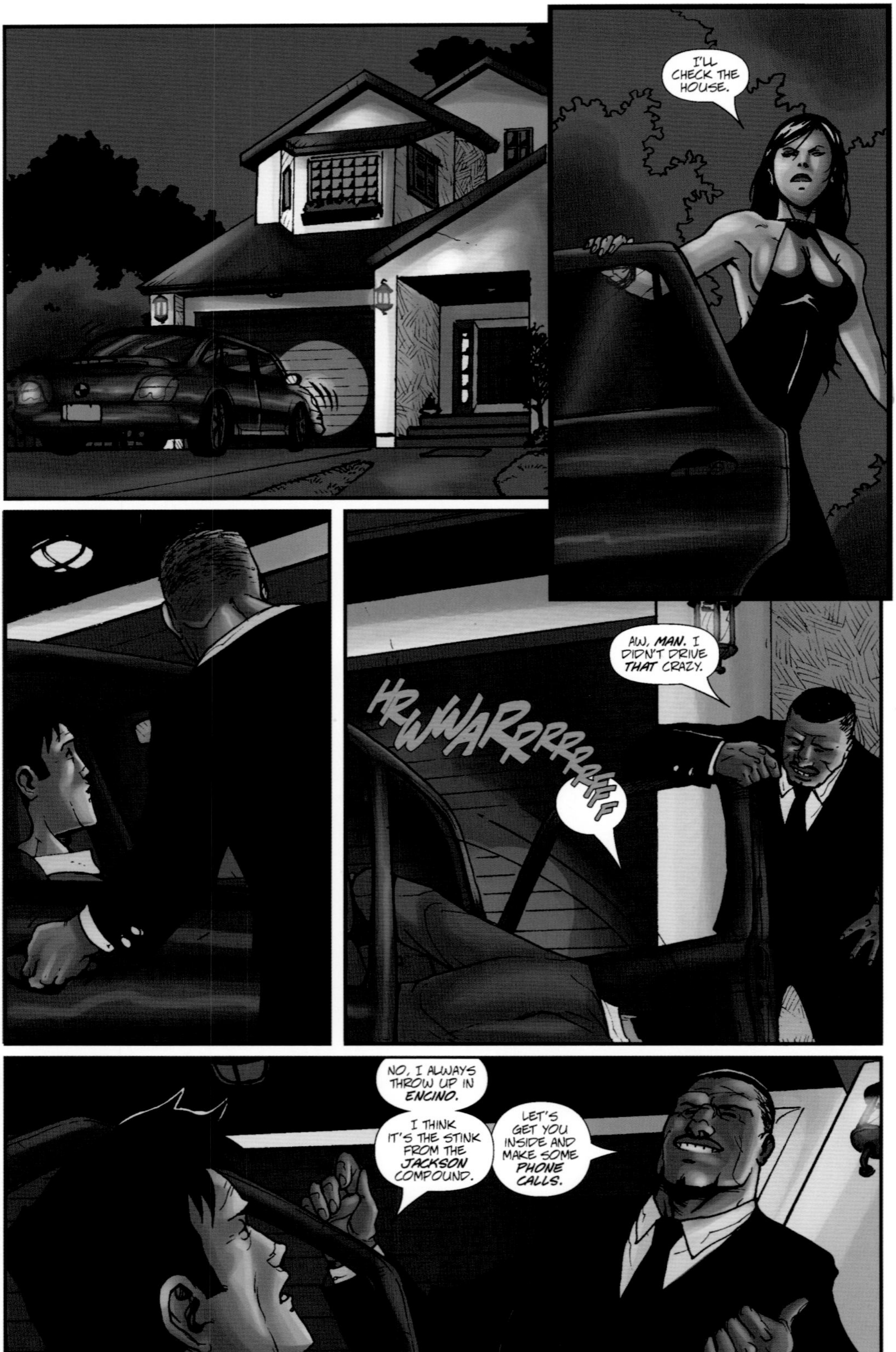
I'LL CHECK THE HOUSE.
AW, MAN. I DIDN'T DRIVE THAT CRAZY.
HRWWARRRRRFFF
NO, I ALWAYS THROW UP IN ENCINO.
I THINK IT'S THE STINK FROM THE JACKSON COMPOUND.
LET'S GET YOU INSIDE AND MAKE SOME PHONE CALLS.

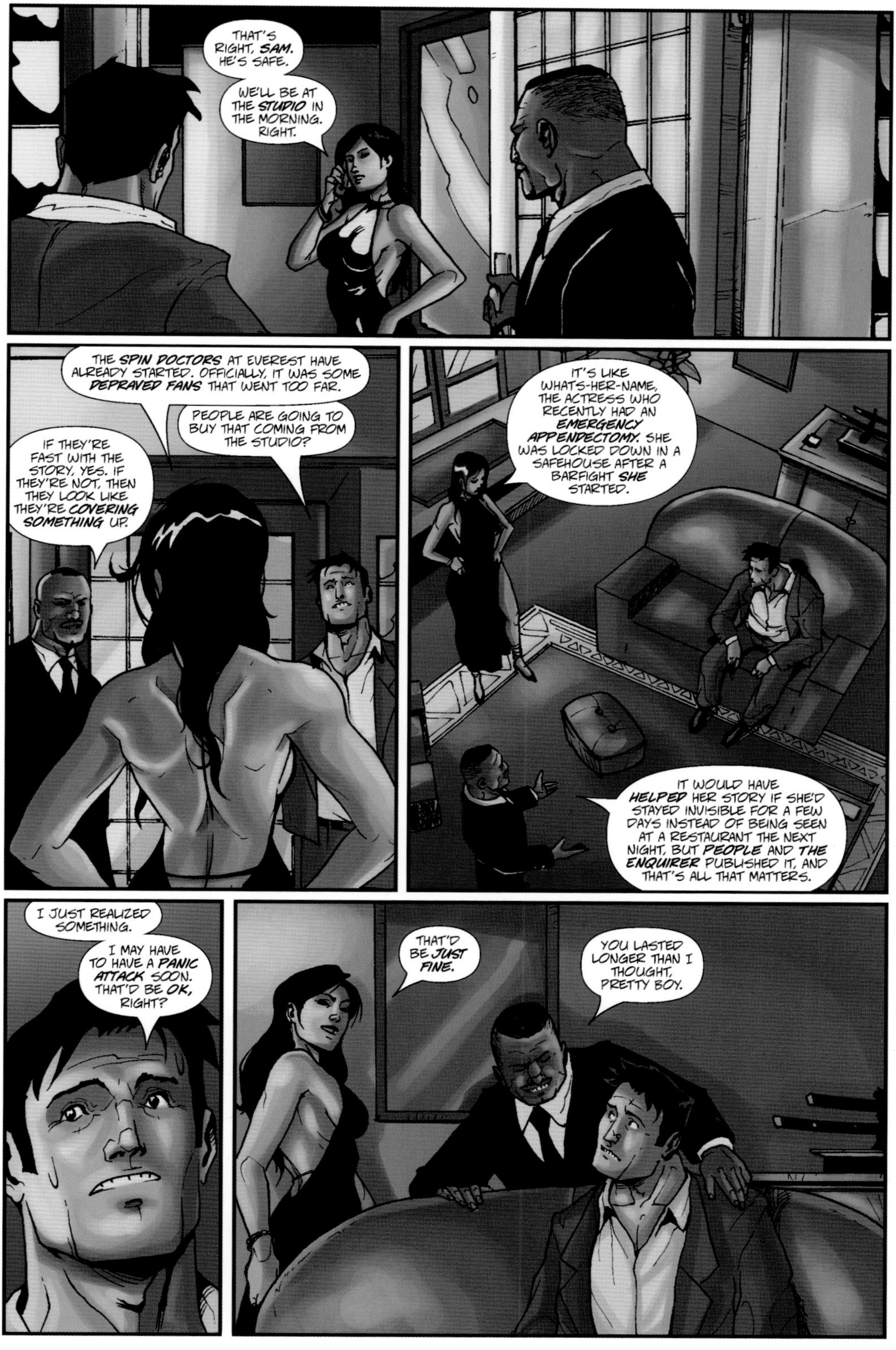
THAT'S RIGHT, SAM. HE'S SAFE.
WE'LL BE AT THE STUDIO IN THE MORNING. RIGHT.
THE SPIN DOCTORS AT EVEREST HAVE ALREADY STARTED. OFFICIALLY, IT WAS SOME DEPRAVED FANS THAT WENT TOO FAR.
PEOPLE ARE GOING TO BUY THAT COMING FROM THE STUDIO?
IF THEY'RE FAST WITH THE STORY, YES. IF THEY'RE NOT, THEN THEY LOOK LIKE THEY'RE COVERING SOMETHING UP.
IT'S LIKE WHATS-HER-NAME, THE ACTRESS WHO RECENTLY HAD AN EMERGENCY APPENDECTOMY. SHE WAS LOCKED DOWN IN A SAFEHOUSE AFTER A BARFIGHT SHE STARTED.
IT WOULD HAVE HELPED HER STORY IF SHE'D STAYED INVISIBLE FOR A FEW DAYS INSTEAD OF BEING SEEN AT A RESTAURANT THE NEXT NIGHT, BUT PEOPLE AND THE ENQUIRER PUBLISHED IT, AND THAT'S ALL THAT MATTERS.
I JUST REALIZED SOMETHING.
I MAY HAVE TO HAVE A PANIC ATTACK SOON. THAT'D BE OK, RIGHT?
THAT'D BE JUST FINE.
YOU LASTED LONGER THAN I THOUGHT, PRETTY BOY.

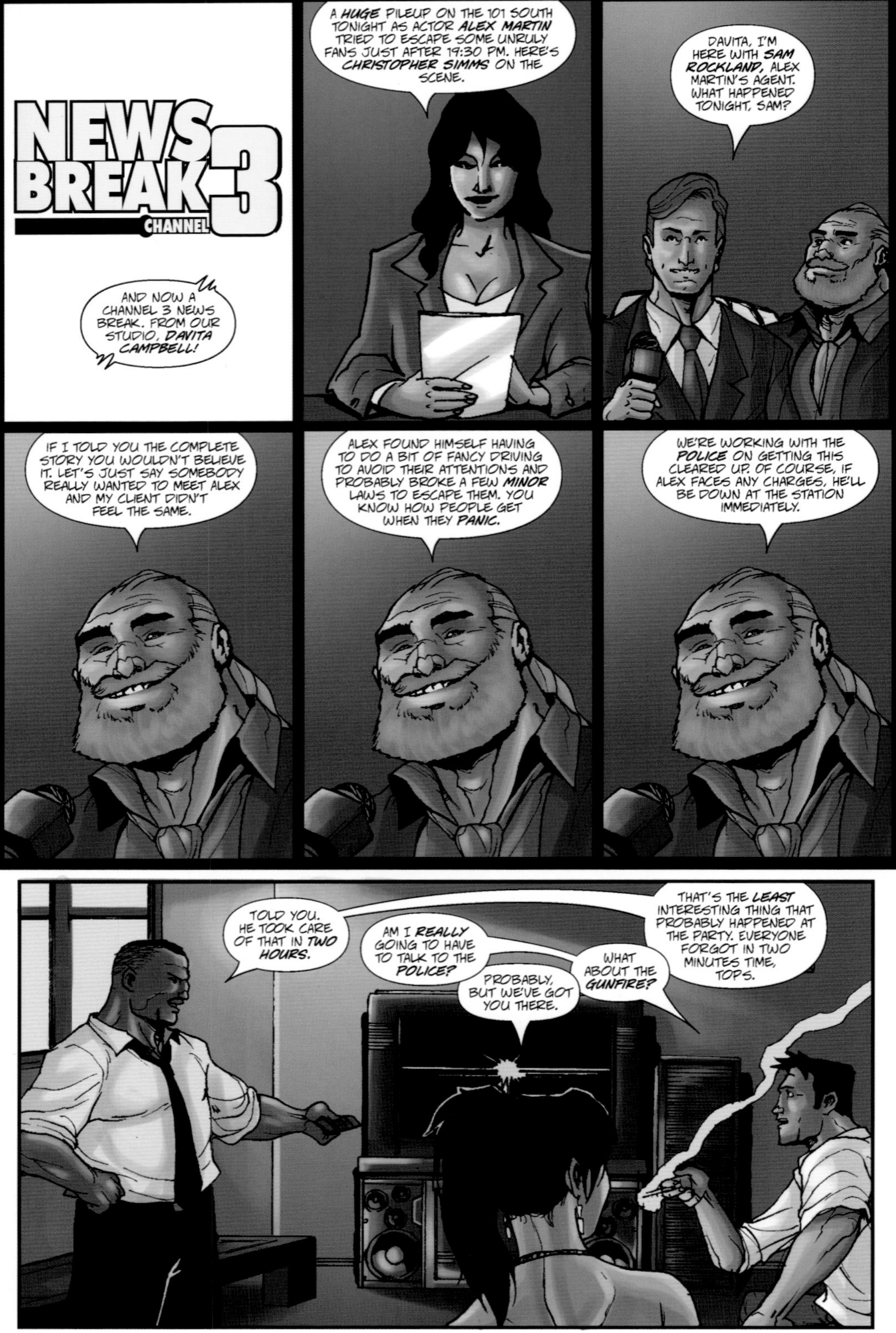
NEWS BREAK CHANNEL 3
AND NOW A CHANNEL 3 NEWS BREAK. FROM OUR STUDIO, DAVITA CAMPBELL!
A HUGE PILEUP ON THE 101 SOUTH TONIGHT AS ACTOR ALEX MARTIN TRIED TO ESCAPE SOME UNRULY FANS JUST AFTER 19:30 PM. HERE'S CHRISTOPHER SIMMS ON THE SCENE.
DAVITA, I'M HERE WITH SAM ROCKLAND, ALEX MARTIN'S AGENT. WHAT HAPPENED TONIGHT, SAM?
IF I TOLD YOU THE COMPLETE STORY YOU WOULDN'T BELIEVE IT. LET'S JUST SAY SOMEBODY REALLY WANTED TO MEET ALEX AND MY CLIENT DIDN'T FEEL THE SAME.
ALEX FOUND HIMSELF HAVING TO DO A BIT OF FANCY DRIVING TO AVOID THEIR ATTENTIONS AND PROBABLY BROKE A FEW MINOR LAWS TO ESCAPE THEM. YOU KNOW HOW PEOPLE GET WHEN THEY PANIC.
WE'RE WORKING WITH THE POLICE ON GETTING THIS CLEARED UP. OF COURSE, IF ALEX FACES ANY CHARGES, HE'LL BE DOWN AT THE STATION IMMEDIATELY.
TOLD YOU. HE TOOK CARE OF THAT IN TWO HOURS.
AM I REALLY GOING TO HAVE TO TALK TO THE POLICE?
PROBABLY, BUT WE'VE GOT YOU THERE.
WHAT ABOUT THE GUNFIRE?
THAT'S THE LEAST INTERESTING THING THAT PROBABLY HAPPENED AT THE PARTY. EVERYONE FORGOT IN TWO MINUTES TIME, TOPS.

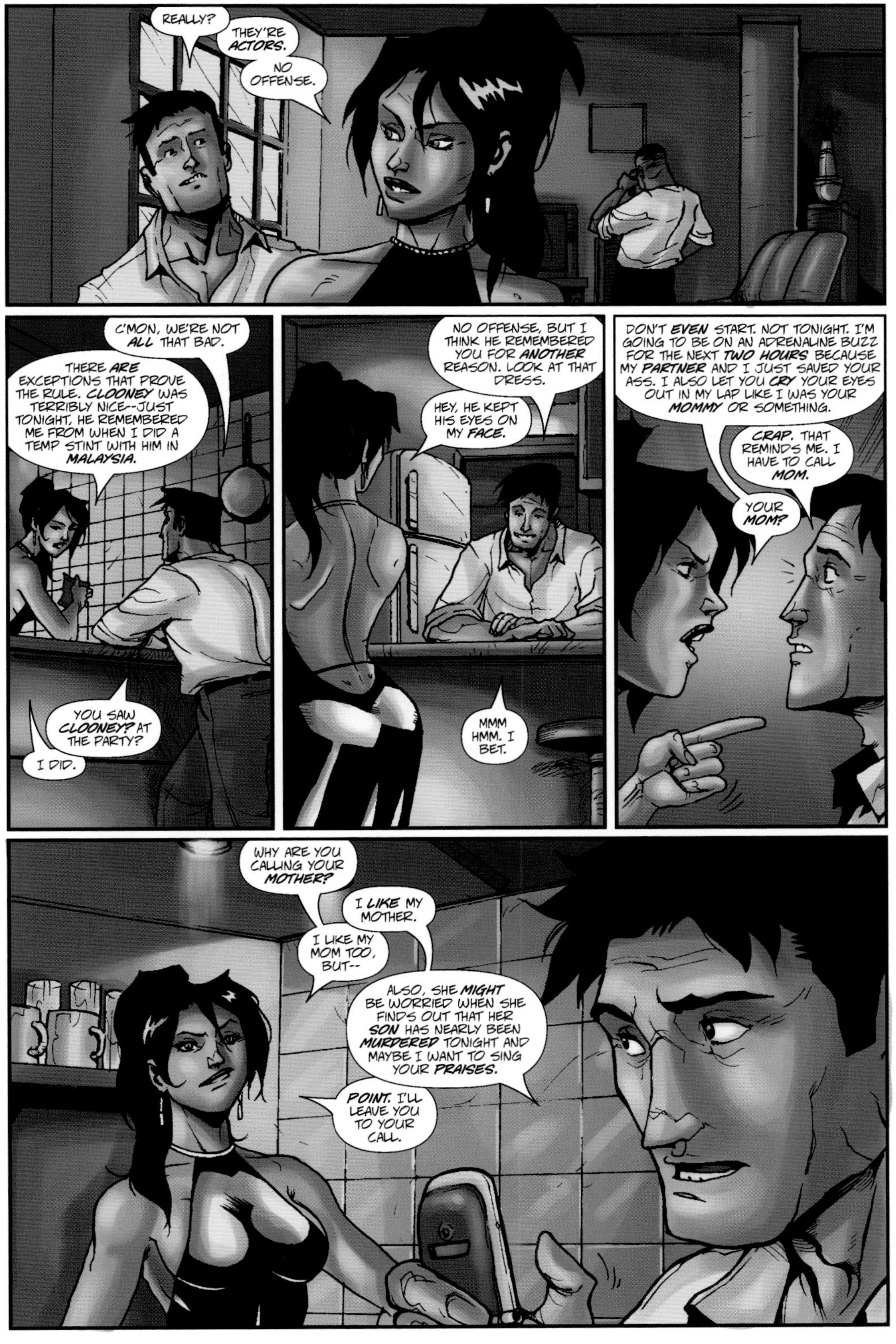
REALLY?
THEY'RE ACTORS.
NO OFFENSE.
C'MON, WE'RE NOT ALL THAT BAD.
THERE ARE EXCEPTIONS THAT PROVE THE RULE. CLOONEY WAS TERRIBLY NICE--JUST TONIGHT, HE REMEMBERED ME FROM WHEN I DID A TEMP STINT WITH HIM IN MALAYSIA.
YOU SAW CLOONEY? AT THE PARTY?
I DID.
NO OFFENSE, BUT I THINK HE REMEMBERED YOU FOR ANOTHER REASON. LOOK AT THAT DRESS.
HEY, HE KEPT HIS EYES ON MY FACE.
MMM HMM. I BET.
DON'T EVEN START. NOT TONIGHT. I'M GOING TO BE ON AN ADRENALINE BUZZ FOR THE NEXT TWO HOURS BECAUSE MY PARTNER AND I JUST SAVED YOUR ASS. I ALSO LET YOU CRY YOUR EYES OUT IN MY LAP LIKE I WAS YOUR MOMMY OR SOMETHING.
CRAP. THAT REMINDS ME. I HAVE TO CALL MOM.
YOUR MOM?
WHY ARE YOU CALLING YOUR MOTHER?
I LIKE MY MOTHER.
I LIKE MY MOM TOO, BUT--
ALSO, SHE MIGHT BE WORRIED WHEN SHE FINDS OUT THAT HER SON HAS NEARLY BEEN MURDERED TONIGHT AND MAYBE I WANT TO SING YOUR PRAISES.
POINT. I'LL LEAVE YOU TO YOUR CALL.

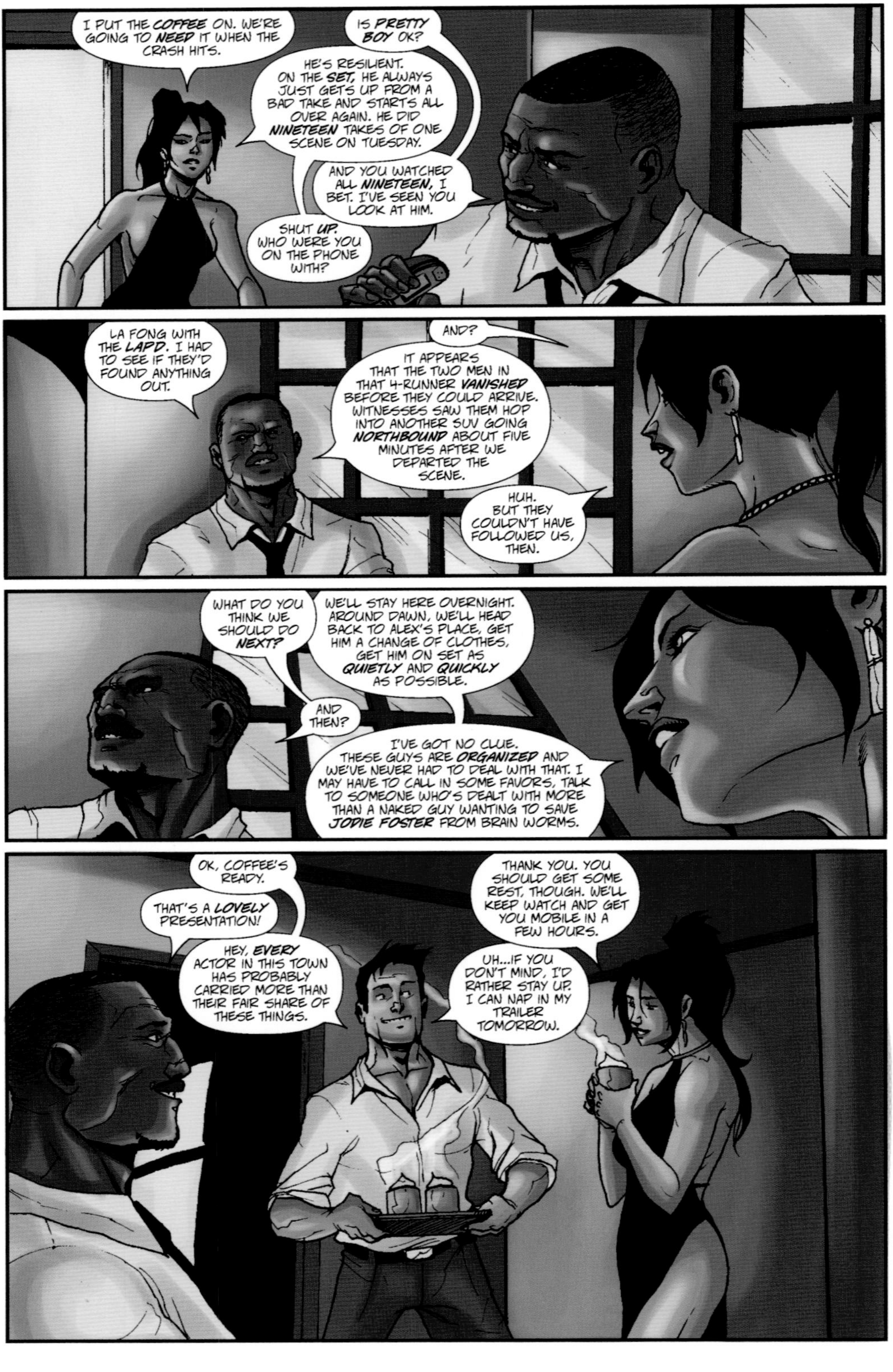
I PUT THE COFFEE ON. WE'RE GOING TO NEED IT WHEN THE CRASH HITS.
IS PRETTY BOY OK?
HE'S RESILIENT. ON THE SET, HE ALWAYS JUST GETS UP FROM A BAD TAKE AND STARTS ALL OVER AGAIN. HE DID NINETEEN TAKES OF ONE SCENE ON TUESDAY.
AND YOU WATCHED ALL NINETEEN, I BET. I'VE SEEN YOU LOOK AT HIM.
SHUT UP. WHO WERE YOU ON THE PHONE WITH?
LA FONG WITH THE LAPD. I HAD TO SEE IF THEY'D FOUND ANYTHING OUT.
AND?
IT APPEARS THAT THE TWO MEN IN THAT 4-RUNNER VANISHED BEFORE THEY COULD ARRIVE. WITNESSES SAW THEM HOP INTO ANOTHER SUV GOING NORTHBOUND ABOUT FIVE MINUTES AFTER WE DEPARTED THE SCENE.
HUH. BUT THEY COULDN'T HAVE FOLLOWED US, THEN.
WHAT DO YOU THINK WE SHOULD DO NEXT?
WE'LL STAY HERE OVERNIGHT. AROUND DAWN, WE'LL HEAD BACK TO ALEX'S PLACE, GET HIM A CHANGE OF CLOTHES, GET HIM ON SET AS QUIETLY AND QUICKLY AS POSSIBLE.
AND THEN?
I'VE GOT NO CLUE. THESE GUYS ARE ORGANIZED AND WE'VE NEVER HAD TO DEAL WITH THAT. I MAY HAVE TO CALL IN SOME FAVORS, TALK TO SOMEONE WHO'S DEALT WITH MORE THAN A NAKED GUY WANTING TO SAVE JODIE FOSTER FROM BRAIN WORMS.
OK, COFFEE'S READY.
THAT'S A LOVELY PRESENTATION!
HEY, EVERY ACTOR IN THIS TOWN HAS PROBABLY CARRIED MORE THAN THEIR FAIR SHARE OF THESE THINGS.
THANK YOU. YOU SHOULD GET SOME REST, THOUGH. WE'LL KEEP WATCH AND GET YOU MOBILE IN A FEW HOURS.
UH...IF YOU DON'T MIND, I'D RATHER STAY UP. I CAN NAP IN MY TRAILER TOMORROW.

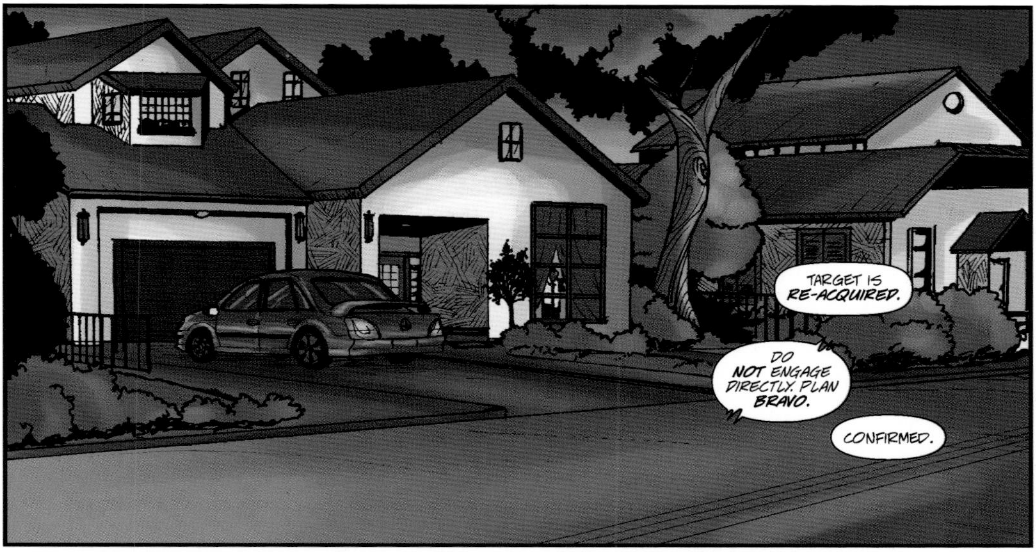
TARGET IS **RE-ACQUIRED.**
DO **NOT** ENGAGE DIRECTLY. PLAN **BRAVO.**
CONFIRMED.

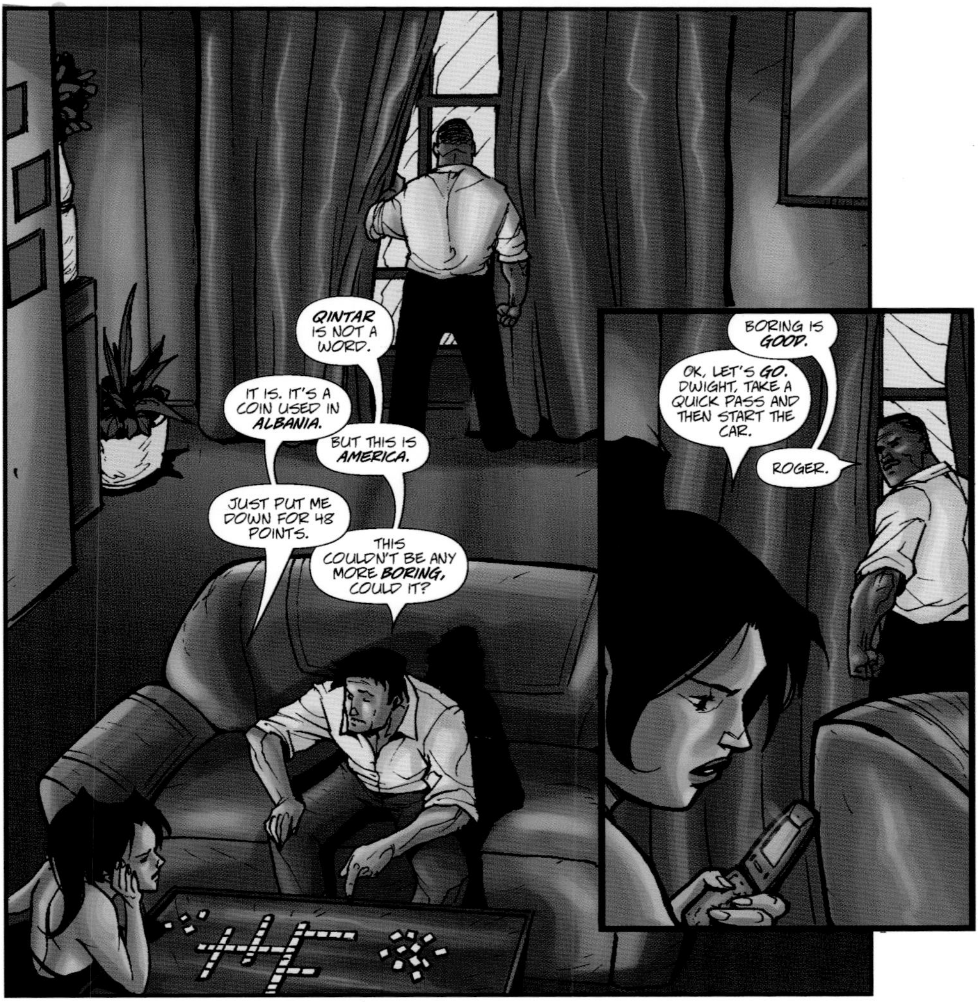
QINTAR IS NOT A WORD.
IT IS. IT'S A COIN USED IN **ALBANIA.**
BUT THIS IS **AMERICA.**
JUST PUT ME DOWN FOR 48 POINTS.
THIS COULDN'T BE ANY MORE **BORING,** COULD IT?
BORING IS **GOOD.**
OK, LET'S **GO.** DWIGHT, TAKE A QUICK PASS AND THEN START THE CAR.
ROGER.

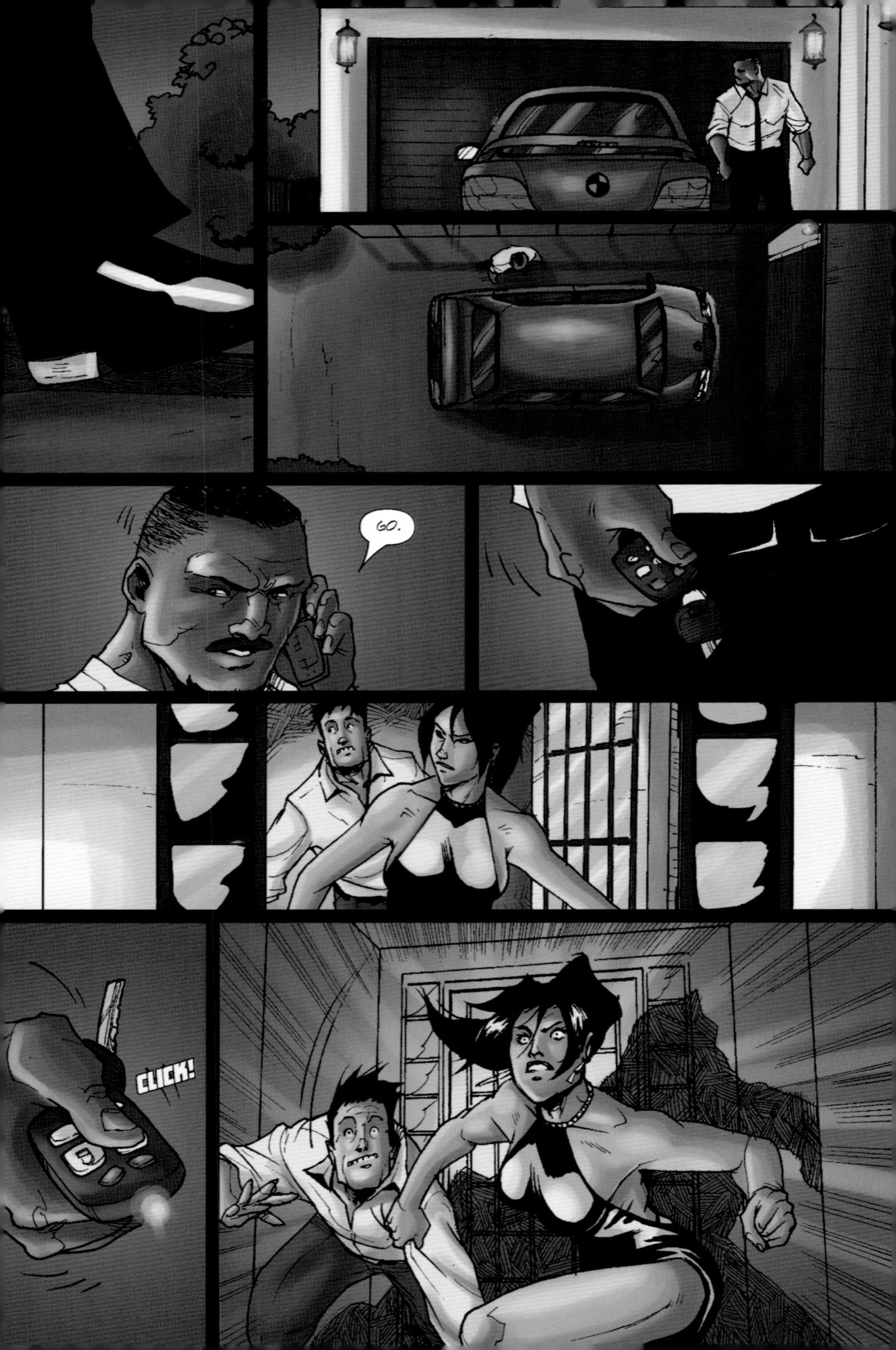
GO.
CLICK!

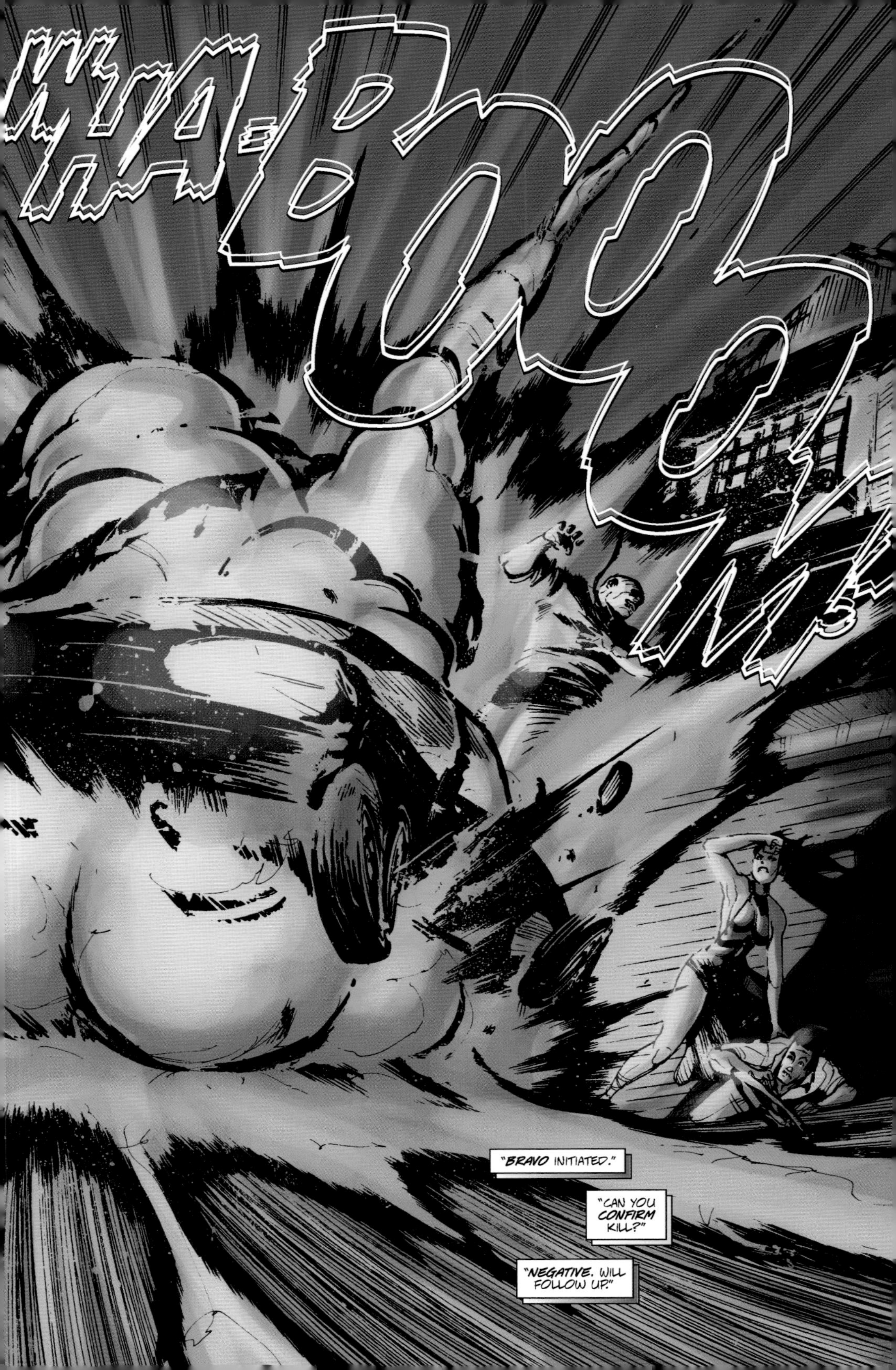
KA-BOOOM!
"BRAVO INITIATED."
"CAN YOU CONFIRM KILL?"
"NEGATIVE. WILL FOLLOW UP."

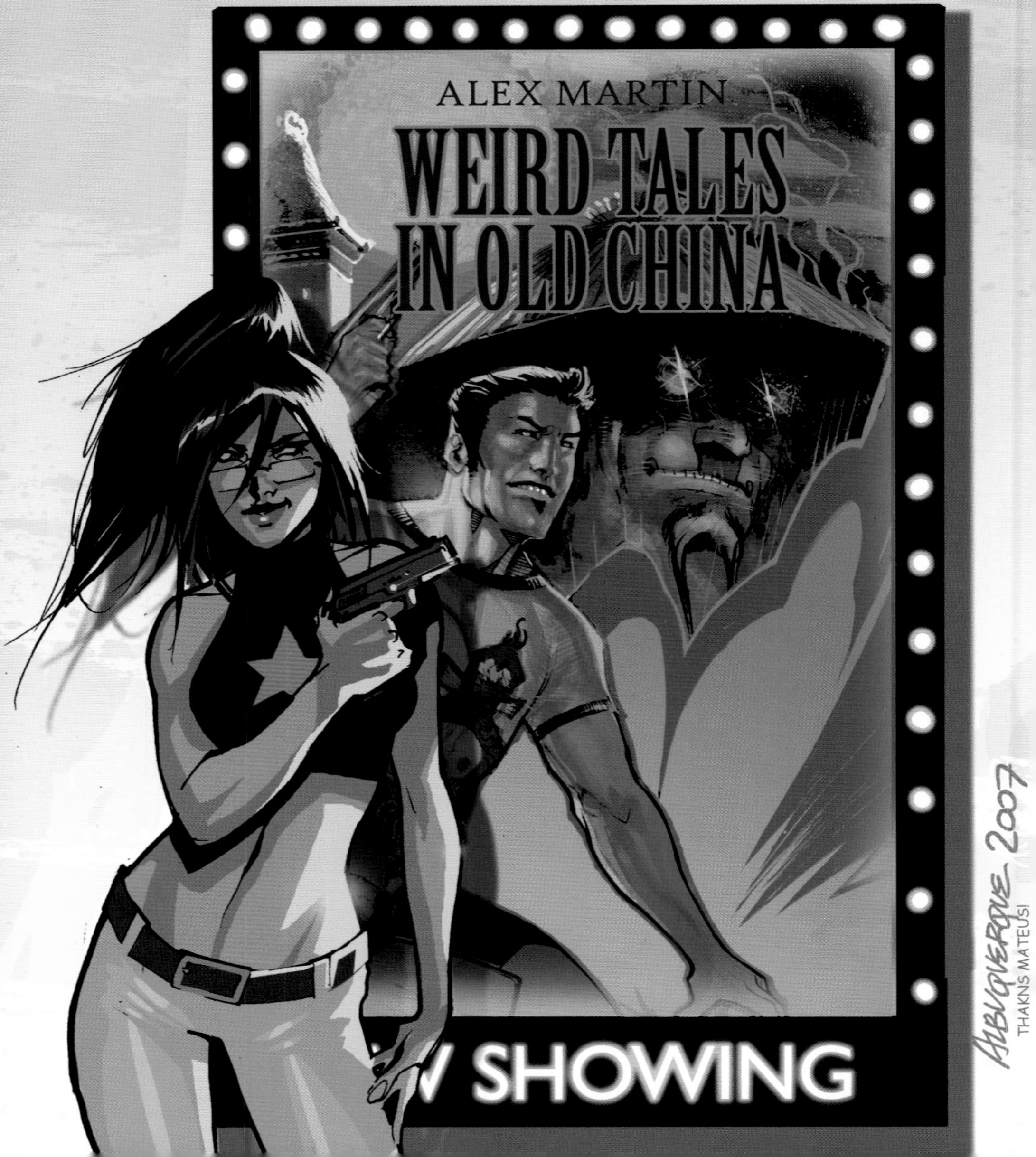
ALEX MARTIN
WEIRD TALES IN OLD CHINA
SHOWING
ALBUQUERQUE 2007
THAKNS MATEUS!

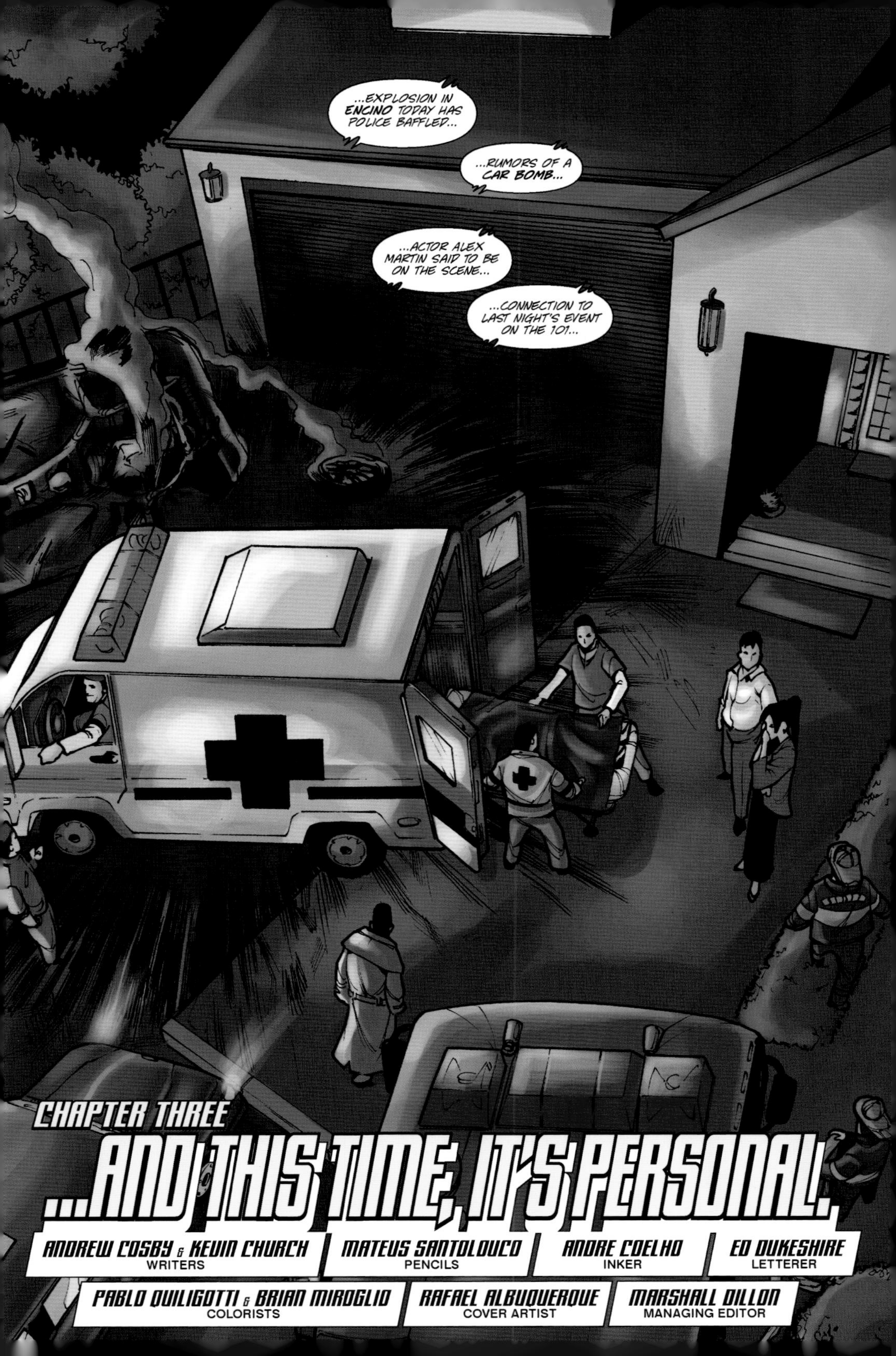
...EXPLOSION IN ENCINO TODAY HAS POLICE BAFFLED...
...RUMORS OF A CAR BOMB...
...ACTOR ALEX MARTIN SAID TO BE ON THE SCENE...
...CONNECTION TO LAST NIGHT'S EVENT ON THE 101...
CHAPTER THREE
...AND THIS TIME, IT'S PERSONAL.
ANDREW COSBY & KEVIN CHURCH
WRITERS
MATEUS SANTOLOUCO
PENCILS
ANDRE COELHO
INKER
ED DUKESHIRE
LETTERER
PABLO QUILIGOTTI & BRIAN MIROGLIO
COLORISTS
RAFAEL ALBUQUERQUE
COVER ARTIST
MARSHALL DILLON
MANAGING EDITOR

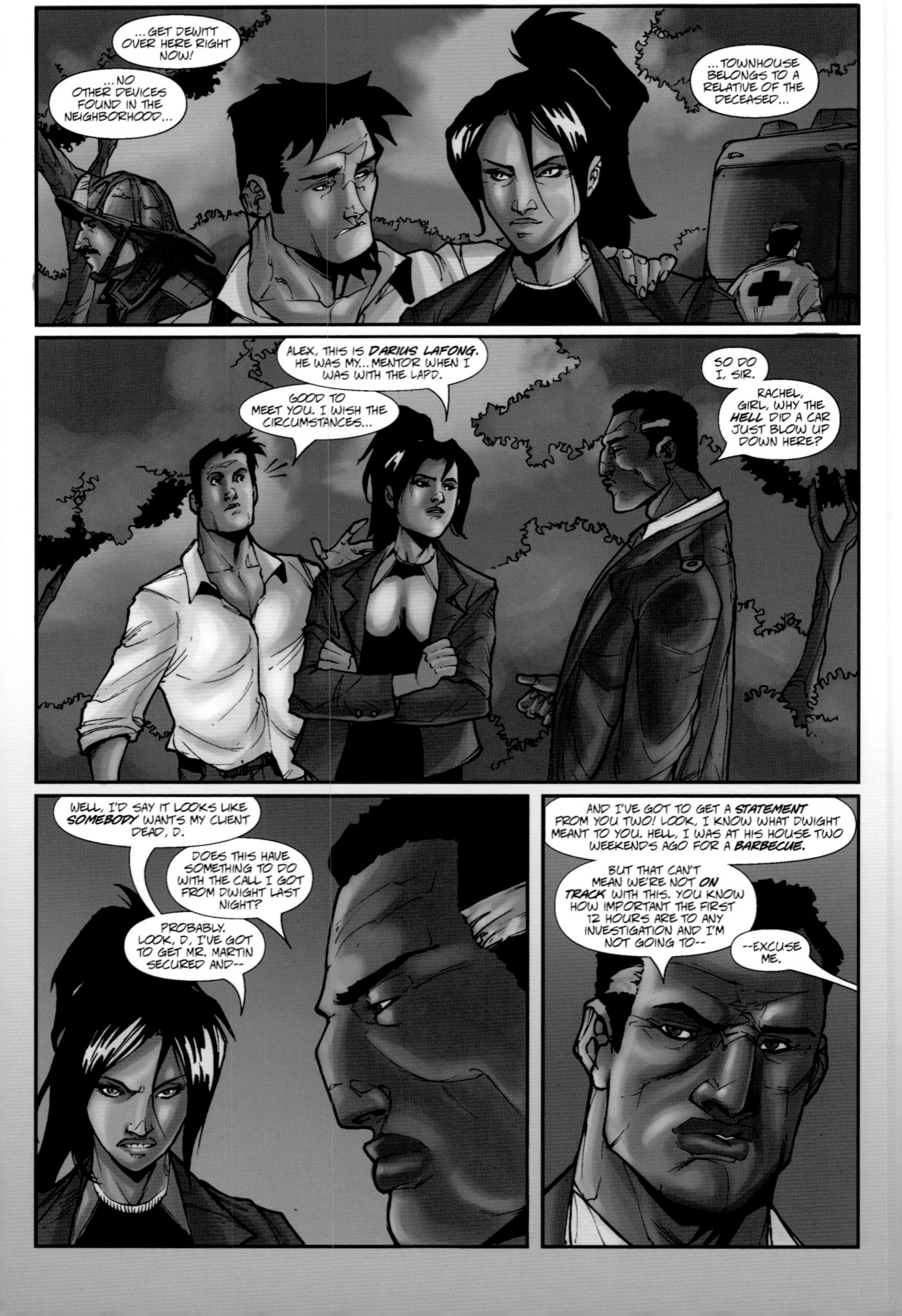
...GET DEWITT OVER HERE RIGHT NOW!
...NO OTHER DEVICES FOUND IN THE NEIGHBORHOOD...
...TOWNHOUSE BELONGS TO A RELATIVE OF THE DECEASED...
ALEX, THIS IS **DARIUS LAFONG.** HE WAS MY...MENTOR WHEN I WAS WITH THE LAPD.
GOOD TO MEET YOU. I WISH THE CIRCUMSTANCES...
SO DO I, SIR.
RACHEL, GIRL, WHY THE **HELL** DID A CAR JUST BLOW UP DOWN HERE?
WELL, I'D SAY IT LOOKS LIKE **SOMEBODY** WANTS MY CLIENT DEAD, D.
DOES THIS HAVE SOMETHING TO DO WITH THE CALL I GOT FROM DWIGHT LAST NIGHT?
PROBABLY. LOOK, D, I'VE GOT TO GET MR. MARTIN SECURED AND--
AND I'VE GOT TO GET A **STATEMENT** FROM YOU TWO! LOOK, I KNOW WHAT DWIGHT MEANT TO YOU. HELL, I WAS AT HIS HOUSE TWO WEEKENDS AGO FOR A **BARBECUE.**
BUT THAT CAN'T MEAN WE'RE NOT **ON TRACK** WITH THIS. YOU KNOW HOW IMPORTANT THE FIRST 12 HOURS ARE TO ANY INVESTIGATION AND I'M NOT GOING TO--
--EXCUSE ME.

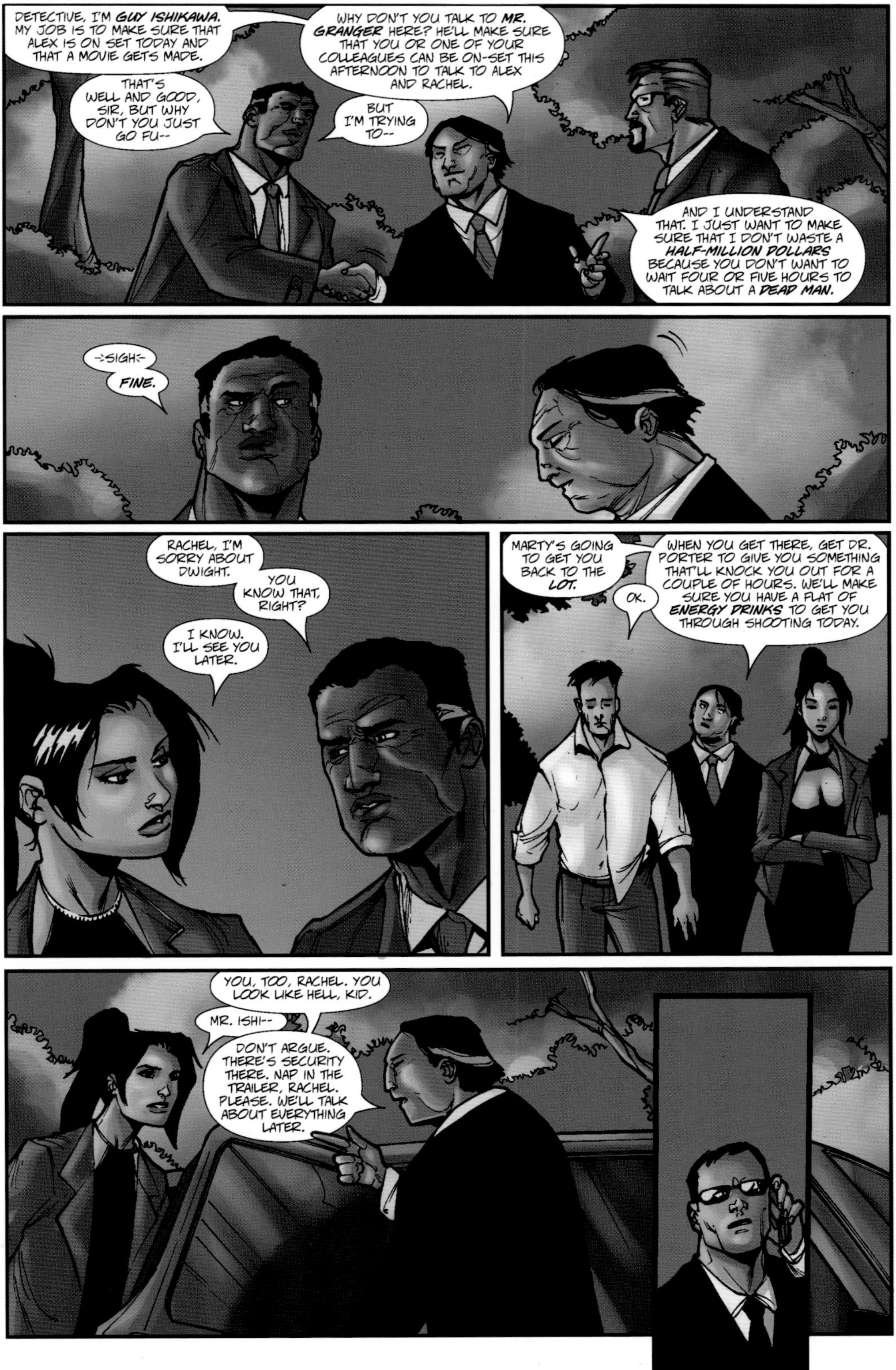
DETECTIVE, I'M GUY ISHIKAWA. MY JOB IS TO MAKE SURE THAT ALEX IS ON SET TODAY AND THAT A MOVIE GETS MADE.
THAT'S WELL AND GOOD, SIR, BUT WHY DON'T YOU JUST GO FU--
WHY DON'T YOU TALK TO MR. GRANGER HERE? HE'LL MAKE SURE THAT YOU OR ONE OF YOUR COLLEAGUES CAN BE ON-SET THIS AFTERNOON TO TALK TO ALEX AND RACHEL.
BUT I'M TRYING TO--
AND I UNDERSTAND THAT. I JUST WANT TO MAKE SURE THAT I DON'T WASTE A HALF-MILLION DOLLARS BECAUSE YOU DON'T WANT TO WAIT FOUR OR FIVE HOURS TO TALK ABOUT A DEAD MAN.
-SIGH-
FINE.
RACHEL, I'M SORRY ABOUT DWIGHT.
YOU KNOW THAT, RIGHT?
I KNOW. I'LL SEE YOU LATER.
MARTY'S GOING TO GET YOU BACK TO THE LOT.
WHEN YOU GET THERE, GET DR. PORTER TO GIVE YOU SOMETHING THAT'LL KNOCK YOU OUT FOR A COUPLE OF HOURS. WE'LL MAKE SURE YOU HAVE A FLAT OF ENERGY DRINKS TO GET YOU THROUGH SHOOTING TODAY.
OK.
YOU, TOO, RACHEL. YOU LOOK LIKE HELL, KID.
MR. ISHI--
DON'T ARGUE. THERE'S SECURITY THERE. NAP IN THE TRAILER, RACHEL. PLEASE. WE'LL TALK ABOUT EVERYTHING LATER.

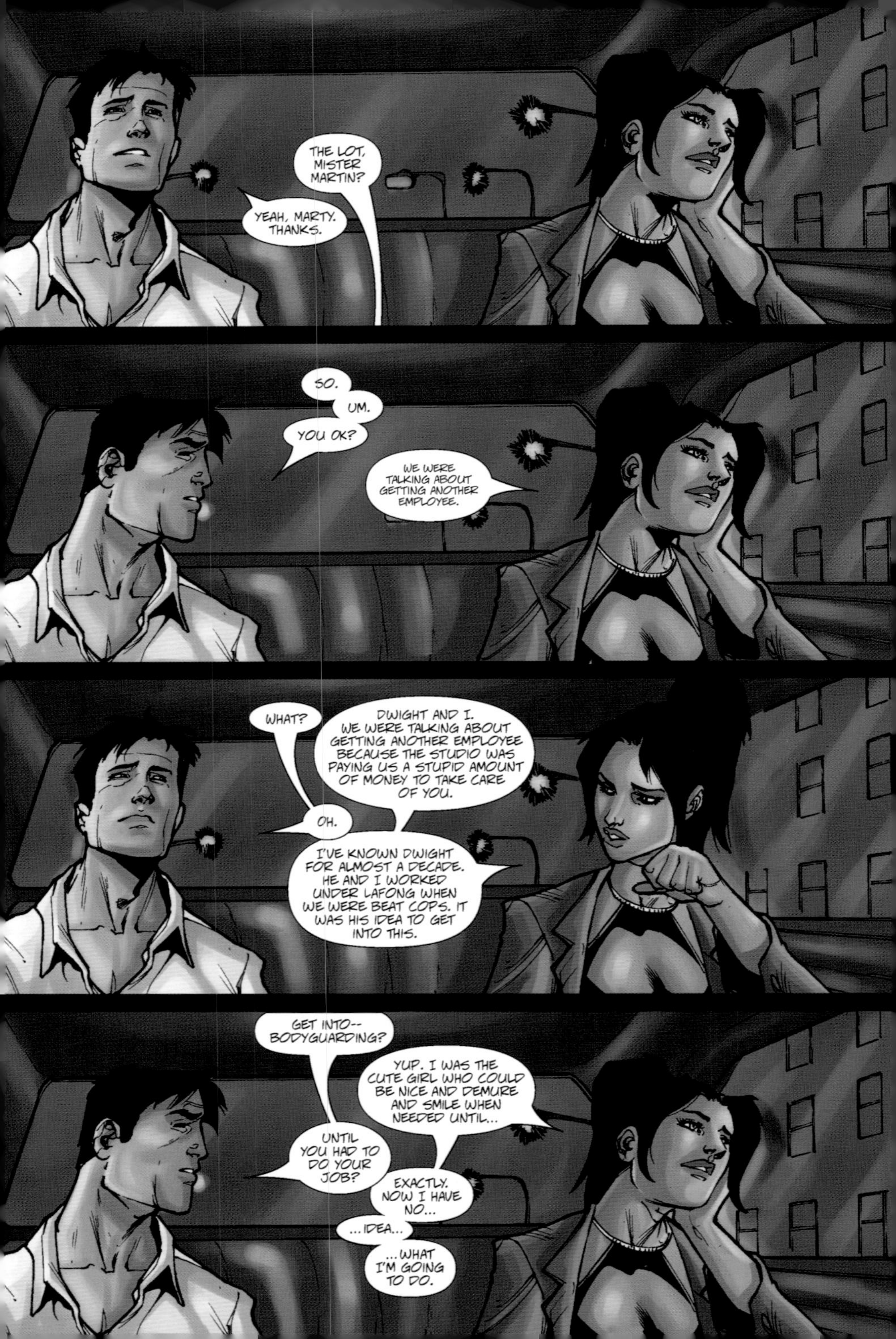
THE LOT, MISTER MARTIN?
YEAH, MARTY. THANKS.
SO.
UM.
YOU OK?
WE WERE TALKING ABOUT GETTING ANOTHER EMPLOYEE.
WHAT?
DWIGHT AND I. WE WERE TALKING ABOUT GETTING ANOTHER EMPLOYEE BECAUSE THE STUDIO WAS PAYING US A STUPID AMOUNT OF MONEY TO TAKE CARE OF YOU.
OH.
I'VE KNOWN DWIGHT FOR ALMOST A DECADE. HE AND I WORKED UNDER LAFONG WHEN WE WERE BEAT COPS. IT WAS HIS IDEA TO GET INTO THIS.
GET INTO-- BODYGUARDING?
YUP. I WAS THE CUTE GIRL WHO COULD BE NICE AND DEMURE AND SMILE WHEN NEEDED UNTIL...
UNTIL YOU HAD TO DO YOUR JOB?
EXACTLY. NOW I HAVE NO...
...IDEA...
...WHAT I'M GOING TO DO.

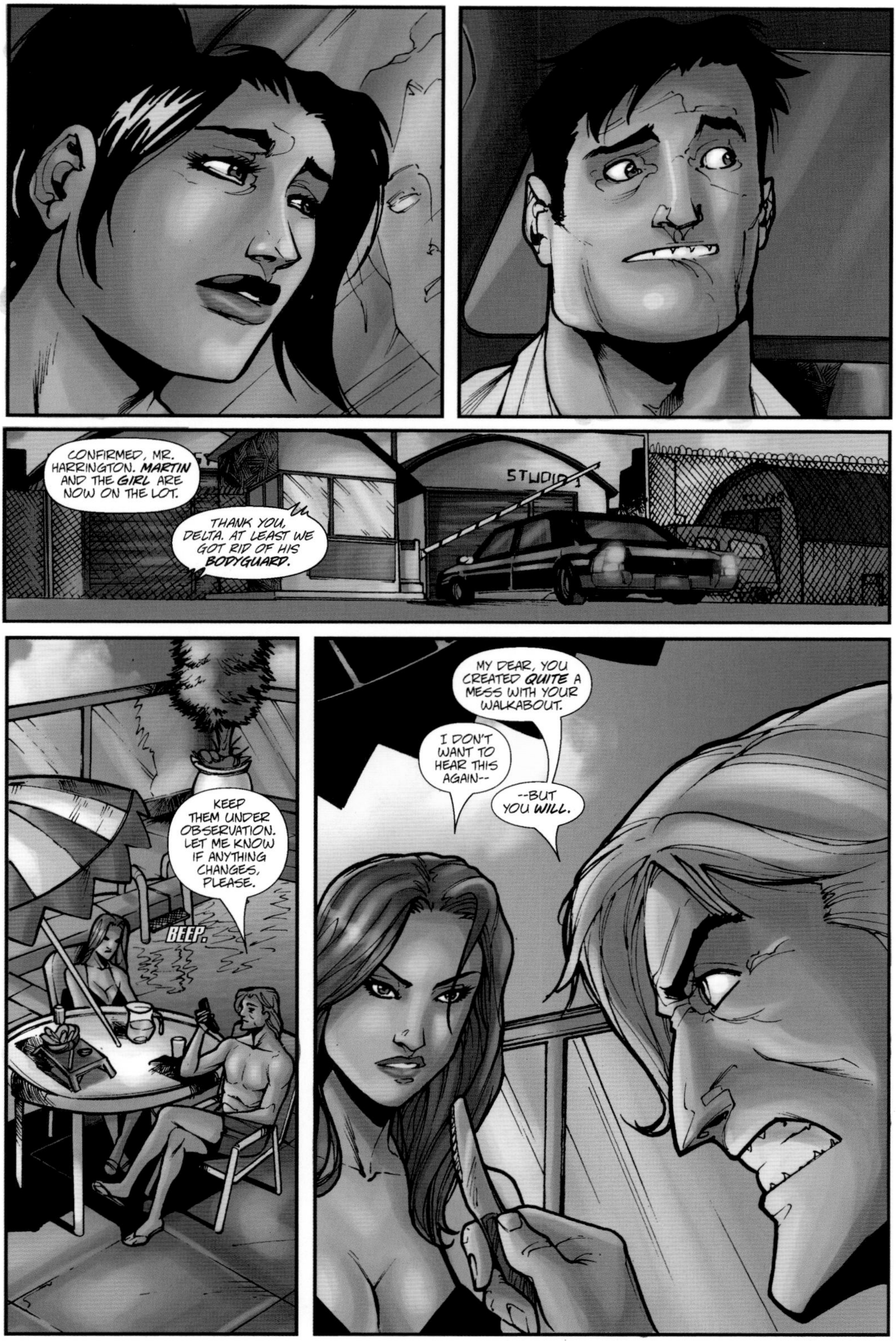
CONFIRMED, MR. HARRINGTON. MARTIN AND THE GIRL ARE NOW ON THE LOT.
STUDIO
THANK YOU, DELTA. AT LEAST WE GOT RID OF HIS BODYGUARD.
KEEP THEM UNDER OBSERVATION. LET ME KNOW IF ANYTHING CHANGES, PLEASE.
BEEP.
MY DEAR, YOU CREATED QUITE A MESS WITH YOUR WALKABOUT.
I DON'T WANT TO HEAR THIS AGAIN--
--BUT YOU WILL.

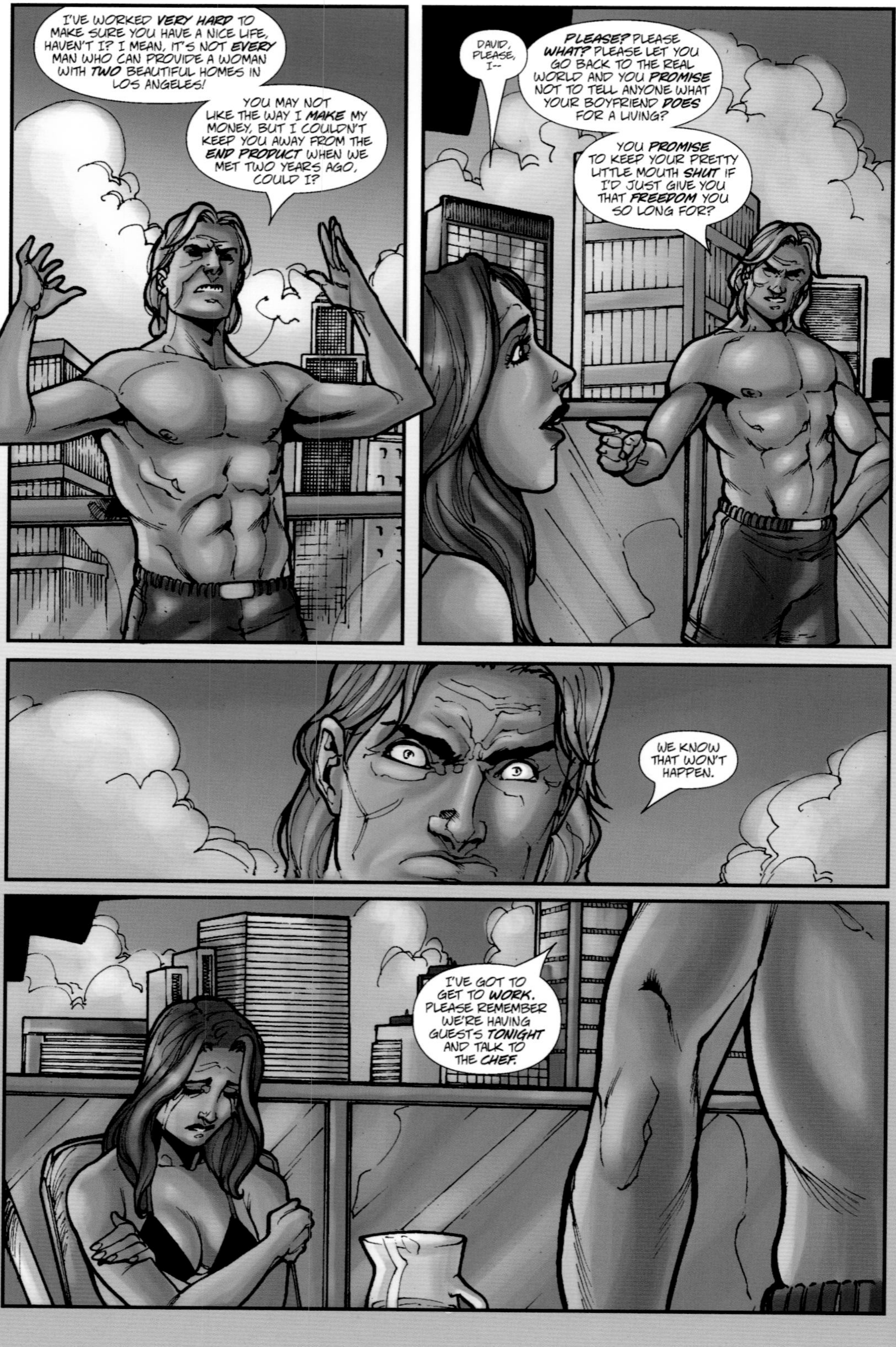
I'VE WORKED VERY HARD TO MAKE SURE YOU HAVE A NICE LIFE, HAVEN'T I? I MEAN, IT'S NOT EVERY MAN WHO CAN PROVIDE A WOMAN WITH TWO BEAUTIFUL HOMES IN LOS ANGELES!
YOU MAY NOT LIKE THE WAY I MAKE MY MONEY, BUT I COULDN'T KEEP YOU AWAY FROM THE END PRODUCT WHEN WE MET TWO YEARS AGO, COULD I?
DAVID, PLEASE, I--
PLEASE? PLEASE WHAT? PLEASE LET YOU GO BACK TO THE REAL WORLD AND YOU PROMISE NOT TO TELL ANYONE WHAT YOUR BOYFRIEND DOES FOR A LIVING?
YOU PROMISE TO KEEP YOUR PRETTY LITTLE MOUTH SHUT IF I'D JUST GIVE YOU THAT FREEDOM YOU SO LONG FOR?
WE KNOW THAT WON'T HAPPEN.
I'VE GOT TO GET TO WORK. PLEASE REMEMBER WE'RE HAVING GUESTS TONIGHT AND TALK TO THE CHEF.

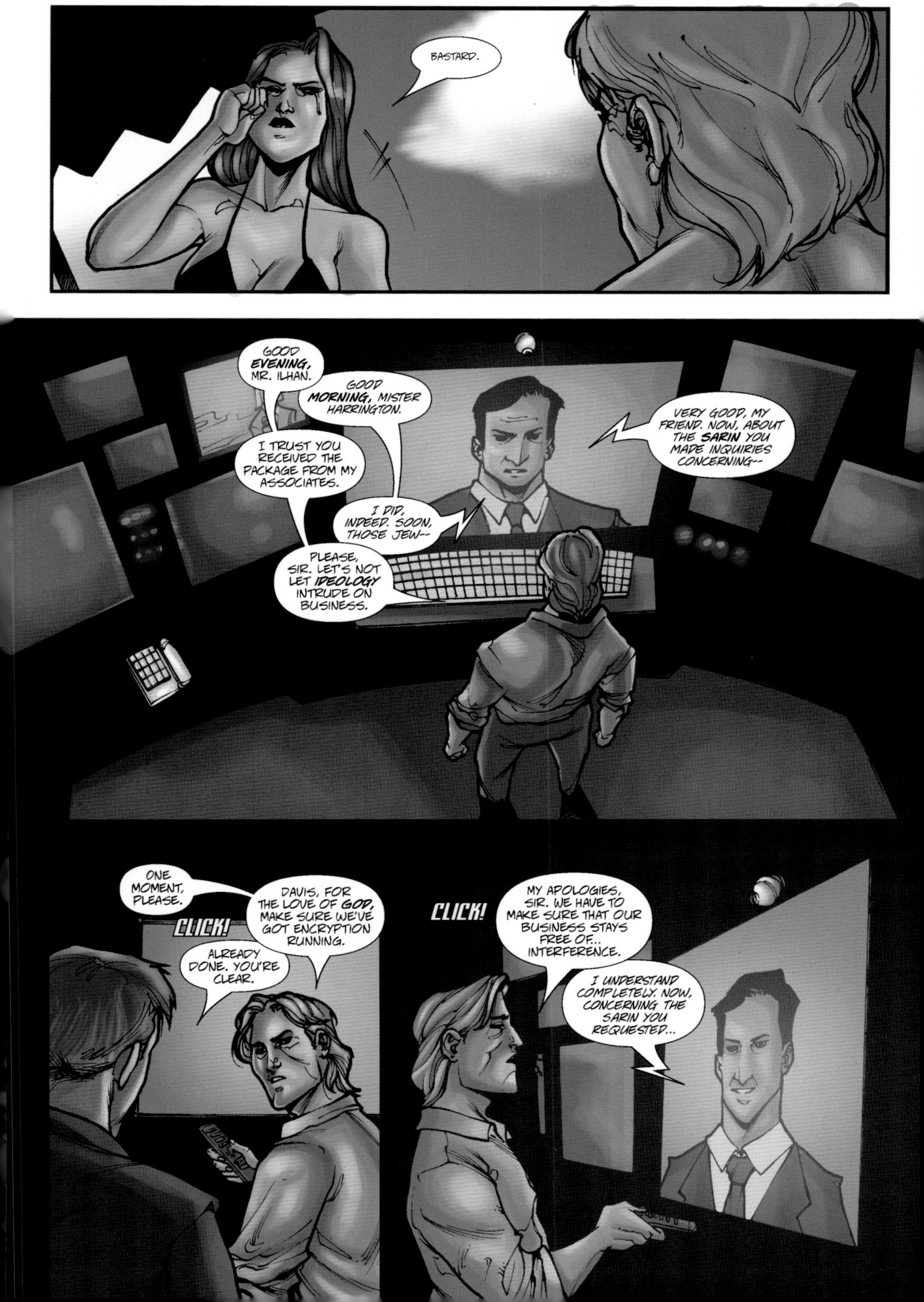
BASTARD.
GOOD EVENING, MR. ILHAN.
GOOD MORNING, MISTER HARRINGTON.
I TRUST YOU RECEIVED THE PACKAGE FROM MY ASSOCIATES.
I DID, INDEED. SOON, THOSE JEW--
PLEASE, SIR. LET'S NOT LET IDEOLOGY INTRUDE ON BUSINESS.
VERY GOOD, MY FRIEND. NOW, ABOUT THE SARIN YOU MADE INQUIRIES CONCERNING--
ONE MOMENT, PLEASE.
CLICK!
DAVIS, FOR THE LOVE OF GOD, MAKE SURE WE'VE GOT ENCRYPTION RUNNING.
ALREADY DONE. YOU'RE CLEAR.
CLICK!
MY APOLOGIES, SIR. WE HAVE TO MAKE SURE THAT OUR BUSINESS STAYS FREE OF... INTERFERENCE.
I UNDERSTAND COMPLETELY. NOW, CONCERNING THE SARIN YOU REQUESTED...

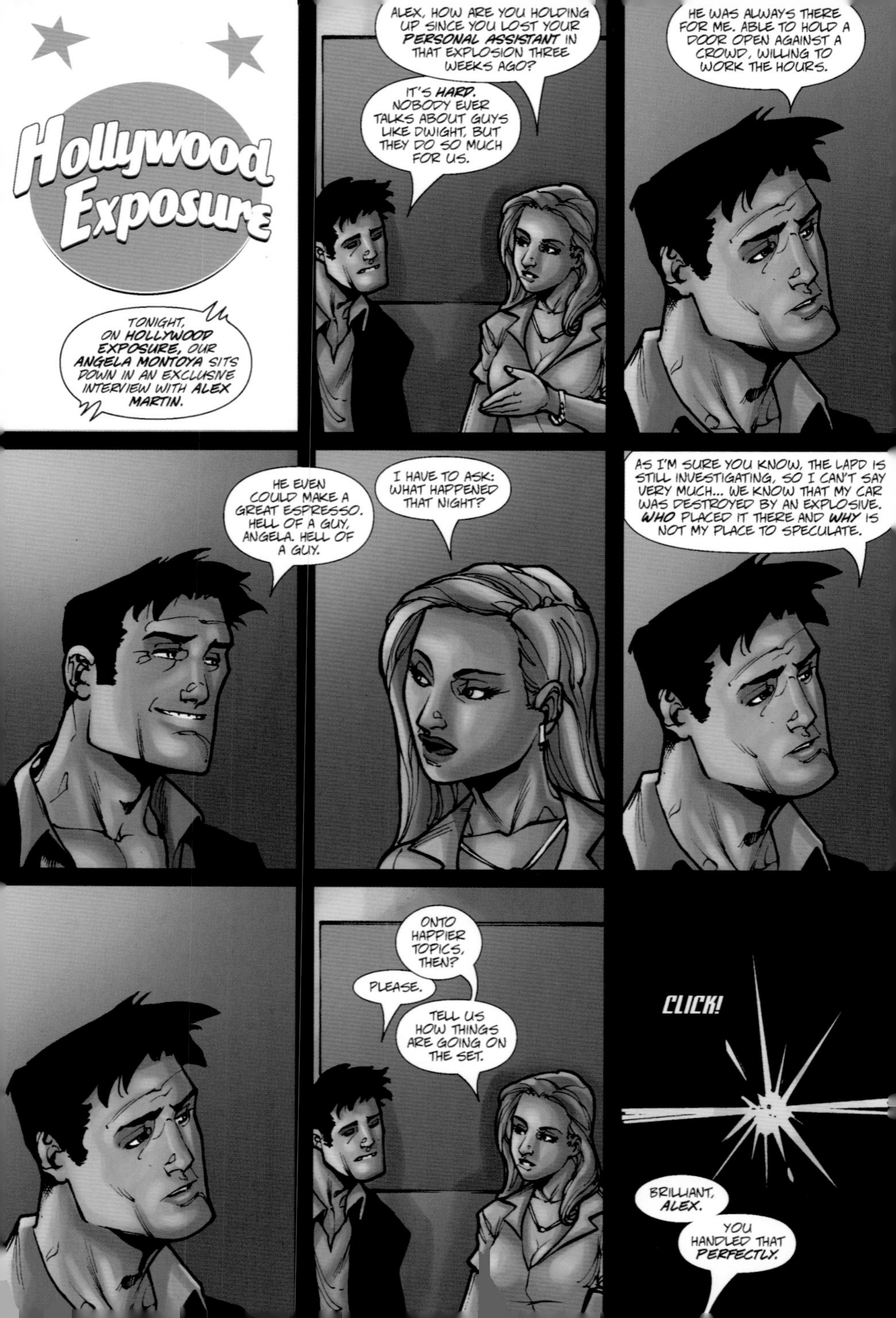
Hollywood Exposure
TONIGHT, ON HOLLYWOOD EXPOSURE, OUR ANGELA MONTOYA SITS DOWN IN AN EXCLUSIVE INTERVIEW WITH ALEX MARTIN.
ALEX, HOW ARE YOU HOLDING UP SINCE YOU LOST YOUR PERSONAL ASSISTANT IN THAT EXPLOSION THREE WEEKS AGO?
IT'S HARD. NOBODY EVER TALKS ABOUT GUYS LIKE DWIGHT, BUT THEY DO SO MUCH FOR US.
HE WAS ALWAYS THERE FOR ME. ABLE TO HOLD A DOOR OPEN AGAINST A CROWD, WILLING TO WORK THE HOURS.
HE EVEN COULD MAKE A GREAT ESPRESSO. HELL OF A GUY, ANGELA. HELL OF A GUY.
I HAVE TO ASK: WHAT HAPPENED THAT NIGHT?
AS I'M SURE YOU KNOW, THE LAPD IS STILL INVESTIGATING, SO I CAN'T SAY VERY MUCH... WE KNOW THAT MY CAR WAS DESTROYED BY AN EXPLOSIVE. WHO PLACED IT THERE AND WHY IS NOT MY PLACE TO SPECULATE.
ONTO HAPPIER TOPICS, THEN?
PLEASE.
TELL US HOW THINGS ARE GOING ON THE SET.
CLICK!
BRILLIANT, ALEX.
YOU HANDLED THAT PERFECTLY.

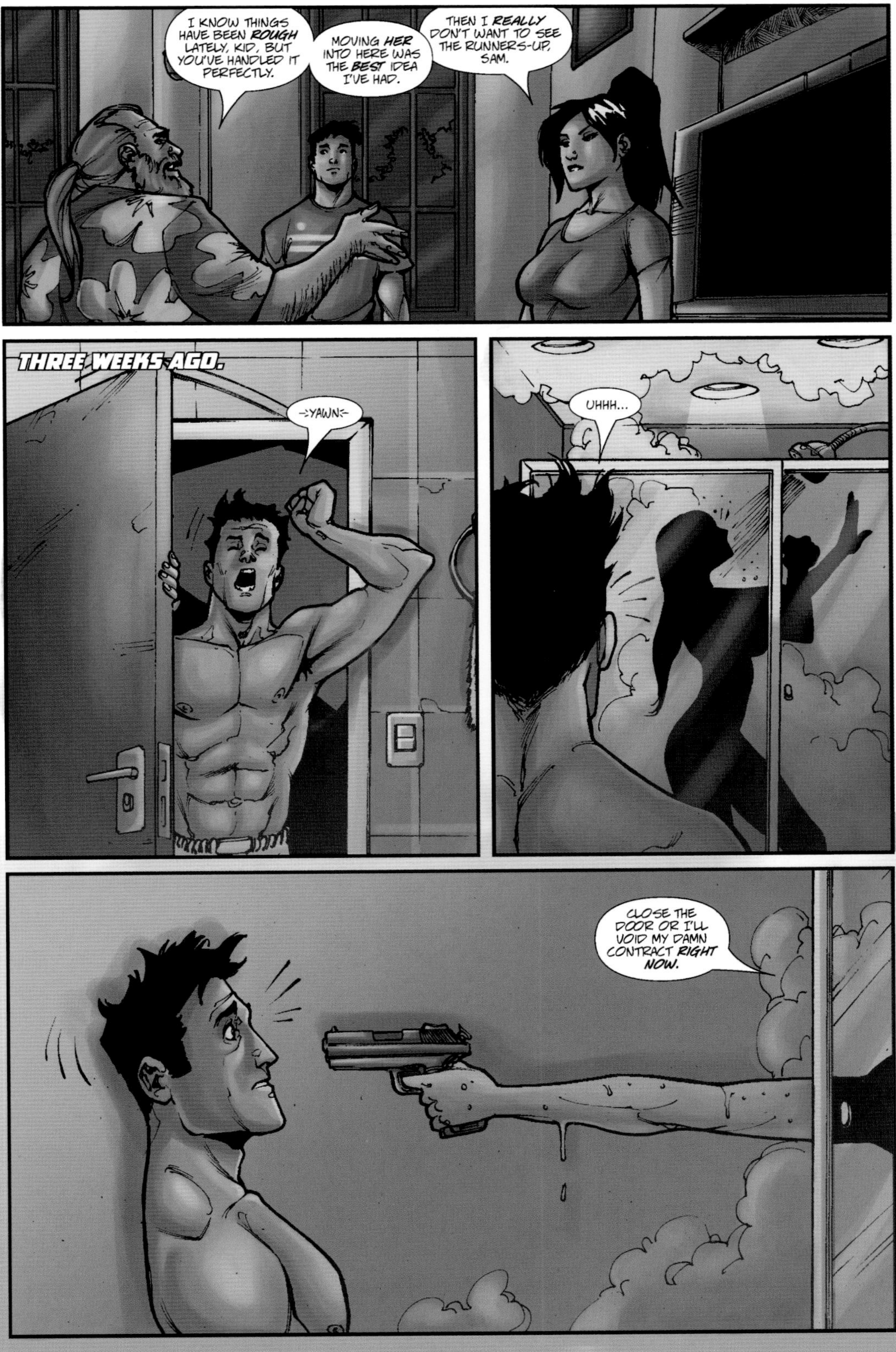
I KNOW THINGS HAVE BEEN ROUGH LATELY, KID, BUT YOU'VE HANDLED IT PERFECTLY.
MOVING HER INTO HERE WAS THE BEST IDEA I'VE HAD.
THEN I REALLY DON'T WANT TO SEE THE RUNNERS-UP, SAM.
THREE WEEKS AGO.
-YAWN-
UHHH...
CLOSE THE DOOR OR I'LL VOID MY DAMN CONTRACT RIGHT NOW.

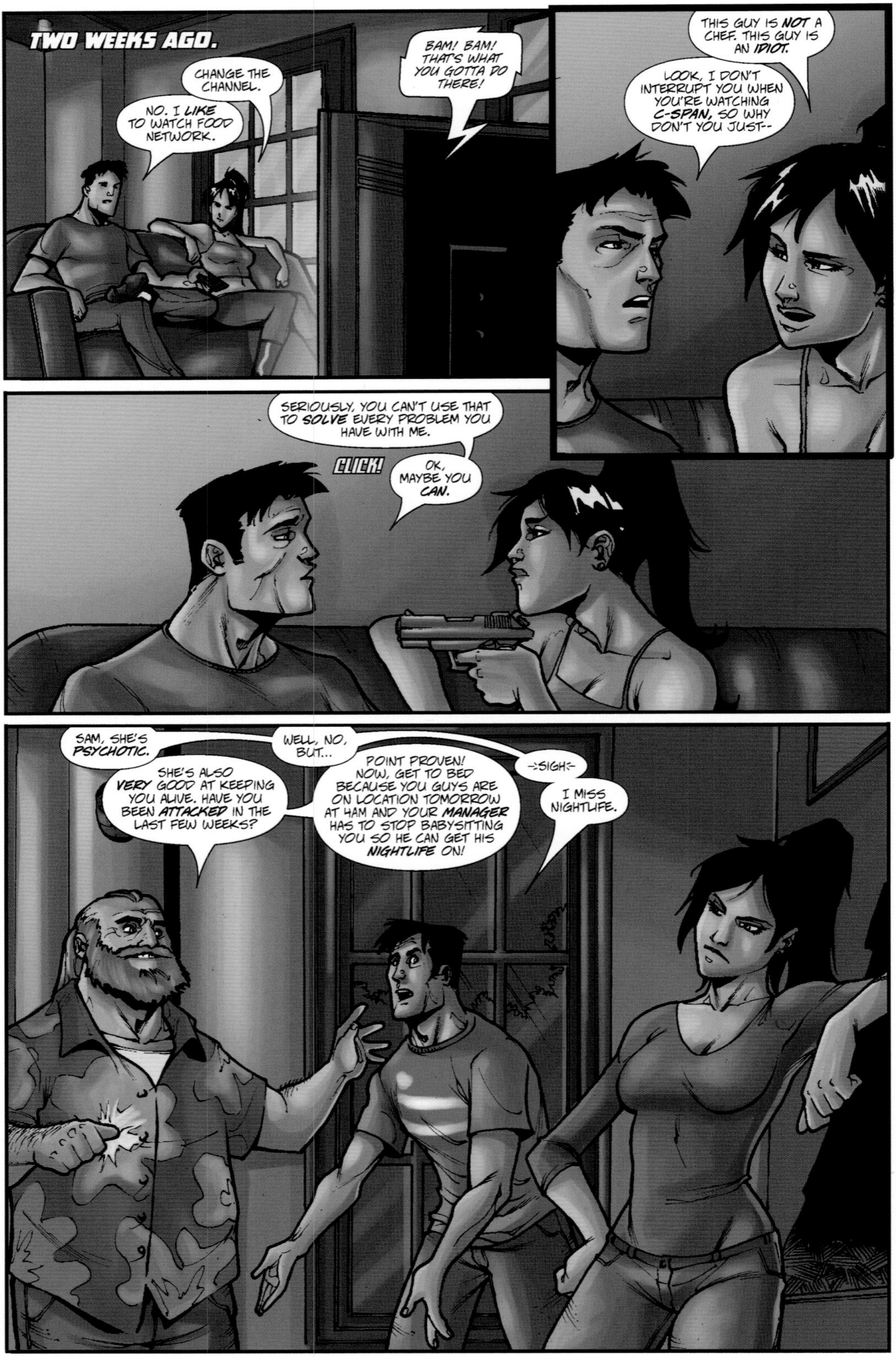
TWO WEEKS AGO.
CHANGE THE CHANNEL.
NO. I LIKE TO WATCH FOOD NETWORK.
BAM! BAM! THAT'S WHAT YOU GOTTA DO THERE!
THIS GUY IS NOT A CHEF. THIS GUY IS AN IDIOT.
LOOK, I DON'T INTERRUPT YOU WHEN YOU'RE WATCHING C-SPAN, SO WHY DON'T YOU JUST--
SERIOUSLY, YOU CAN'T USE THAT TO SOLVE EVERY PROBLEM YOU HAVE WITH ME.
CLICK!
OK, MAYBE YOU CAN.
SAM, SHE'S PSYCHOTIC.
SHE'S ALSO VERY GOOD AT KEEPING YOU ALIVE. HAVE YOU BEEN ATTACKED IN THE LAST FEW WEEKS?
WELL, NO, BUT...
POINT PROVEN! NOW, GET TO BED BECAUSE YOU GUYS ARE ON LOCATION TOMORROW AT 4AM AND YOUR MANAGER HAS TO STOP BABYSITTING YOU SO HE CAN GET HIS NIGHTLIFE ON!
-SIGH-
I MISS NIGHTLIFE.

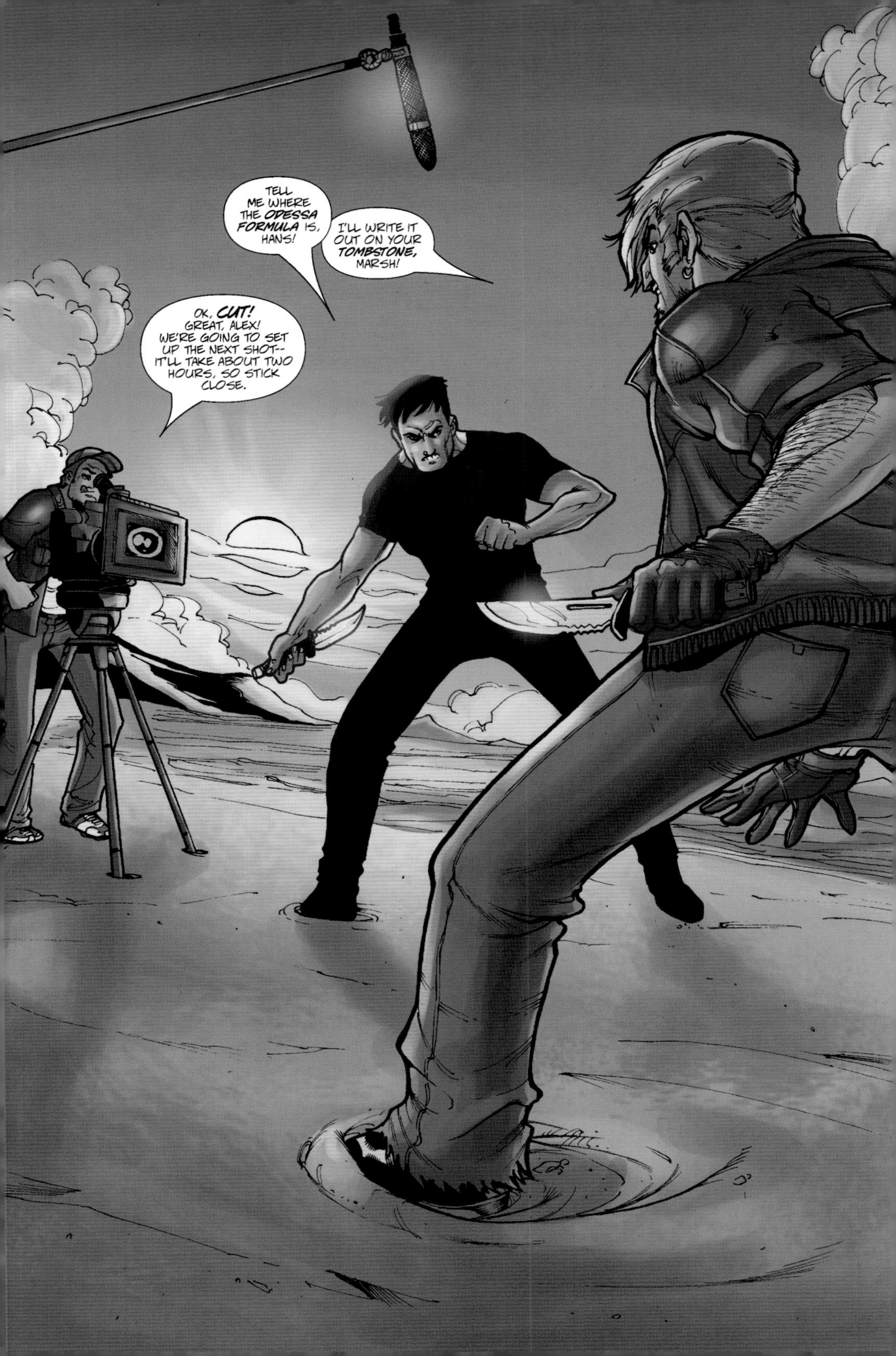
TELL ME WHERE THE ODESSA FORMULA IS, HANS!
I'LL WRITE IT OUT ON YOUR TOMBSTONE, MARSH!
OK, CUT! GREAT, ALEX! WE'RE GOING TO SET UP THE NEXT SHOT-- IT'LL TAKE ABOUT TWO HOURS, SO STICK CLOSE.

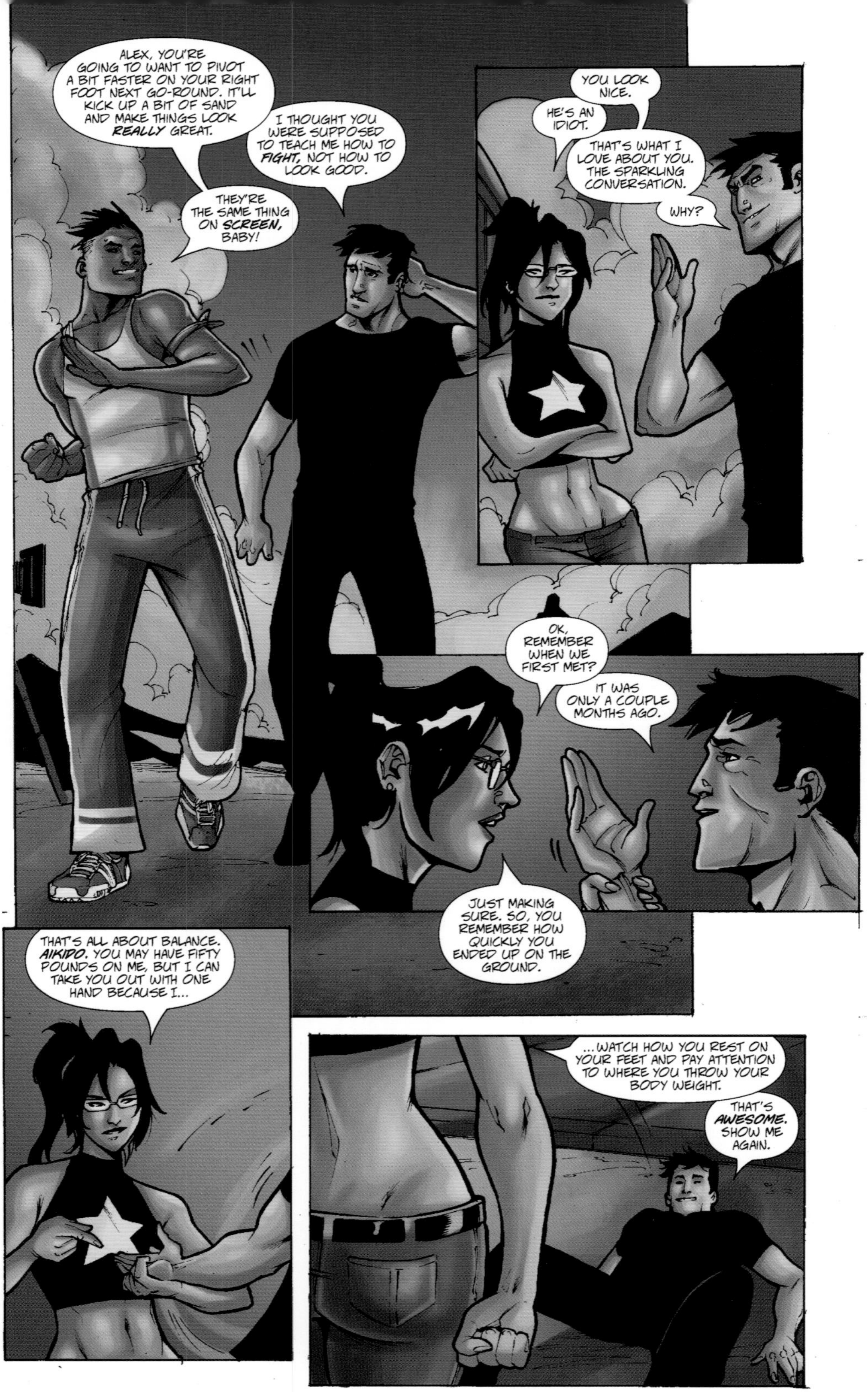
ALEX, YOU'RE GOING TO WANT TO PIVOT A BIT FASTER ON YOUR RIGHT FOOT NEXT GO-ROUND. IT'LL KICK UP A BIT OF SAND AND MAKE THINGS LOOK REALLY GREAT.
I THOUGHT YOU WERE SUPPOSED TO TEACH ME HOW TO FIGHT, NOT HOW TO LOOK GOOD.
THEY'RE THE SAME THING ON SCREEN, BABY!
YOU LOOK NICE.
HE'S AN IDIOT.
THAT'S WHAT I LOVE ABOUT YOU. THE SPARKLING CONVERSATION.
WHY?
OK, REMEMBER WHEN WE FIRST MET?
IT WAS ONLY A COUPLE MONTHS AGO.
JUST MAKING SURE. SO, YOU REMEMBER HOW QUICKLY YOU ENDED UP ON THE GROUND.
THAT'S ALL ABOUT BALANCE. AIKIDO. YOU MAY HAVE FIFTY POUNDS ON ME, BUT I CAN TAKE YOU OUT WITH ONE HAND BECAUSE I...
...WATCH HOW YOU REST ON YOUR FEET AND PAY ATTENTION TO WHERE YOU THROW YOUR BODY WEIGHT.
THAT'S AWESOME. SHOW ME AGAIN.

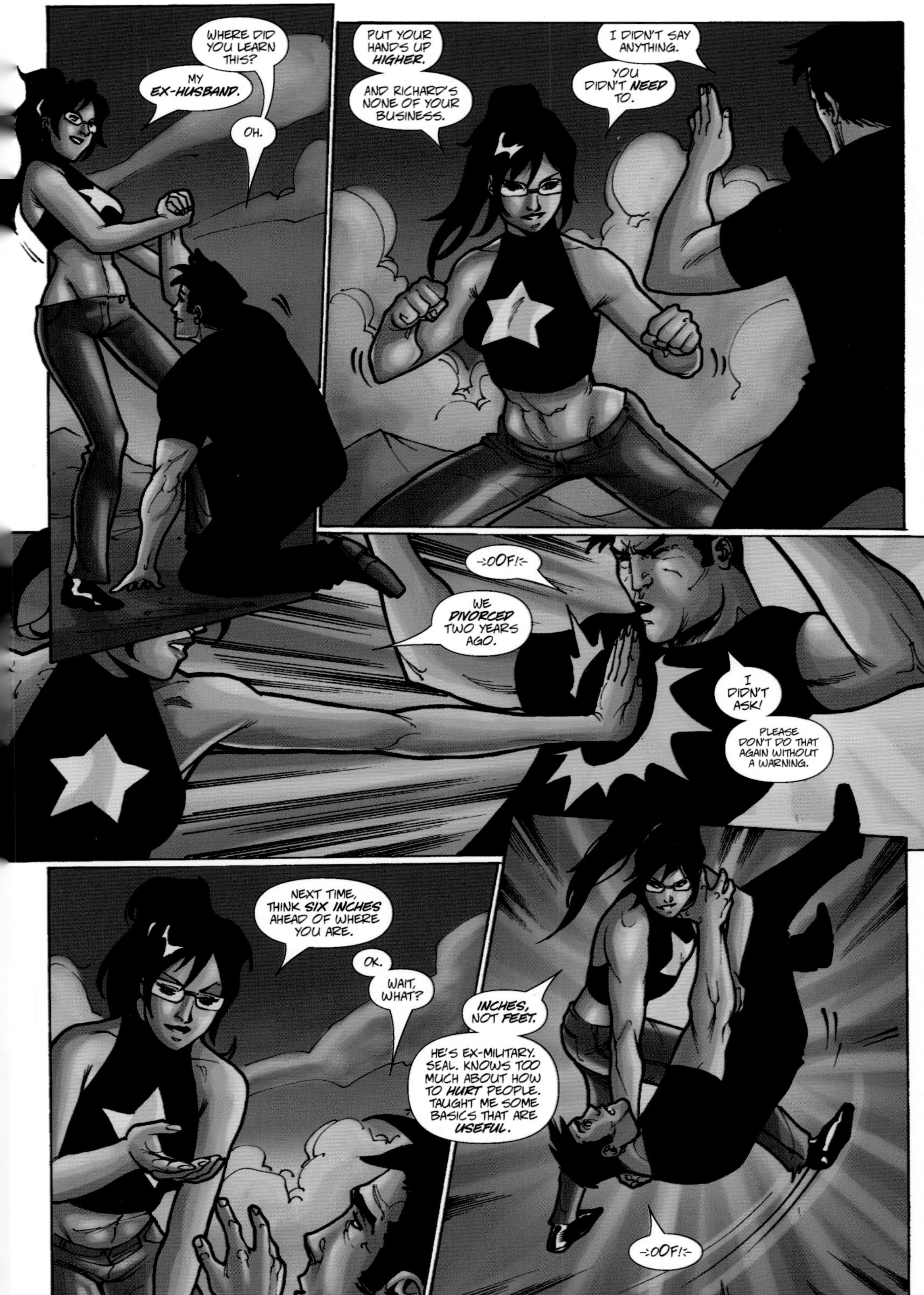
WHERE DID YOU LEARN THIS?
MY EX-HUSBAND.
OH.
PUT YOUR HANDS UP HIGHER.
AND RICHARD'S NONE OF YOUR BUSINESS.
I DIDN'T SAY ANYTHING.
YOU DIDN'T NEED TO.
-:OOF!:-
WE DIVORCED TWO YEARS AGO.
I DIDN'T ASK!
PLEASE DON'T DO THAT AGAIN WITHOUT A WARNING.
NEXT TIME, THINK SIX INCHES AHEAD OF WHERE YOU ARE.
OK.
WAIT, WHAT?
INCHES, NOT FEET.
HE'S EX-MILITARY. SEAL. KNOWS TOO MUCH ABOUT HOW TO HURT PEOPLE. TAUGHT ME SOME BASICS THAT ARE USEFUL.
-:OOF!:-

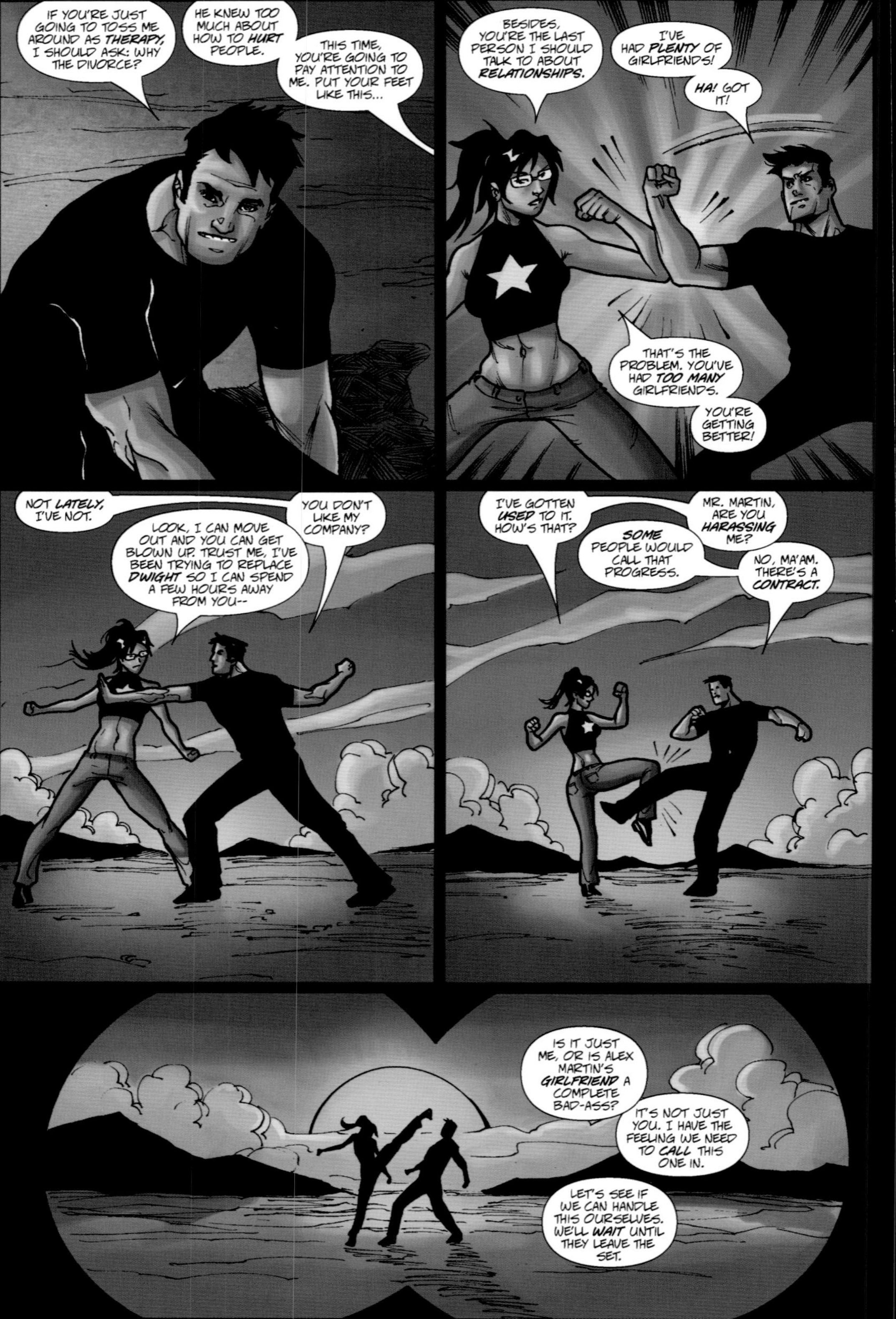
IF YOU'RE JUST GOING TO TOSS ME AROUND AS THERAPY, I SHOULD ASK: WHY THE DIVORCE?
HE KNEW TOO MUCH ABOUT HOW TO HURT PEOPLE.
THIS TIME, YOU'RE GOING TO PAY ATTENTION TO ME. PUT YOUR FEET LIKE THIS...
BESIDES, YOU'RE THE LAST PERSON I SHOULD TALK TO ABOUT RELATIONSHIPS.
I'VE HAD PLENTY OF GIRLFRIENDS!
HA! GOT IT!
THAT'S THE PROBLEM. YOU'VE HAD TOO MANY GIRLFRIENDS.
YOU'RE GETTING BETTER!
NOT LATELY, I'VE NOT.
YOU DON'T LIKE MY COMPANY?
LOOK, I CAN MOVE OUT AND YOU CAN GET BLOWN UP. TRUST ME, I'VE BEEN TRYING TO REPLACE DWIGHT SO I CAN SPEND A FEW HOURS AWAY FROM YOU--
I'VE GOTTEN USED TO IT. HOW'S THAT?
MR. MARTIN, ARE YOU HARASSING ME?
SOME PEOPLE WOULD CALL THAT PROGRESS.
NO, MA'AM. THERE'S A CONTRACT.
IS IT JUST ME, OR IS ALEX MARTIN'S GIRLFRIEND A COMPLETE BAD-ASS?
IT'S NOT JUST YOU. I HAVE THE FEELING WE NEED TO CALL THIS ONE IN.
LET'S SEE IF WE CAN HANDLE THIS OURSELVES. WE'LL WAIT UNTIL THEY LEAVE THE SET.

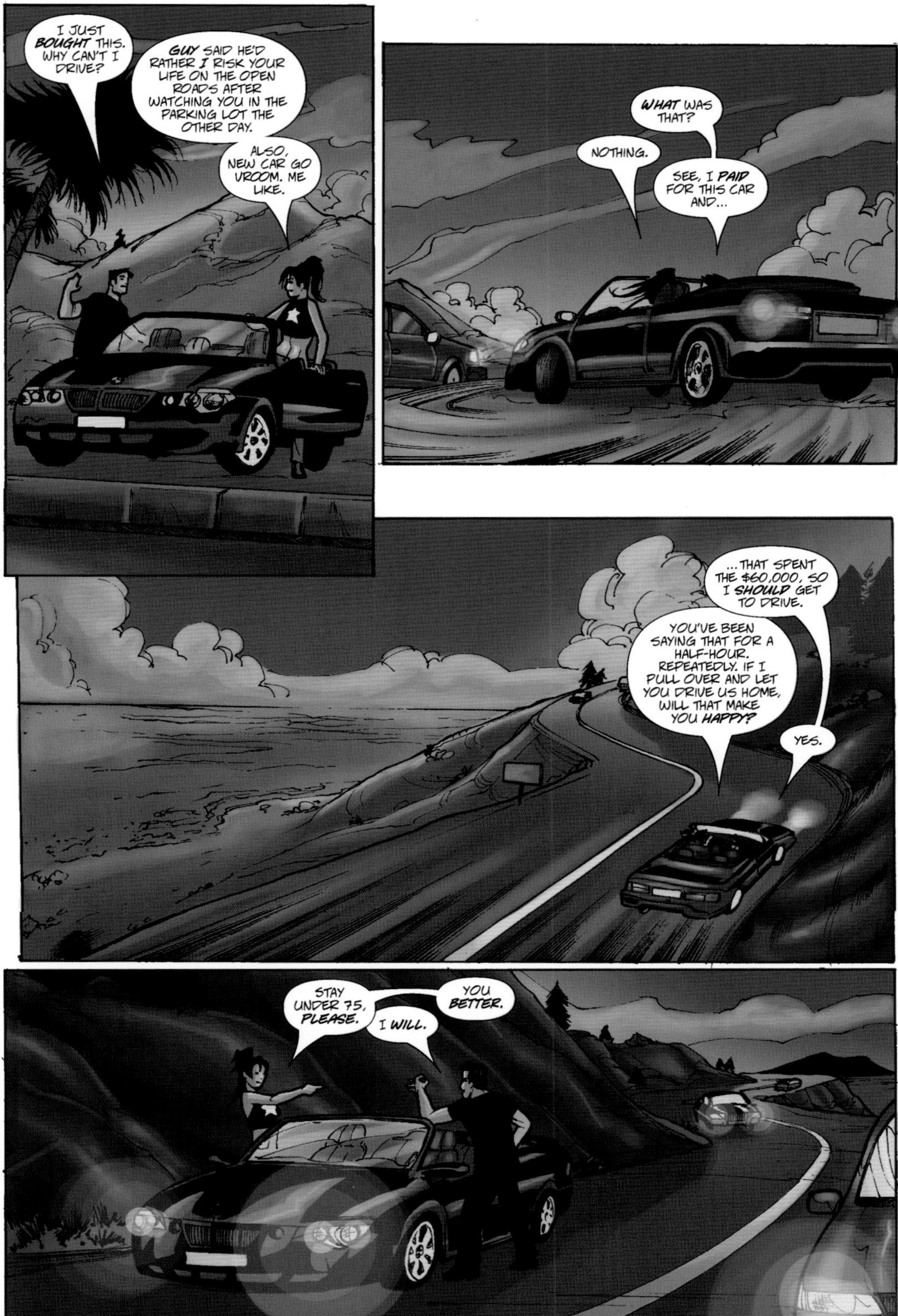
I JUST **BOUGHT** THIS. WHY CAN'T I DRIVE?
GUY SAID HE'D RATHER **I** RISK YOUR LIFE ON THE OPEN ROADS AFTER WATCHING YOU IN THE PARKING LOT THE OTHER DAY.
ALSO, NEW CAR GO VROOM. ME LIKE.
WHAT WAS THAT?
NOTHING.
SEE, I **PAID** FOR THIS CAR AND...
...THAT SPENT THE $60,000, SO I **SHOULD** GET TO DRIVE.
YOU'VE BEEN SAYING THAT FOR A HALF-HOUR. REPEATEDLY. IF I PULL OVER AND LET YOU DRIVE US HOME, WILL THAT MAKE YOU **HAPPY?**
YES.
STAY UNDER 75, **PLEASE.**
I **WILL.**
YOU **BETTER.**

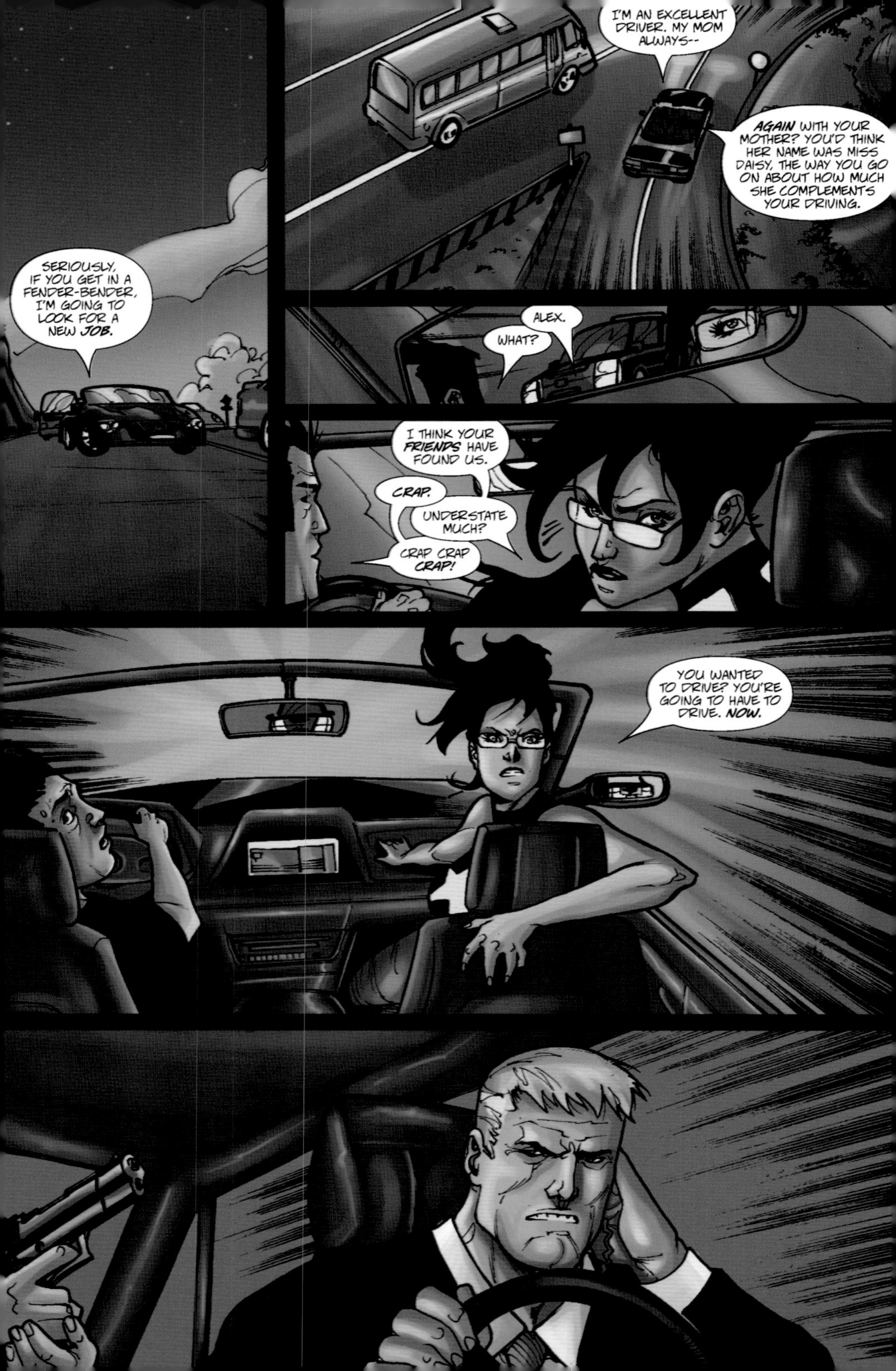

SERIOUSLY, IF YOU GET IN A FENDER-BENDER, I'M GOING TO LOOK FOR A NEW **JOB**.
I'M AN EXCELLENT DRIVER. MY MOM ALWAYS--
AGAIN WITH YOUR MOTHER? YOU'D THINK HER NAME WAS MISS DAISY, THE WAY YOU GO ON ABOUT HOW MUCH SHE COMPLEMENTS YOUR DRIVING.
ALEX.
WHAT?
I THINK YOUR **FRIENDS** HAVE FOUND US.
CRAP.
UNDERSTATE MUCH?
CRAP CRAP **CRAP!**
YOU WANTED TO DRIVE? YOU'RE GOING TO HAVE TO DRIVE. **NOW.**

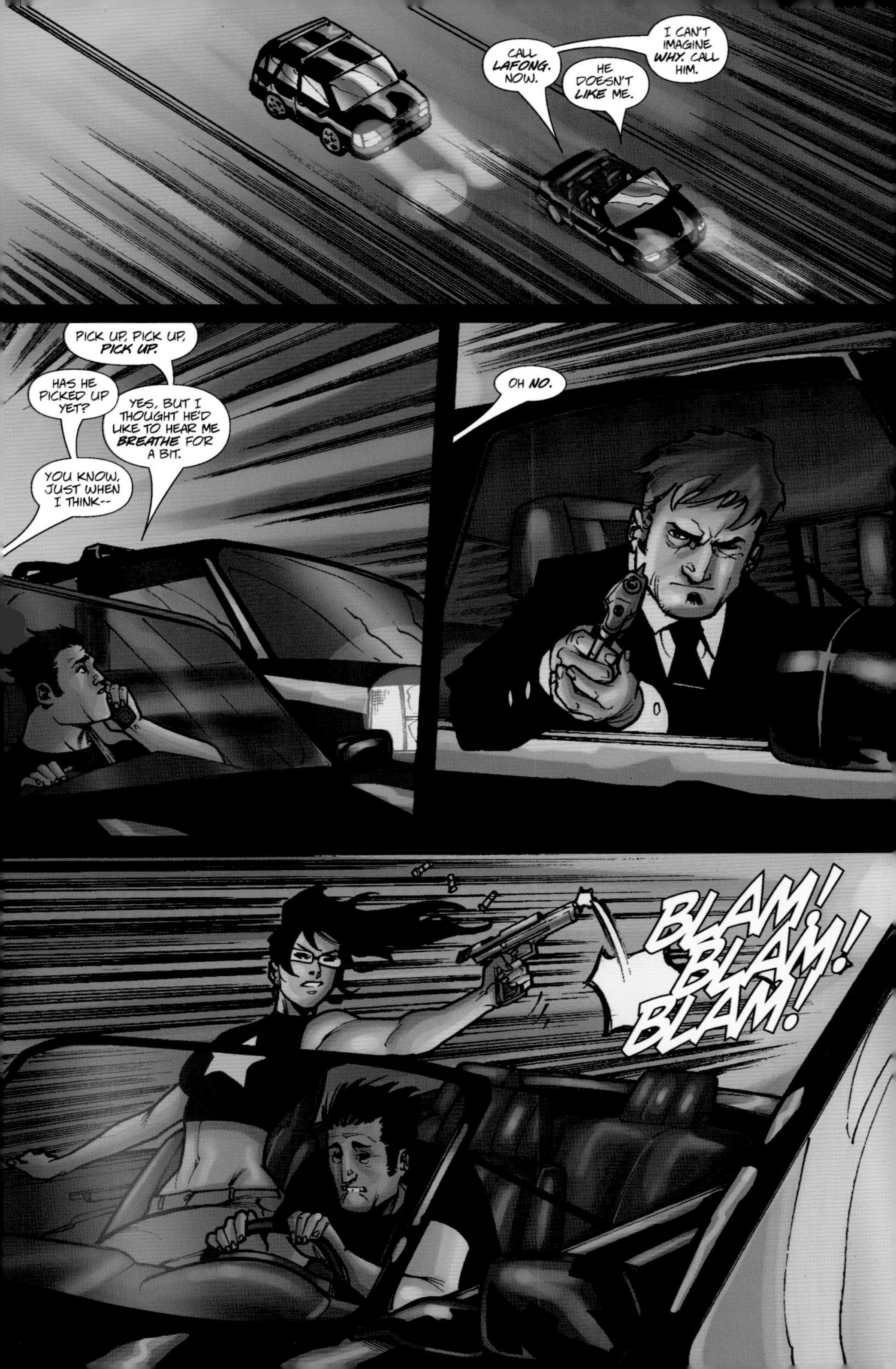
CALL LAFONG. NOW.
HE DOESN'T LIKE ME.
I CAN'T IMAGINE WHY. CALL HIM.
PICK UP, PICK UP, PICK UP.
HAS HE PICKED UP YET?
YES, BUT I THOUGHT HE'D LIKE TO HEAR ME BREATHE FOR A BIT.
YOU KNOW, JUST WHEN I THINK--
OH NO.
BLAM! BLAM! BLAM!

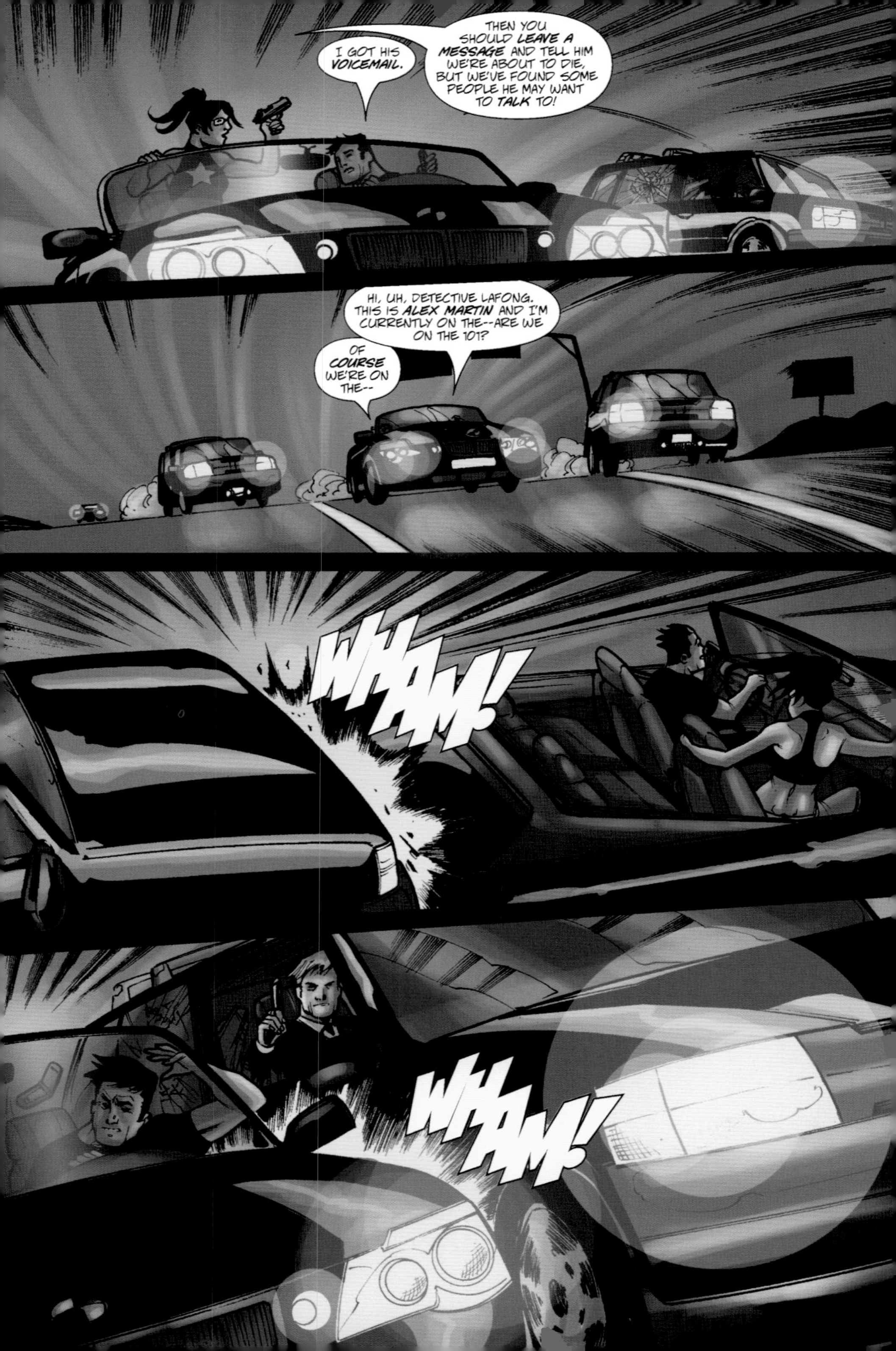
I GOT HIS **VOICEMAIL.**
THEN YOU SHOULD **LEAVE A MESSAGE** AND TELL HIM WE'RE ABOUT TO DIE, BUT WE'VE FOUND SOME PEOPLE HE MAY WANT TO **TALK** TO!
HI, UH, DETECTIVE LAFONG. THIS IS **ALEX MARTIN** AND I'M CURRENTLY ON THE--ARE WE ON THE 101?
OF **COURSE** WE'RE ON THE--
WHAM!
WHAM!

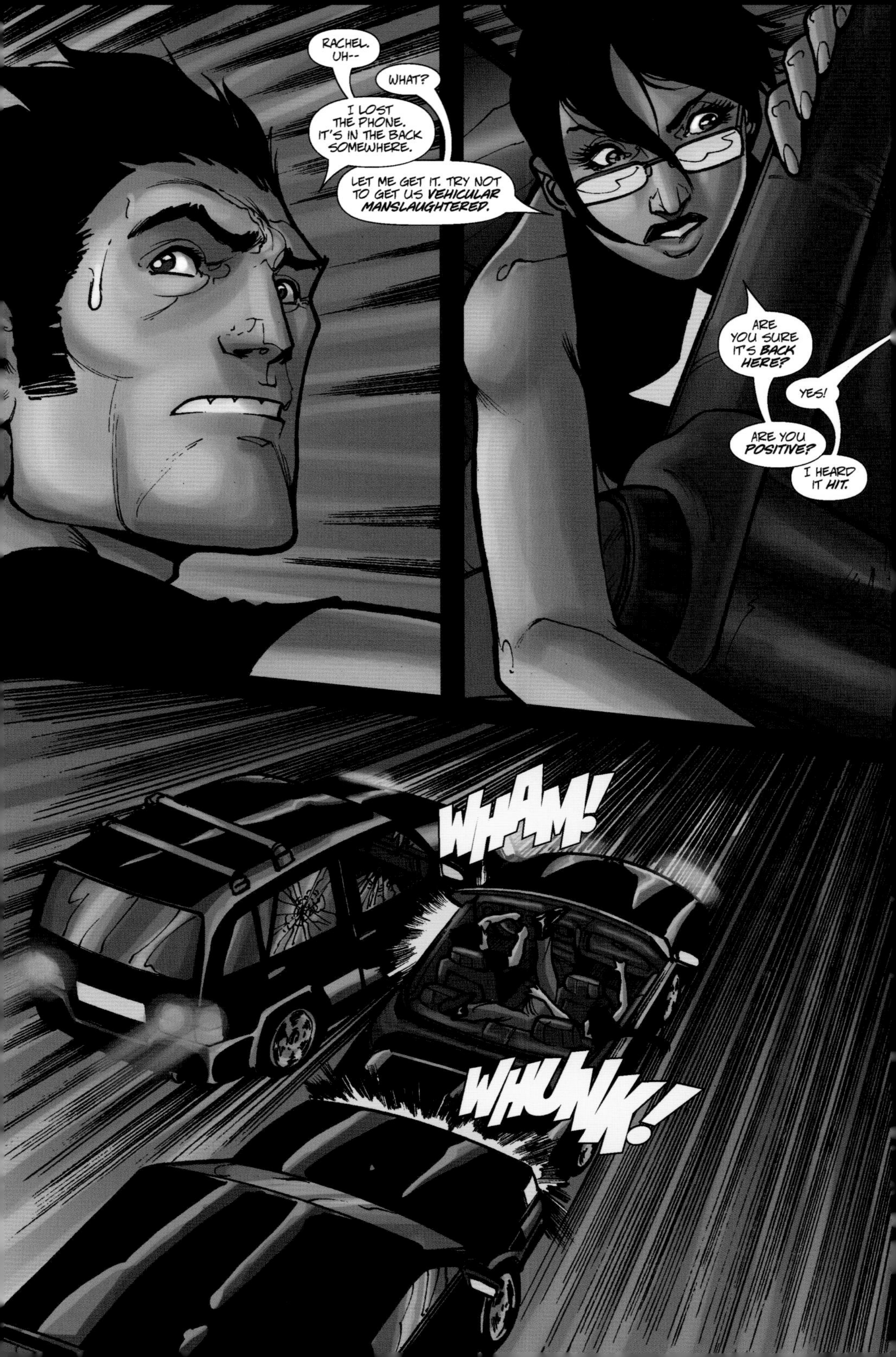
RACHEL. UH--
WHAT?
I LOST THE PHONE. IT'S IN THE BACK SOMEWHERE.
LET ME GET IT. TRY NOT TO GET US VEHICULAR MANSLAUGHTERED.
ARE YOU SURE IT'S BACK HERE?
YES!
ARE YOU POSITIVE?
I HEARD IT HIT.
WHAM!
WHUNK!

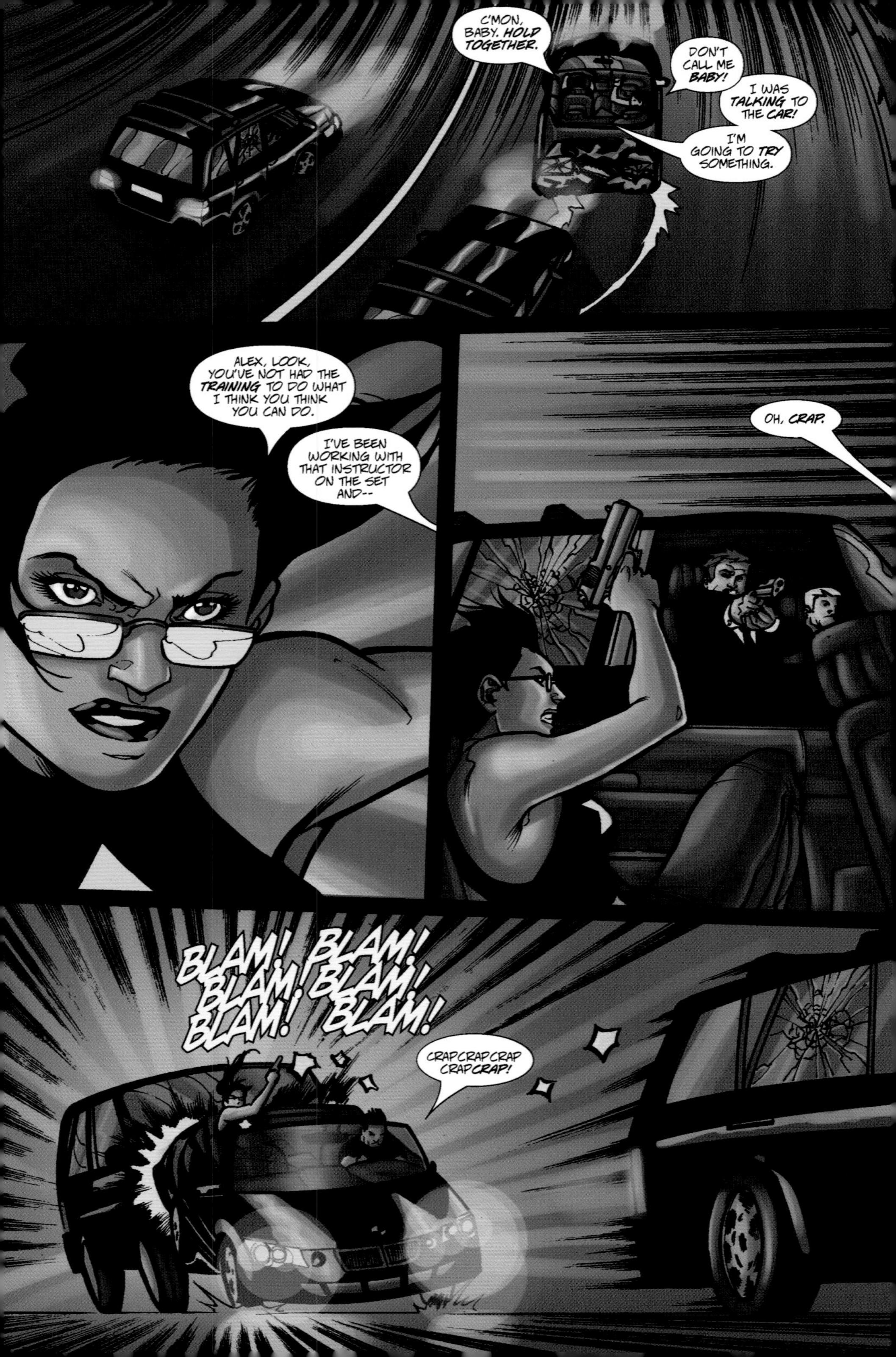
C'MON, BABY. HOLD TOGETHER.
DON'T CALL ME BABY!
I WAS TALKING TO THE CAR!
I'M GOING TO TRY SOMETHING.
ALEX, LOOK, YOU'VE NOT HAD THE TRAINING TO DO WHAT I THINK YOU THINK YOU CAN DO.
I'VE BEEN WORKING WITH THAT INSTRUCTOR ON THE SET AND--
OH, CRAP.
BLAM! BLAM! BLAM! BLAM! BLAM! BLAM!
CRAPCRAPCRAP CRAPCRAP!

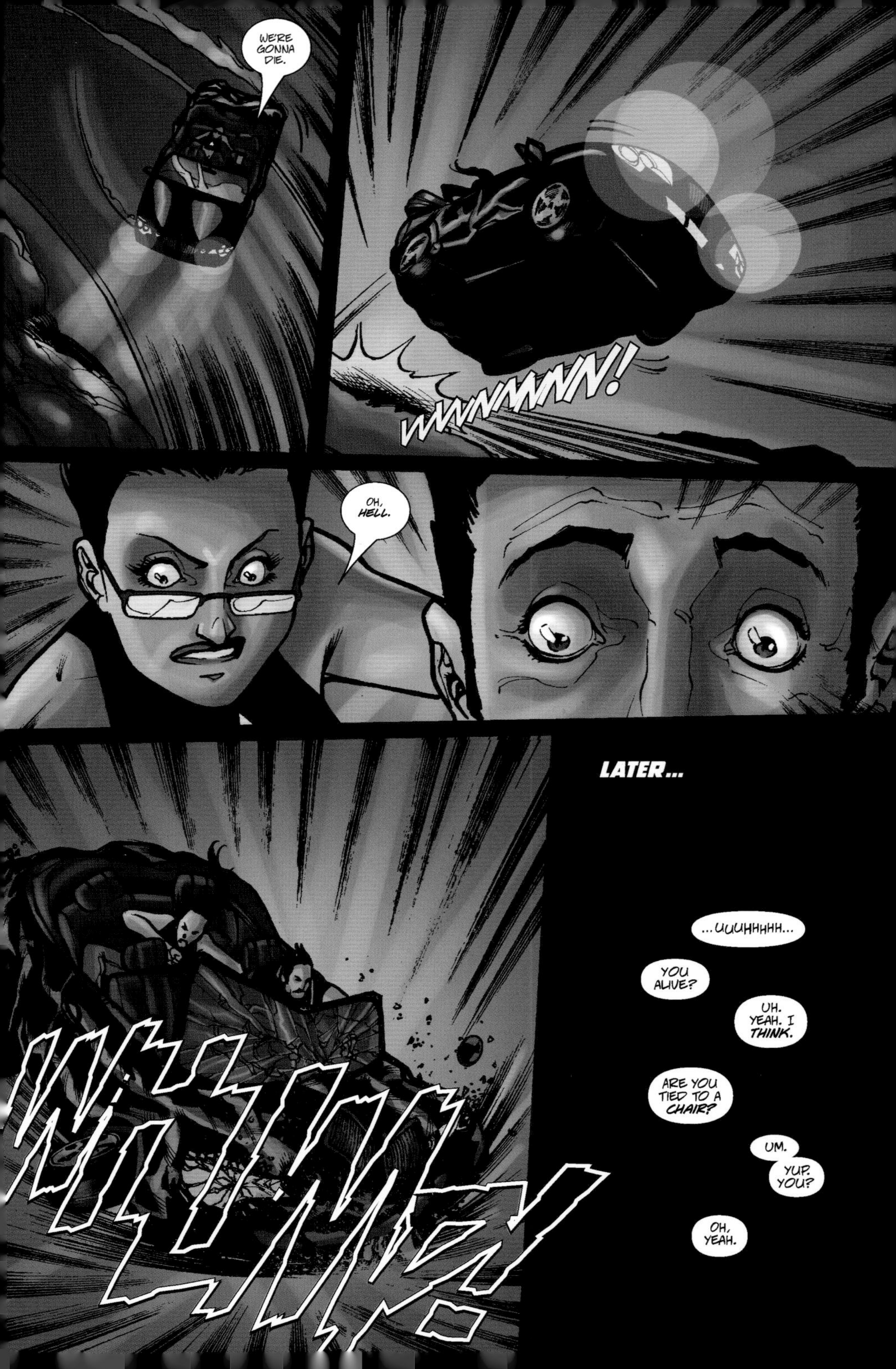
WE'RE GONNA DIE.
OH, HELL.
LATER...
...UUUHHHHH...
YOU ALIVE?
UH. YEAH. I THINK.
ARE YOU TIED TO A CHAIR?
UM.
YUP. YOU?
OH, YEAH.

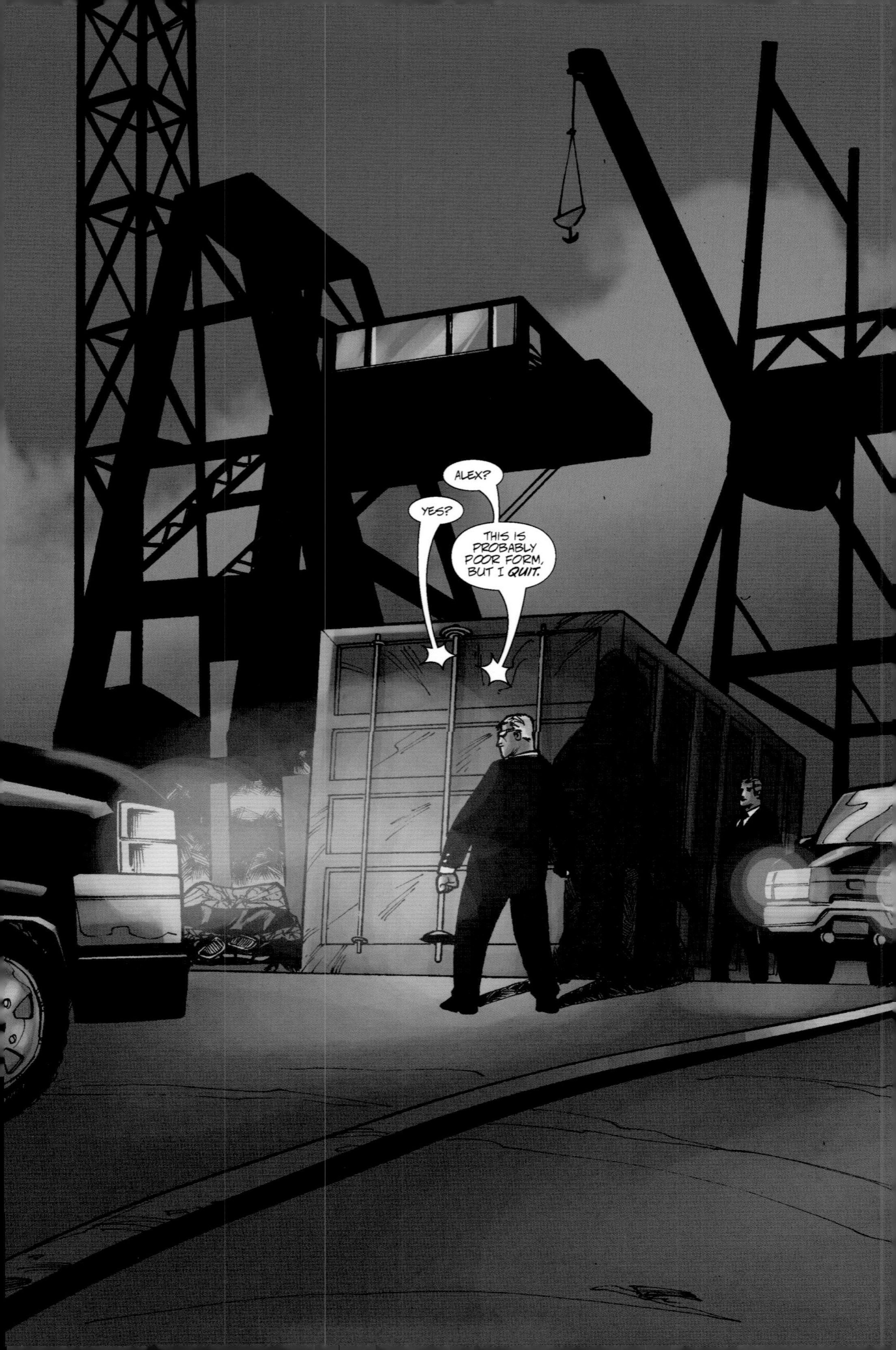
ALEX?
YES?
THIS IS PROBABLY POOR FORM, BUT I QUIT.

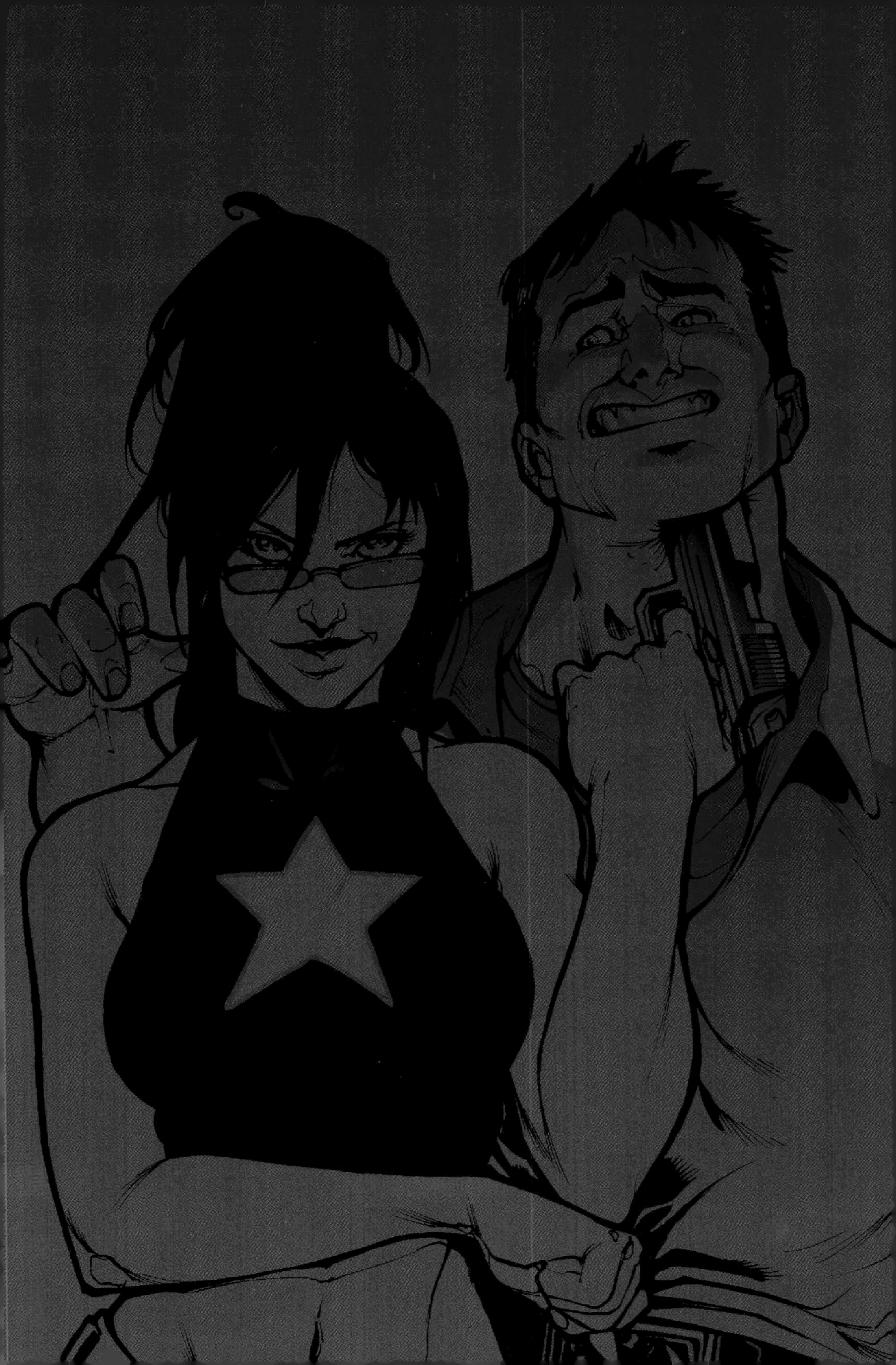

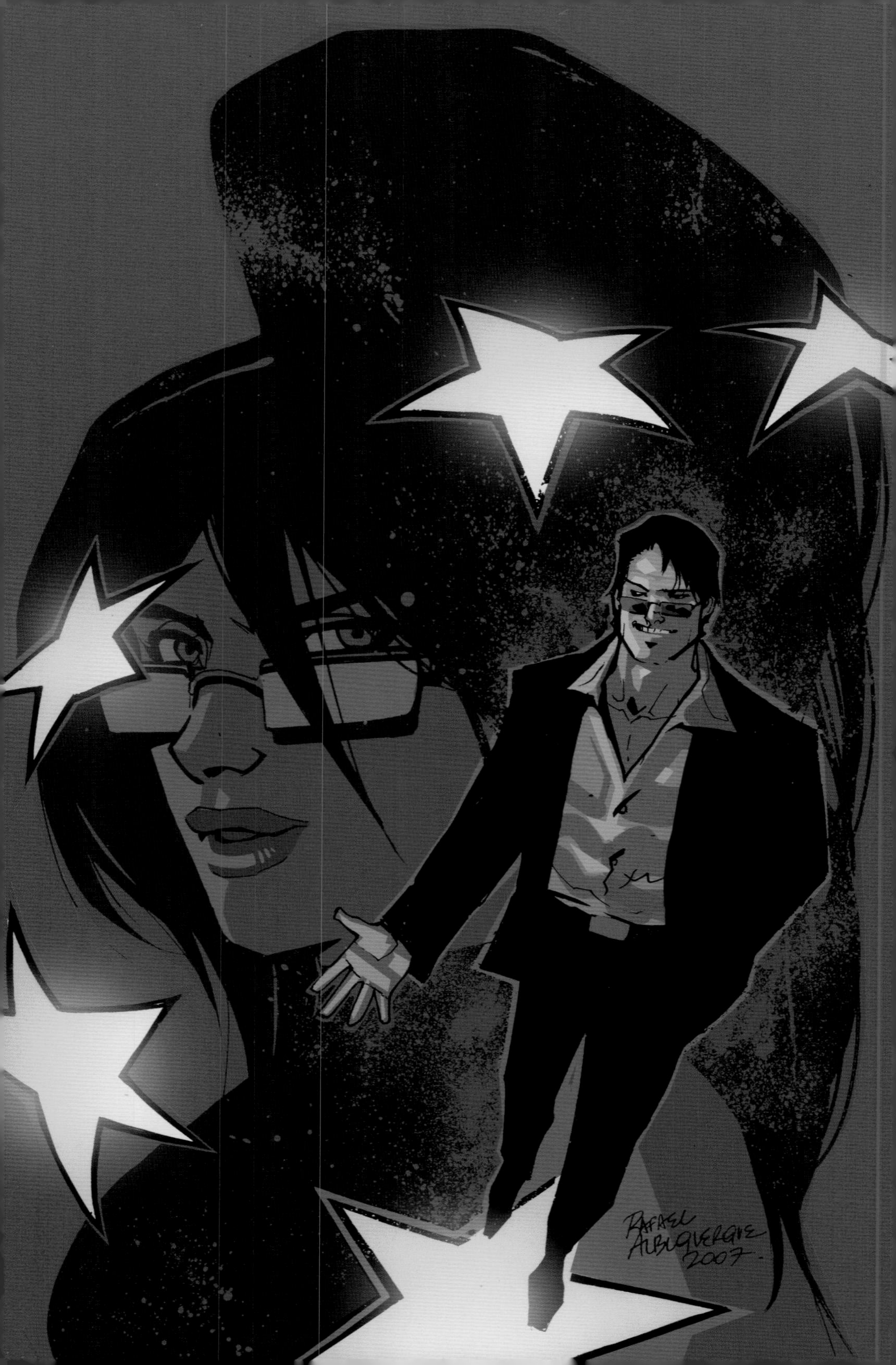
RAFAEL ALBUQUERQUE 2007.

YOU KNOW, RIGHT NOW, I THINK I HATE YOU.

NO, ALEX. I *KNOW* I HATE YOU.

I FIND THAT REMARKABLY UNFAIR. IT'S NOT MY FAULT WE WERE IN YET *ANOTHER* CAR CHASE.

WE LIVE IN LOS ANGELES. YOU'RE OBVIOUSLY WANTED BY WHOEVER CAPTURED US. YOU WEREN'T THINKING TO YOURSELF "HEY, MAYBE I'LL LET THE BODYGUARD HIRED BY THE STUDIO WHO MANAGED TO SAVE MY ASS ONCE ALREADY ON THE ROAD *KEEP ON DRIVING* UNTIL WE SORT OUT ALL THAT CRAP?"

HEY, LOOK, I *BOUGHT* THE CAR.

AND THE STUDIO BOUGHT *YOU* AND THEN HIRED ME, WHICH MEANS THAT YOU ARE *MY* RESPONSIBILITY.

FINE.

FINE.

CHAPTER FOUR
L.A. CONFIDENTIAL

ANDREW COSBY & KEVIN CHURCH
WRITERS

MATEUS SANTOLOUCO
PENCILS

ANDRE COELHO
INKER

ED DUKESHIRE
LETTERER

PABLO QUILIGOTTI & BRIAN MIROGLIO
COLORISTS

RAFAEL ALBUQUERQUE
COVER ARTIST

MARSHALL DILLON
MANAGING EDITOR

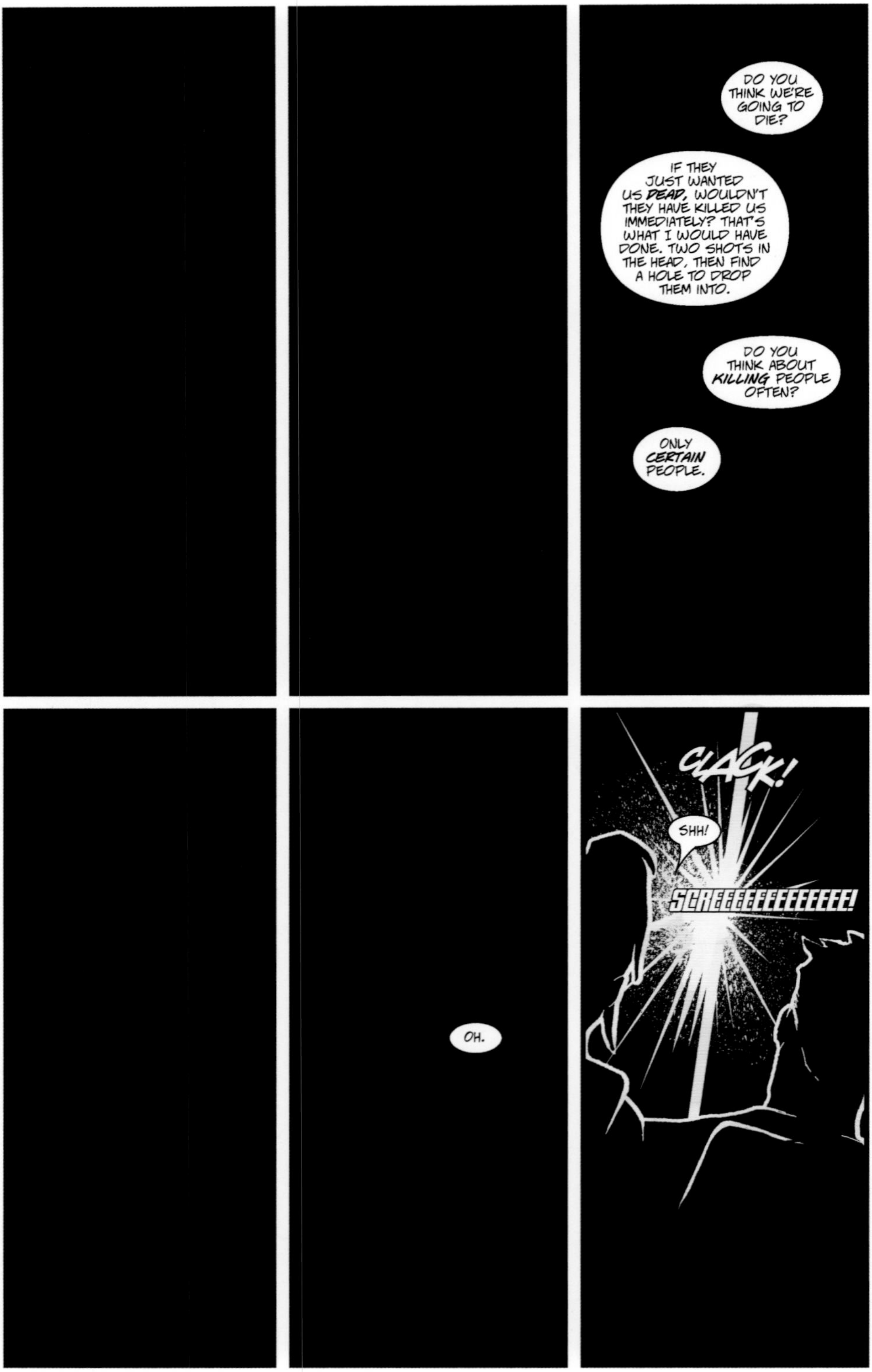
DO YOU THINK WE'RE GOING TO DIE?
IF THEY JUST WANTED US DEAD, WOULDN'T THEY HAVE KILLED US IMMEDIATELY? THAT'S WHAT I WOULD HAVE DONE. TWO SHOTS IN THE HEAD, THEN FIND A HOLE TO DROP THEM INTO.
DO YOU THINK ABOUT KILLING PEOPLE OFTEN?
ONLY CERTAIN PEOPLE.
OH.
CLACK!
SHH!
SCREEEEEEEEEEEEE!

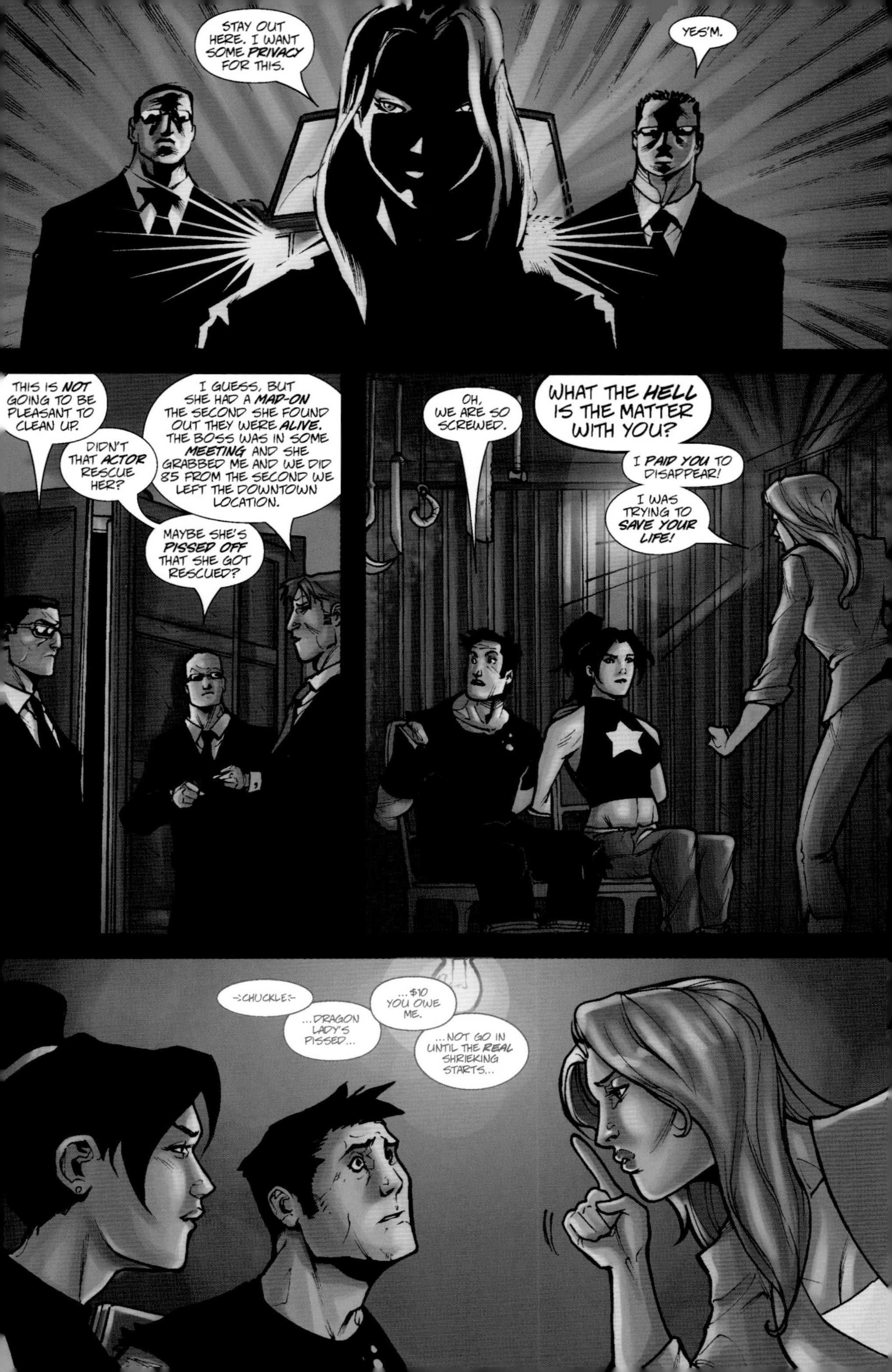

STAY OUT HERE. I WANT SOME PRIVACY FOR THIS.
YES'M.
THIS IS NOT GOING TO BE PLEASANT TO CLEAN UP.
DIDN'T THAT ACTOR RESCUE HER?
I GUESS, BUT SHE HAD A MAD-ON THE SECOND SHE FOUND OUT THEY WERE ALIVE. THE BOSS WAS IN SOME MEETING AND SHE GRABBED ME AND WE DID 85 FROM THE SECOND WE LEFT THE DOWNTOWN LOCATION.
MAYBE SHE'S PISSED OFF THAT SHE GOT RESCUED?
OH, WE ARE SO SCREWED.
WHAT THE HELL IS THE MATTER WITH YOU?
I PAID YOU TO DISAPPEAR!
I WAS TRYING TO SAVE YOUR LIFE!
-:CHUCKLE:-
...DRAGON LADY'S PISSED...
...$10 YOU OWE ME.
...NOT GO IN UNTIL THE REAL SHRIEKING STARTS...

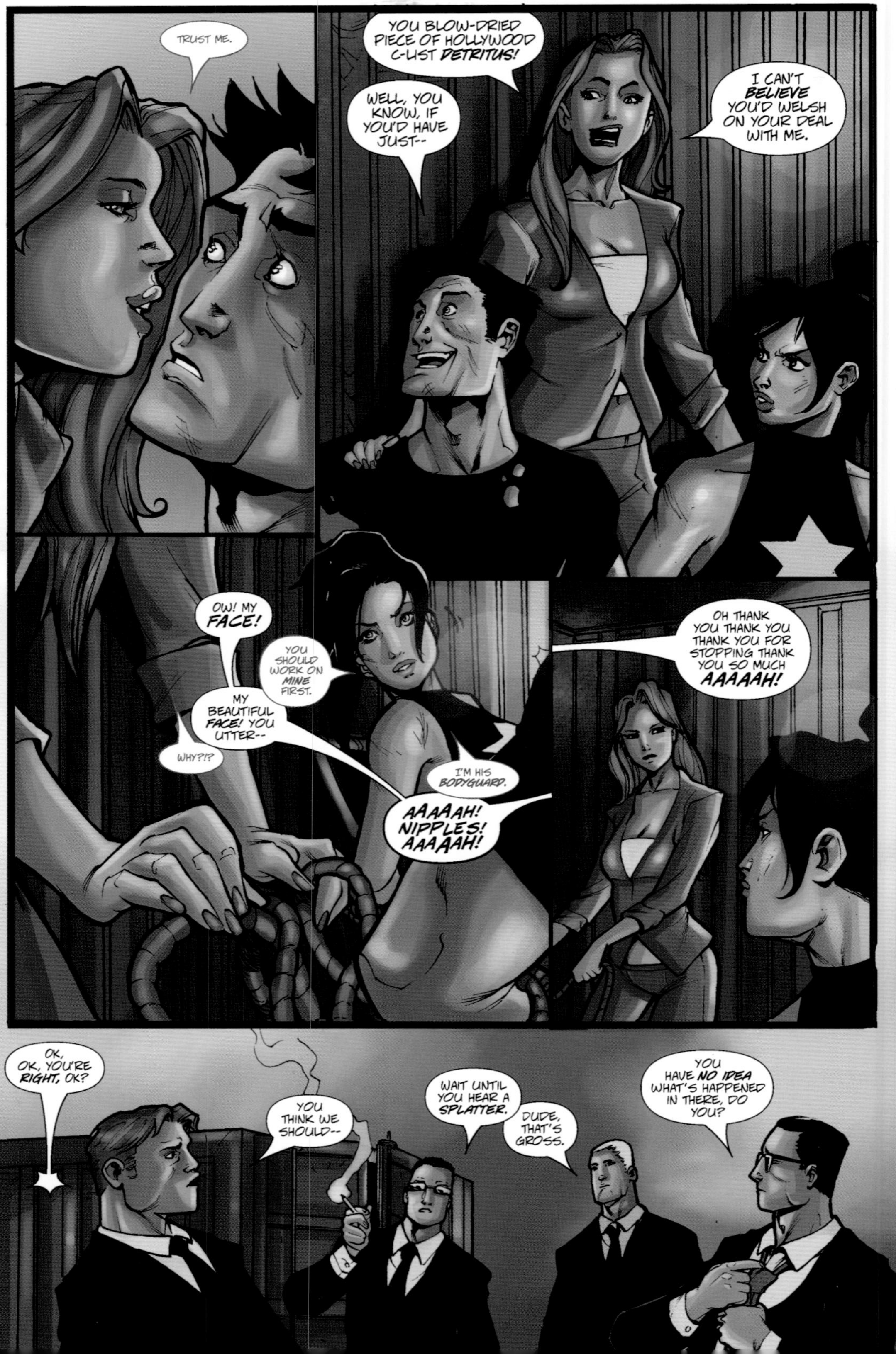
TRUST ME.
YOU BLOW-DRIED PIECE OF HOLLYWOOD C-LIST DETRITUS!
WELL, YOU KNOW, IF YOU'D HAVE JUST--
I CAN'T BELIEVE YOU'D WELSH ON YOUR DEAL WITH ME.
OW! MY FACE!
YOU SHOULD WORK ON MINE FIRST.
MY BEAUTIFUL FACE! YOU UTTER--
WHY?!?
I'M HIS BODYGUARD.
AAAAAH! NIPPLES! AAAAAH!
OH THANK YOU THANK YOU THANK YOU FOR STOPPING THANK YOU SO MUCH AAAAAH!
OK, OK, YOU'RE RIGHT, OK?
YOU THINK WE SHOULD--
WAIT UNTIL YOU HEAR A SPLATTER.
DUDE, THAT'S GROSS.
YOU HAVE NO IDEA WHAT'S HAPPENED IN THERE, DO YOU?

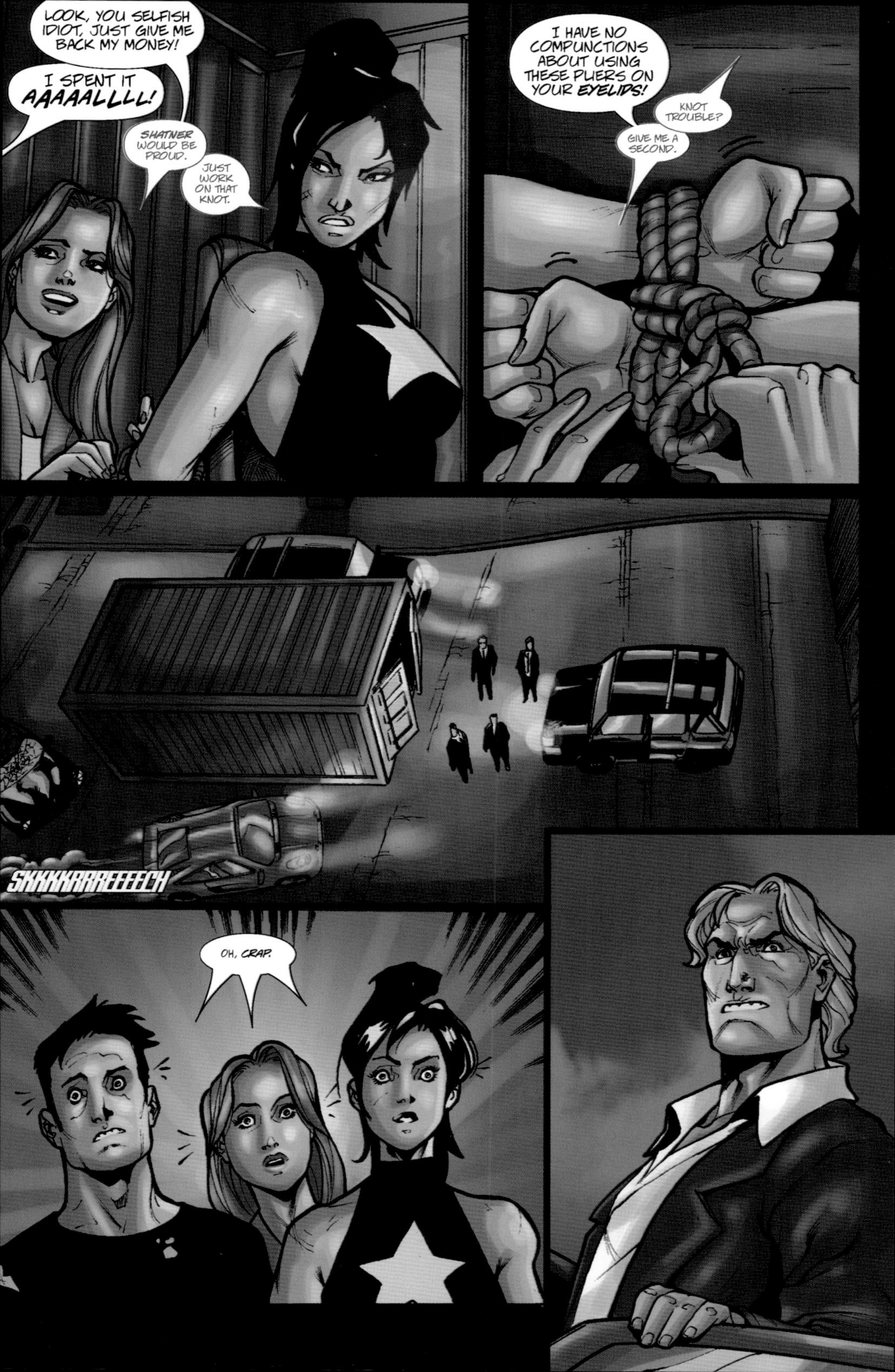
LOOK, YOU SELFISH IDIOT, JUST GIVE ME BACK MY MONEY!
I SPENT IT AAAAALLLL!
SHATNER WOULD BE PROUD.
JUST WORK ON THAT KNOT.
I HAVE NO COMPUNCTIONS ABOUT USING THESE PLIERS ON YOUR EYELIDS!
KNOT TROUBLE?
GIVE ME A SECOND.
SKKKKRRREEEEECH
OH, CRAP.

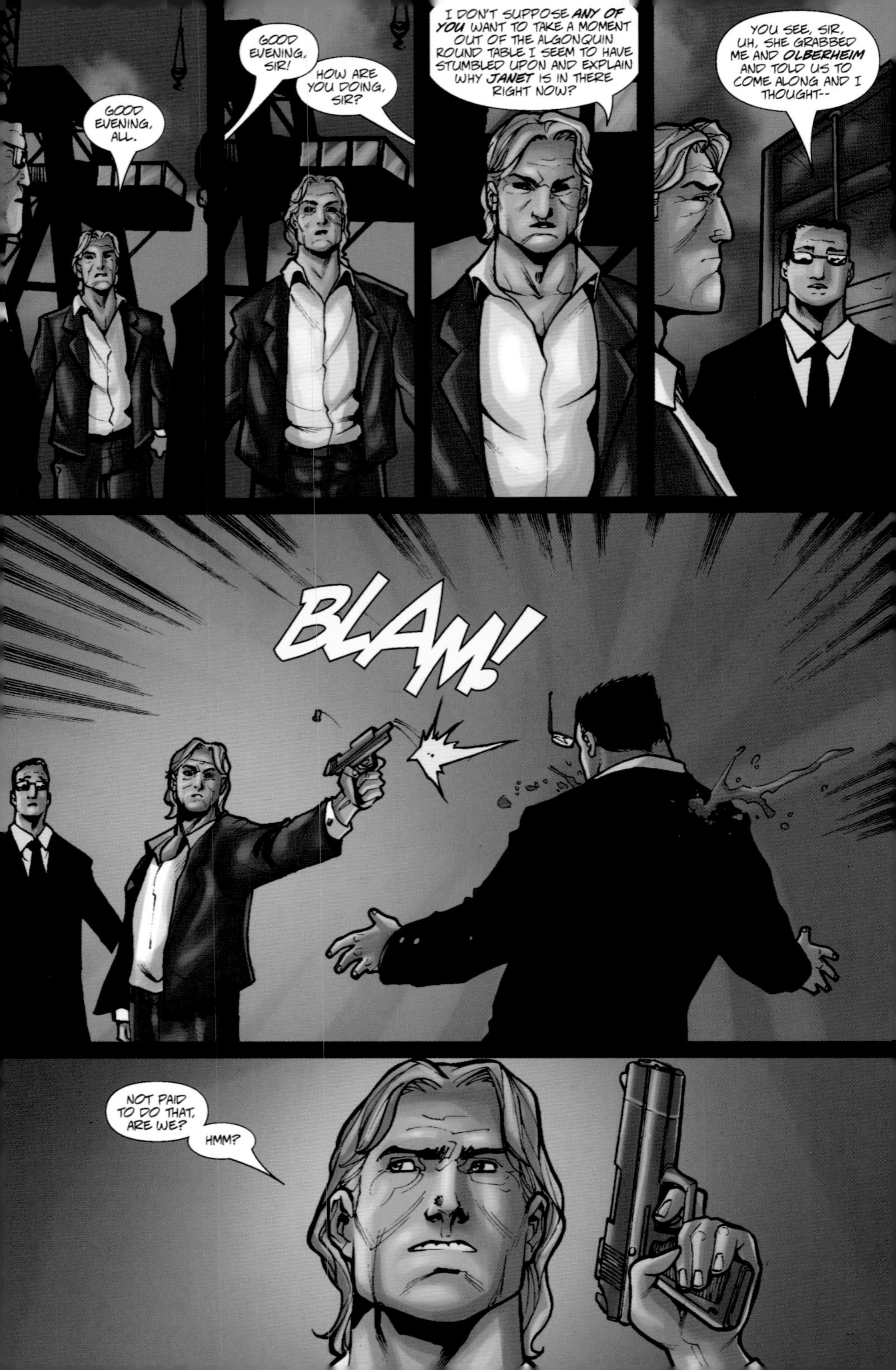
GOOD EVENING, ALL.
GOOD EVENING, SIR!
HOW ARE YOU DOING, SIR?
I DON'T SUPPOSE ANY OF YOU WANT TO TAKE A MOMENT OUT OF THE ALGONQUIN ROUND TABLE I SEEM TO HAVE STUMBLED UPON AND EXPLAIN WHY JANET IS IN THERE RIGHT NOW?
YOU SEE, SIR, UH, SHE GRABBED ME AND OLBERHEIM AND TOLD US TO COME ALONG AND I THOUGHT--
BLAM!
NOT PAID TO DO THAT, ARE WE?
HMM?

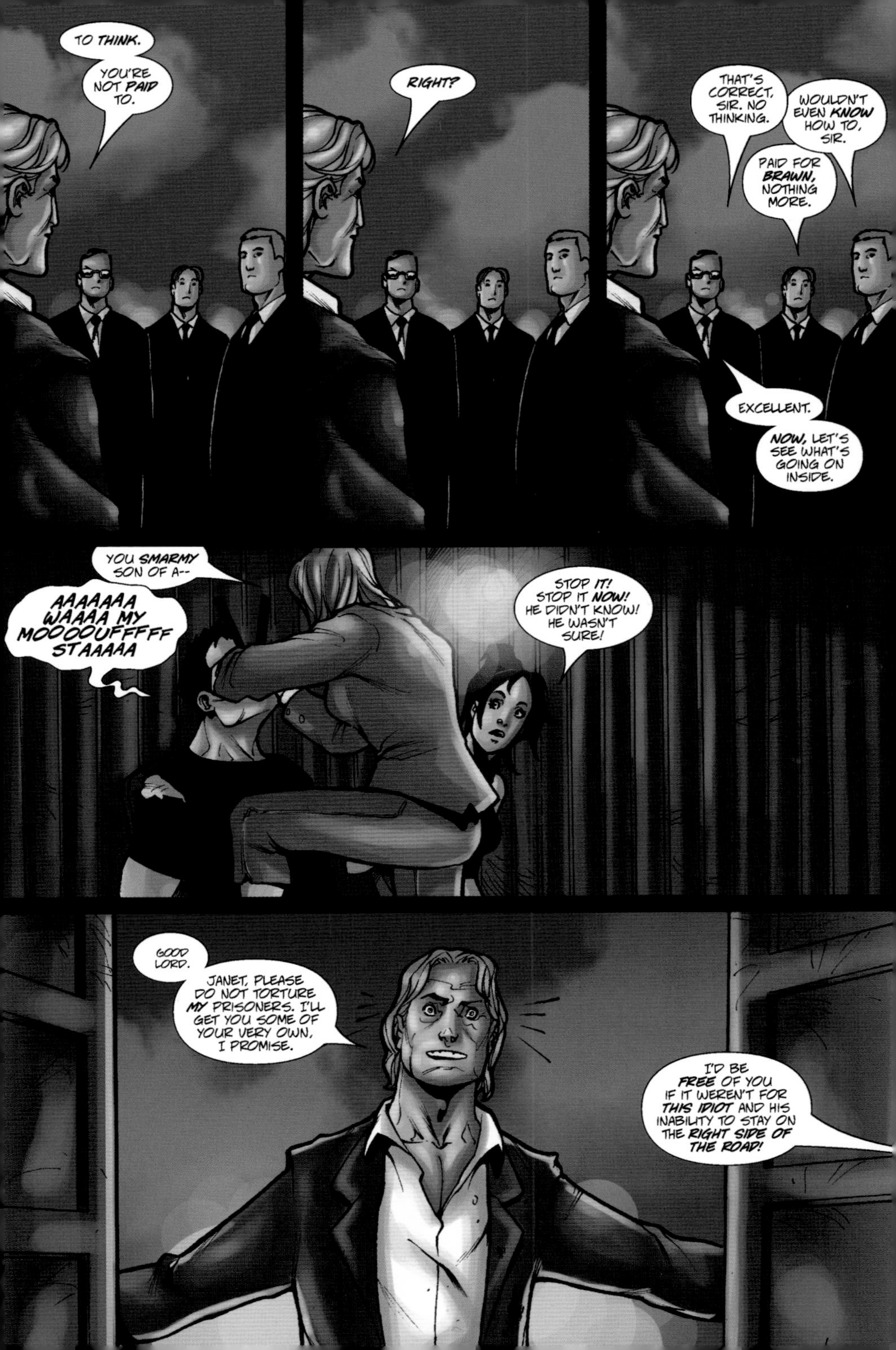
TO THINK.
YOU'RE NOT PAID TO.
RIGHT?
THAT'S CORRECT, SIR. NO THINKING.
WOULDN'T EVEN KNOW HOW TO, SIR.
PAID FOR BRAWN, NOTHING MORE.
EXCELLENT.
NOW, LET'S SEE WHAT'S GOING ON INSIDE.
YOU SMARMY SON OF A--
AAAAAAA WAAAA MY MOOOOUFFFFFF STAAAAA
STOP IT! STOP IT NOW! HE DIDN'T KNOW! HE WASN'T SURE!
GOOD LORD.
JANET, PLEASE DO NOT TORTURE MY PRISONERS. I'LL GET YOU SOME OF YOUR VERY OWN, I PROMISE.
I'D BE FREE OF YOU IF IT WEREN'T FOR THIS IDIOT AND HIS INABILITY TO STAY ON THE RIGHT SIDE OF THE ROAD!

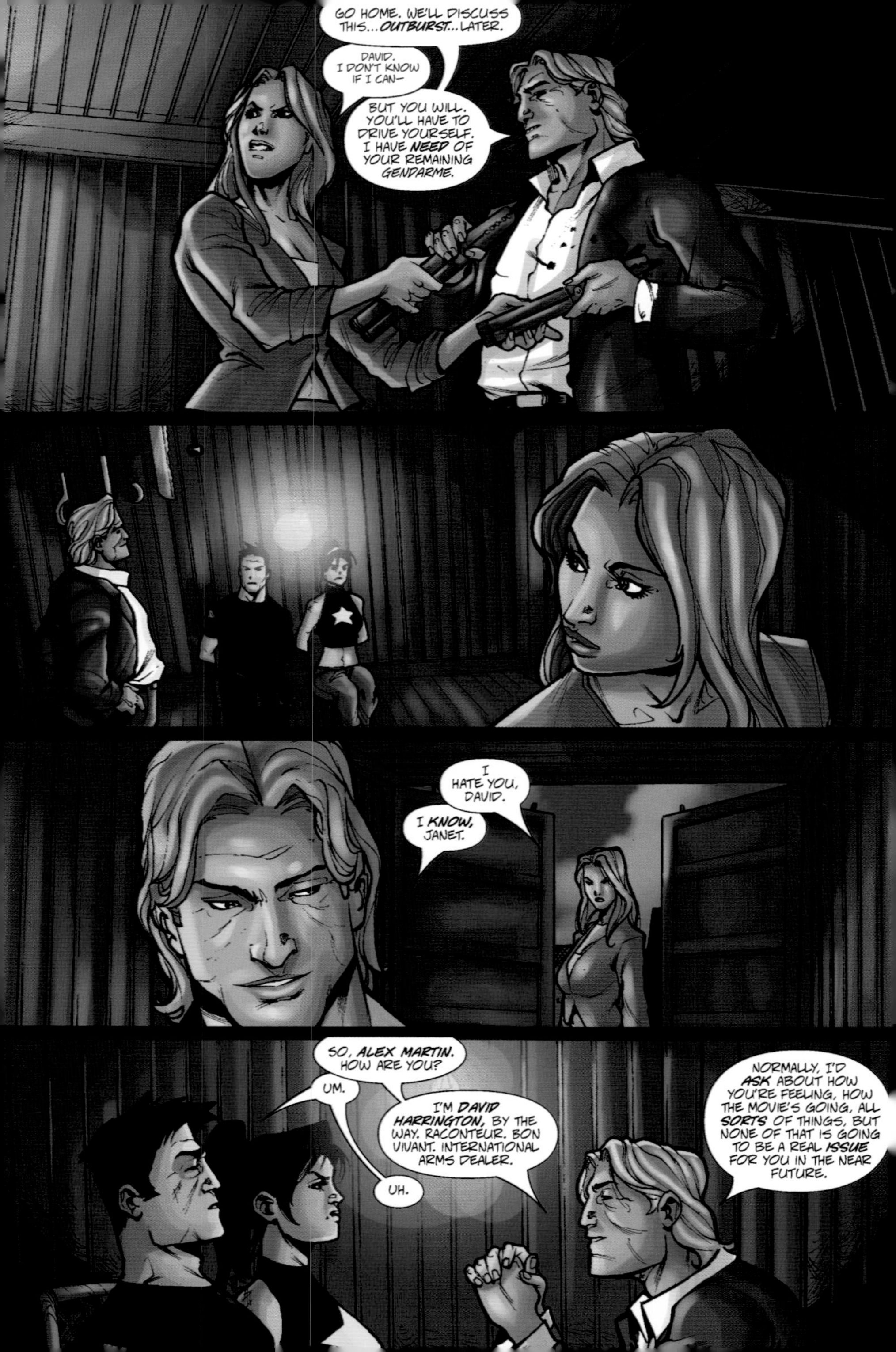
GO HOME. WE'LL DISCUSS THIS... OUTBURST... LATER.
DAVID. I DON'T KNOW IF I CAN—
BUT YOU WILL. YOU'LL HAVE TO DRIVE YOURSELF. I HAVE NEED OF YOUR REMAINING GENDARME.
I HATE YOU, DAVID.
I KNOW, JANET.
SO, ALEX MARTIN. HOW ARE YOU?
UM.
I'M DAVID HARRINGTON, BY THE WAY. RACONTEUR. BON VIVANT. INTERNATIONAL ARMS DEALER.
UH.
NORMALLY, I'D ASK ABOUT HOW YOU'RE FEELING, HOW THE MOVIE'S GOING, ALL SORTS OF THINGS, BUT NONE OF THAT IS GOING TO BE A REAL ISSUE FOR YOU IN THE NEAR FUTURE.

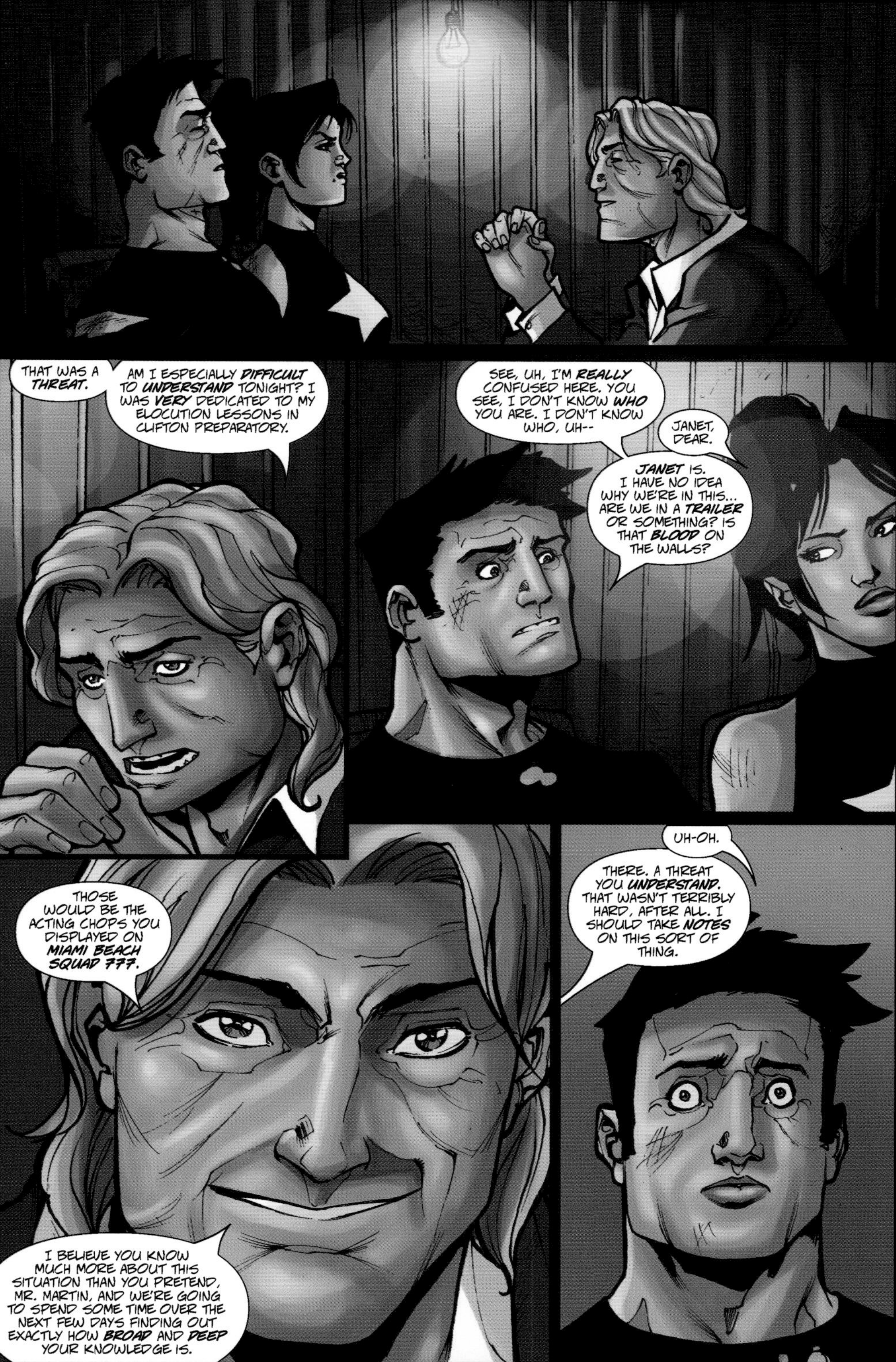
THAT WAS A THREAT.
AM I ESPECIALLY DIFFICULT TO UNDERSTAND TONIGHT? I WAS VERY DEDICATED TO MY ELOCUTION LESSONS IN CLIFTON PREPARATORY.
SEE, UH, I'M REALLY CONFUSED HERE. YOU SEE, I DON'T KNOW WHO YOU ARE. I DON'T KNOW WHO, UH--
JANET, DEAR.
JANET IS. I HAVE NO IDEA WHY WE'RE IN THIS... ARE WE IN A TRAILER OR SOMETHING? IS THAT BLOOD ON THE WALLS?
THOSE WOULD BE THE ACTING CHOPS YOU DISPLAYED ON MIAMI BEACH SQUAD 777.
I BELIEVE YOU KNOW MUCH MORE ABOUT THIS SITUATION THAN YOU PRETEND, MR. MARTIN, AND WE'RE GOING TO SPEND SOME TIME OVER THE NEXT FEW DAYS FINDING OUT EXACTLY HOW BROAD AND DEEP YOUR KNOWLEDGE IS.
UH-OH.
THERE. A THREAT YOU UNDERSTAND. THAT WASN'T TERRIBLY HARD, AFTER ALL. I SHOULD TAKE NOTES ON THIS SORT OF THING.

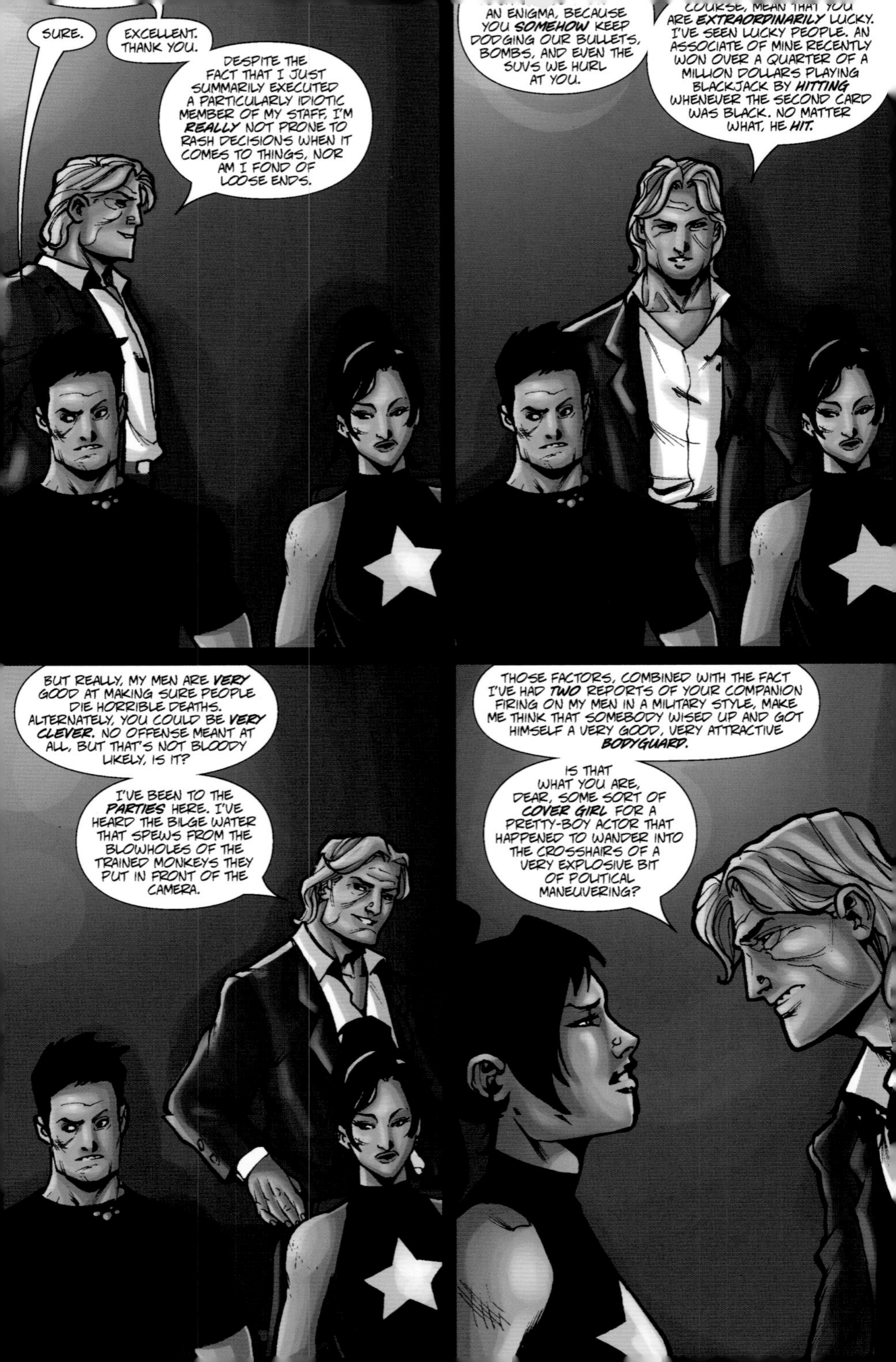

SURE.
EXCELLENT. THANK YOU.
DESPITE THE FACT THAT I JUST SUMMARILY EXECUTED A PARTICULARLY IDIOTIC MEMBER OF MY STAFF, I'M ***REALLY*** NOT PRONE TO RASH DECISIONS WHEN IT COMES TO THINGS, NOR AM I FOND OF LOOSE ENDS.
AN ENIGMA, BECAUSE YOU ***SOMEHOW*** KEEP DODGING OUR BULLETS, BOMBS, AND EVEN THE SUVS WE HURL AT YOU.
COURSE, MEAN THAT YOU ARE ***EXTRAORDINARILY*** LUCKY. I'VE SEEN LUCKY PEOPLE. AN ASSOCIATE OF MINE RECENTLY WON OVER A QUARTER OF A MILLION DOLLARS PLAYING BLACKJACK BY ***HITTING*** WHENEVER THE SECOND CARD WAS BLACK. NO MATTER WHAT, HE ***HIT.***
BUT REALLY, MY MEN ARE ***VERY*** GOOD AT MAKING SURE PEOPLE DIE HORRIBLE DEATHS. ALTERNATELY, YOU COULD BE ***VERY CLEVER.*** NO OFFENSE MEANT AT ALL, BUT THAT'S NOT BLOODY LIKELY, IS IT?
I'VE BEEN TO THE ***PARTIES*** HERE. I'VE HEARD THE BILGE WATER THAT SPEWS FROM THE BLOWHOLES OF THE TRAINED MONKEYS THEY PUT IN FRONT OF THE CAMERA.
THOSE FACTORS, COMBINED WITH THE FACT I'VE HAD ***TWO*** REPORTS OF YOUR COMPANION FIRING ON MY MEN IN A MILITARY STYLE, MAKE ME THINK THAT SOMEBODY WISED UP AND GOT HIMSELF A VERY GOOD, VERY ATTRACTIVE ***BODYGUARD.***
IS THAT WHAT YOU ARE, DEAR, SOME SORT OF ***COVER GIRL*** FOR A PRETTY-BOY ACTOR THAT HAPPENED TO WANDER INTO THE CROSSHAIRS OF A VERY EXPLOSIVE BIT OF POLITICAL MANEUVERING?

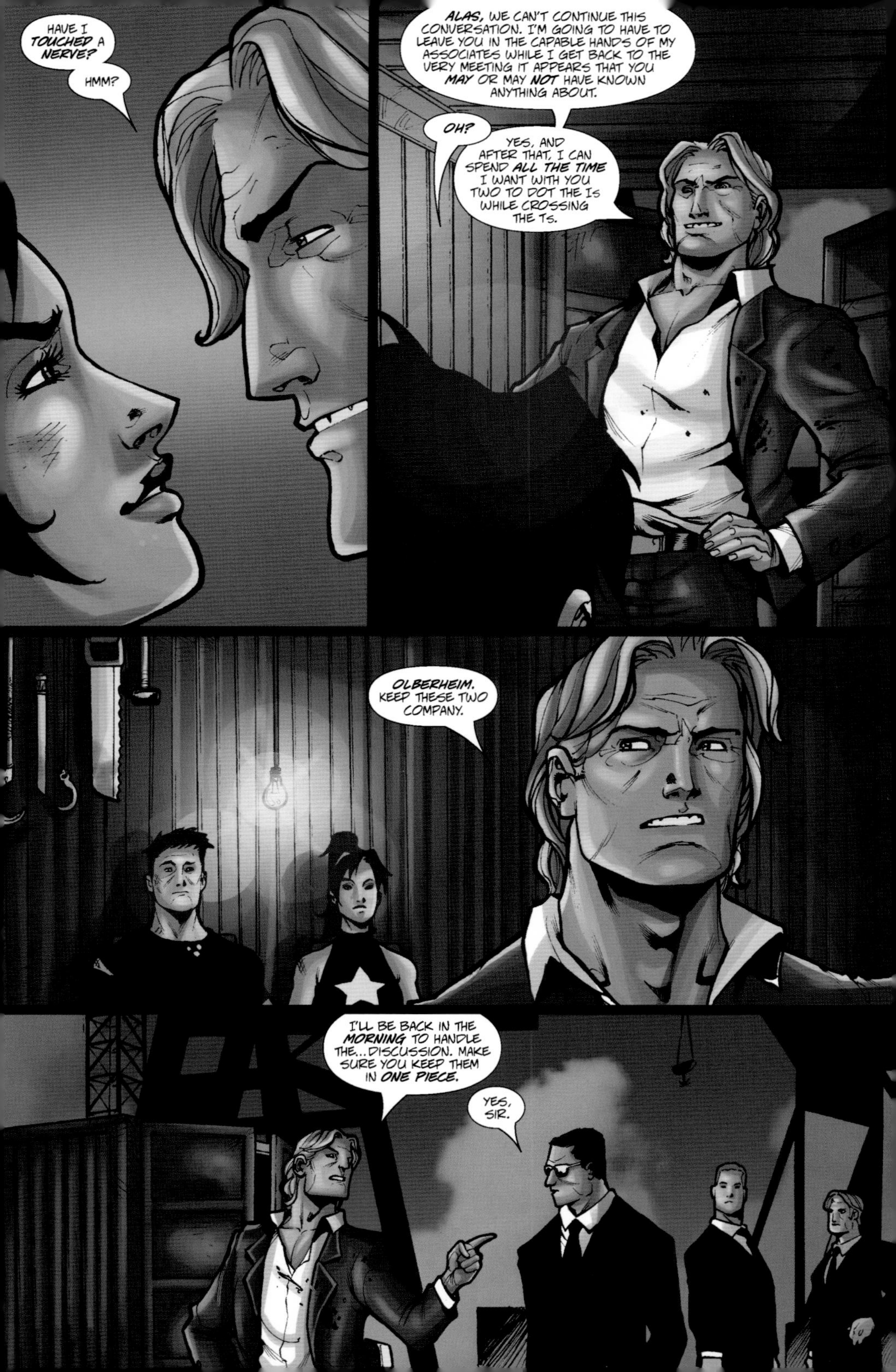
HAVE I TOUCHED A NERVE?
HMM?
ALAS, WE CAN'T CONTINUE THIS CONVERSATION. I'M GOING TO HAVE TO LEAVE YOU IN THE CAPABLE HANDS OF MY ASSOCIATES WHILE I GET BACK TO THE VERY MEETING IT APPEARS THAT YOU MAY OR MAY NOT HAVE KNOWN ANYTHING ABOUT.
OH?
YES, AND AFTER THAT, I CAN SPEND ALL THE TIME I WANT WITH YOU TWO TO DOT THE Is WHILE CROSSING THE Ts.
OLBERHEIM. KEEP THESE TWO COMPANY.
I'LL BE BACK IN THE MORNING TO HANDLE THE...DISCUSSION. MAKE SURE YOU KEEP THEM IN ONE PIECE.
YES, SIR.

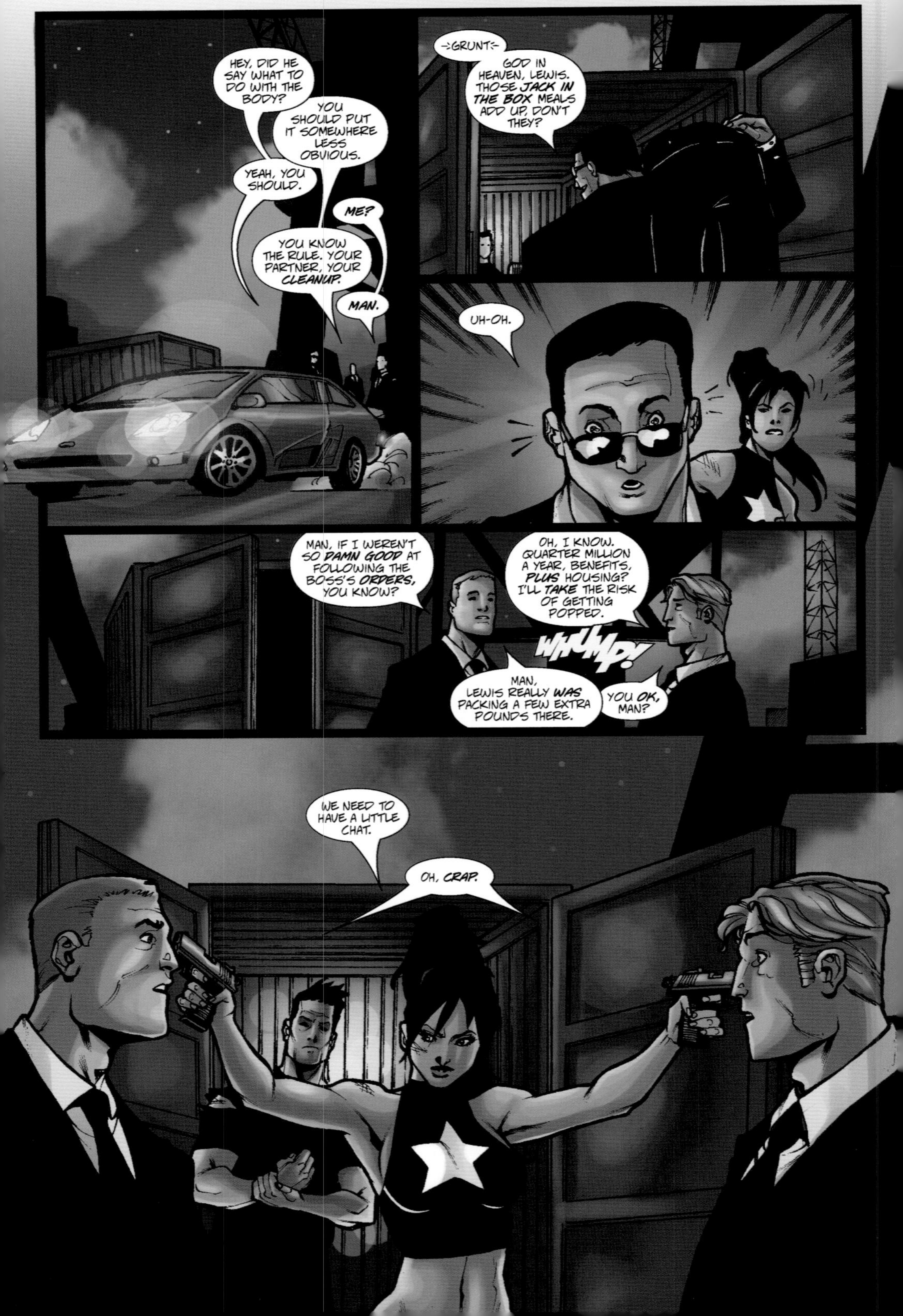
HEY, DID HE SAY WHAT TO DO WITH THE BODY?
YOU SHOULD PUT IT SOMEWHERE LESS OBVIOUS.
YEAH, YOU SHOULD.
ME?
YOU KNOW THE RULE. YOUR PARTNER, YOUR CLEANUP.
MAN.
-GRUNT-
GOD IN HEAVEN, LEWIS. THOSE JACK IN THE BOX MEALS ADD UP, DON'T THEY?
UH-OH.
MAN, IF I WEREN'T SO DAMN GOOD AT FOLLOWING THE BOSS'S ORDERS, YOU KNOW?
OH, I KNOW. QUARTER MILLION A YEAR, BENEFITS, PLUS HOUSING? I'LL TAKE THE RISK OF GETTING POPPED.
WHUMP!
MAN, LEWIS REALLY WAS PACKING A FEW EXTRA POUNDS THERE.
YOU OK, MAN?
WE NEED TO HAVE A LITTLE CHAT.
OH, CRAP.

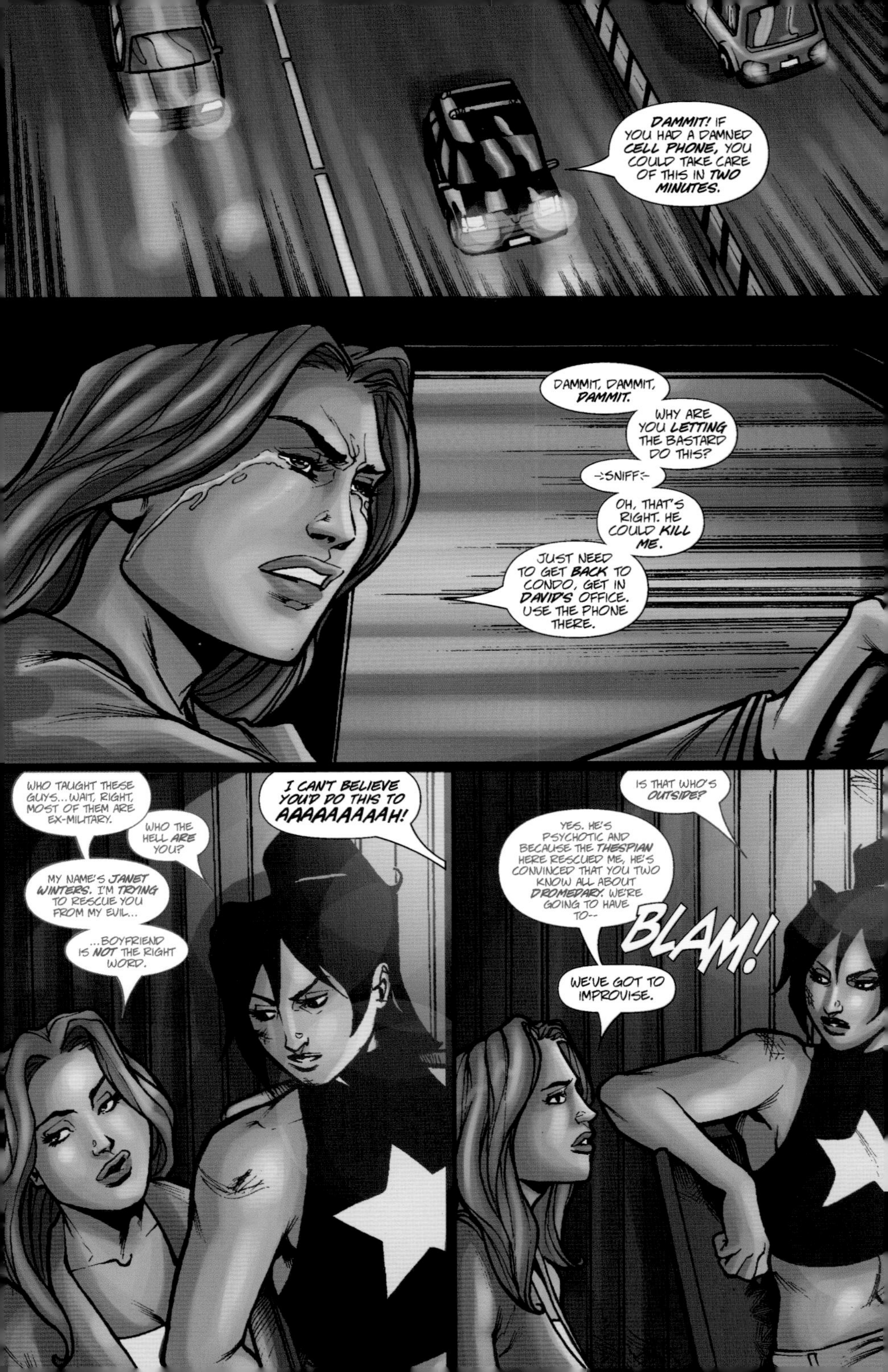
DAMMIT! IF YOU HAD A DAMNED CELL PHONE, YOU COULD TAKE CARE OF THIS IN TWO MINUTES.
DAMMIT, DAMMIT, DAMMIT.
WHY ARE YOU LETTING THE BASTARD DO THIS?
-SNIFF-
OH, THAT'S RIGHT. HE COULD KILL ME.
JUST NEED TO GET BACK TO CONDO, GET IN DAVID'S OFFICE. USE THE PHONE THERE.
WHO TAUGHT THESE GUYS...WAIT, RIGHT, MOST OF THEM ARE EX-MILITARY.
I CAN'T BELIEVE YOU'D DO THIS TO AAAAAAAAAH!
WHO THE HELL ARE YOU?
MY NAME'S JANET WINTERS. I'M TRYING TO RESCUE YOU FROM MY EVIL...
...BOYFRIEND IS NOT THE RIGHT WORD.
IS THAT WHO'S OUTSIDE?
YES. HE'S PSYCHOTIC AND BECAUSE THE THESPIAN HERE RESCUED ME, HE'S CONVINCED THAT YOU TWO KNOW ALL ABOUT DROMEDARY. WE'RE GOING TO HAVE TO--
BLAM!
WE'VE GOT TO IMPROVISE.

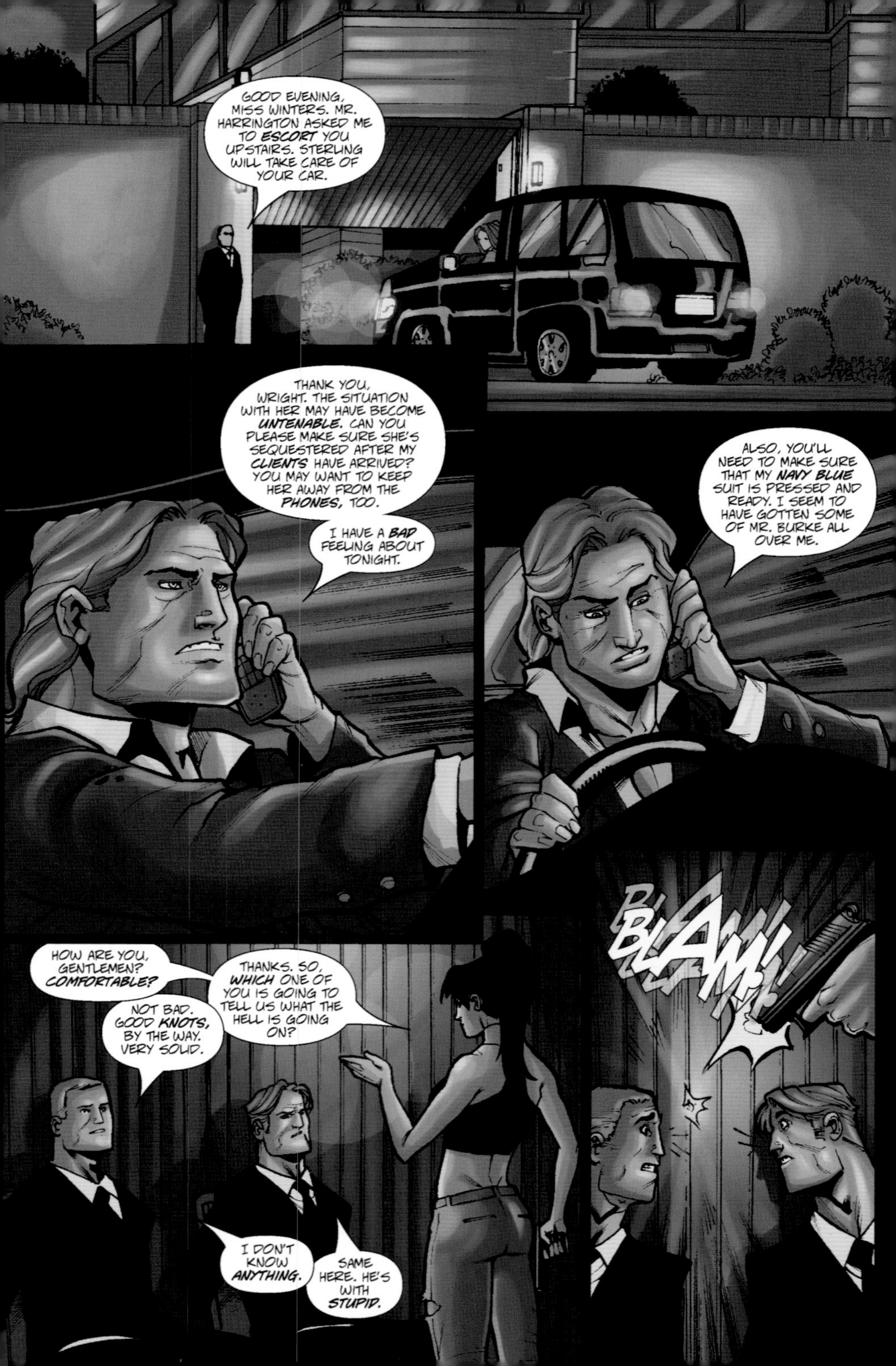
GOOD EVENING, MISS WINTERS. MR. HARRINGTON ASKED ME TO ESCORT YOU UPSTAIRS. STERLING WILL TAKE CARE OF YOUR CAR.
THANK YOU, WRIGHT. THE SITUATION WITH HER MAY HAVE BECOME UNTENABLE. CAN YOU PLEASE MAKE SURE SHE'S SEQUESTERED AFTER MY CLIENTS HAVE ARRIVED? YOU MAY WANT TO KEEP HER AWAY FROM THE PHONES, TOO.
I HAVE A BAD FEELING ABOUT TONIGHT.
ALSO, YOU'LL NEED TO MAKE SURE THAT MY NAVY BLUE SUIT IS PRESSED AND READY. I SEEM TO HAVE GOTTEN SOME OF MR. BURKE ALL OVER ME.
HOW ARE YOU, GENTLEMEN? COMFORTABLE?
NOT BAD. GOOD KNOTS, BY THE WAY. VERY SOLID.
THANKS. SO, WHICH ONE OF YOU IS GOING TO TELL US WHAT THE HELL IS GOING ON?
I DON'T KNOW ANYTHING.
SAME HERE. HE'S WITH STUPID.
BLAM!

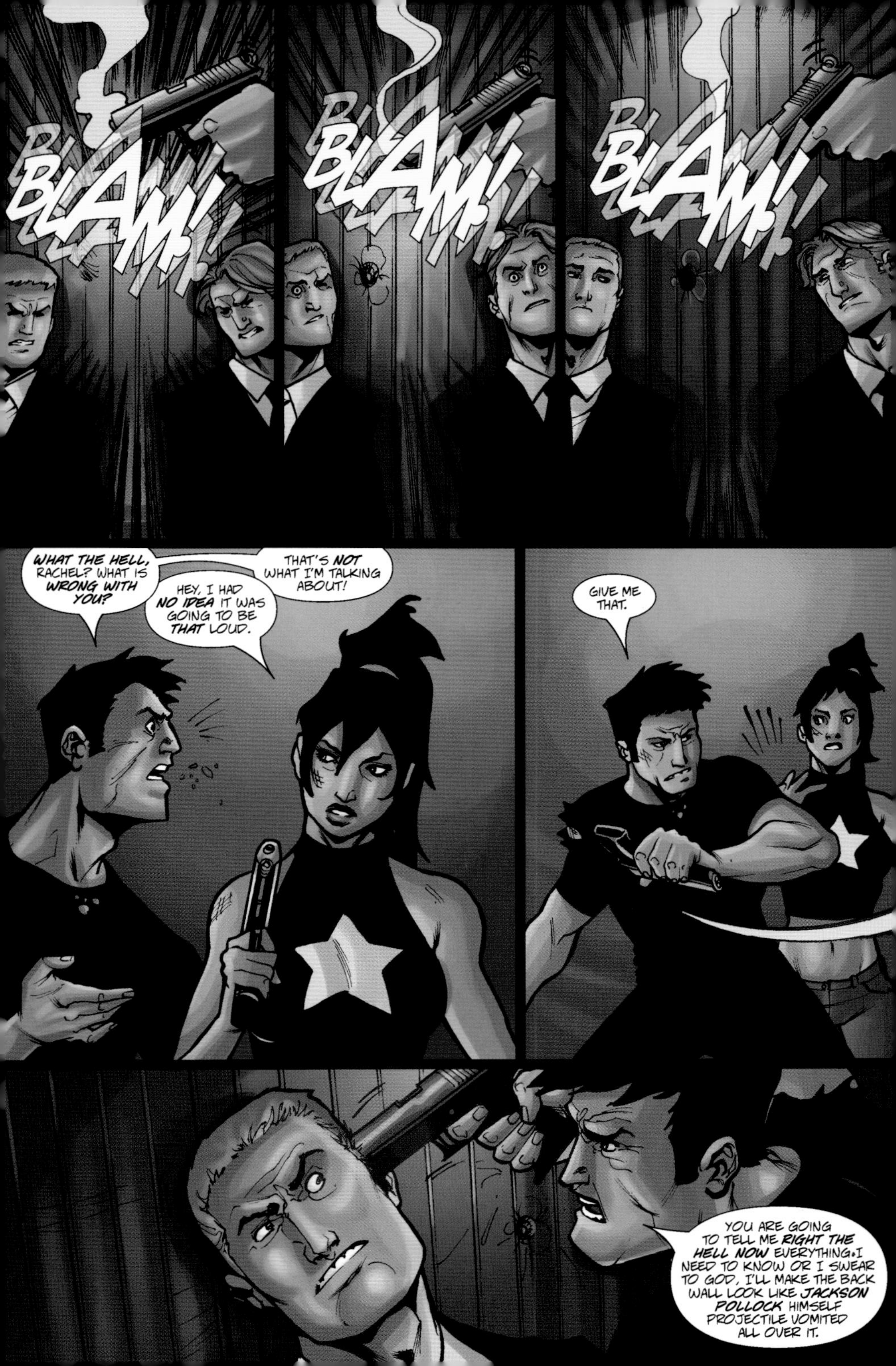
BLAM!
BLAM!
BLAM!
WHAT THE HELL, RACHEL? WHAT IS WRONG WITH YOU?
HEY, I HAD NO IDEA IT WAS GOING TO BE THAT LOUD.
THAT'S NOT WHAT I'M TALKING ABOUT!
GIVE ME THAT.
YOU ARE GOING TO TELL ME RIGHT THE HELL NOW EVERYTHING I NEED TO KNOW OR I SWEAR TO GOD, I'LL MAKE THE BACK WALL LOOK LIKE JACKSON POLLOCK HIMSELF PROJECTILE VOMITED ALL OVER IT.

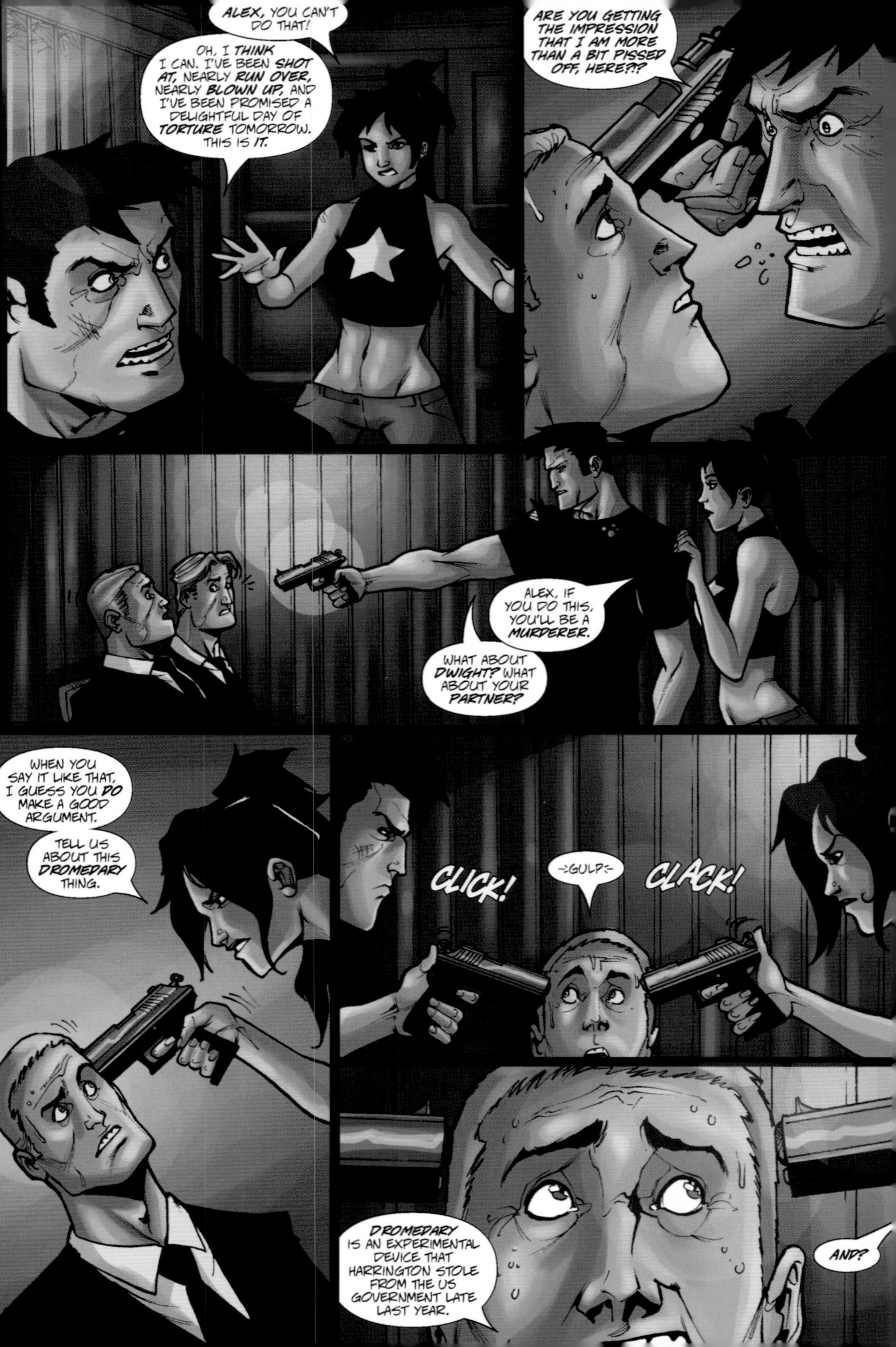
ALEX, YOU CAN'T DO THAT!
OH, I THINK I CAN. I'VE BEEN SHOT AT, NEARLY RUN OVER, NEARLY BLOWN UP, AND I'VE BEEN PROMISED A DELIGHTFUL DAY OF TORTURE TOMORROW. THIS IS IT.
ARE YOU GETTING THE IMPRESSION THAT I AM MORE THAN A BIT PISSED OFF, HERE?!?
ALEX, IF YOU DO THIS, YOU'LL BE A MURDERER.
WHAT ABOUT DWIGHT? WHAT ABOUT YOUR PARTNER?
WHEN YOU SAY IT LIKE THAT, I GUESS YOU DO MAKE A GOOD ARGUMENT.
TELL US ABOUT THIS DROMEDARY THING.
CLICK!
GULP
CLACK!
DROMEDARY IS AN EXPERIMENTAL DEVICE THAT HARRINGTON STOLE FROM THE US GOVERNMENT LATE LAST YEAR.
AND?

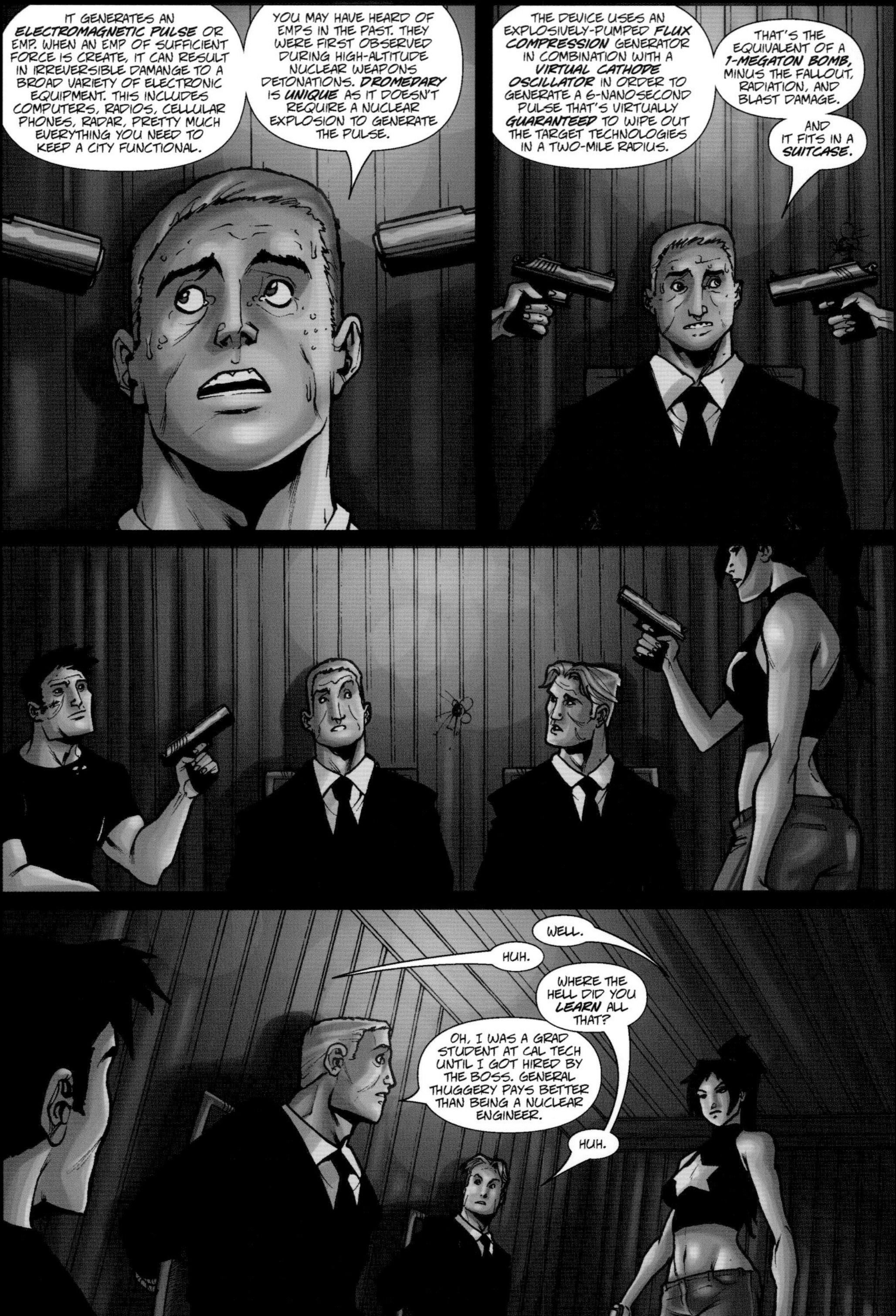
IT GENERATES AN **ELECTROMAGNETIC PULSE** OR EMP. WHEN AN EMP OF SUFFICIENT FORCE IS CREATE, IT CAN RESULT IN IRREVERSIBLE DAMANGE TO A BROAD VARIETY OF ELECTRONIC EQUIPMENT. THIS INCLUDES COMPUTERS, RADIOS, CELLULAR PHONES, RADAR, PRETTY MUCH EVERYTHING YOU NEED TO KEEP A CITY FUNCTIONAL.
YOU MAY HAVE HEARD OF EMPS IN THE PAST. THEY WERE FIRST OBSERVED DURING HIGH-ALTITUDE NUCLEAR WEAPONS DETONATIONS. **DROMEDARY** IS **UNIQUE** AS IT DOESN'T REQUIRE A NUCLEAR EXPLOSION TO GENERATE THE PULSE.
THE DEVICE USES AN EXPLOSIVELY-PUMPED **FLUX COMPRESSION** GENERATOR IN COMBINATION WITH A **VIRTUAL CATHODE OSCILLATOR** IN ORDER TO GENERATE A 6-NANOSECOND PULSE THAT'S VIRTUALLY **GUARANTEED** TO WIPE OUT THE TARGET TECHNOLOGIES IN A TWO-MILE RADIUS.
THAT'S THE EQUIVALENT OF A **1-MEGATON BOMB,** MINUS THE FALLOUT, RADIATION, AND BLAST DAMAGE.
AND IT FITS IN A **SUITCASE.**
WELL.
HUH.
WHERE THE HELL DID YOU **LEARN** ALL THAT?
OH, I WAS A GRAD STUDENT AT CAL TECH UNTIL I GOT HIRED BY THE BOSS. GENERAL THUGGERY PAYS BETTER THAN BEING A NUCLEAR ENGINEER.
HUH.

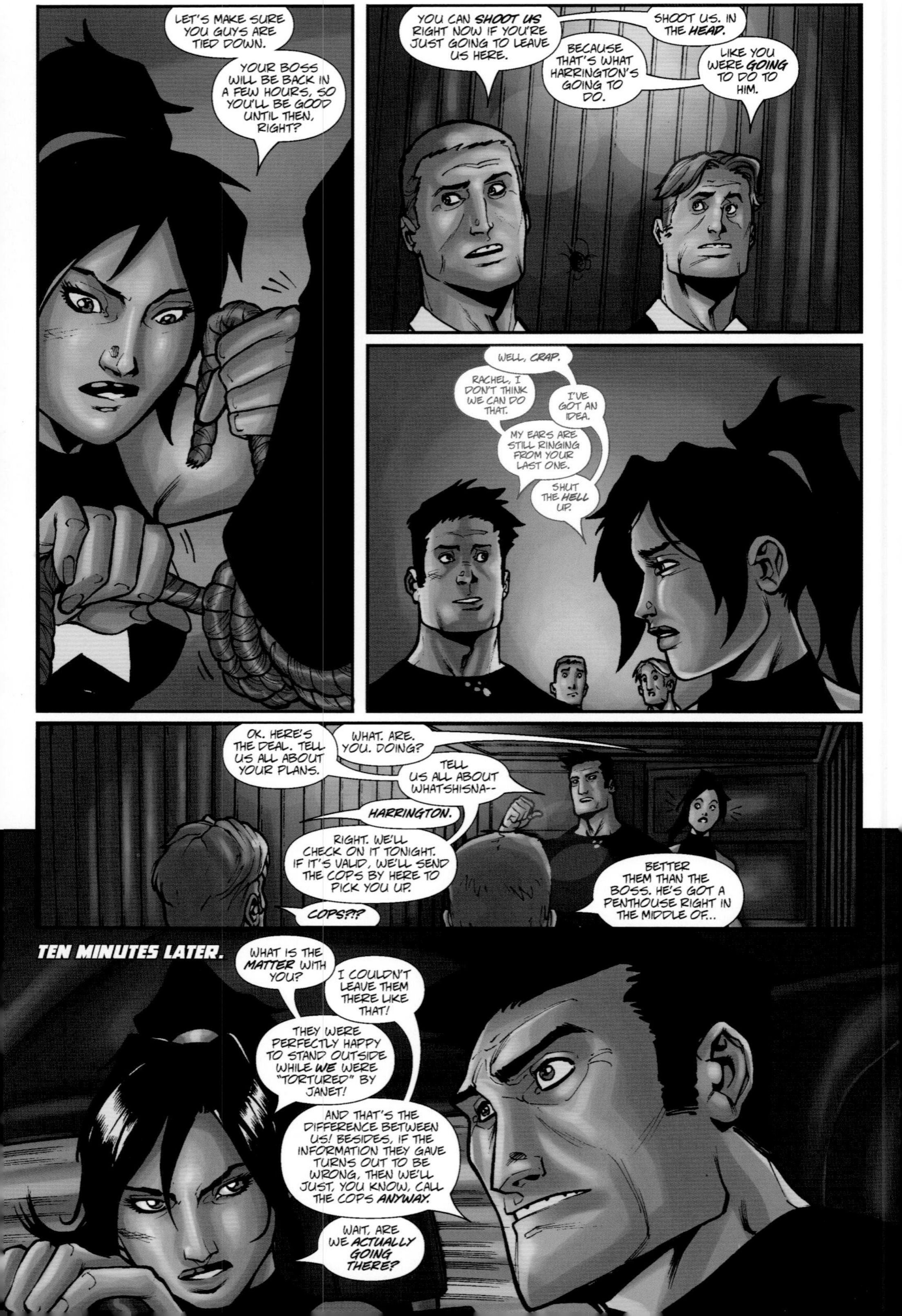
LET'S MAKE SURE YOU GUYS ARE TIED DOWN.
YOUR BOSS WILL BE BACK IN A FEW HOURS, SO YOU'LL BE GOOD UNTIL THEN, RIGHT?
YOU CAN SHOOT US RIGHT NOW IF YOU'RE JUST GOING TO LEAVE US HERE.
SHOOT US. IN THE HEAD.
BECAUSE THAT'S WHAT HARRINGTON'S GOING TO DO.
LIKE YOU WERE GOING TO DO TO HIM.
WELL, CRAP.
RACHEL, I DON'T THINK WE CAN DO THAT.
I'VE GOT AN IDEA.
MY EARS ARE STILL RINGING FROM YOUR LAST ONE.
SHUT THE HELL UP.
OK. HERE'S THE DEAL. TELL US ALL ABOUT YOUR PLANS.
WHAT. ARE. YOU. DOING?
TELL US ALL ABOUT WHATSHISNA--
HARRINGTON.
RIGHT. WE'LL CHECK ON IT TONIGHT. IF IT'S VALID, WE'LL SEND THE COPS BY HERE TO PICK YOU UP.
COPS?!?
BETTER THEM THAN THE BOSS. HE'S GOT A PENTHOUSE RIGHT IN THE MIDDLE OF...
TEN MINUTES LATER.
WHAT IS THE MATTER WITH YOU?
I COULDN'T LEAVE THEM THERE LIKE THAT!
THEY WERE PERFECTLY HAPPY TO STAND OUTSIDE WHILE WE WERE "TORTURED" BY JANET!
AND THAT'S THE DIFFERENCE BETWEEN US! BESIDES, IF THE INFORMATION THEY GAVE TURNS OUT TO BE WRONG, THEN WE'LL JUST, YOU KNOW, CALL THE COPS ANYWAY.
WAIT, ARE WE ACTUALLY GOING THERE?

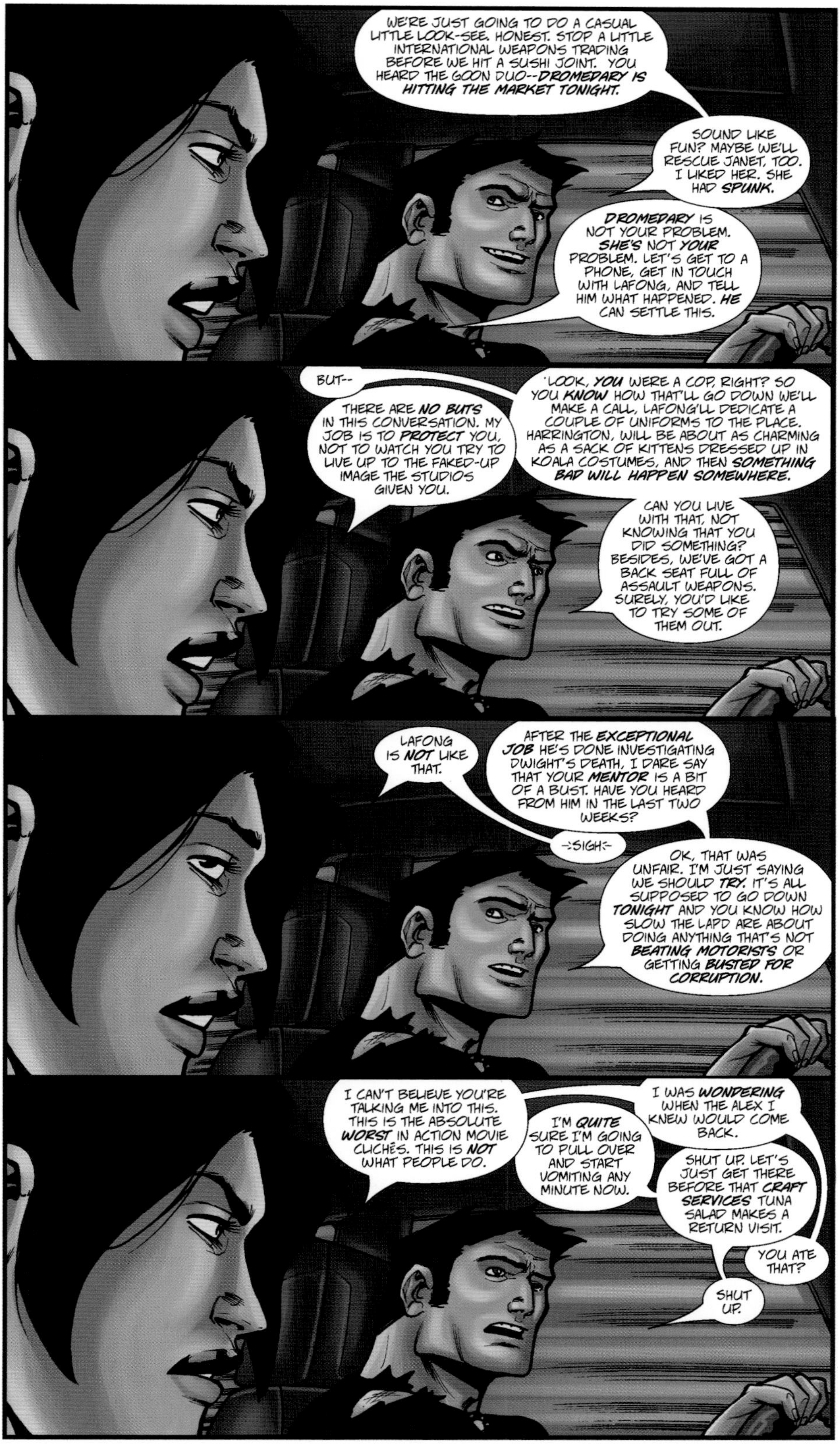
WE'RE JUST GOING TO DO A CASUAL LITTLE LOOK-SEE. HONEST. STOP A LITTLE INTERNATIONAL WEAPONS TRADING BEFORE WE HIT A SUSHI JOINT. YOU HEARD THE GOON DUO--DROMEDARY IS HITTING THE MARKET TONIGHT.
SOUND LIKE FUN? MAYBE WE'LL RESCUE JANET, TOO. I LIKED HER. SHE HAD SPUNK.
DROMEDARY IS NOT YOUR PROBLEM. SHE'S NOT YOUR PROBLEM. LET'S GET TO A PHONE, GET IN TOUCH WITH LAFONG, AND TELL HIM WHAT HAPPENED. HE CAN SETTLE THIS.
BUT--
THERE ARE NO BUTS IN THIS CONVERSATION. MY JOB IS TO PROTECT YOU, NOT TO WATCH YOU TRY TO LIVE UP TO THE FAKED-UP IMAGE THE STUDIOS GIVEN YOU.
'LOOK, YOU WERE A COP, RIGHT? SO YOU KNOW HOW THAT'LL GO DOWN WE'LL MAKE A CALL, LAFONG'LL DEDICATE A COUPLE OF UNIFORMS TO THE PLACE. HARRINGTON, WILL BE ABOUT AS CHARMING AS A SACK OF KITTENS DRESSED UP IN KOALA COSTUMES, AND THEN SOMETHING BAD WILL HAPPEN SOMEWHERE.
CAN YOU LIVE WITH THAT, NOT KNOWING THAT YOU DID SOMETHING? BESIDES, WE'VE GOT A BACK SEAT FULL OF ASSAULT WEAPONS. SURELY, YOU'D LIKE TO TRY SOME OF THEM OUT.
LAFONG IS NOT LIKE THAT.
AFTER THE EXCEPTIONAL JOB HE'S DONE INVESTIGATING DWIGHT'S DEATH, I DARE SAY THAT YOUR MENTOR IS A BIT OF A BUST. HAVE YOU HEARD FROM HIM IN THE LAST TWO WEEKS?
-SIGH-
OK, THAT WAS UNFAIR. I'M JUST SAYING WE SHOULD TRY. IT'S ALL SUPPOSED TO GO DOWN TONIGHT AND YOU KNOW HOW SLOW THE LAPD ARE ABOUT DOING ANYTHING THAT'S NOT BEATING MOTORISTS OR GETTING BUSTED FOR CORRUPTION.
I CAN'T BELIEVE YOU'RE TALKING ME INTO THIS. THIS IS THE ABSOLUTE WORST IN ACTION MOVIE CLICHÉS. THIS IS NOT WHAT PEOPLE DO.
I WAS WONDERING WHEN THE ALEX I KNEW WOULD COME BACK.
I'M QUITE SURE I'M GOING TO PULL OVER AND START VOMITING ANY MINUTE NOW.
SHUT UP. LET'S JUST GET THERE BEFORE THAT CRAFT SERVICES TUNA SALAD MAKES A RETURN VISIT.
YOU ATE THAT?
SHUT UP.

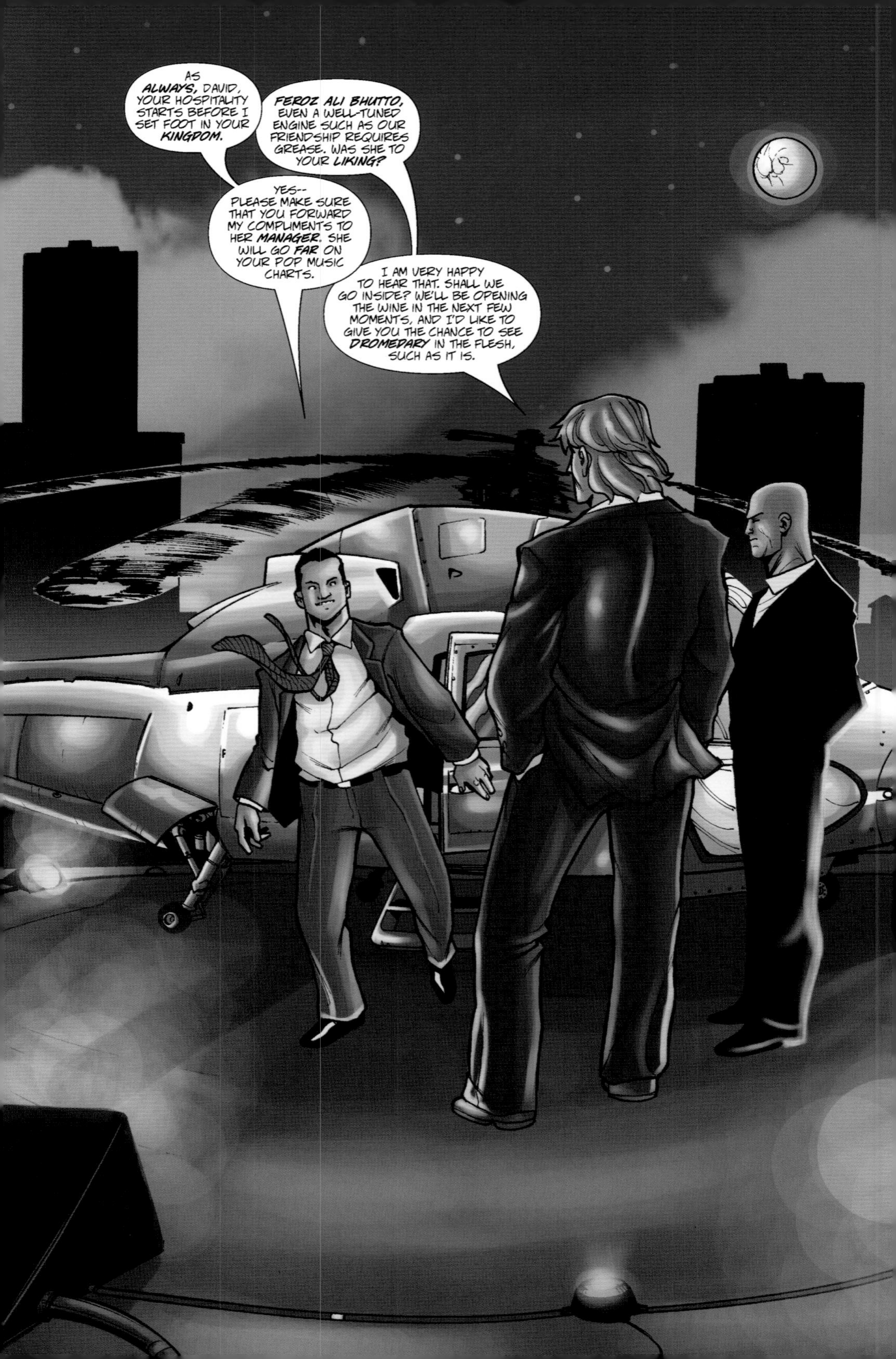
AS ALWAYS, DAVID, YOUR HOSPITALITY STARTS BEFORE I SET FOOT IN YOUR KINGDOM.
FEROZ ALI BHUTTO, EVEN A WELL-TUNED ENGINE SUCH AS OUR FRIENDSHIP REQUIRES GREASE. WAS SHE TO YOUR LIKING?
YES-- PLEASE MAKE SURE THAT YOU FORWARD MY COMPLIMENTS TO HER MANAGER. SHE WILL GO FAR ON YOUR POP MUSIC CHARTS.
I AM VERY HAPPY TO HEAR THAT. SHALL WE GO INSIDE? WE'LL BE OPENING THE WINE IN THE NEXT FEW MOMENTS, AND I'D LIKE TO GIVE YOU THE CHANCE TO SEE DROMEDARY IN THE FLESH, SUCH AS IT IS.

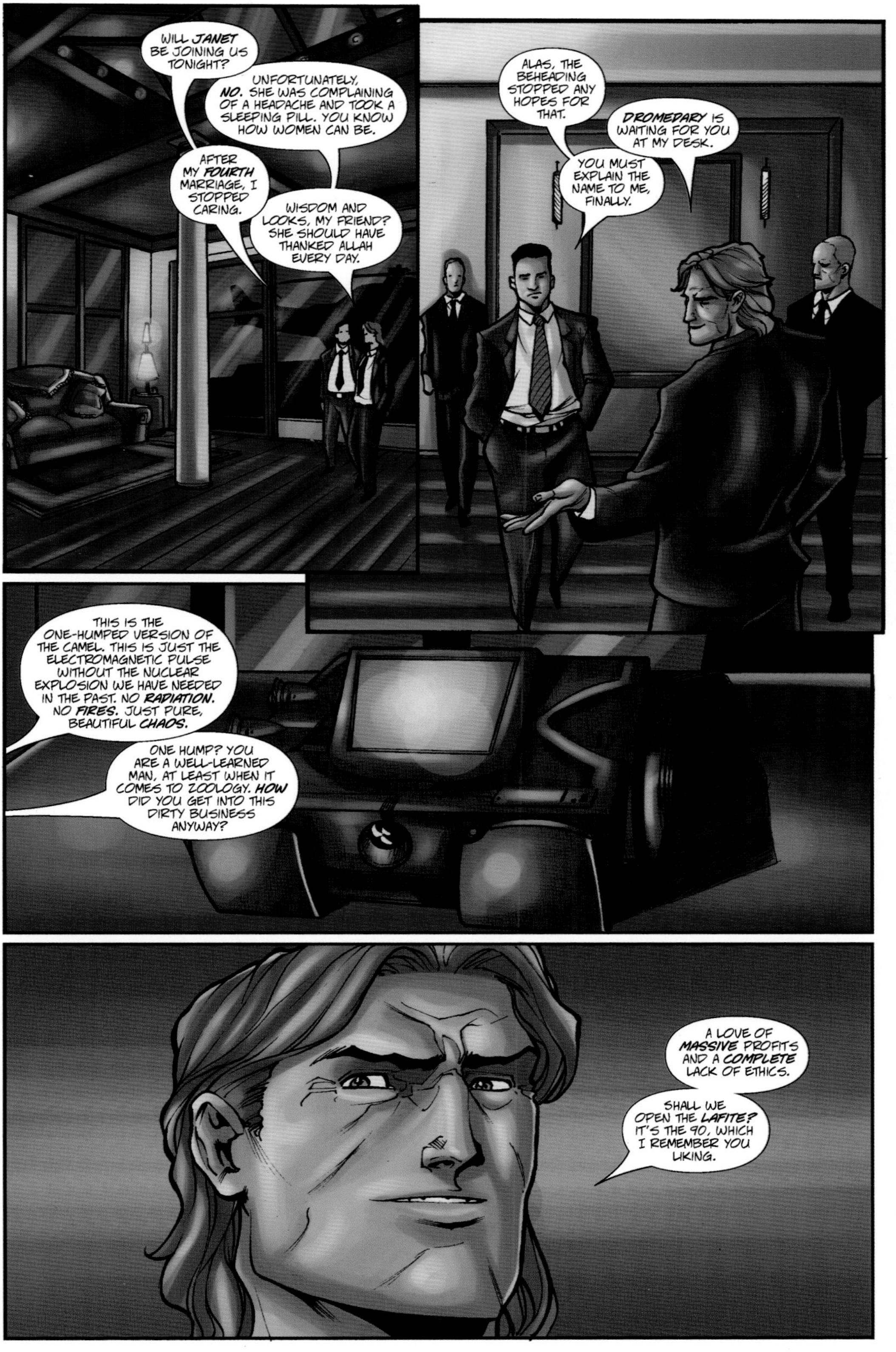
WILL JANET BE JOINING US TONIGHT?
UNFORTUNATELY, NO. SHE WAS COMPLAINING OF A HEADACHE AND TOOK A SLEEPING PILL. YOU KNOW HOW WOMEN CAN BE.
AFTER MY FOURTH MARRIAGE, I STOPPED CARING.
WISDOM AND LOOKS, MY FRIEND? SHE SHOULD HAVE THANKED ALLAH EVERY DAY.
ALAS, THE BEHEADING STOPPED ANY HOPES FOR THAT.
DROMEDARY IS WAITING FOR YOU AT MY DESK.
YOU MUST EXPLAIN THE NAME TO ME, FINALLY.
THIS IS THE ONE-HUMPED VERSION OF THE CAMEL. THIS IS JUST THE ELECTROMAGNETIC PULSE WITHOUT THE NUCLEAR EXPLOSION WE HAVE NEEDED IN THE PAST. NO RADIATION. NO FIRES. JUST PURE, BEAUTIFUL CHAOS.
ONE HUMP? YOU ARE A WELL-LEARNED MAN, AT LEAST WHEN IT COMES TO ZOOLOGY. HOW DID YOU GET INTO THIS DIRTY BUSINESS ANYWAY?
A LOVE OF MASSIVE PROFITS AND A COMPLETE LACK OF ETHICS.
SHALL WE OPEN THE LAFITE? IT'S THE 90, WHICH I REMEMBER YOU LIKING.

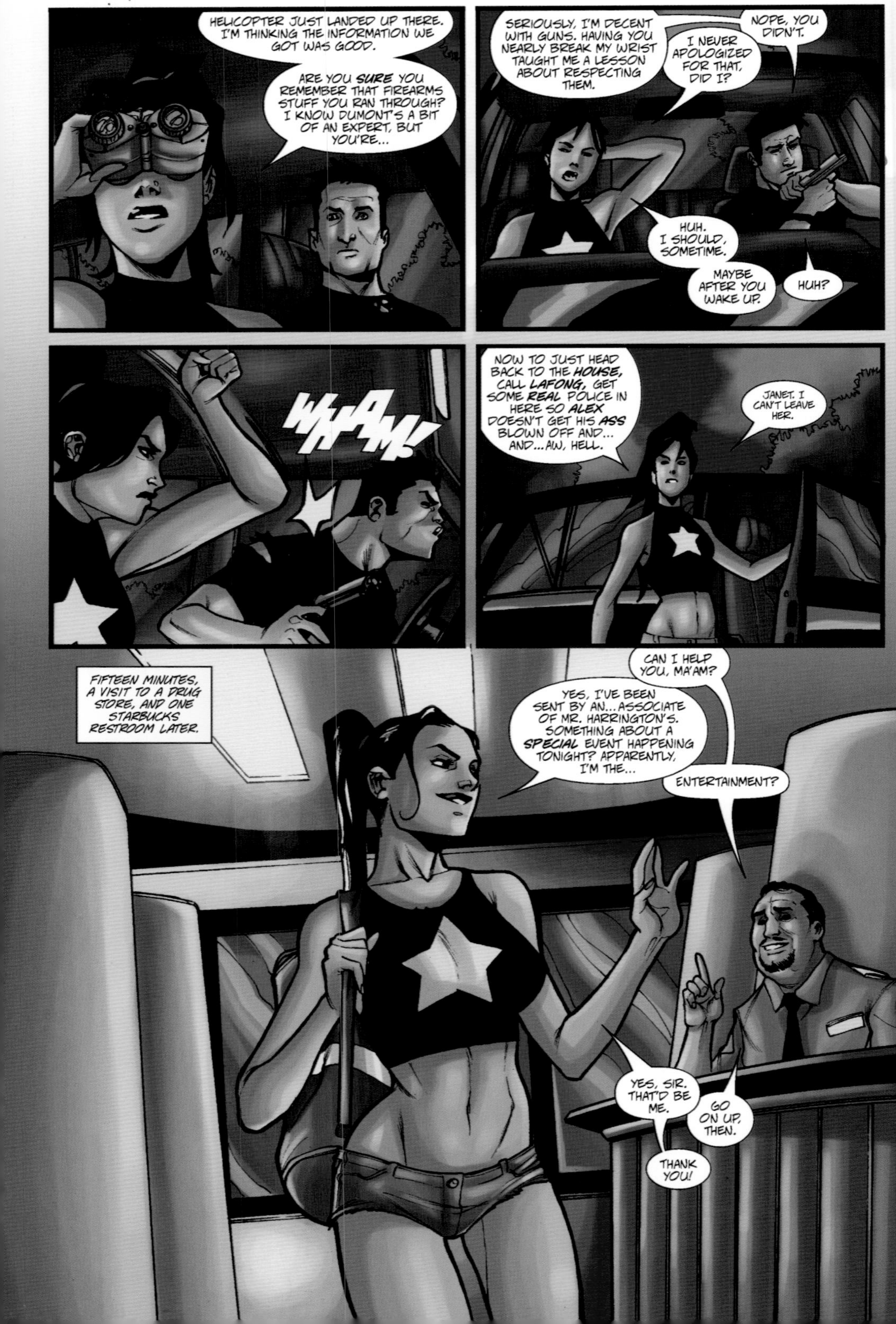

HELICOPTER JUST LANDED UP THERE. I'M THINKING THE INFORMATION WE GOT WAS GOOD.
ARE YOU SURE YOU REMEMBER THAT FIREARMS STUFF YOU RAN THROUGH? I KNOW DUMONT'S A BIT OF AN EXPERT, BUT YOU'RE...
SERIOUSLY, I'M DECENT WITH GUNS. HAVING YOU NEARLY BREAK MY WRIST TAUGHT ME A LESSON ABOUT RESPECTING THEM.
I NEVER APOLOGIZED FOR THAT, DID I?
NOPE, YOU DIDN'T.
HUH. I SHOULD, SOMETIME.
MAYBE AFTER YOU WAKE UP.
HUH?
WHAM!
NOW TO JUST HEAD BACK TO THE HOUSE, CALL LAFONG, GET SOME REAL POLICE IN HERE SO ALEX DOESN'T GET HIS ASS BLOWN OFF AND... AND...AW, HELL.
JANET. I CAN'T LEAVE HER.
FIFTEEN MINUTES, A VISIT TO A DRUG STORE, AND ONE STARBUCKS RESTROOM LATER.
CAN I HELP YOU, MA'AM?
YES, I'VE BEEN SENT BY AN...ASSOCIATE OF MR. HARRINGTON'S. SOMETHING ABOUT A SPECIAL EVENT HAPPENING TONIGHT? APPARENTLY, I'M THE...
ENTERTAINMENT?
YES, SIR. THAT'D BE ME.
GO ON UP, THEN.
THANK YOU!

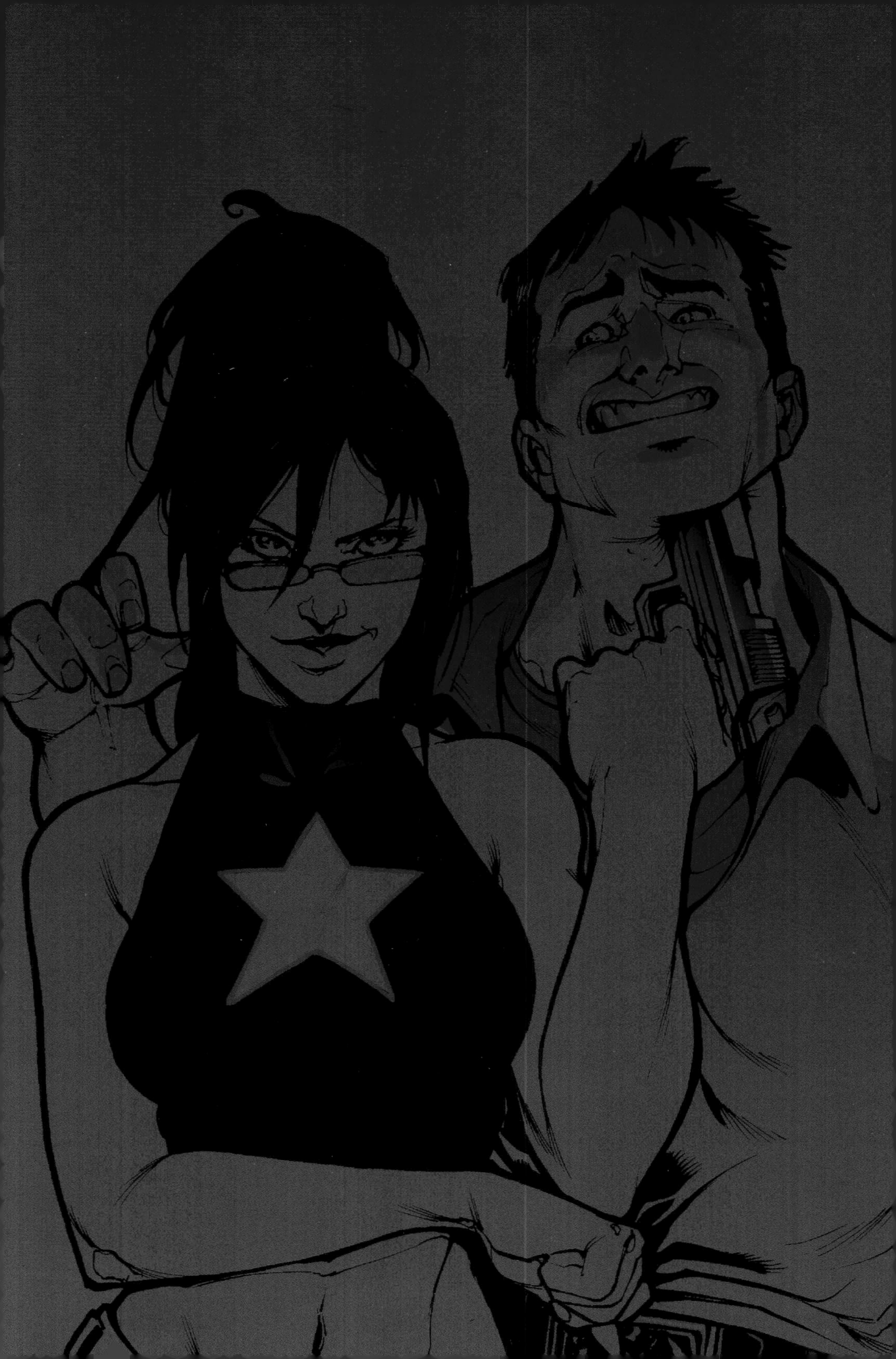

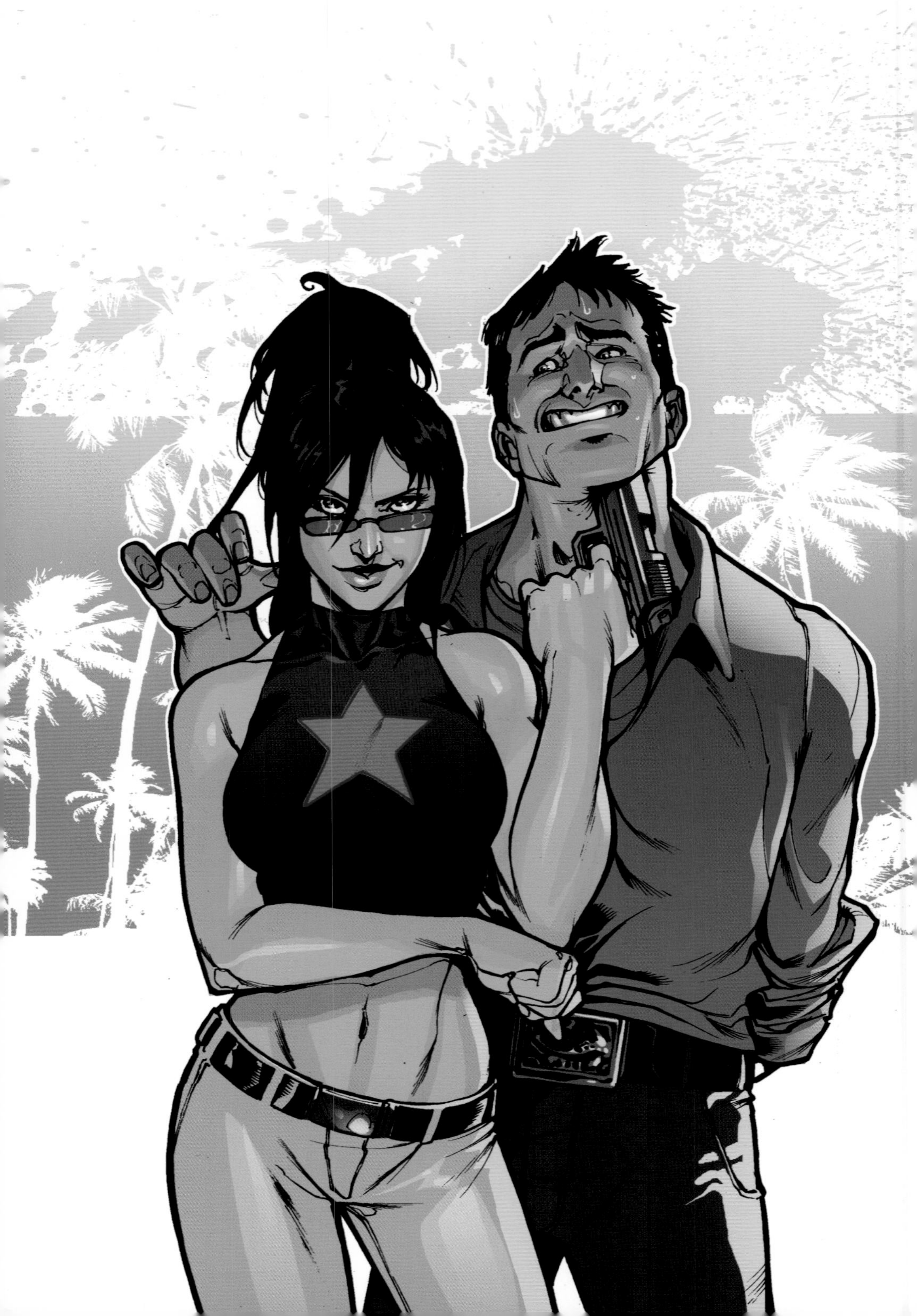

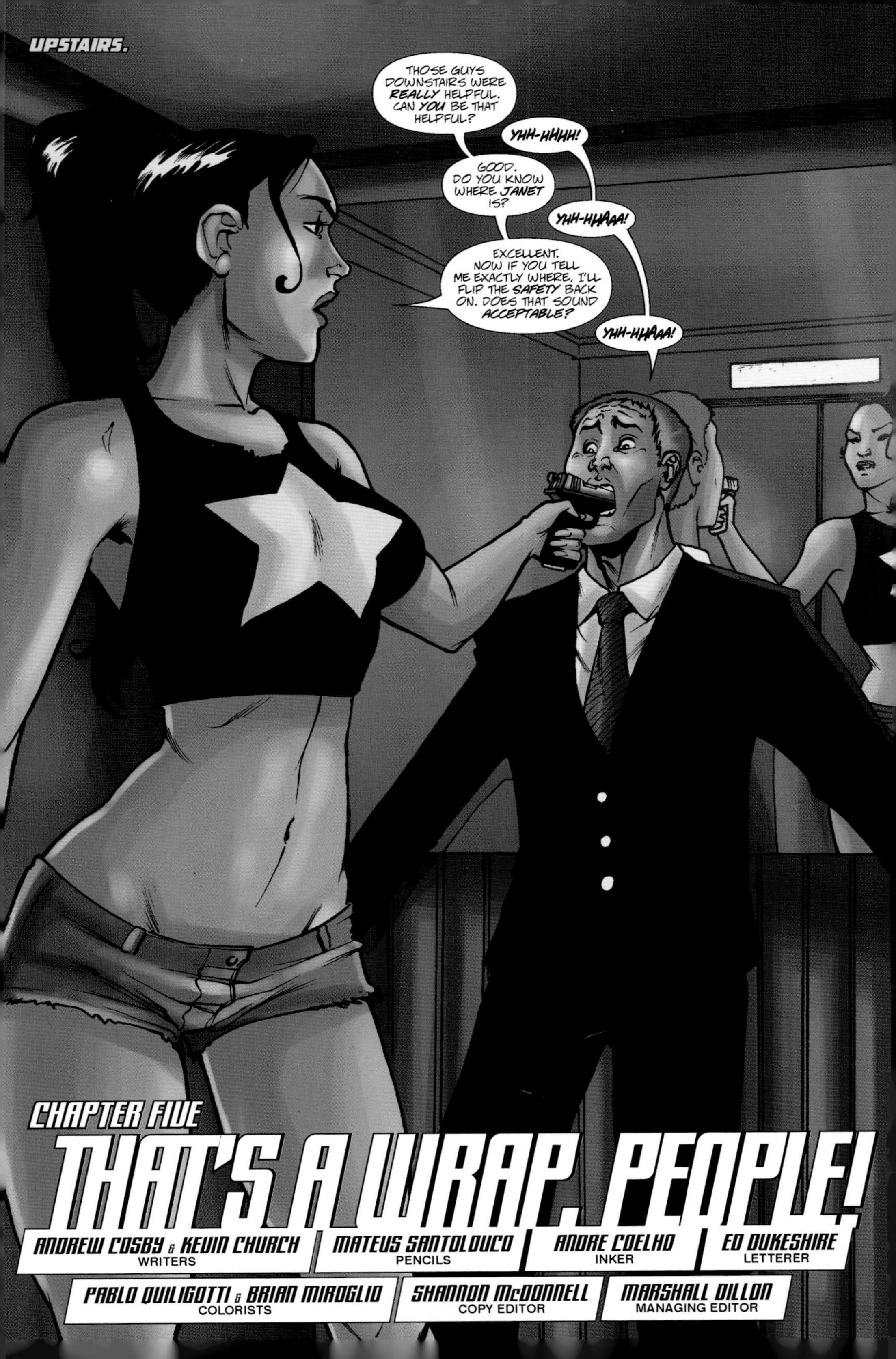
UPSTAIRS.
THOSE GUYS DOWNSTAIRS WERE REALLY HELPFUL. CAN YOU BE THAT HELPFUL?
YHH-HHHH!
GOOD. DO YOU KNOW WHERE JANET IS?
YHH-HHAAA!
EXCELLENT. NOW IF YOU TELL ME EXACTLY WHERE, I'LL FLIP THE SAFETY BACK ON. DOES THAT SOUND ACCEPTABLE?
YHH-HHAAA!
CHAPTER FIVE
THAT'S A WRAP, PEOPLE!
ANDREW COSBY & KEVIN CHURCH
WRITERS
MATEUS SANTOLOUCO
PENCILS
ANDRE COELHO
INKER
ED DUKESHIRE
LETTERER
PABLO QUILIGOTTI & BRIAN MIROGLIO
COLORISTS
SHANNON McDONNELL
COPY EDITOR
MARSHALL DILLON
MANAGING EDITOR

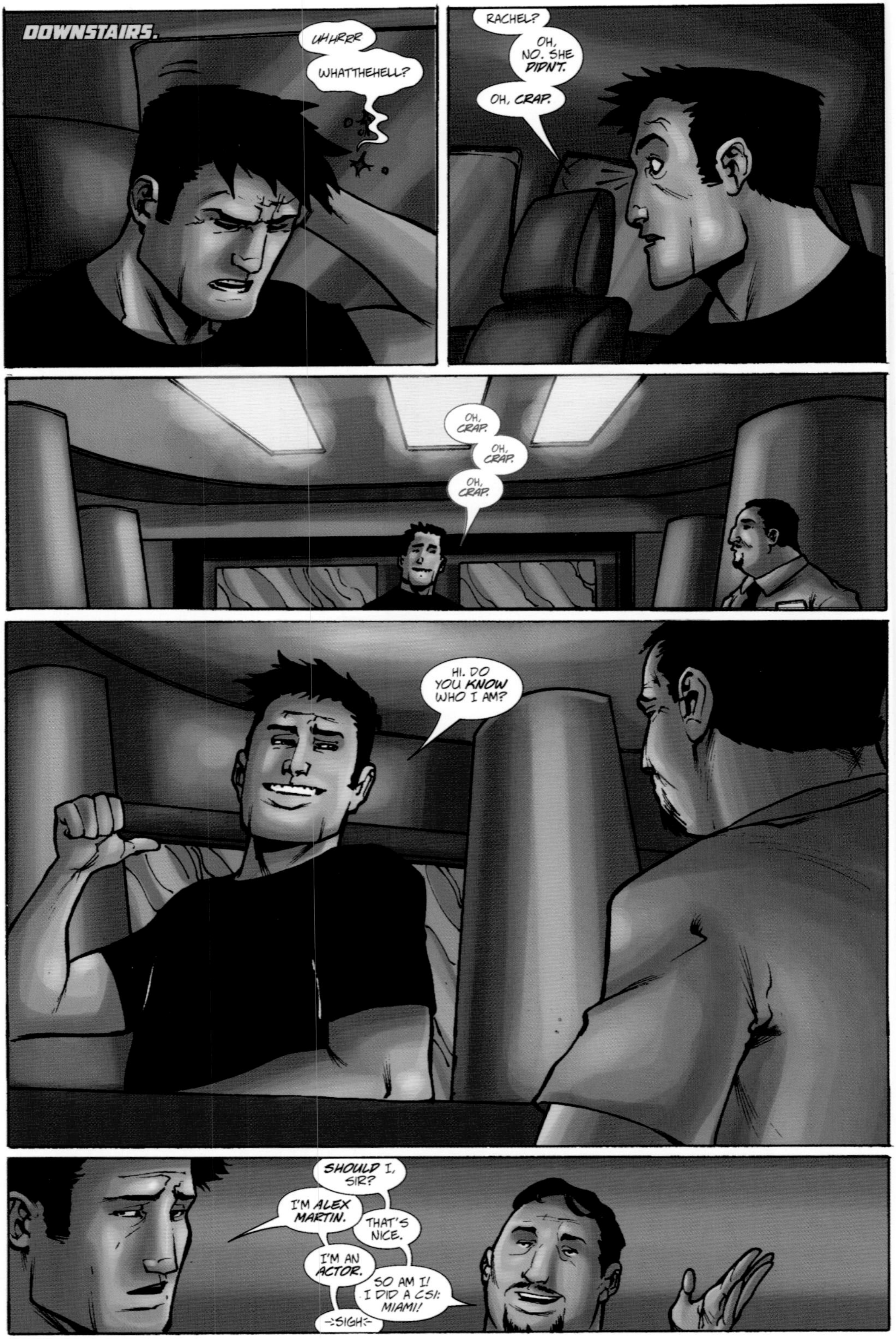
DOWNSTAIRS.
UHHRRR
WHATTHEHELL?
RACHEL?
OH, NO. SHE DIDN'T.
OH, CRAP.
OH, CRAP.
OH, CRAP.
OH, CRAP.
HI. DO YOU KNOW WHO I AM?
SHOULD I, SIR?
I'M ALEX MARTIN.
THAT'S NICE.
I'M AN ACTOR.
SO AM I! I DID A CSI: MIAMI!
-SIGH-

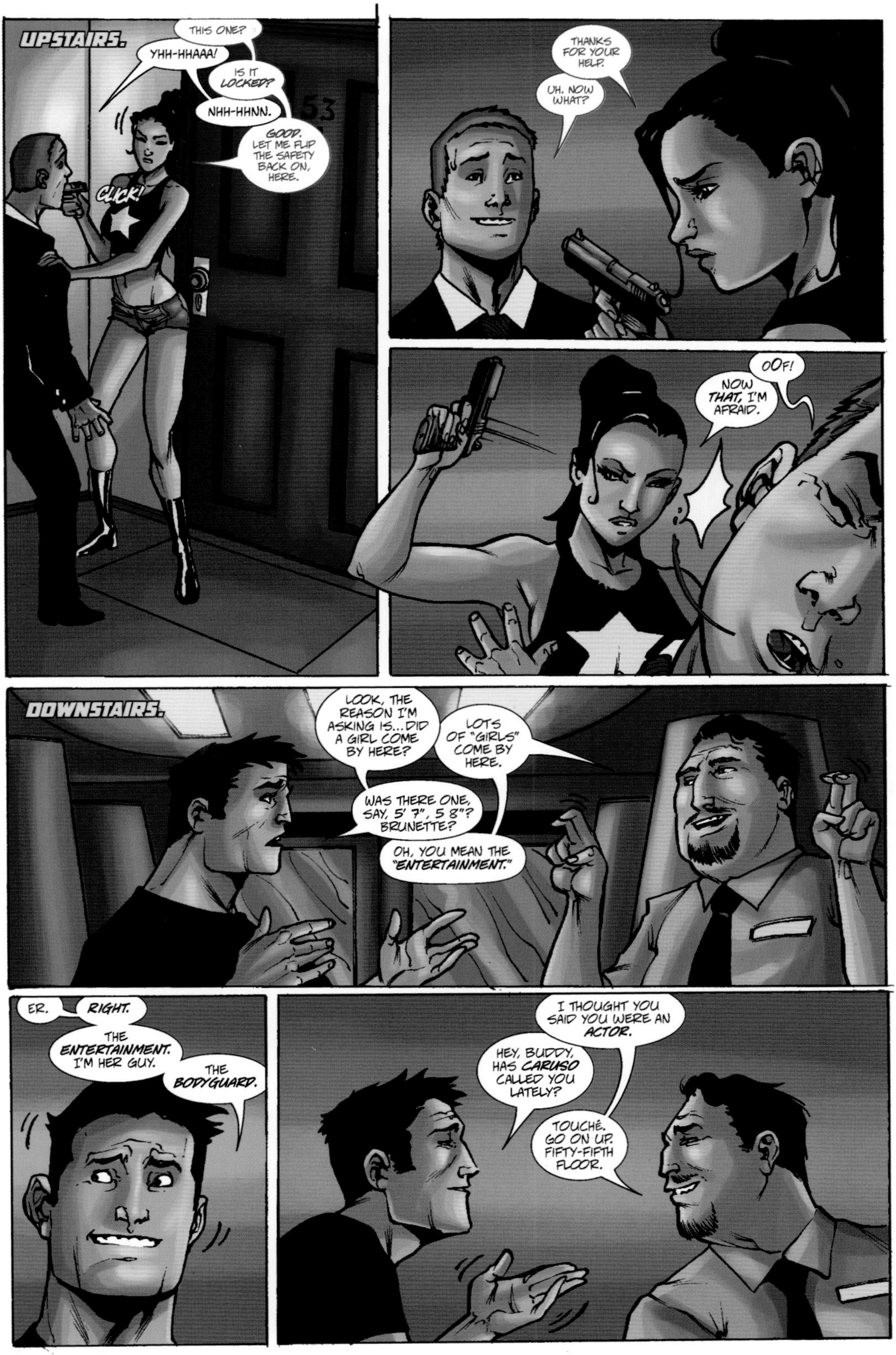
UPSTAIRS.
THIS ONE?
YHH-HHAAA!
IS IT LOCKED?
NHH-HHNN.
GOOD. LET ME FLIP THE SAFETY BACK ON, HERE.
CLICK!
THANKS FOR YOUR HELP.
UH. NOW WHAT?
NOW THAT, I'M AFRAID.
OOF!
DOWNSTAIRS.
LOOK, THE REASON I'M ASKING IS... DID A GIRL COME BY HERE?
LOTS OF "GIRLS" COME BY HERE.
WAS THERE ONE, SAY, 5' 7", 5 8"? BRUNETTE?
OH, YOU MEAN THE "ENTERTAINMENT."
ER.
RIGHT.
THE ENTERTAINMENT. I'M HER GUY.
THE BODYGUARD.
I THOUGHT YOU SAID YOU WERE AN ACTOR.
HEY, BUDDY, HAS CARUSO CALLED YOU LATELY?
TOUCHÉ. GO ON UP. FIFTY-FIFTH FLOOR.

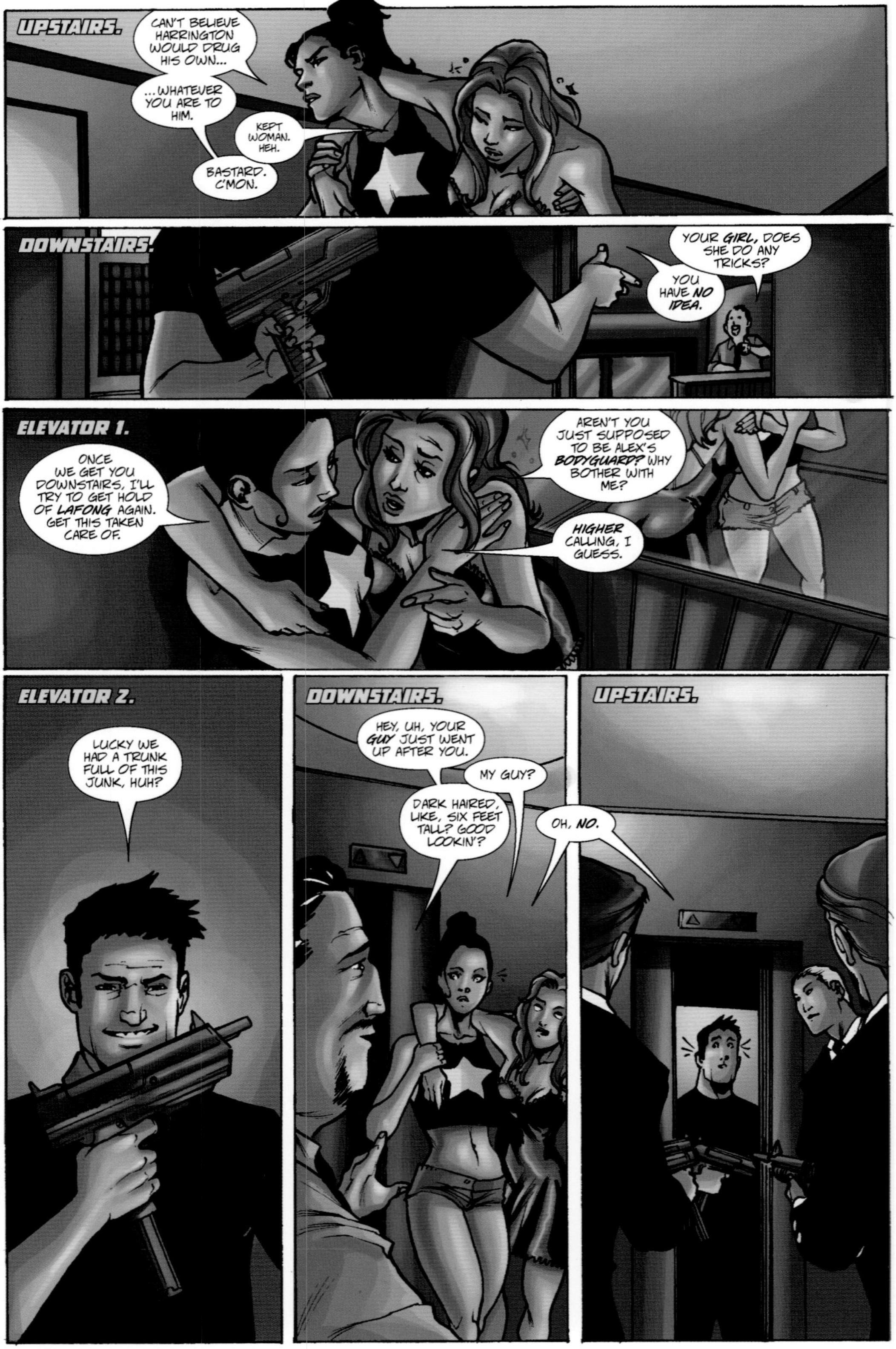
UPSTAIRS.
CAN'T BELIEVE HARRINGTON WOULD DRUG HIS OWN...
...WHATEVER YOU ARE TO HIM.
KEPT WOMAN. HEH.
BASTARD. C'MON.
DOWNSTAIRS.
YOUR GIRL, DOES SHE DO ANY TRICKS?
YOU HAVE NO IDEA.
ELEVATOR 1.
ONCE WE GET YOU DOWNSTAIRS, I'LL TRY TO GET HOLD OF LAFONG AGAIN. GET THIS TAKEN CARE OF.
AREN'T YOU JUST SUPPOSED TO BE ALEX'S BODYGUARD? WHY BOTHER WITH ME?
HIGHER CALLING, I GUESS.
ELEVATOR 2.
LUCKY WE HAD A TRUNK FULL OF THIS JUNK, HUH?
DOWNSTAIRS.
HEY, UH, YOUR GUY JUST WENT UP AFTER YOU.
MY GUY?
DARK HAIRED, LIKE, SIX FEET TALL? GOOD LOOKIN'?
OH, NO.
UPSTAIRS.

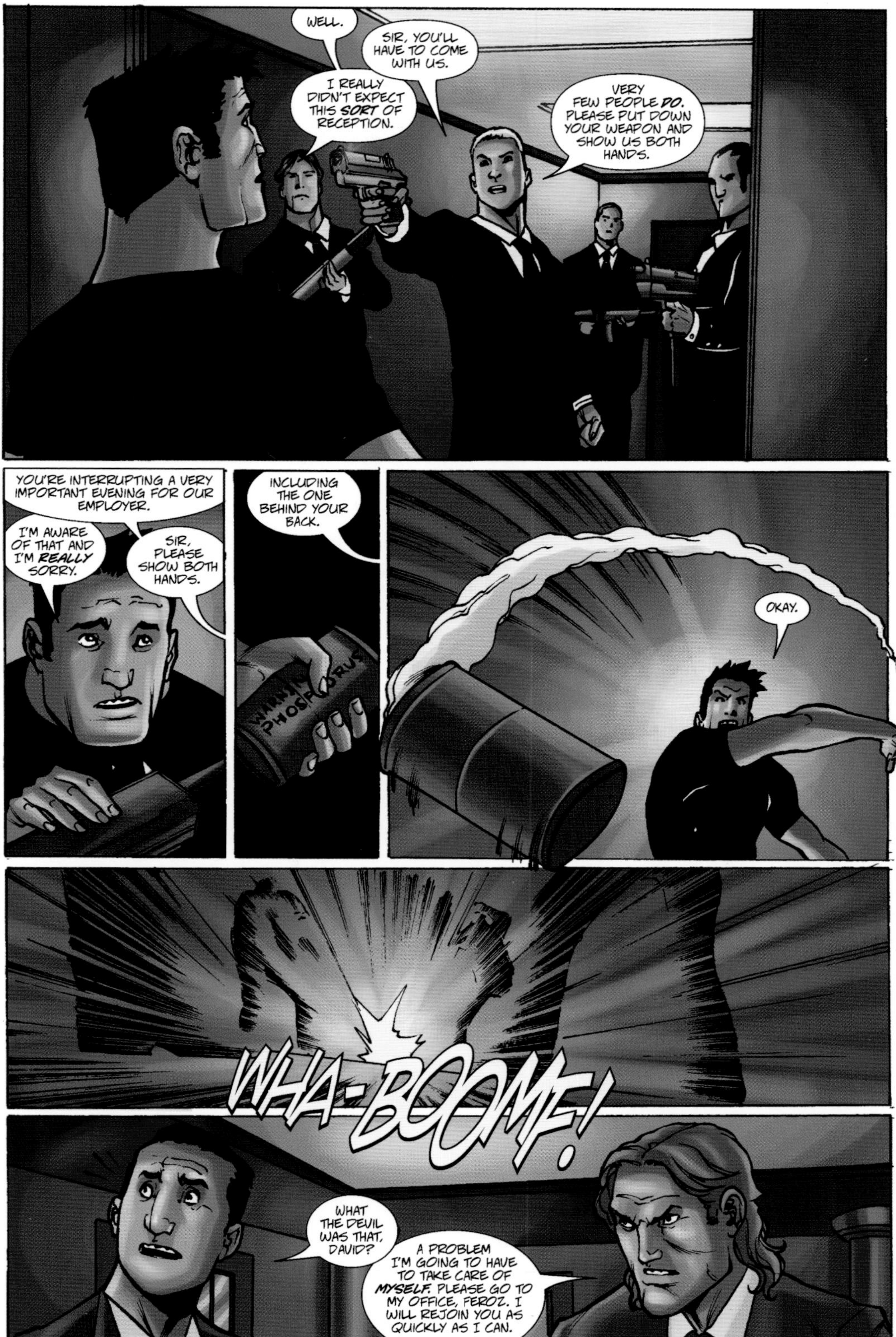
WELL.
I REALLY DIDN'T EXPECT THIS *SORT* OF RECEPTION.
SIR, YOU'LL HAVE TO COME WITH US.
VERY FEW PEOPLE *DO*. PLEASE PUT DOWN YOUR WEAPON AND SHOW US BOTH HANDS.
YOU'RE INTERRUPTING A VERY IMPORTANT EVENING FOR OUR EMPLOYER.
I'M AWARE OF THAT AND I'M *REALLY* SORRY.
SIR, PLEASE SHOW BOTH HANDS.
INCLUDING THE ONE BEHIND YOUR BACK.
PHOSPHORUS
OKAY.
WHA-BOOMF!
WHAT THE DEVIL WAS THAT, DAVID?
A PROBLEM I'M GOING TO HAVE TO TAKE CARE OF *MYSELF*. PLEASE GO TO MY OFFICE, FEROZ. I WILL REJOIN YOU AS QUICKLY AS I CAN.

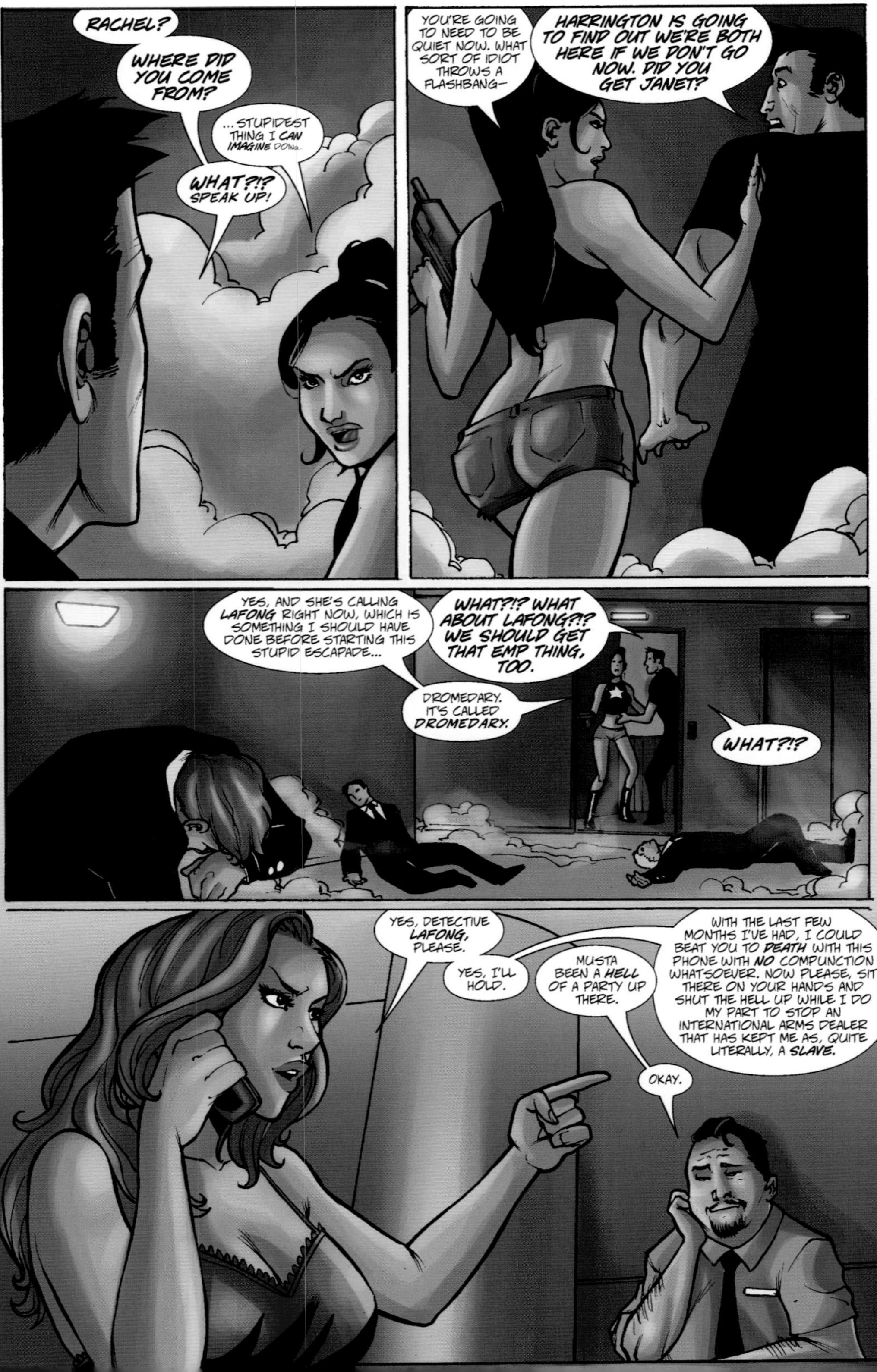

RACHEL?
WHERE DID YOU COME FROM?
...STUPIDEST THING I CAN IMAGINE DOING...
WHAT?!? SPEAK UP!
YOU'RE GOING TO NEED TO BE QUIET NOW. WHAT SORT OF IDIOT THROWS A FLASHBANG–
HARRINGTON IS GOING TO FIND OUT WE'RE BOTH HERE IF WE DON'T GO NOW. DID YOU GET JANET?
YES, AND SHE'S CALLING LAFONG RIGHT NOW, WHICH IS SOMETHING I SHOULD HAVE DONE BEFORE STARTING THIS STUPID ESCAPADE...
WHAT?!? WHAT ABOUT LAFONG?!? WE SHOULD GET THAT EMP THING, TOO.
DROMEDARY. IT'S CALLED DROMEDARY.
WHAT?!?
YES, DETECTIVE LAFONG, PLEASE.
YES, I'LL HOLD.
MUSTA BEEN A HELL OF A PARTY UP THERE.
WITH THE LAST FEW MONTHS I'VE HAD, I COULD BEAT YOU TO DEATH WITH THIS PHONE WITH NO COMPUNCTION WHATSOEVER. NOW PLEASE, SIT THERE ON YOUR HANDS AND SHUT THE HELL UP WHILE I DO MY PART TO STOP AN INTERNATIONAL ARMS DEALER THAT HAS KEPT ME AS, QUITE LITERALLY, A SLAVE.
OKAY.

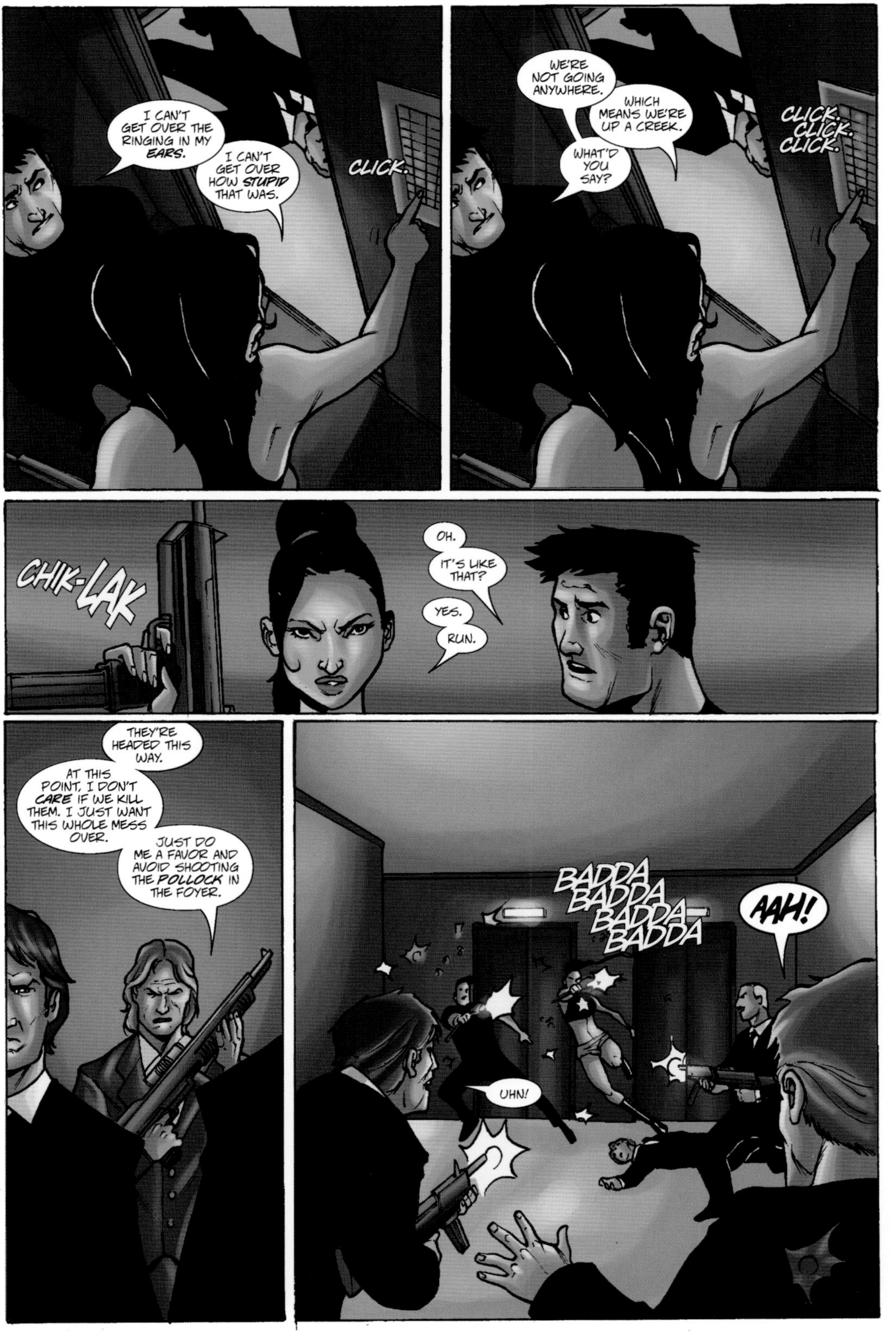
I CAN'T GET OVER THE RINGING IN MY EARS.
I CAN'T GET OVER HOW STUPID THAT WAS.
CLICK.
WE'RE NOT GOING ANYWHERE.
WHICH MEANS WE'RE UP A CREEK.
WHAT'D YOU SAY?
CLICK. CLICK. CLICK.
CHIK-LAK
OH.
IT'S LIKE THAT?
YES.
RUN.
THEY'RE HEADED THIS WAY.
AT THIS POINT, I DON'T CARE IF WE KILL THEM. I JUST WANT THIS WHOLE MESS OVER.
JUST DO ME A FAVOR AND AVOID SHOOTING THE POLLOCK IN THE FOYER.
BADDA BADDA BADDA-BADDA
AAH!
UHN!

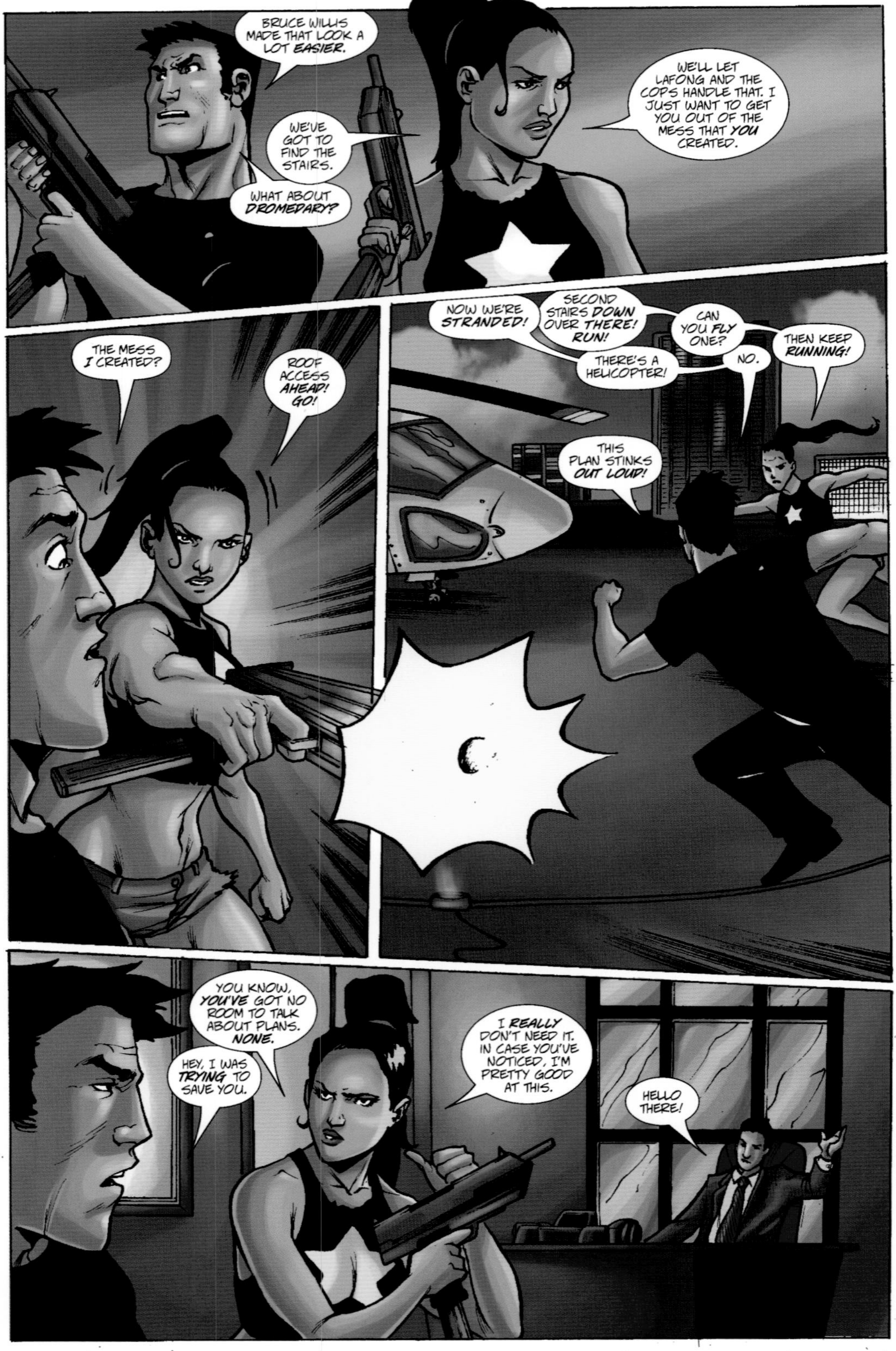
BRUCE WILLIS MADE THAT LOOK A LOT EASIER.
WE'VE GOT TO FIND THE STAIRS.
WHAT ABOUT DROMEDARY?
WE'LL LET LAFONG AND THE COPS HANDLE THAT. I JUST WANT TO GET YOU OUT OF THE MESS THAT YOU CREATED.
THE MESS I CREATED?
ROOF ACCESS AHEAD! GO!
NOW WE'RE STRANDED!
THERE'S A HELICOPTER!
SECOND STAIRS DOWN OVER THERE! RUN!
CAN YOU FLY ONE?
NO.
THEN KEEP RUNNING!
THIS PLAN STINKS OUT LOUD!
YOU KNOW, YOU'VE GOT NO ROOM TO TALK ABOUT PLANS. NONE.
HEY, I WAS TRYING TO SAVE YOU.
I REALLY DON'T NEED IT. IN CASE YOU'VE NOTICED, I'M PRETTY GOOD AT THIS.
HELLO THERE!

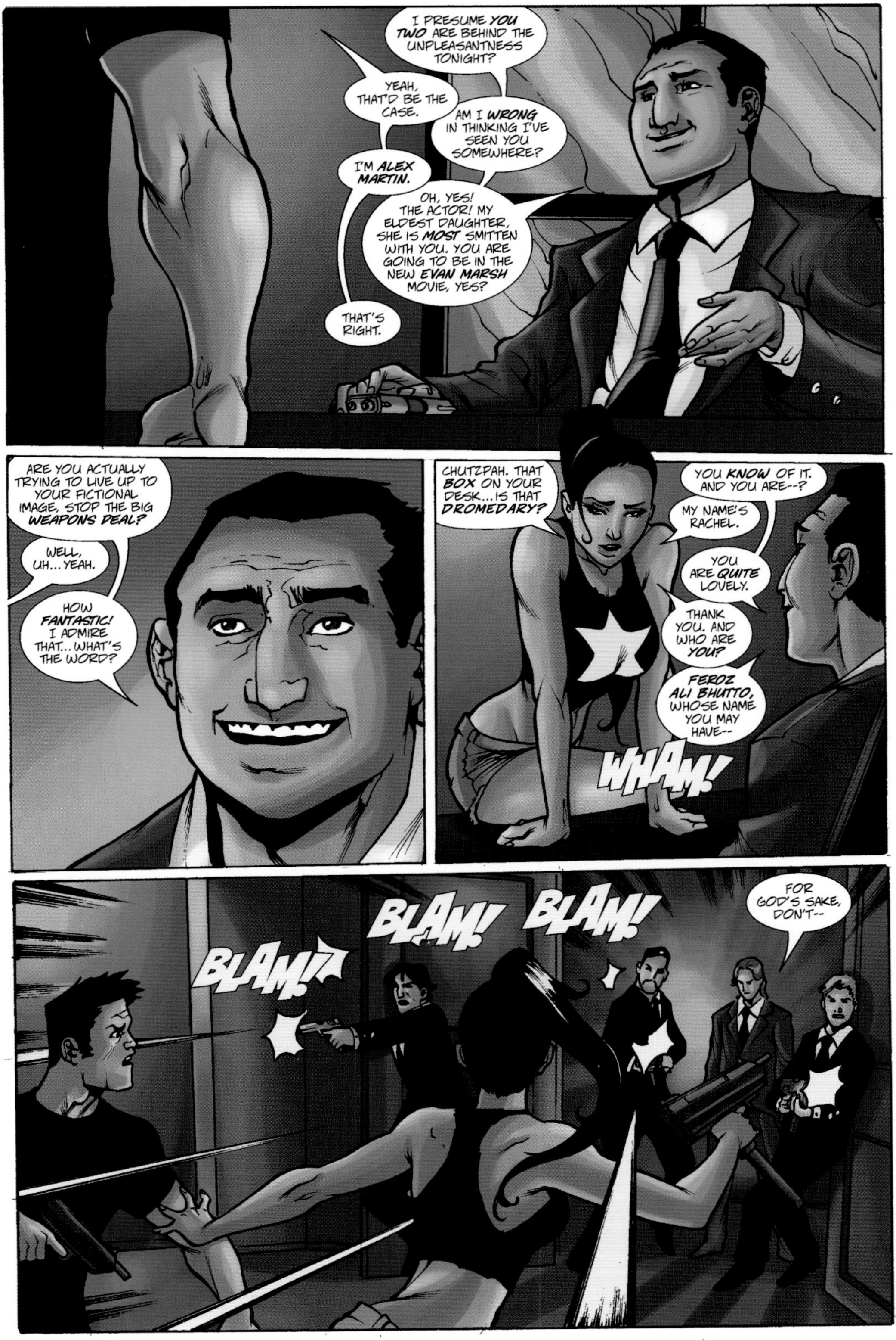
I PRESUME YOU TWO ARE BEHIND THE UNPLEASANTNESS TONIGHT?
YEAH, THAT'D BE THE CASE.
AM I WRONG IN THINKING I'VE SEEN YOU SOMEWHERE?
I'M ALEX MARTIN.
OH, YES! THE ACTOR! MY ELDEST DAUGHTER, SHE IS MOST SMITTEN WITH YOU. YOU ARE GOING TO BE IN THE NEW EVAN MARSH MOVIE, YES?
THAT'S RIGHT.
ARE YOU ACTUALLY TRYING TO LIVE UP TO YOUR FICTIONAL IMAGE, STOP THE BIG WEAPONS DEAL?
WELL, UH... YEAH.
HOW FANTASTIC! I ADMIRE THAT... WHAT'S THE WORD?
CHUTZPAH. THAT BOX ON YOUR DESK... IS THAT DROMEDARY?
YOU KNOW OF IT. AND YOU ARE--?
MY NAME'S RACHEL.
YOU ARE QUITE LOVELY.
THANK YOU. AND WHO ARE YOU?
FEROZ ALI BHUTTO, WHOSE NAME YOU MAY HAVE--
WHAM!
BLAM!
BLAM!
BLAM!
FOR GOD'S SAKE, DON'T--

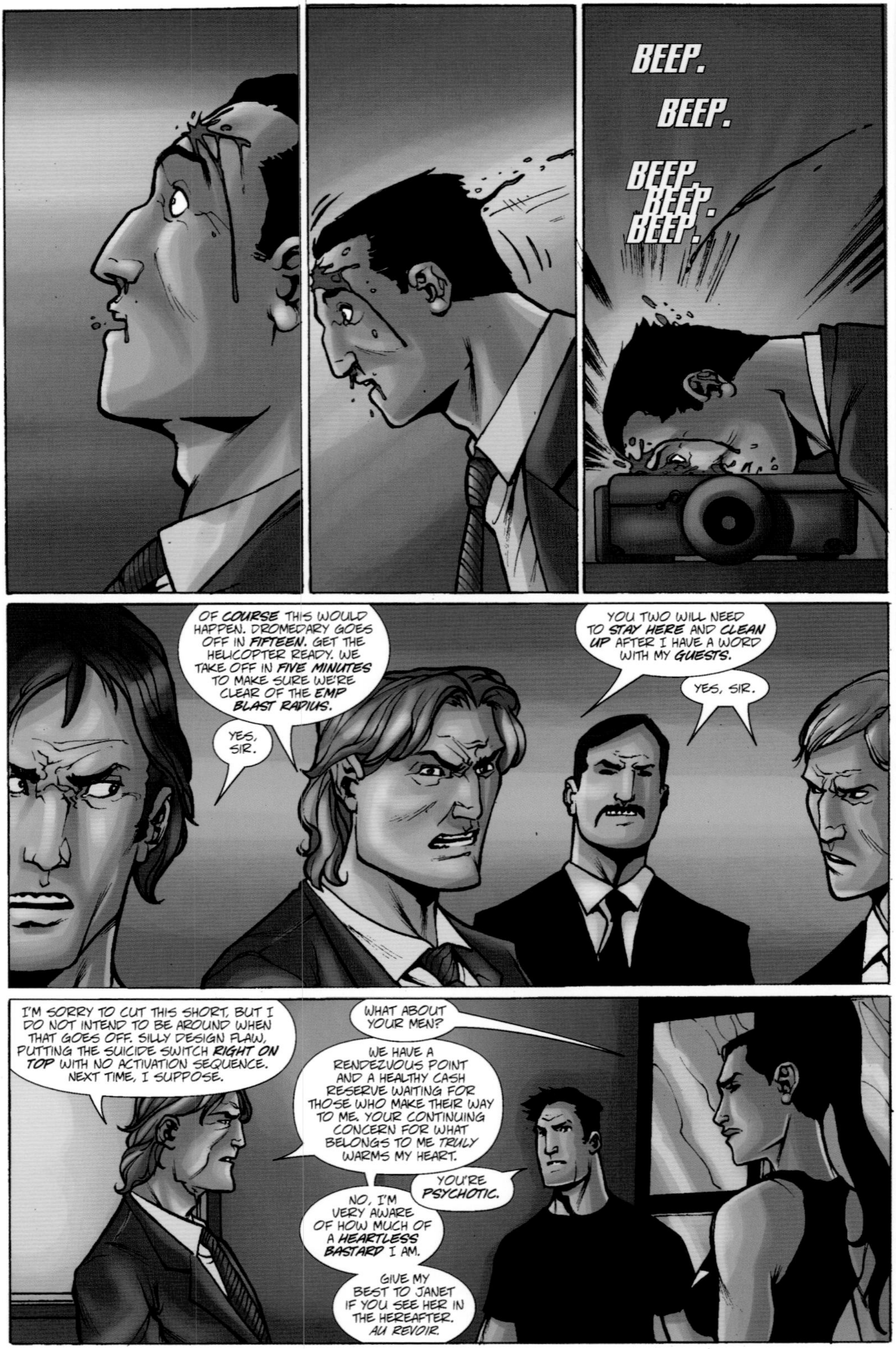

BEEP.
BEEP.
BEEP. BEEP. BEEP.
OF COURSE THIS WOULD HAPPEN. DROMEDARY GOES OFF IN FIFTEEN. GET THE HELICOPTER READY. WE TAKE OFF IN FIVE MINUTES TO MAKE SURE WE'RE CLEAR OF THE EMP BLAST RADIUS.
YES, SIR.
YOU TWO WILL NEED TO STAY HERE AND CLEAN UP AFTER I HAVE A WORD WITH MY GUESTS.
YES, SIR.
I'M SORRY TO CUT THIS SHORT, BUT I DO NOT INTEND TO BE AROUND WHEN THAT GOES OFF. SILLY DESIGN FLAW, PUTTING THE SUICIDE SWITCH RIGHT ON TOP WITH NO ACTIVATION SEQUENCE. NEXT TIME, I SUPPOSE.
WHAT ABOUT YOUR MEN?
WE HAVE A RENDEZVOUS POINT AND A HEALTHY CASH RESERVE WAITING FOR THOSE WHO MAKE THEIR WAY TO ME. YOUR CONTINUING CONCERN FOR WHAT BELONGS TO ME TRULY WARMS MY HEART.
YOU'RE PSYCHOTIC.
NO, I'M VERY AWARE OF HOW MUCH OF A HEARTLESS BASTARD I AM.
GIVE MY BEST TO JANET IF YOU SEE HER IN THE HEREAFTER. AU REVOIR.

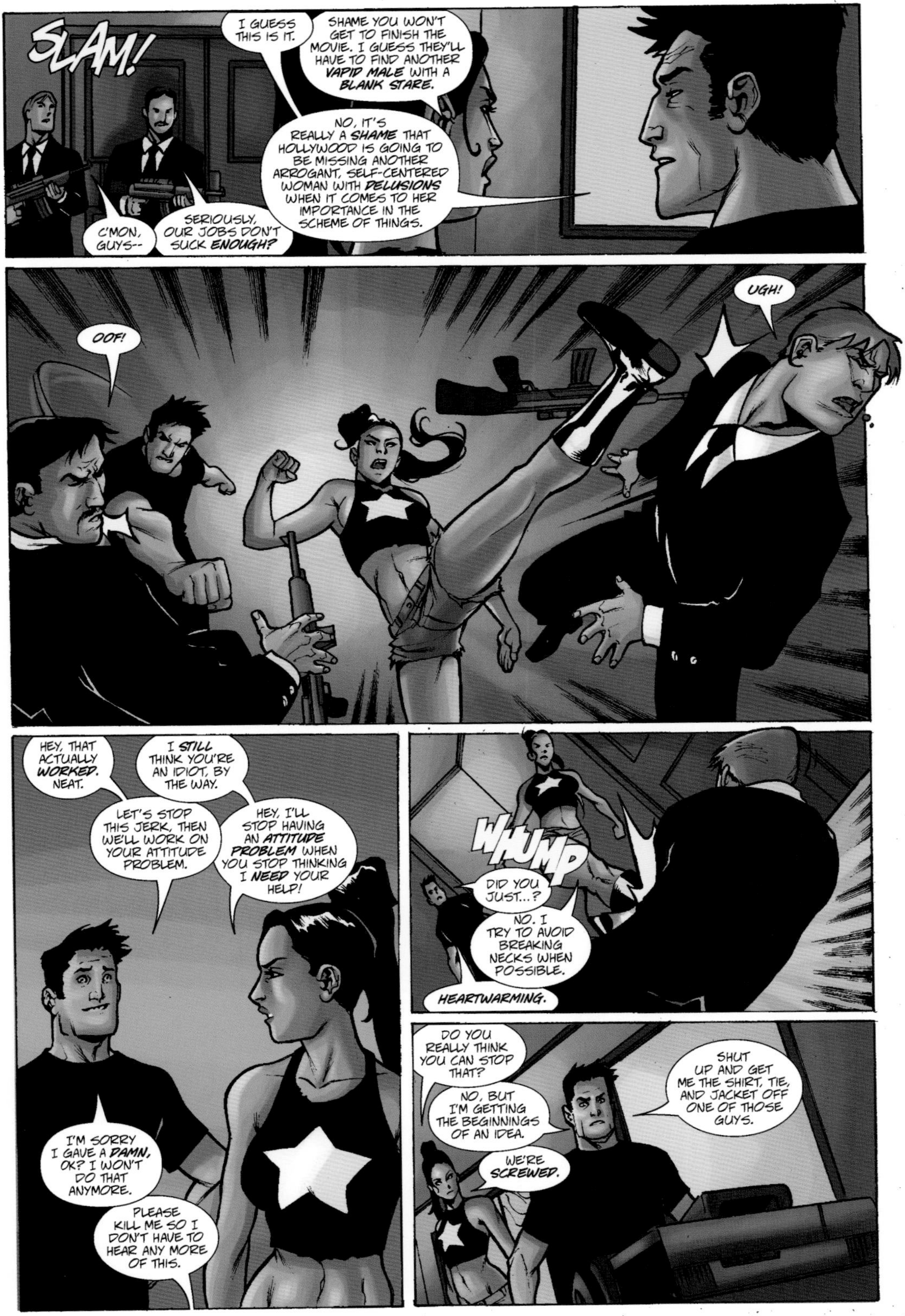
SLAM!
I GUESS THIS IS IT.
SHAME YOU WON'T GET TO FINISH THE MOVIE. I GUESS THEY'LL HAVE TO FIND ANOTHER VAPID MALE WITH A BLANK STARE.
NO, IT'S REALLY A SHAME THAT HOLLYWOOD IS GOING TO BE MISSING ANOTHER ARROGANT, SELF-CENTERED WOMAN WITH DELUSIONS WHEN IT COMES TO HER IMPORTANCE IN THE SCHEME OF THINGS.
C'MON, GUYS--
SERIOUSLY, OUR JOBS DON'T SUCK ENOUGH?
OOF!
UGH!
HEY, THAT ACTUALLY WORKED. NEAT.
I STILL THINK YOU'RE AN IDIOT, BY THE WAY.
LET'S STOP THIS JERK, THEN WE'LL WORK ON YOUR ATTITUDE PROBLEM.
HEY, I'LL STOP HAVING AN ATTITUDE PROBLEM WHEN YOU STOP THINKING I NEED YOUR HELP!
I'M SORRY I GAVE A DAMN, OK? I WON'T DO THAT ANYMORE.
PLEASE KILL ME SO I DON'T HAVE TO HEAR ANY MORE OF THIS.
WHUMP
DID YOU JUST...?
NO. I TRY TO AVOID BREAKING NECKS WHEN POSSIBLE.
HEARTWARMING.
DO YOU REALLY THINK YOU CAN STOP THAT?
NO, BUT I'M GETTING THE BEGINNINGS OF AN IDEA.
SHUT UP AND GET ME THE SHIRT, TIE, AND JACKET OFF ONE OF THOSE GUYS.
WE'RE SCREWED.

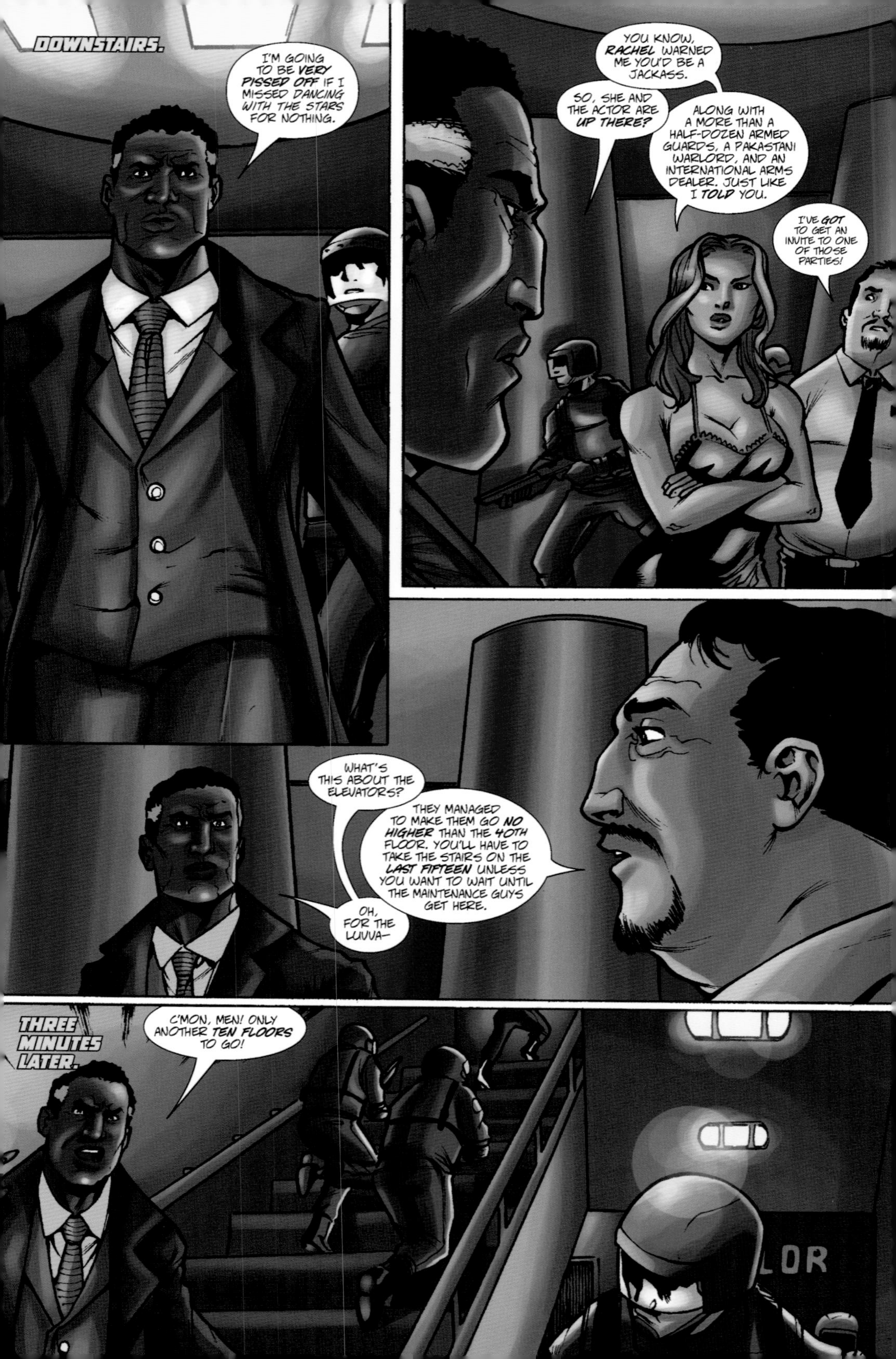
DOWNSTAIRS.
I'M GOING TO BE VERY PISSED OFF IF I MISSED DANCING WITH THE STARS FOR NOTHING.
YOU KNOW, RACHEL WARNED ME YOU'D BE A JACKASS.
SO, SHE AND THE ACTOR ARE UP THERE?
ALONG WITH A MORE THAN A HALF-DOZEN ARMED GUARDS, A PAKASTANI WARLORD, AND AN INTERNATIONAL ARMS DEALER. JUST LIKE I TOLD YOU.
I'VE GOT TO GET AN INVITE TO ONE OF THOSE PARTIES!
WHAT'S THIS ABOUT THE ELEVATORS?
THEY MANAGED TO MAKE THEM GO NO HIGHER THAN THE 40TH FLOOR. YOU'LL HAVE TO TAKE THE STAIRS ON THE LAST FIFTEEN UNLESS YOU WANT TO WAIT UNTIL THE MAINTENANCE GUYS GET HERE.
OH, FOR THE LUVVA-
THREE MINUTES LATER.
C'MON, MEN! ONLY ANOTHER TEN FLOORS TO GO!
LOR

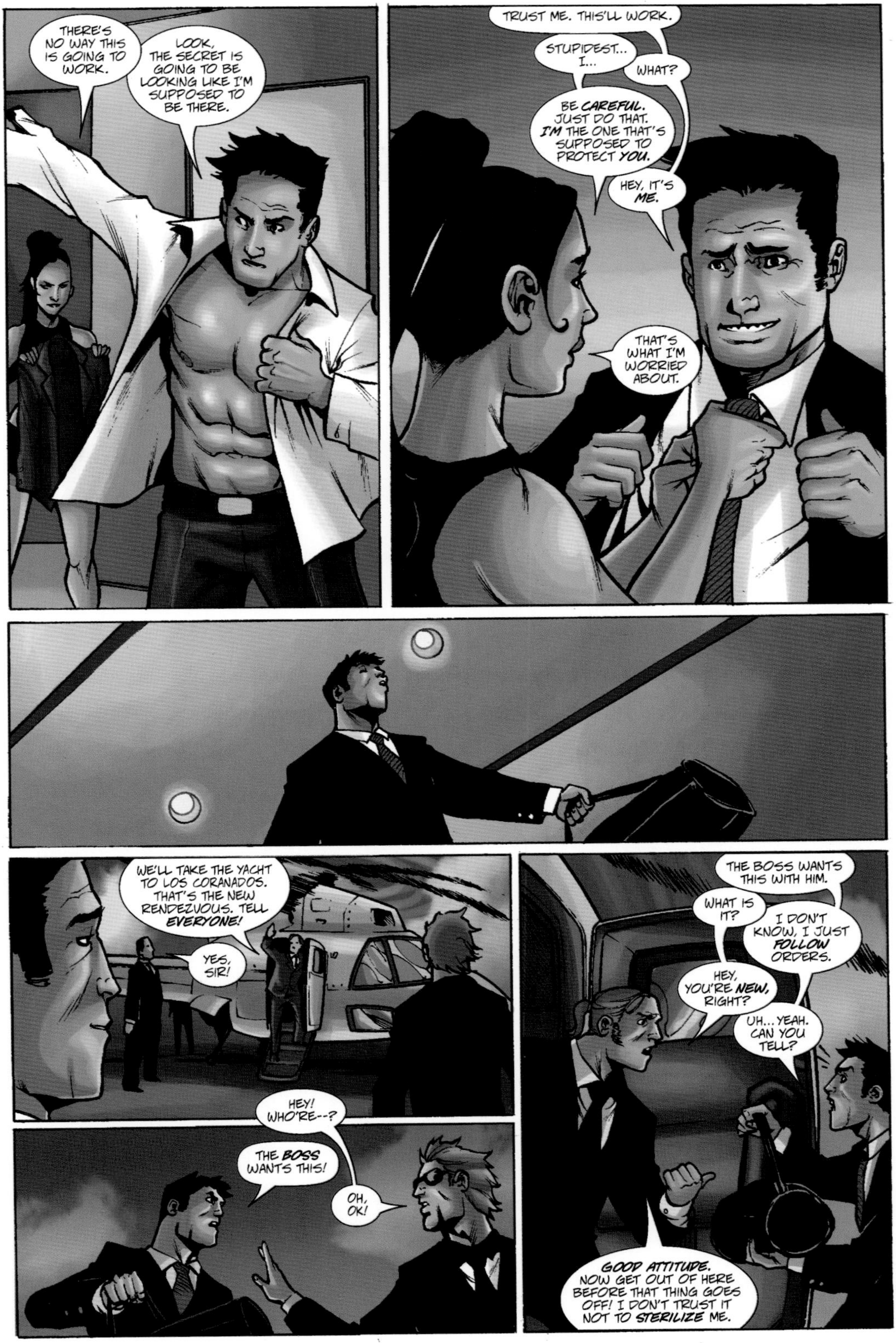
THERE'S NO WAY THIS IS GOING TO WORK.
LOOK, THE SECRET IS GOING TO BE LOOKING LIKE I'M SUPPOSED TO BE THERE.
TRUST ME. THIS'LL WORK.
STUPIDEST... I...
WHAT?
BE CAREFUL. JUST DO THAT. I'M THE ONE THAT'S SUPPOSED TO PROTECT YOU.
HEY, IT'S ME.
THAT'S WHAT I'M WORRIED ABOUT.
WE'LL TAKE THE YACHT TO LOS CORANADOS. THAT'S THE NEW RENDEZVOUS. TELL EVERYONE!
YES, SIR!
HEY! WHO'RE--?
THE BOSS WANTS THIS!
OH, OK!
THE BOSS WANTS THIS WITH HIM.
WHAT IS IT?
I DON'T KNOW, I JUST FOLLOW ORDERS.
HEY, YOU'RE NEW, RIGHT?
UH... YEAH. CAN YOU TELL?
GOOD ATTITUDE. NOW GET OUT OF HERE BEFORE THAT THING GOES OFF! I DON'T TRUST IT NOT TO STERILIZE ME.

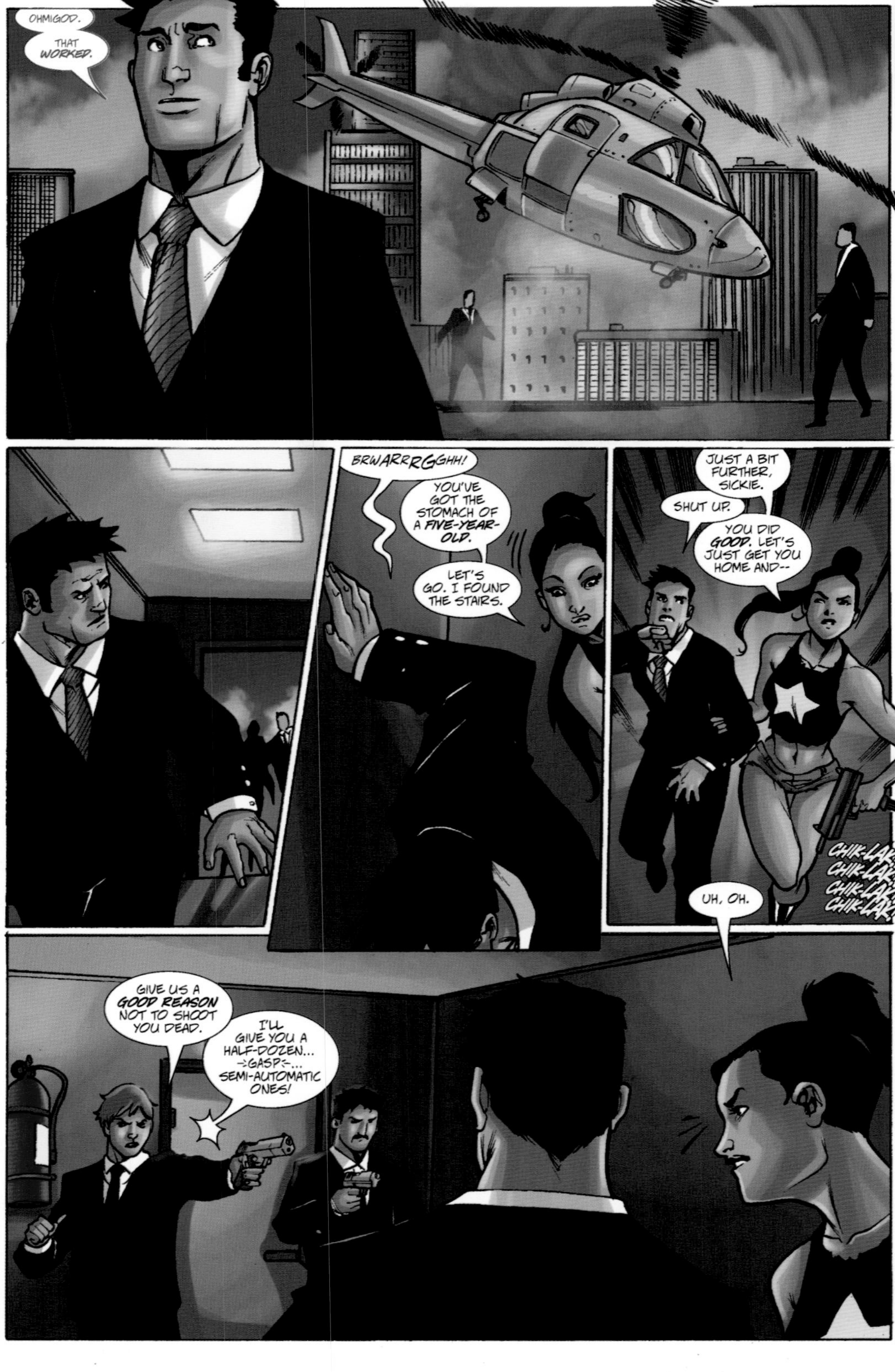
OHMIGOD.
THAT WORKED.
BRWARRRGGHH!
YOU'VE GOT THE STOMACH OF A FIVE-YEAR-OLD.
LET'S GO. I FOUND THE STAIRS.
JUST A BIT FURTHER, SICKIE.
SHUT UP.
YOU DID GOOD. LET'S JUST GET YOU HOME AND--
CHIK-LAK! CHIK-LAK! CHIK-LAK! CHIK-LAK!
UH, OH.
GIVE US A GOOD REASON NOT TO SHOOT YOU DEAD.
I'LL GIVE YOU A HALF-DOZEN... -GASP-... SEMI-AUTOMATIC ONES!

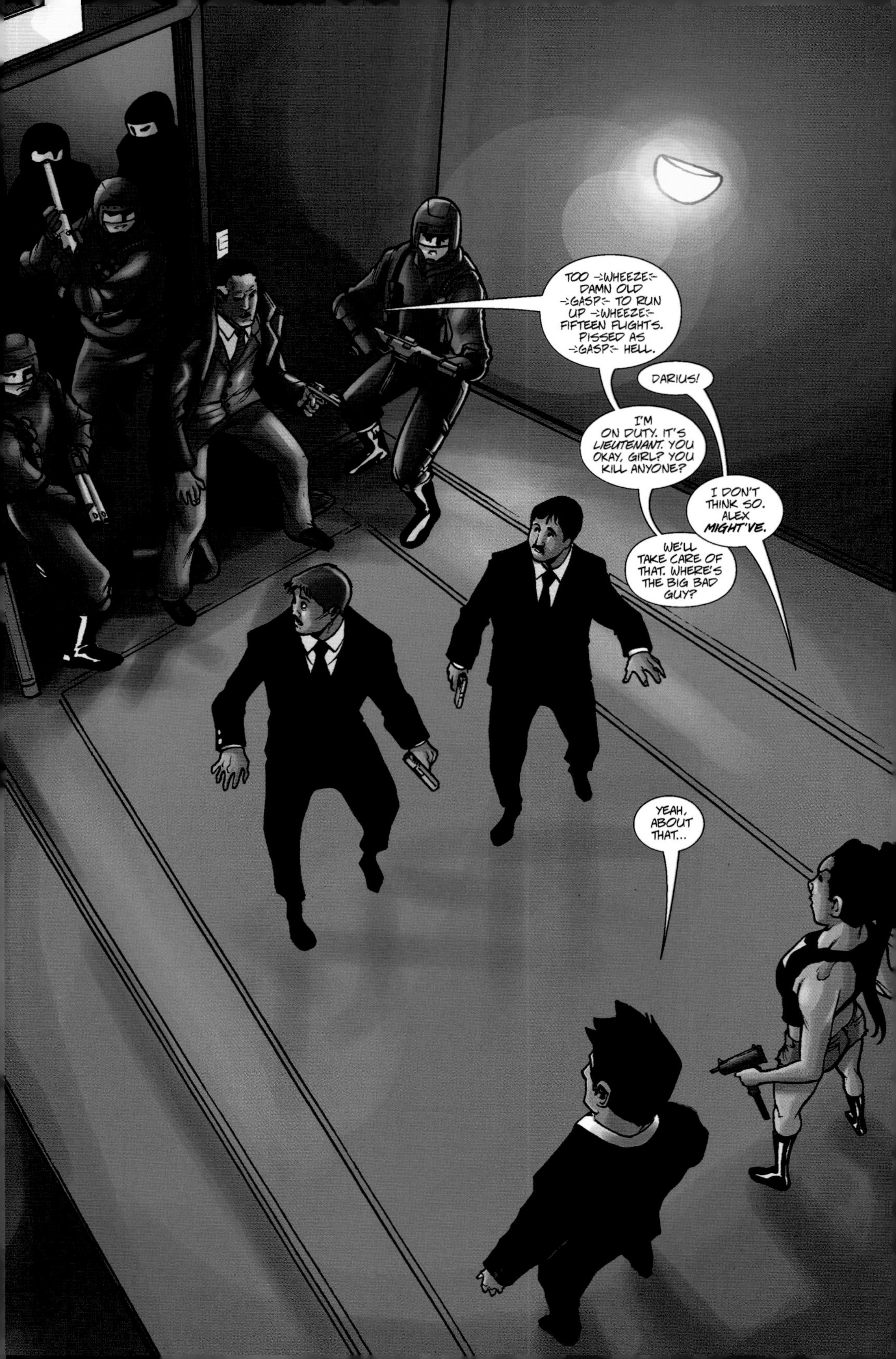
TOO -WHEEZE- DAMN OLD -GASP- TO RUN UP -WHEEZE- FIFTEEN FLIGHTS. PISSED AS -GASP- HELL.
DARIUS!
I'M ON DUTY. IT'S *LIEUTENANT*. YOU OKAY, GIRL? YOU KILL ANYONE?
I DON'T THINK SO. ALEX ***MIGHT'VE.***
WE'LL TAKE CARE OF THAT. WHERE'S THE BIG BAD GUY?
YEAH, ABOUT THAT...

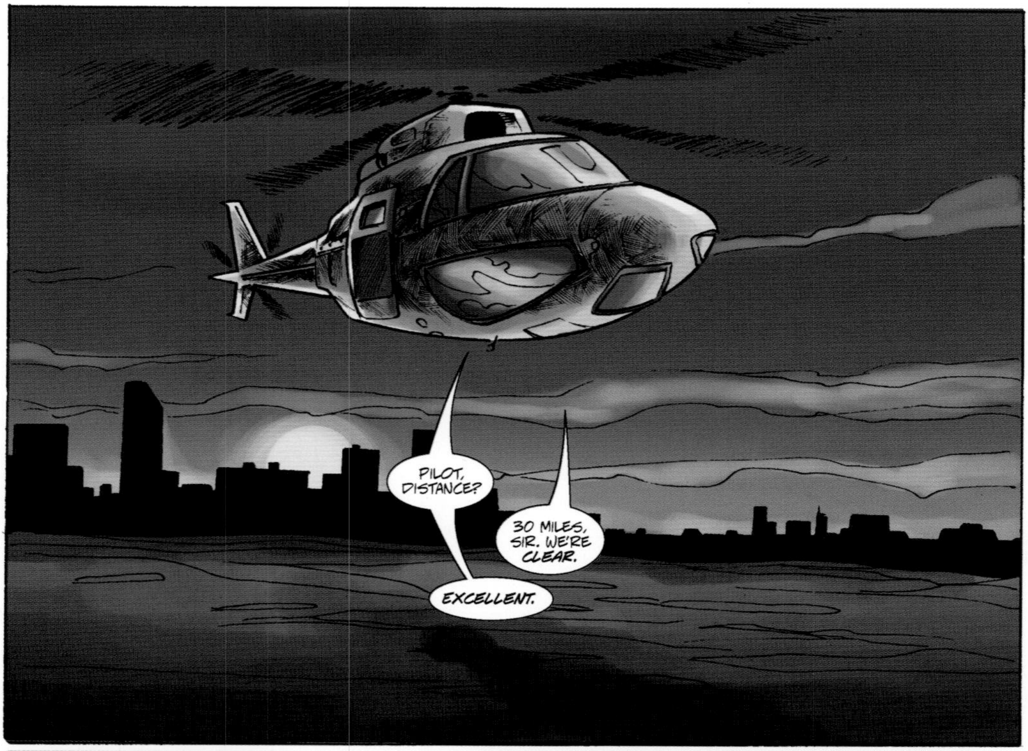
PILOT, DISTANCE?
30 MILES, SIR. WE'RE CLEAR.
EXCELLENT.

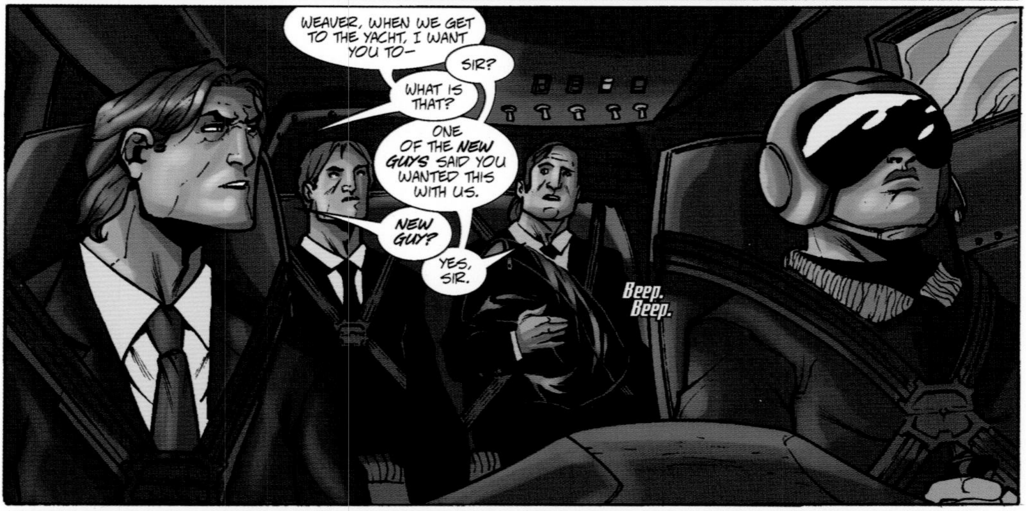
WEAVER, WHEN WE GET TO THE YACHT, I WANT YOU TO—
SIR?
WHAT IS THAT?
ONE OF THE NEW GUYS SAID YOU WANTED THIS WITH US.
NEW GUY?
YES, SIR.
Beep. Beep.

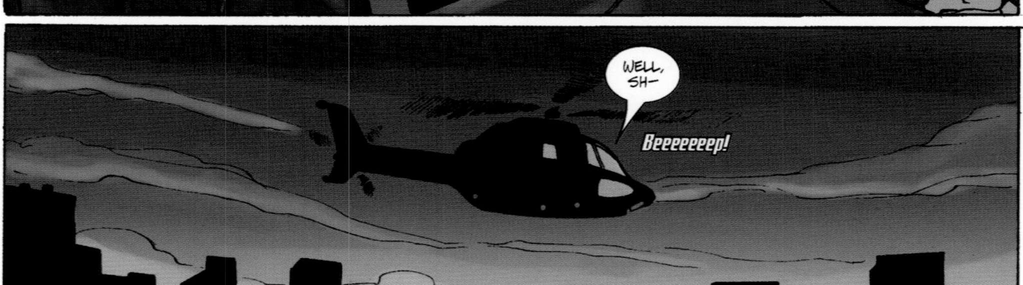
WELL, SH—
Beeeeeeep!

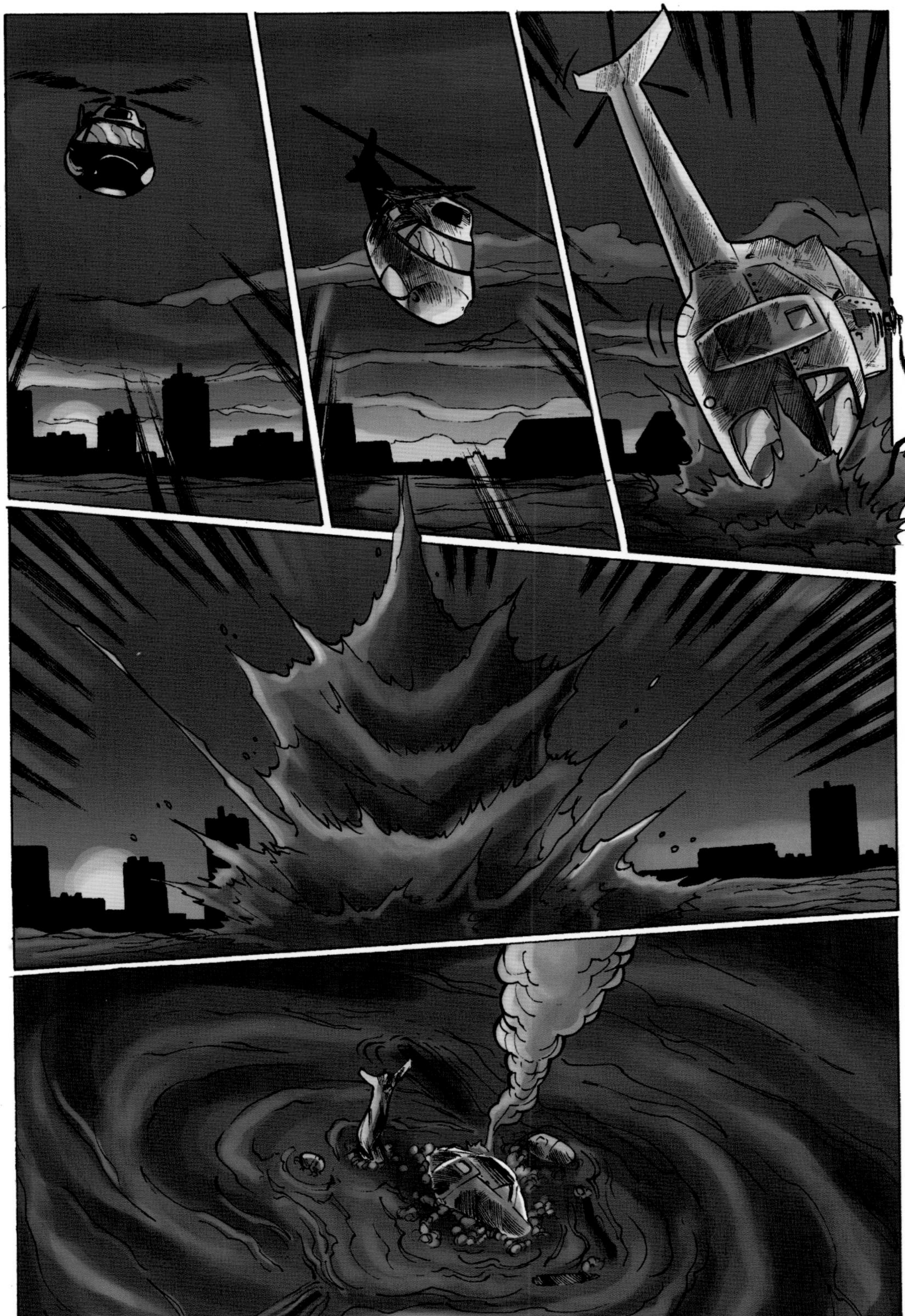

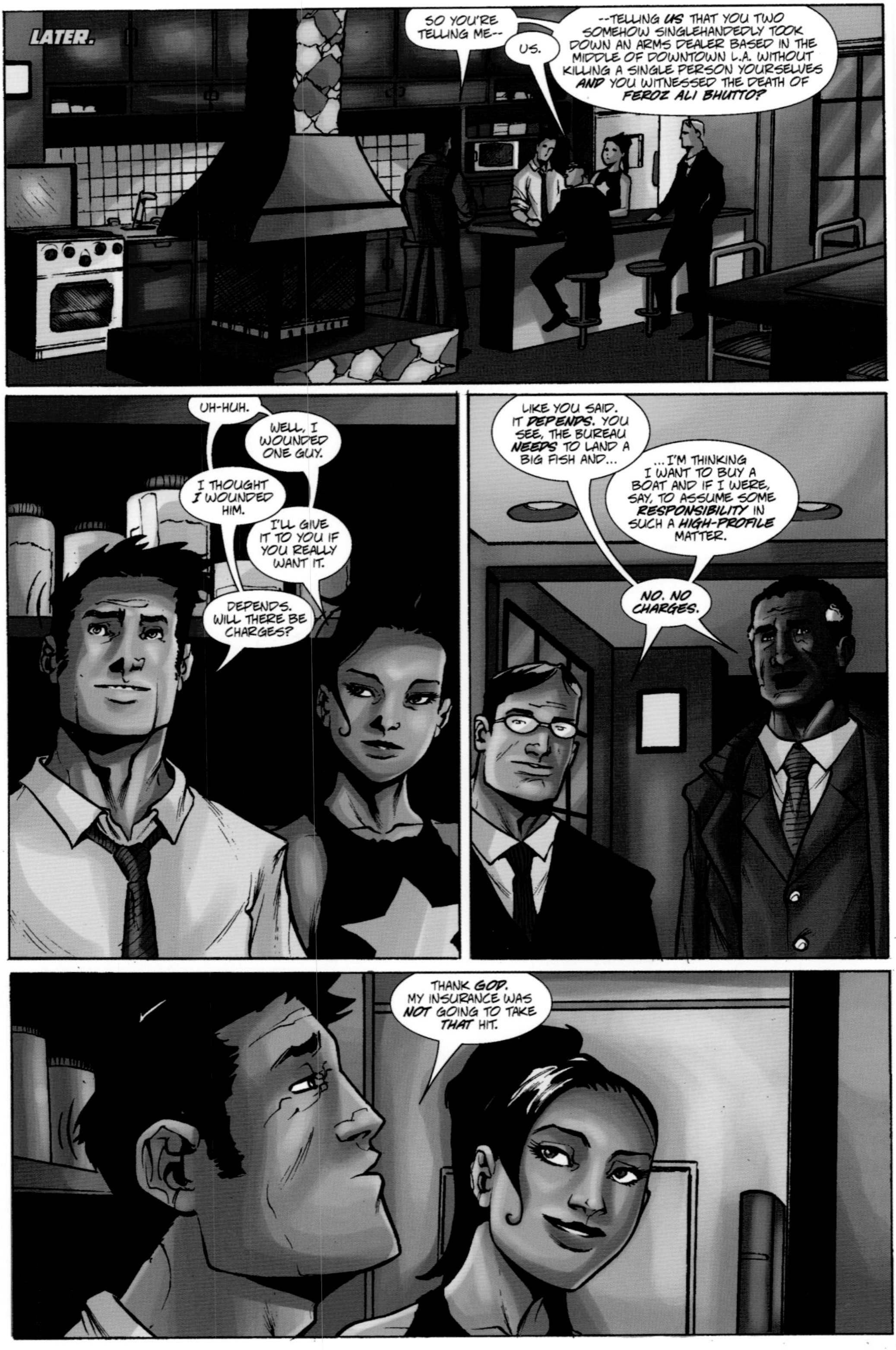
LATER.
SO YOU'RE TELLING ME--
US.
--TELLING US THAT YOU TWO SOMEHOW SINGLEHANDEDLY TOOK DOWN AN ARMS DEALER BASED IN THE MIDDLE OF DOWNTOWN L.A. WITHOUT KILLING A SINGLE PERSON YOURSELVES AND YOU WITNESSED THE DEATH OF FEROZ ALI BHUTTO?
UH-HUH.
WELL, I WOUNDED ONE GUY.
I THOUGHT I WOUNDED HIM.
I'LL GIVE IT TO YOU IF YOU REALLY WANT IT.
DEPENDS. WILL THERE BE CHARGES?
LIKE YOU SAID. IT DEPENDS. YOU SEE, THE BUREAU NEEDS TO LAND A BIG FISH AND...
...I'M THINKING I WANT TO BUY A BOAT AND IF I WERE, SAY, TO ASSUME SOME RESPONSIBILITY IN SUCH A HIGH-PROFILE MATTER.
NO. NO CHARGES.
THANK GOD. MY INSURANCE WAS NOT GOING TO TAKE THAT HIT.

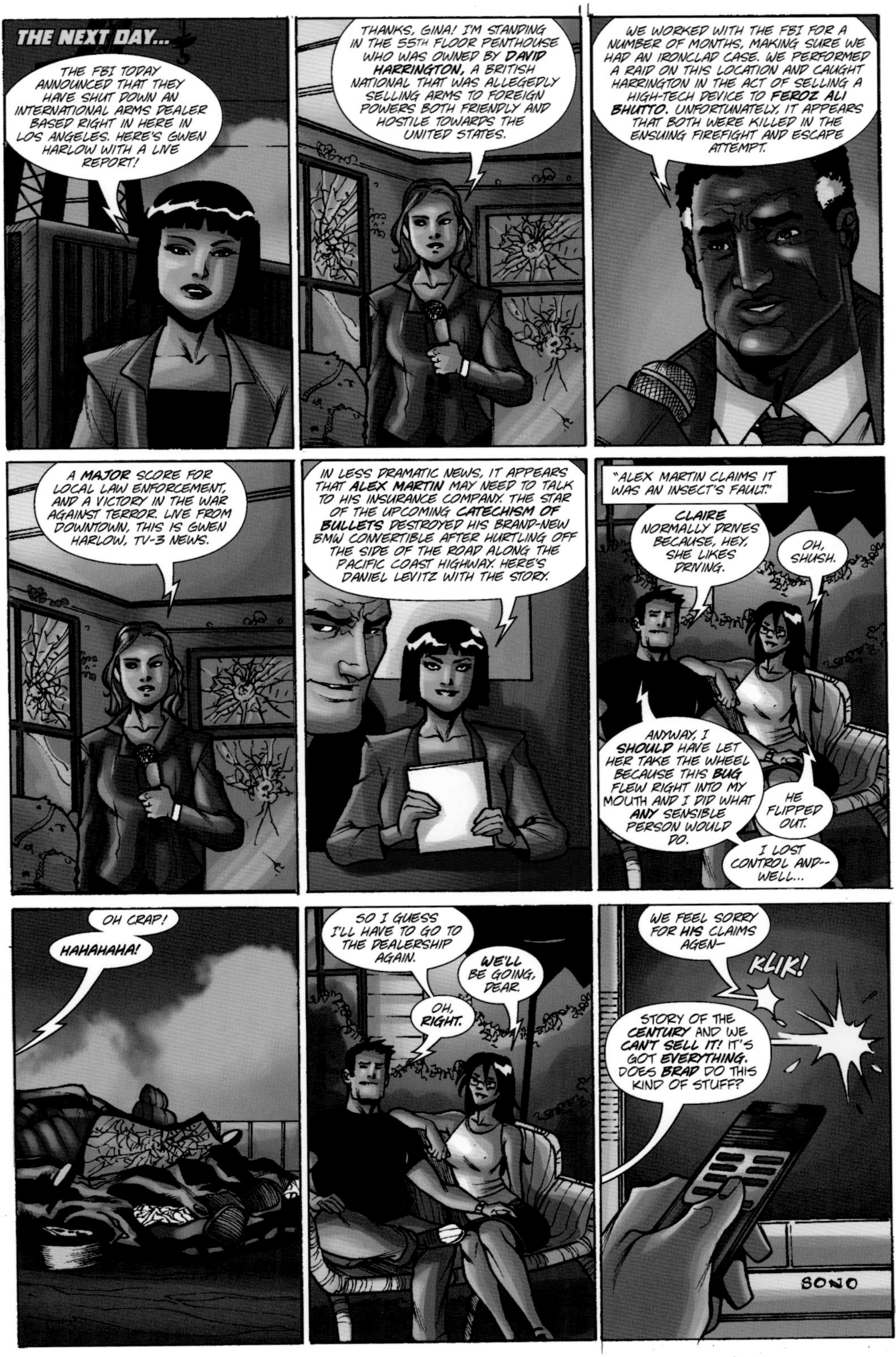

THE NEXT DAY...
THE FBI TODAY ANNOUNCED THAT THEY HAVE SHUT DOWN AN INTERNATIONAL ARMS DEALER BASED RIGHT IN HERE IN LOS ANGELES. HERE'S GWEN HARLOW WITH A LIVE REPORT!
THANKS, GINA! I'M STANDING IN THE 55TH FLOOR PENTHOUSE WHO WAS OWNED BY DAVID HARRINGTON, A BRITISH NATIONAL THAT WAS ALLEGEDLY SELLING ARMS TO FOREIGN POWERS BOTH FRIENDLY AND HOSTILE TOWARDS THE UNITED STATES.
WE WORKED WITH THE FBI FOR A NUMBER OF MONTHS, MAKING SURE WE HAD AN IRONCLAD CASE. WE PERFORMED A RAID ON THIS LOCATION AND CAUGHT HARRINGTON IN THE ACT OF SELLING A HIGH-TECH DEVICE TO FEROZ ALI BHUTTO. UNFORTUNATELY, IT APPEARS THAT BOTH WERE KILLED IN THE ENSUING FIREFIGHT AND ESCAPE ATTEMPT.
A MAJOR SCORE FOR LOCAL LAW ENFORCEMENT, AND A VICTORY IN THE WAR AGAINST TERROR. LIVE FROM DOWNTOWN, THIS IS GWEN HARLOW, TV-3 NEWS.
IN LESS DRAMATIC NEWS, IT APPEARS THAT ALEX MARTIN MAY NEED TO TALK TO HIS INSURANCE COMPANY. THE STAR OF THE UPCOMING CATECHISM OF BULLETS DESTROYED HIS BRAND-NEW BMW CONVERTIBLE AFTER HURTLING OFF THE SIDE OF THE ROAD ALONG THE PACIFIC COAST HIGHWAY. HERE'S DANIEL LEVITZ WITH THE STORY.
"ALEX MARTIN CLAIMS IT WAS AN INSECT'S FAULT."
CLAIRE NORMALLY DRIVES BECAUSE, HEY, SHE LIKES DRIVING.
OH, SHUSH.
ANYWAY, I SHOULD HAVE LET HER TAKE THE WHEEL BECAUSE THIS BUG FLEW RIGHT INTO MY MOUTH AND I DID WHAT ANY SENSIBLE PERSON WOULD DO.
HE FLIPPED OUT.
I LOST CONTROL AND-- WELL...
OH CRAP!
HAHAHAHA!
SO I GUESS I'LL HAVE TO GO TO THE DEALERSHIP AGAIN.
OH, RIGHT.
WE'LL BE GOING, DEAR.
WE FEEL SORRY FOR HIS CLAIMS AGEN—
KLIK!
STORY OF THE CENTURY AND WE CAN'T SELL IT! IT'S GOT EVERYTHING. DOES BRAD DO THIS KIND OF STUFF?
SONO

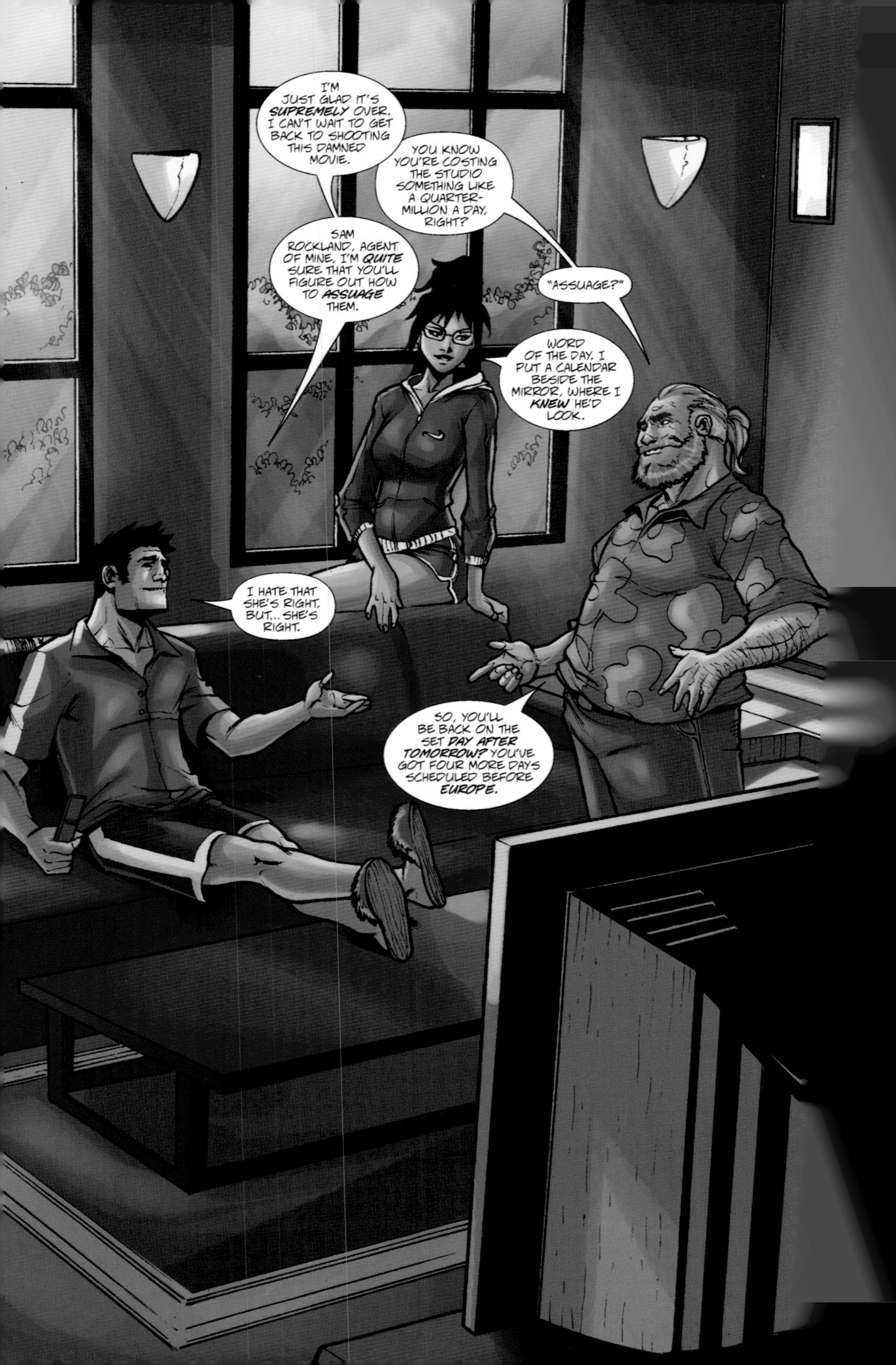
I'M JUST GLAD IT'S SUPREMELY OVER. I CAN'T WAIT TO GET BACK TO SHOOTING THIS DAMNED MOVIE.
YOU KNOW YOU'RE COSTING THE STUDIO SOMETHING LIKE A QUARTER-MILLION A DAY, RIGHT?
SAM ROCKLAND, AGENT OF MINE, I'M QUITE SURE THAT YOU'LL FIGURE OUT HOW TO ASSUAGE THEM.
"ASSUAGE?"
WORD OF THE DAY. I PUT A CALENDAR BESIDE THE MIRROR, WHERE I KNEW HE'D LOOK.
I HATE THAT SHE'S RIGHT, BUT... SHE'S RIGHT.
SO, YOU'LL BE BACK ON THE SET DAY AFTER TOMORROW? YOU'VE GOT FOUR MORE DAYS SCHEDULED BEFORE EUROPE.

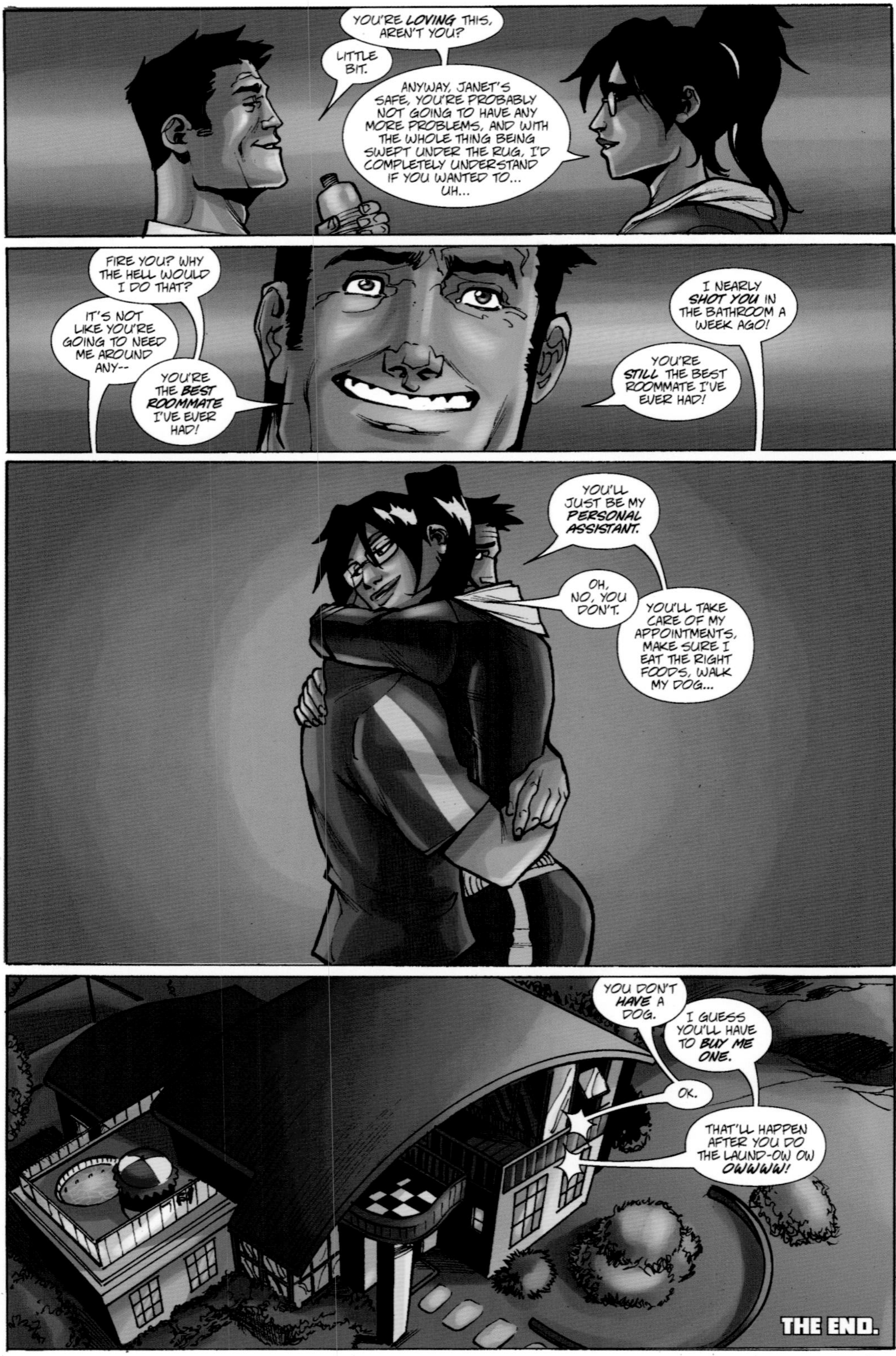
YOU'RE LOVING THIS, AREN'T YOU?
LITTLE BIT.
ANYWAY, JANET'S SAFE, YOU'RE PROBABLY NOT GOING TO HAVE ANY MORE PROBLEMS, AND WITH THE WHOLE THING BEING SWEPT UNDER THE RUG, I'D COMPLETELY UNDERSTAND IF YOU WANTED TO... UH...
FIRE YOU? WHY THE HELL WOULD I DO THAT?
IT'S NOT LIKE YOU'RE GOING TO NEED ME AROUND ANY--
YOU'RE THE BEST ROOMMATE I'VE EVER HAD!
I NEARLY SHOT YOU IN THE BATHROOM A WEEK AGO!
YOU'RE STILL THE BEST ROOMMATE I'VE EVER HAD!
YOU'LL JUST BE MY PERSONAL ASSISTANT.
OH, NO, YOU DON'T.
YOU'LL TAKE CARE OF MY APPOINTMENTS, MAKE SURE I EAT THE RIGHT FOODS, WALK MY DOG...
YOU DON'T HAVE A DOG.
I GUESS YOU'LL HAVE TO BUY ME ONE.
OK.
THAT'LL HAPPEN AFTER YOU DO THE LAUND-OW OW OWWWW!
THE END.

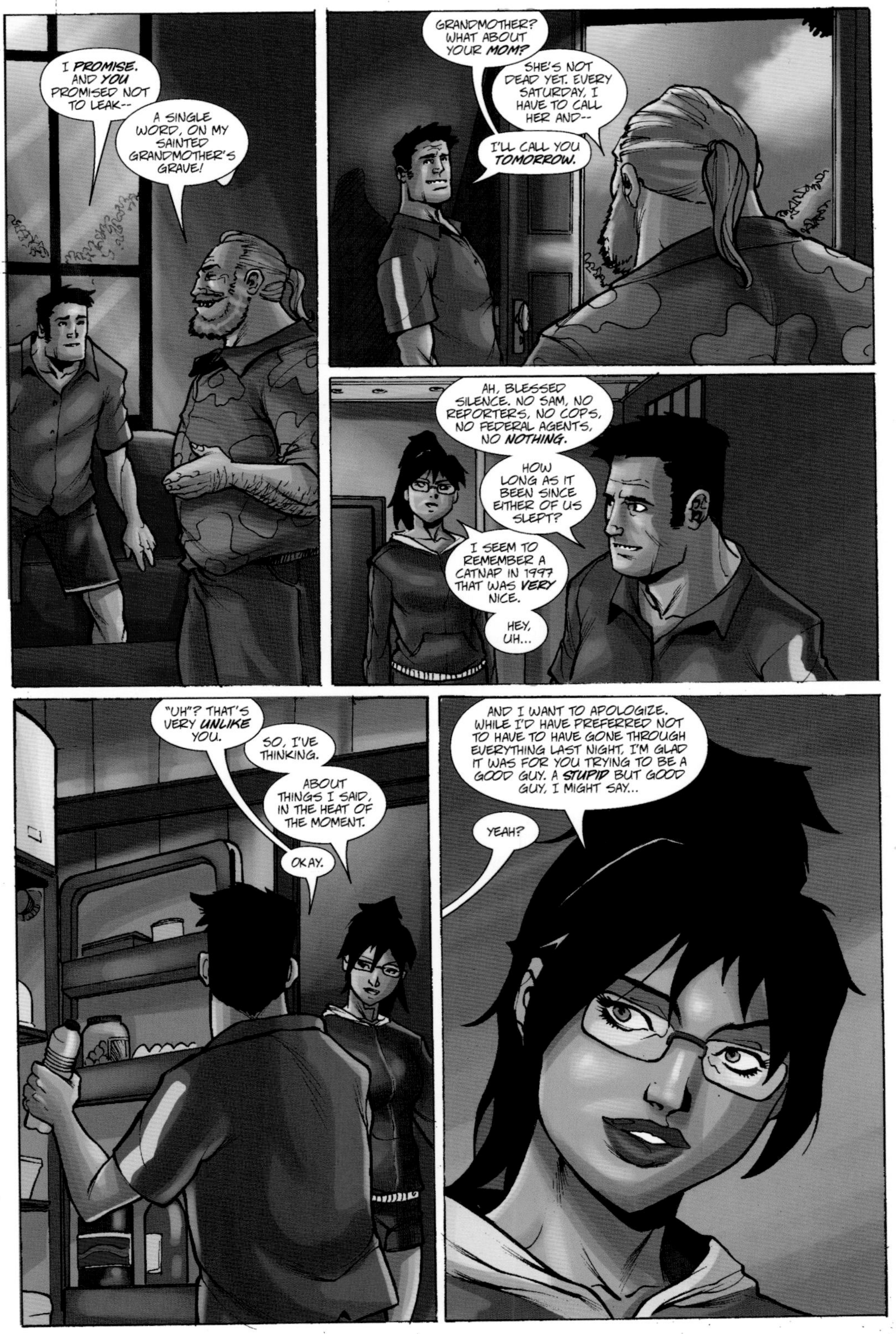

I **PROMISE.** AND **YOU** PROMISED NOT TO LEAK--
A SINGLE WORD, ON MY SAINTED GRANDMOTHER'S GRAVE!
GRANDMOTHER? WHAT ABOUT YOUR **MOM?**
SHE'S NOT DEAD YET. EVERY SATURDAY, I HAVE TO CALL HER AND--
I'LL CALL YOU **TOMORROW.**
AH, BLESSED SILENCE. NO SAM, NO REPORTERS, NO COPS, NO FEDERAL AGENTS, NO **NOTHING.**
HOW LONG AS IT BEEN SINCE EITHER OF US SLEPT?
I SEEM TO REMEMBER A CATNAP IN 1997 THAT WAS **VERY** NICE.
HEY, UH...
"UH"? THAT'S VERY **UNLIKE** YOU.
SO, I'VE THINKING.
ABOUT THINGS I SAID, IN THE HEAT OF THE MOMENT.
OKAY.
AND I WANT TO APOLOGIZE. WHILE I'D HAVE PREFERRED NOT TO HAVE TO HAVE GONE THROUGH EVERYTHING LAST NIGHT, I'M GLAD IT WAS FOR YOU TRYING TO BE A GOOD GUY. A **STUPID** BUT GOOD GUY, I MIGHT SAY...
YEAH?

TRADE PAPERBACKS

ANDREW COSBY · JOHANNA STOKES · RHOALD MARCELLUS
DEATH VALLEY
Travis Klein
Ryan Zimmerman
Samantha Lyons
Death Valley High Yearbook - photography by Kaare Andrews

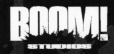

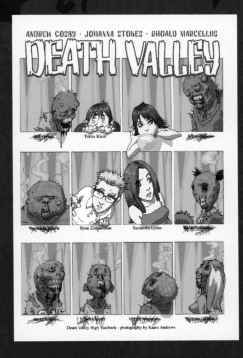

DEATH VALLEY

written by Johanna Stokes
and Andrew Cosby
drawn by Rhoald Marcellus
cover by Kaare Andrews
$14.99, full color, 128 pages

ISBN13: 978-1-934506-08-0

Samantha's graduating from high school in the Valley - getting together with her pals to throw an End of the World party to celebrate, everyone ends up accidentally locked in a bomb shelter. When Samantha and her pals emerge, they find that the entire world has changed, and the dead now walk the Earth... It's Dawn of the Dead by way of The O.C.! From EUREKA TV show writers writers Andrew Cosby and Johanna Stokes (Mr. Stuffins and The Savage Brothers)!

Giffen and DeMatteis'
PLANETARY BRIGADE

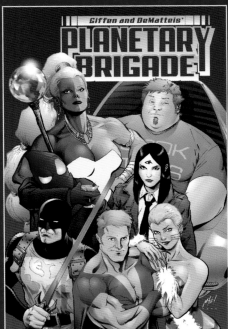

PLANETARY BRIGADE

written by Keith Giffen
and J.M. DeMatteis
drawn by various
$14.99, full color, 128 pages

ISBN13: 978-1-934506-10-3

More Giffen and DeMatteis Bwaha-ha-ha hilarity! From the hit-writers of Justice League International comes their own, quirky, turn on a league of super-heroes! The Planetary Brigade is a group of heroes fronted by Hero Squared's Captain Valor and Grim Knight. Meet Mr. Brilliant - Earth has never met a smarter, or more smug, hero. Earth Goddess - by day, she's a sweet, unassuming wallflower, but when the Earth needs her, she turns into a gargantuan guardian of the planet. Purring Pussycat -sweet, sexy... what's she hiding? The Third Eye - spiritual mystic. The Mauve Visitor - strange visitor from another world, or cute little Smurf-like dude? Together, they're in a league all their own.

GIFFEN • DEMATTEIS • ABRAHAM
HERO
SQUARED

HERO SQUARED VOLUME 1

Written by Keith Giffen
and J.M. DeMatteis
Drawn by Joe Abraham
$14.99, full color, 136 pages

ISBN13: 978-1-934506-00-4

Collecting the sold-out X-Tra Sized Special one-shot - which was such a success that it lead to a three issue miniseries - this book is packed with extras. In print for the first time will be the popular web comic promotion that Keith Giffen plotted and penciled, and which DeMatteis scripted along with Giffen's original character designs and Joe Abraham's concept sketches. Also in print for the first time is a Keith Giffen plot, which can now be compared side-by-side with DeMatteis' final script!

ZOMBIE TALES
JOHNSON

ZOMBIE TALES

written and drawn by various
$14.99, full color, 144 pages

ISBN13: 978-1-934506-02-8

The best-selling zombie anthology finally gets collected, featuring work from the best of the best: material written by Mark Waid, Keith Giffen, Eureka creator Andrew Cosby, Transformers The Movie writer John Rogers, Eureka TV show writer Johanna Stokes, Fall of Cthulhu writer Michael Alan Nelson, and more! Artists featured are a non-stop constellation of names: Keith Giffen, Fallen Angel's J.K. Woodward, Painkiller Jane's Lee Moder, 100 Bullets' Dave Johnson, Mark Badger, and many many more! This edition collects Zombie Tales #1, Zombie Tales: Oblivion, and Zombie Tales: The Dead. Don't wait 28 days later for the new dawn of the walking dead!

BOOM! STUDIOS

TRADE PAPERBACKS

WHAT'S THE BIG IDEA?
www.BOOM-STUDIOS.com

From the creators of ABADAZAD!
the Stardust Kid
J.M. DeMatteis & Mike Ploog
with Nick Bell & Dave Lanphear

STARDUST KID

written by J.M. DeMatteis
drawn by Mike Ploog
$14.99, full color, 128 pages

ISBN13: 978-1-934506-04-2

From the best-selling creative team behind Abadazad comes the collection of their conceptual sequel! Last night, when Cody DiMarco went to bed, life was the same as it's always been. This morning, when he woke up, the world he knew...was gone. A Magic older than Time. An ancient evil. And four children whose only chance to restore their families, and their world, is to solve the mystery of...The Stardust Kid. Twelve year old Cody DiMaro's best friend is Paul Brightfield and Paul Brightfield isn't human: He's the last of The Old Ones, ancient elemental beings from The Time Before.

SECOND WAVE

SECOND WAVE

written by Michael Alan Nelson
drawn by Chee
$14.99, full color, 144 pages

ISBN13: 978-1-934506-06-6

Mankind held the first invasion back. But then the second wave came... Mitch was an ordinary man living an ordinary suburban life, but alien invaders took his home and his wife away. Now that they're back, how have they grown immune to mankind's defenses? And what key role does Mitch play in the invasion? What's his link to this extra-terrestrial threat? This edition collects issues 1 to 6 of the critically acclaimed series.

TALENT
GOLDEN · SNIEGOSKI · AZACETA

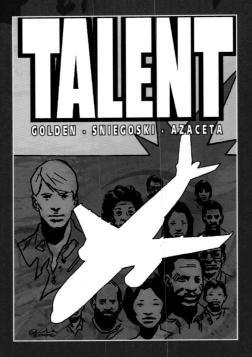

TALENT
written by Christopher Golden
and Tom Sniegoski
drawn by Paul Azaceta
$14.99, full color, 128 pages

ISBN13: 978-1-934506-05-9

The sold-out sensation is finally collected! Optioned in a five way studio bidding war by Universal Pictures, Talent tracks Nicholas Dane, miraculous sole survior of a plane crash. As mysterious men arrive to kill Dane, he discovers he can channel the talents of the victims of the crash! Discover why Ain't It Cool News said "Since the company's inception, Boom! has been creating quite a rumble in the comics world, but with Talent, they're definitely living up to their name. Highly recommended."

KEITH GIFFEN · ALAN GRANT
JEREMIAH
HARM

JEREMIAH HARM
written by Keith Giffen
and Alan Grant
drawn by Rael Lyra
and Rafael Albuquerque
$14.99, full color, 128 pages

ISBN13: 978-1-934506-12-7

From Keith Giffen (52, Annihilation) and Alan Grant (Batman, Lobo) comes this hard-hitting sci- fi series with a gritty tone and a brutal anti-hero as the lead! When three of the galaxy's most fearsome criminals escape confinement on a prison planet and wind up on Earth, the authorities have no choice but to free the most wanted man in the universe - Jeremiah Harm - to track these fugitives down and stop them. He doesn't love you, he doesn't want to be your friend, he isn't your super-hero - and God help you if you find yourself in Harm's way! Featuring art from Rael Lyra (Dragonlance: Legend of Huma) and Rafael Albuquerque (Blue Beetle).

GIFFEN · LEIB · ROGERS · COSBY · WARD
WHAT WERE THEY THINKING?!
CLASSIC COMICS REMIXED
A BOOM STUDIOS PRODUCTION BS
GLUB!
GLUB-UBBA!
GLUB!
GLUB! GLUBBA! GLUB-UB!
GLUBBA!
KEITH GIFFEN & COMPANY GO NUTS AND CHANGE THE WORD BALLOONS ON AN OLD COMIC!

WHAT WERE THEY THINKING?!

written by various
drawn by various
$14.99, full color, 128 pages

ISBN13: 978-1-934506-07-3

Led by Keith Giffen and Eureka series creator Andrew Cosby, with Transformers the Movie writer John Rogers and Eureka series writer Johanna Stokes, this collection features a wild array of Golden Age comics, all re-written to make their word balloons comedic! It's a Mystery Science Theater 3000 turn on venerable Golden Age funnybooks! It's What's Up, Tiger Lily? with the funny pages! This well-reviewed edition collects What Were They Thinking?! #1, WWTT: Some People Never Learn, WWTT: Monster Mash-Up, and WWTT: Go West Young Man.

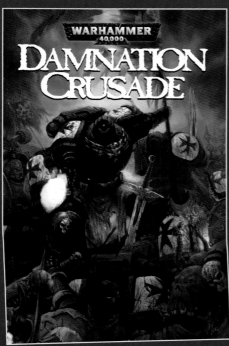

WARHAMMER 40,000
DAMNATION CRUSADE

WARHAMMER 40,000: DAMNATION CRUSADE

written by Dan Abnett
and Ian Edginton
$14.99 full color 136 pages

ISBN13: 978-1-934506-11-0

In the nightmare future of the 41st millennium, Mankind teeters upon the brink of extinction. The galaxy-spanning Imperium of Man is beset on all sides by ravening aliens, and threatened from within by malevolent creatures and heretic rebels. Only the strength of the Immortal Emperor of Terra stands between Humanity and its annihilation. Foremost amongst servants of the Imperium stand the Space Marines, mentally and physically engineered to be the supreme fighting force, the ultimate protectors of Mankind. The Black Templars are fearless champions and unforgiving crusaders against the enemies of the Emperor.

WHAT'S THE BIG IDEA?
www.BOOM-STUDIOS.com

BOOM! STUDIOS

TRADE PAPERBACKS

COSBY · NELSON · SCOTT
X ISLE

X ISLE
written by Andrew Cosby
and Michael Alan Nelson
drawn by Greg Scott
$14.99, full color, 128 pages

ISBN13: 978-1-934506-09-7

From EUREKA TV show creator Andrew Cosby and Michael Alan Nelson (Fall of Cthulhu, Second Wave) comes this tale of survival horror! A team of researchers drift on the ocean, lost, in their quest for an enigmatic island that's never been explored. Washing on its shores, they find a dense, terrifying jungle populated with animal and plant life that has evolved along a completely different path. What secret does this isle hold? Why are the life forms there so dangerous –and so alien? In the tradition of Alien and the recent horror-hit The Descent! Featuring art

GIFFEN CHAMBERLAIN CREE
Tag

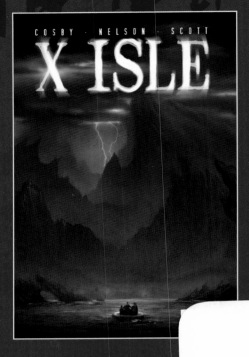